THE MERCENARY'S BOUNTY

AGE OF THE ANDINNA

KRISTEN BANET

Copyright © 2019 by Kristen Banet

All rights reserved.

Cover Illustration by Merilliza Chan

No part of this book may be reproduced in any form or by any electronic or mechanical means, including information storage and retrieval systems, without written permission from the author, except for the use of brief quotations in a book review.

This is a work of fiction. Names, characters, businesses, places, events, locales, and incidents are either the products of the author's imagination or used in a fictitious manner. Any resemblance to actual persons, living or dead, or actual events is purely coincidental.

❀ Created with Vellum

*Don't let anyone tell you
what you're worth.
They're probably wrong,
because the answer should always be
priceless.*

1

TREVAN

Trevan coughed up the dirt he ate when he hit the ground. As he tried to push himself up, a sharp kick to his ribs had him groaning in pain.

"Get up, Elvasi. Fight me," the Andinna snarled.

He wasn't going to go further than his hands and knees. He knew better than to try. His best bet was to wait for training, get better, get stronger, and hope he won against the Andinna when the day of monthly games came. Until then, he just needed to survive. By not fighting back, he was just keeping himself from getting more injured. They couldn't kill him without getting themselves into more trouble than they could handle.

"He's a coward, like the rest of his people," another one spat.

A coward. He gave up wealth and privilege to become a guard in the worst place in the Empire. He gave up the security of his position in the military to save a few slaves from their own deaths. The same slaves now beating him.

Yet they called him a coward.

Of course they did. They didn't know or care what he'd given up or why he'd done it.

"Break it up!" a guard yelled. "Break it up before I have all of you beaten!"

The Andinna scattered, growling and snapping at every Elvasi they saw as they left. They wouldn't pick a fight or start a riot over this, just posture and be pissed off.

"You. Get up." The guard was sneering down at him.

Trevan pushed up slowly, leaning against the earth wall to look at an old brother at arms. Without saying anything, the guard threw a punch to his gut. Trevan coughed, the air knocked out of him. While the Andinna hadn't been armed, his Elvasi brothers were. With gauntlets on their fists and steel on their boots, their beatings were worse.

Trevan sank back down, groaning.

"Eventually, the Empress is going to have you killed. I'm going to be first in line. For Gentry."

Trevan began to chuckle.

"What are you laughing about?" another guard snapped, kicking his leg.

"Gentry was high that night," he answered. He found it funny, anyway. Everyone was so upset by the guards who were killed when he'd gotten the Andinna out of the pits. They had been drunk, high, and done with whoring. So honorable. Some heroes.

"Leave him," a rougher voice ordered. "He's not worth it. He wasted his time saving a few of the fucking Andinna, and look where it's left him. I'm happy the Empress didn't have him executed."

"Why?" the first one asked incredulously.

"He fucking saved the Champion. He's in the pits with his own worst enemies now. *Hers.*"

Trevan tried to ignore the spit that hit his face.

Three weeks of this. Three weeks of living in the hellhole that he had spent six hundred years guarding. He'd thought he could survive it, but he didn't have anything he once had. No armor, no weapons, no backup.

He was alone.

All he had was a glimmer of hope that when he died, his gods would judge him fairly. Once, the Elvasi gods had been about the balance of living things. About fairness and kindness. They hadn't been a warrior people, but a peaceful one. They weren't built for brutality. It's why they were so high and mighty with the Andinna.

But their gods were about balance and goodness. For every justice, there was injustice. For every good, there was evil. For life, there was death. He just hoped he'd done enough good in the world that his hell ended when he died.

He slowly and silently walked to a tiny room he was using to sleep, hidden from the Andinna and the guards he was now living with. He hunkered down.

Three weeks.

She had survived a thousand years. He held onto that. She had been strong enough to suffer and grow stronger. She had done everything she could to live. He just needed to channel whatever that had been. He just needed to hope she didn't need whatever inner strength that was anymore. He hoped her life was better and that strength wasn't necessary anymore.

That would make his thousand years in the pits worth it.

Right?

He passed out, trying to imagine the better life she had and he was paying for. It was all he had left.

2

MAVE

Mave spun, remembering to keep her wings close to her back as she slashed her blade through the air. The sing of steel called to her soul, a promise of violence and a release of frustration. She cut downward and across, killing an invisible foe before turning to take out another enemy in the imaginary battle she fought. With sea water spraying her, she kicked back enemies and gutted them. Sailors talked amongst themselves, ignoring her and her practice in the dead of night. She could pretend it was just her and the sands for a moment. The cool, salty water hit her skin in the same way sand used to when it was kicked up.

And she slowly worked out every ounce of frustration that she carried.

She continued to fight until her arms felt heavy and her legs moved too slowly. Even her tail was sluggish. She stopped, breathing hard. She had no idea what time it was, but for a moment, she enjoyed the cool night air of the sea. Closing her eyes, she let the feel of this new place wash over her again. She wasn't in the pits anymore. She hadn't been in the pits for over three weeks. Her longest time away from them since she had been tossed into them.

"Impressive," a male commented politely.

Mave's eyes flew open and she looked back over her shoulder to see Alchan watching her. His amber eyes, a rare color for their people, seemed to glow in the night.

"Care to join me?" she asked, just as politely. Not that she particularly wanted to spar with him, but he was her boss. He was one of the two leaders of the Ivory Shadow Mercenary Company, something she was now a member of. Not that she had done much to earn it. She was pretty certain they offered it to her out of pity and because she could kill well. She didn't particularly care, though. It wasn't the pits. She wasn't going to turn them down at any point or leave, and they knew it.

"No. I came out because I noticed Luykas was sweating again in his sleep, tossing and turning. Come inside and do something less strenuous. You can do this during the training sessions I host in the afternoons, but I don't want you staying up all night out here." He was diplomatic and professional, not showing her any of the asshole she had come to know him as. She knew it would come out if she pressed, though.

"Fine." She sheathed the blades and picked up her shirt from the deck, having discarded it when it became drenched in sweat. She had an undershirt on, but it only covered the important bits so the sailors didn't whistle, leaving most of her flesh exposed to the cool night air.

Glancing at Alchan, she didn't feel self-conscious about her state of undress.

At least I wear a shirt, unlike every damned male on this boat.

"Why are you out here?" he asked as she drew closer, with what almost sounded like a shred of concern. Almost. She looked at the door that led below deck, already planning her escape, and watched him slowly slide between her and her destination.

Looks like I'm talking to Alchan for a moment.

"I was practicing my Andena earlier. I grew frustrated and needed to work it out before getting into my Common and Elvasi reading."

She saw no reason to lie about it. She met his amber eyes and tried to push him out of her way with sheer force of will.

Andinna were naturally a pushy, temperamental race, and eye contact was a constant game of dominance and submission. She was hoping he would submit and move out of her way. Instead, he held the gaze almost without effort. He was one of two males she had ever met who could.

She always got pissed off when either of them did it. The other one, Alchan's brother Luykas, was smart enough to drop his gaze even if he didn't feel the need. Alchan wasn't nearly as intelligent.

"Well, try to get some sleep tonight." Neither of them broke the gaze and showed submission. The right response would have been to look down. Alchan's eyes went up, a clear sign he wasn't willing to fight with her over it, but wasn't backing down from any future challenges.

"I got some," she said, stepping around him.

She left him on the deck and went to her shared room with Matesh. She ignored his large form on the floor and pulled out two books from a small chest she had been given. Settling in on a stripped bed, with no mattress or anything else, she opened the first book. Realizing it was too dark, she fumbled around to light a secured lantern that filled the room with the light she needed. Then she decided her clothing was too sweaty to be comfortable, so she got up one more time and stripped. There was no way to bathe, but that was just how life was on the ship. She had never thought she would be in a place less clean than the pits. She threw her dirty clothing onto a small pile in the far corner. They would need to be washed as best they could be when the sun came up. She could get Mat to do it.

Finally, she began to read. At first, she was confused by the letters, but she remembered the sheets of information Luykas and Leshaun gave her. She sounded out the first word, smiling as the word came to life, rolling off her tongue.

"Common," Mave murmured, staring intently at the book, finally parsing it enough to know which language it was. "This is Common.

Nearly all of the short-lived races speak it, as do the long-lived races. Humans don't have the time to learn the age-old nuances of Andena or Elvasi. Nothing looks like Andena, but Elvasi shares some letters with Common."

"What are you talking about?"

She jumped, remembering she wasn't alone in the small room. She looked down at the floor from her spot on the bed and saw that Matesh was awake, only half-covered by the blankets that had ended up down there. It left his large chest bare and much of his stomach, with well-defined muscles, and when he shifted a little, she was given a teasing glimpse of what she knew was under the blankets. There was nothing she found unattractive about Matesh, even his broken horn.

"I'm...reading," she answered tentatively. "And this book is in Common. Luykas says my Common reading is coming along really well, but it still takes me a moment to really figure out which language is which. There's just so much to learn."

"So you were mumbling facts about Common versus Andena and Elvasi to yourself?" He sat up, yawning. "What time is it, Mave?"

"I don't know. It's not dawn yet, but there's enough light from the lantern that I can read." She shrugged. "I wanted to practice more."

"I thought you would sleep longer after the night we had," he commented, giving her that arrogant smirk.

"Maybe you should work a little harder," she retorted, sending him a taunting smile back.

With a growl, he pushed out of their pile of blankets and pillows. That's what their two beds had become. The mattresses were on the clean floor, covered in every linen he could find, and she was sure he stole half those pillows from other Andinna. Sometimes two or three of them would go missing for a couple of days, then they would be back.

There was a silent war going on, but she was staying firmly out of it. She didn't particularly care about all the creature comforts Matesh had filled the room with. They were nice, but unnecessary in her mind. *The only thing I need in this room at night is him. I wonder if he knows that.*

No. I can't tell him. His ego will explode.

She leaned back as he drew closer, his beautifully nude male form looking appealing in the dim light of her lantern. From the heat in those emerald eyes, she knew he had noticed that she wasn't wearing anything either.

"Come back to bed," he crooned, continuing to draw closer until their lips touched. The kiss was tender, but there was a power beneath it she knew well now. He was a strong male with firm hands that knew just how to grab her body to make it sing. And she didn't miss the note of arrogance in his order, like he knew everything she was thinking.

As good as that idea sounds, I can't spend all my time fucking him.

"I want to get this down before we're there. I only have a week left." It was the same answer she gave every morning. While on the ship, she sank into her studies, only doing enough physical work to keep her body maintained. She could admit she liked not having to train three or more times a day now. She could study. She could learn.

So she did.

"You are completely fluent in Common and Elvasi. You're getting better at the alphabets every day for those two languages. You can read anything in Common and most things in Elvasi. That's a lot done in just three weeks. You can spare a moment to come join me in bed." He made it sound like she had nothing to worry about.

But they both knew she had a lot to worry about.

He didn't bring up Andena, because I'm terrible at it. They're all worried I'll never pick it up well enough to have a real conversation. I'll always be a weird, Elvasi-speaking Andinna.

"I'm not stopping because you woke up hard," she told him simply. "It's nice, this." She waved the book around. "You can help me. I have a few words in this one I'm sure I'm pronouncing wrong."

He nodded slowly, eyeing her carefully.

She shifted, holding her wings tight to her body so he could sit next to her. Their tails trailed to the floor and she resisted smiling as his wrapped around hers. She liked the casual touching he did, a simple contact that didn't distract. The further from the Empire they got, the more he touched her. They had grown close in the pits, but now they were becoming truly comfortable. Well, she was, at least, and he never said anything about it.

I've never been this comfortable with anyone before, especially not a male.

She downright hated casual touch, but here she was, enjoying every touch he gave her. Only Rain came close to how this male made her feel, and Rain's was familial, not the low fire constantly burning between her and Matesh.

"What are you having trouble with?" he asked softly, leaning close enough for their horns to touch. Their closed wings were pressed together until he shifted one over to cocoon her in their own little bubble. In that moment, like every time he did it, she felt like it could just be the two of them in the world, private and intimate in ways she didn't understand.

It felt good.

"This one. How do you pronounce it? I feel like I'm forgetting a rule or something." She pointed to the word. It was a name, which made it even more difficult.

He sounded it out with her several times. It was the captain's first name. She had heard it before, but never seen it written down. They were teaching her with every scroll and book they could get their hands on, which was usually the ship's manifests and other business documents to make the enterprise legitimate. Not that it was actually legitimate, but appearances mattered.

They continued until there was a soft knock on the door. Matesh was patient and didn't try to stop her from practicing after that first attempt to get her back into bed.

But once that knock came, he stole the book from her and closed it.

"Come in!" he called, sliding the book away before wrapping an arm around her waist. She didn't say anything as he held her possessively as the door opened.

Rainev poked his head in, smiling at them. "Breakfast is nearly ready. I didn't want Mave to miss it again."

"Oh!" She jumped up, ignoring her nakedness. "Thank you, *illi bodyr*."

"No problem, *illo amyr*," he replied, his smile turning into a grin. She couldn't help but return it. "Now put some clothes on."

"Fine." She waved him away and the door closed with a thud. "Come on, Mat, let's get something to eat."

"I know what I want for breakfast," Mat purred, looking over her. She narrowed her eyes at him as he rose onto his knees. She didn't resist when he grabbed her hips and pulled her closer, kissing just under her belly button. "It won't take long," he promised, moving lower. His nose pressed against her thigh and he inhaled deeply, then bit down on the flesh with just enough pressure to make her notice. Her pulse jumped as her world focused on his hot breath caressing her skin. One of his hands reached around to cup her ass as he licked the spot he'd nibbled on.

Her stomach growled.

"You are relentless," she mumbled, running her fingers through his hair. Then she grabbed his horns and pushed him back from her. Looking down at him, she liked how the broken horn made him look rougher, less perfect than the day they had met. "But I am hungry and I missed breakfast yesterday, only to regret it."

"A male has to try, right?" He was laughing as he stood up. She didn't miss how he somehow kept his hand on her ass, letting it slide to her lower back and holding her.

She only rolled her eyes. She enjoyed his attempts, even when she wasn't going to accept his offers every single time. They made her feel wanted and appreciated. She also wondered how much of this he held back in the pits.

Anxiety crept in as they got dressed, like it did on occasion. She didn't know what life was about anymore. Would Matesh still want her when they were off the ship and he had other options? No male ever wanted her when there were other options.

Skies, no male ever really wanted me before.

She tried to shake it and never spoke of it, but for three weeks, the anxiety over it had settled in. It was one of the reasons she was pushing so hard to learn before they landed in Olost - one of many internal and external pressures to get through this. This was why she had been out on the deck in the middle of the night, forcing the frustration to leave her body.

She didn't say anything as Matesh buckled the back of her shirt for her. He did it every morning without commenting. One day he'd caught her struggling to reach it, and he was there quickly. Since then, he was just always there.

"Make sure to stretch your wings after breakfast," he reminded her softly. "You're supposed to do it when you wake up."

"Thank you." She'd forgotten to when she left the bed earlier. "I'll make sure to get to it before lessons with your uncle." She tried to hide the bite in the sentence, but nothing could cover up the dread she felt at another day with Leshaun, poring over Andena scrolls.

"Is my *bodrya* giving you a hard time?" Matesh grabbed her forearm, holding her before she could retreat.

"No, I just..." She shook her head. It wasn't Leshaun. It was her. "I don't like feeling like I'm failing, and I am."

"Just the language lessons, right? You're fine with everything else?" He seemed so concerned. "I know it's been hard for you, but I don't think you need to worry. It's not failing; it's just difficult. You're making progress, too. I know you are. So does everyone else."

"The history is whatever. He wants to bring Varon in to teach me about the gods soon as well. Not like I give a damn about them-"

"Mave." Matesh's voice was full of warning. He didn't appreciate when she spat on their gods. It was a sticking point.

"All right," she conceded. It at least stopped the conversation about Andena and how she was bad at it. "Let's go get breakfast before it's cold."

"Let's," he agreed, nodding. He didn't release her, not for several long seconds. Even then, she noticed how his fingers lingered. At least one thing hadn't changed; she was still as observant as ever. She liked noticing the small nuances of the people around her just as much as always.

They walked to the dining area together, and she immediately did a head count when she walked in. Alchan and Luykas were together, pouring over papers she didn't care about. Nevyn and Varon were both yawning as if they had gotten no sleep, sitting close together much like she and Matesh had. She knew they were in a relationship, but she didn't know much else. She didn't speak to them much.

Next, she saw Rainev with two empty seats on his right. On his left, his father. Zayden. That man. She didn't feel like dealing with the cranky man this early so she sat in the further seat, leaving Matesh closer to the father and son duo. It left her with Matesh on one side and Bryn on the other. Leshaun was the last to enter, using a cane, something she saw nearly every day now. He grabbed a spot next to Luykas and ignored everyone as he pulled out his own reading material.

"Good mornin'," Bryn said brightly to her, smiling.

"Good morning," she replied, not saying anything else as he continued to stare at her. She made no attempt to keep talking and waited to see if he would try. She knew he wanted to get to know her. She wanted to get to know him too, but she was also unsure how to make it happen.

If anything, he made her nervous. A rogue, another prior slave, another gladiator. And one who kept giving her small gifts and not so small ones, like the gold sun. She didn't know much else about him other than that, even after three weeks on the ship.

Then again, I haven't tried getting to know any of them.

It was second nature for her. Surrounded by males in tight spaces, her natural reflex was to keep her distance and try to be safe. The only reason she ever spoke to them was because she was going to be working with them.

As the newest member of the Ivory Shadow Mercenary Company, of all things. One of the most infamous groups to give the Empire a hard time in the last thousand years.

Bryn's bright smile disappeared as he looked back to his plate, proving her gaze was the more dominant one, even if it was unintentional on her part. It was the same every morning. He would try to be friendly and she would shut down. She wished she could think more about how easy it was in those first few days. She had been easier with all of them when the trip had first started. Time and the environment had forced her back into old habits she wasn't sure how to break.

She felt guilty for it. This wasn't like Rainev and Matesh in the pits. There, she had been in her place, knew the rules of engagement, and outside forces pushed them together. Here, she was trying to swim and failing at it. She had no experience to draw from to grow these new relationships thrust upon her.

Distance was easy. It was her best defense mechanism - and one she wished she could get rid of.

She ate slowly, listening in on conversations. Matesh and Zayden were teasing Rainev about a boy back home until something flew across the table and nailed Zayden in the forehead with perfect accuracy.

"Varon," Alchan chastised softly. Males chuckled, but in the end, Matesh and Zayden stopped teasing the young male.

"Mave, remember to get your stretches done," Matesh said to her as she finished eating. There was a pause before he added anything further. "Before you settle in for lessons."

"I didn't forget." She took the last piece of jerky off his plate and bit into it. She felt the heat explode in her mouth, but she was getting used to the spices and seasonings they used every meal. The sailors on board made every meal to how the Andinna liked their food, and she just had to get used to it.

Along with fucking everything else.

"I'll come out with you," Brynec offered, pushing his plate away. She shook her head quickly.

"No…" She rejected the offer every time. She knew if she accepted it, they would probably have a better opportunity to talk, but it also meant someone new would be touching her. "Um…" She saw the sad acceptance at her rejection in the rogue's eyes. She wasn't sure what to do with it.

"I'll come out with you!" Rain jumped up, grabbing her plate from in front of her and walking away. "I don't want to have to listen to those two all morning." He jerked his head towards Matesh and his father.

"Good idea." She smiled at him and together, they walked out of the dining area and to the main deck. "Thank you."

"I know you don't like other people touching you. Matesh normally does the stretches with you, right? Or Leshaun?"

"Yeah. I can do them by myself sometimes, but it's nice to have someone helping work out the cramps as they come, before they send me to the floor." She began to extend her right wing, making Rainev jump into action. His hands weren't as skilled as the old male's or full of tension like Mat's. He went through the motions, helping her.

"You know, if you let Bryn do this, then you might progress a lot faster. You are doing really well, from what I've heard, but he's got the practical experience of having done it before. He's been where you are. He knows how it hurts better than anyone and what ends up being the weakest section that needs work."

"I don't want him touching me. He's not bad, but…"

"You're nervous around everyone. We can tell." Rain chuckled. "Well, you aren't nervous around me or Mat, of course, but you are with them."

"I'm not sure how to just…talk to people." She sighed. "Well, we're long-lived. I don't need to learn tomorrow right?" *Well, I do. I needed to know Andena by yesterday if I want any chance.*

"Is that why you're always in your room?"

"No, I'm always in my room because I've been practicing the things I do need to learn. I can't get off this boat without knowing how to read at least Common. I'm nearly there, though. It's much easier than Andena."

"Andena isn't hard. You just have no experience in it."

"Andena is hard and I'm very bad at it." She was feeling snarly at just the idea of it.

"No, you aren't. You didn't think you would learn it just on this trip, right?"

"I mean…" She had. "It's not like I have anything else to do. I can dedicate all my time to it, and I do and yet…"

"I thought you were more patient than this," he commented, raising an eyebrow as he moved in front of her. "Look, there's really no reason to beat yourself up over this."

Yes, there is. Not knowing Andena makes me an outcast. I don't want to be one of those anymore.

"We'll talk about it later. Tell me about this boy they were teasing you about." Her tone left no room for him to argue with her. As *illo amyr*, she was learning she had a level of authority over him, even in the eyes of the other Andinna on board. They all respected the adopted familial terms as if she had always been his big sister, including Zayden, who also made it clear she was *not* his 'daughter.' Whatever relationship she had with Rain was between her and Rain. Just another thing she hadn't expected from her people.

"Let's finish your stretches before Leshaun comes out looking for you," he said quickly, moving back behind her, ignoring what she had brought up. Two could play at that game, so the silence continued.

They kept going with her extensions as Rain massaged out the muscles, helping them get through the exercise without cramping, until the old male himself walked out, tapping his cane on the deck. She heard the same tapping every morning when he came to look for her.

Here we go. Another day of this.

"Let's get to work, Maevana," he called. She bared her teeth, glad she was turned away from him. She was going to rip his throat out one day for refusing to use her chosen name. No, he would only use her full name or female. Damned old pigeon. Quickly, she remembered why she wasn't ever going to hurt the old man. He was Matesh's uncle, his blood uncle at that, and his last real family.

Other than always calling me that, he's kind. That's keeping him alive more than anything else.

"Have a good lesson," Rain told her as she went to follow Leshaun back into the ship.

The old male moved slowly and with care, his cane supporting his left leg. She didn't remark on it. To live so long, to see as much as he must have, it was something to be respected. Many Andinna no longer lived past their prime, cut down too young. She knew from experience.

She grabbed the door to his room for him, holding it open. He narrowed his pale green eyes at her in response to the gesture and walked in first. Once they were closed into the room together, he sat slowly on his bed and pulled out a book she was familiar with, but hadn't yet read.

"Begin," he ordered. She took it without comment and sat down on the other bed in his room, opening it up. Andena used symbols she wasn't familiar with. Elvasi and Common shared some between the two languages, making them easier to learn, and she was moving quickly with those studies since she could already speak it.

Andena, however, was like nothing she had encountered before.

"You know I hate this type of lesson," she reminded him as he handed her a second book.

"Yes, but this is the one that helps you build the most skills at once. Read the Common and then read the Andena version. I'll assist as you go through." He was patient, watching her carefully. "And if I have to repeat a previous lesson, I will. It takes time to build the vocabulary, and our language isn't easy, I know that. We use glyphs that grow more complex as the word grows complex, more meaningful. When we were a young race, we developed Andena by scratching on cavern walls. Those places have become holy sites. Did you know that?"

"No," she answered. She hadn't been expecting the history lesson so early in the morning. "Can I get started?"

"Ah yes. I just love the interesting nuances of our language compared to others."

She groaned. She opened her mouth and started but was quickly cut off. She threw up her hands as Leshaun kept talking.

"Also, before we get off this ship, you're going to sit down with me and Luykas. We're not going to start your Blackblood training until we get to the village, but that doesn't mean you can't have the lessons and rules of it before then. It will only prepare you more for the future."

"*Oldura*," she muttered petulantly, growing angry at even the idea of spending time with Luykas. After they talked about what the blood bond entailed, they smartly started avoiding each other. Her ability to create emotional distance from people only helped encourage the separation.

Leshaun just reached out with his cane and smacked her shin, causing her to wince.

She rubbed her leg as she looked over the pages. She started reading before he could stop her again. "'The Dragons raised the Spine, and with it divided the land, protecting the territory of their people, the Andinna, and their beasts, the wyverns.'"

"Very good," he said kindly. She even dared a smile at his words, even though it was slightly pained from his cane. He was a tough old man, but she liked impressing him because of it. A compliment from Leshaun was rare and earned. "Now, the Andena."

With a deep breath, she looked over the Andena and began desperately trying to sound out the glyphs into the right words. She grew more frustrated with each word he had to correct, telling her how each word was said. Dragon was simple. *Andin*. It was important to their people, the people of dragons, of flight, of the skies. Wyvern was *andinno*. The siblings, the other, the beast. Others proved more difficult, like territory or protecting.

"Remember, Andena heavily uses root words. Take soul. It's

semara, a combination of skies, *sema*, and *mara*, which is life. We believe the soul comes from those two things."

She nodded, understanding that part. This was a lesson he had given her several times before, but she appreciated the time he took to repeat it, reshow it. Appreciated him for it. She hated herself for needing it.

"So…" He pulled out a loose scroll and a quill. She watched him deftly open some ink and write both words, *sema* and *mara*. Then he wrote *semara*. She studied it, knowing what he was showing her. *Semara* was just made out of the glyphs of those two root words.

"What if I learn all the roots? I'm better at those than anything else." She liked things she was good at. Didn't everyone?

"Then you'll understand about half of our language. There's many words that needed unique terms. Those will trip you up, which is why you need to learn all the glyphs and how to pronounce them as they are brought together." He pointed back to the book. "Keep that in mind, though. It will help you."

She went on to the next sentence, swallowing before she read it in Common and then butchered it in Andena. She snarled when she slipped up on a word she knew, screwing up how to say it. It changed the meaning of the word and she was embarrassed by the mistake. When she did it a third time, she held onto the books a bit tighter.

She hated this. She hated Andena, but she needed it. She would never fit in if she didn't know it. Never. She wouldn't bother trying until she could speak to them and not be the weird Andinna who didn't know her own language.

She was more than ready to stop when he snatched both books from her and began to put them away. She had been getting snappier with every word, every time he had to correct her, until at one point, he just stopped trying to help her at all, leaving her to flounder and grow more frustrated.

"Go eat lunch," he ordered. "Then I recommend working out your frustration with the others on the deck before coming back and getting back to this."

Thank the fucking Skies. I was about to rip those damned books to shreds.

She didn't say that out loud for good reason. Leshaun would have whacked her with his cane again. She retreated as quickly as she could and went to the dining area, sliding into a seat next to Matesh. He put a plate down in front of her immediately.

"Thank you," she said softly.

"How was the lesson today?"

"Well, I didn't make the rookie mistake of trying to read it sideways," she answered, causing Matesh and half the table to begin chuckling. "Yeah, laugh at *me*," she muttered, glaring. "Who in the world decided Andena needed to read from top to bottom and not left to right like every other language?"

That had Matesh in a fit, leaning over until his head hit the table, his unbroken horn scratching into the wood without care.

I should have kept my mouth shut.

"At least you're getting better," Luykas said from his place further down the table. "That's good. By the time we reach the village, you should have a passing reading skill. Maybe we can start speaking more in Andena, though I think total immersion from the village will help with that."

"I was thinking the same thing," Leshaun agreed, sitting down with the brothers.

"Want to stretch your wings after you eat?" Brynec asked, leaning closer to her from his spot. She didn't miss how Matesh straightened up quickly and tensed ever so slightly next to her. "Rainev was saying you're making good progress, but he wanted me to get my eyes on them."

"Say yes," Leshaun ordered her from his spot. Then he nodded Bryn's way. "That's a good idea. You've got the most experience after me. You can bring me a progress report on how she's doing with her wings. I haven't looked at them in the last two weeks."

She gritted her teeth but nodded. "That sounds good. I was hoping to start stretching them more often." *Damn it, Rain. You've thrown me to the wolves.*

Finally, they all stopped talking to her and let her eat. This was just a day like any other, and she was only halfway through it. The Company males weren't the males from the pits, but some part of her still felt the sting of what she used to be.

Ensam. A word she had learned that described everything she once and still was. An Andinna without a community, an outcast.

Even here, she still was one, and every time they laughed, she felt it cut deep to her bones, a reminder that while they weren't cruel like the gladiators, she was still different. They launched into conversations in Andena and forgot she existed. She had no idea what they were saying and didn't blame them for it. She just stopped listening, knowing she couldn't figure it out. They spoke more in Andena the further they got from the Empire. It was their native tongue. It was supposed to be hers.

She had never felt so lonely.

"LET'S GET STARTED, AYE?" Bryn grinned at her, spinning a finger to have Mave turn around. She did as he wanted, hoping they would be done with this quickly. Already, the rest of the Company was moving to get into their afternoon training. She had no idea why they enjoyed training during the worst of the heat, only that they did it every day. Personally, she spent years dealing with that and thought it was stupid. They could train at night and not have a problem with the overbearing sun or the shine of it on the waters. The sailors were always watching as well. She liked the men who worked the nights more. They were quieter, more out of the way than the rowdy day crew.

"How do they look?" she asked. He hadn't even touched her yet and she was already tense.

"Open 'em up and show me," he replied.

With a steady breath, she did as he asked, spreading both her wings at the same time. There was an ache, but no cramps yet. She figured since this was her second time stretching them for the day, they were already loose.

"Look at that. Yer wings are lookin' great. Now, I just need ya to relax. Think you can do that?" His voice was full of humor and patience. It was a simple request for her to relax.

"You know I don't like being touched," she said, feeling a bit snappy.

"I do," he murmured. She wished she could see his face or what he was doing. His tone had changed with those two words. "Trust, remember? Ya can trust us."

"I do," she mumbled. She thought she did, anyway.

How does someone just trust? I mean, I don't think they're going to kill me in my sleep. That's trust, right?

"Okay." He ran his hands over her wings after that, touching every muscle, every tendon, and feeling out every bone. "Yer wings are weak, but that's normal. I think yer ready for workouts, though. Ain't no reason to hold off. If ya can do an extension without cramping, ya can start working them."

"I still cramp at the beginning of the day. It's not like I can do this without help all the time."

"Ya won't be able to until they're flexible and strong. We've been building the flexibility since it had to come first, but now we need to work on both. Build flexibility and muscle, so the muscle is flexible." Bryn ran a hand over her left wing. "Ya have no scars or deformities. We'll have ya flying in less than a year."

She believed him. Every second he touched her, something eased that fear she had. Her shoulders relaxed.

"Ya will now flap your wings. Steady pace, until I say stop. If you can only do ten, ya stop. Hear me?"

"Yeah."

"Get started." He pulled his hand off her, leaving her bereft of anyone's help in case her wings cramped and took her down.

The movement felt both natural and unnatural. Her wings did exactly as they were supposed to, extending, flapping in the air, kicking up a small wind, and then smoothly moving into the next. The problem was, she had never experienced the feeling. Her wings had never moved this much. She felt like they were huge, and clumsy. She wasn't sure if she was really doing it right, only trying what felt natural.

"Three." Brynec kept count from behind her. "Four."

She closed her eyes, ignoring the burn in her back and wings as those unworked muscles worked for the first time in a very long time. At six, her right wing tensed up, but she pushed on. Physical work, she could handle. This was just like working any part of her body. She could remember when she was young and in the pits. Every exercise had hurt, but it was pushing past the burn that made her stronger. Physical strength was just overcoming the signs the body sent when it felt too weak.

"Ten. Eleven."

This felt like more progress than she had in weeks. She might never learn her own language, but she could become stronger - and she would. She held that belief to her as she pushed on, as her body began to shake from the exertion.

"Fifteen. Stop."

She did exactly as he asked, panting. She let her wings close back up, looking for a position they were comfortable in. Tight to her back, like normal.

"Good job, Mave!" Bryn walked around her, grinning. "Fifteen is more than I could do in a month. I told ya that ya would move faster than me."

She grinned back, feeling an indescribable pride. She was making progress. Three weeks ago, she couldn't open her wings. "Thank you, Bryn. I know you and Leshaun set out this schedule for me…" It was why she was progressing. She might not have let him help her before, but she knew he had a hand in it.

He waved a hand dismissively. "Ah, nah, Mave. Yer the one who needs the credit. Now if we could just get you speaking Andena. If ya need any help with flyin' or that, ya know where to find me."

He said it lightly, without any pressure. Just a simple comment, but something about it tore her short-lived good mood into pieces. She could only nod and turn away from him again. Turning only confronted her with seeing the entire Company, with Alchan and Luykas giving them orders in Andena as they went through a rough afternoon training. She knew she should go jump in, remembering what Leshaun had said, but she didn't feel up for it. She didn't feel up for confronting the fact that they would need to switch languages for her to understand, and how that special need would make her feel.

"I'm heading in," she told Brynec quickly, walking away before he could stop her. She ignored how he called out her name, confused. She was inside and going below deck as quickly as she could. Every step was ridden by the same thing it was every day. She was still a damned outcast, but now it wasn't because they forced her out for who she was. Now it was because of her own idiocy.

She went straight to her room and decided to work on what she could deal with. Elvasi and Common. She worked on Common before breakfast so she went Elvasi this time. It made her feel dirty, being better at it than Andena, but she could at least do it.

Every second she worked on it, she felt the gap growing between her and the men upstairs. Every single word she knew and could write in messy letters was another piece of her that was too different.

3

MATESH

"*Ahae, bodrya,*" Matesh greeted his uncle in Andena as the older male walked out from below deck. Matesh was lying back, enjoying the sun with the other males. With afternoon training done, they weren't really sure what to do with themselves. Ships were always the worst for the Company, as they grew stagnant, bored from trying to find things to do.

"*Ahae,* nephew," his uncle greeted back. "Do me a favor."

"Yes?"

"Stop stealing my extra pillows. I'm old. I need them."

Matesh groaned, letting his head fall back to the wood as the others began to laugh and call to him to stop stealing theirs as well.

"Anything else, uncle?"

"Yes…" Leshaun looked him over carefully. "Mave didn't train with you all, did she?"

"No. She walked away after I finished givin' her wings a workout. Seemed in a bit of a mood," Brynec said from the shade. Mat had thought he was asleep, but apparently the rogue was just pretending.

"Hm." Leshaun tapped his cane against the deck, a sign he was thinking about something. "I had wanted her out here with you. Matesh, why didn't you go get her?"

"Because she deserves her own time?" He frowned. "She comes and works out before the sun is up. We all know that. Why would I force her to come out during the hottest time of the day? She's lived that for a thousand years."

"Because I want her to be out here spending time with the Company." Leshaun growled, a cranky old man growl. "I want her absorbing you all speaking Andena and trying to learn. It's why I've asked you all to start using it during meals and workouts. So she can be immersed in it."

"Instead, she's shutting down," Bryn accused. "Good thinking."

Matesh raised an eyebrow. He knew Bryn was feeling some sort of kindred thing with her, wanting to get to know another gladiator, someone who went through things like him. He hadn't been expecting that sort of thing to come out of his mouth.

"You are a conniving old man," Zayden accused. "I mean, I like it, but fuck. Don't ever let me get on your bad side."

"You've been on my bad side since the day you and Matesh decided to be friends," Leshaun retorted. Mat started laughing as Zayden grumbled and growled, saying Mat was the bad one getting him into trouble, not the other way around.

"I'm worried about her when she gets to the village," Alchan commented. "If she can't fit in with us, then she's going to have a hell of a time with the other Andinna."

"She'll be fine," Matesh growled. "Just have some faith in her." He didn't like how Alchan always went to that. How she would always be some *ensam*. She wasn't anymore. He was in her *mayara*. She had him. She had Rain. She wasn't an outcast. Just because she didn't fall in and become friends with everyone didn't mean she was an *ensam*. She didn't need to be all community-oriented. He liked her the way she was.

Plus, she would never leave him if she continued like this. He knew it was a selfish thought, but he was dreading going to the village, having her meet all the other Andinna. What if she decided she didn't want the Company? What if she decided she didn't want *him*?

I'll just keep making her a comfortable bed. It's all I can do right now.

He knew the rules. Males were supposed to bring things back to prove they were worth more than their bodies in bed. He had to prove to her that he was worth keeping, irreplaceable for what he offered her.

It hadn't been something he worried about before. He'd never wanted to be in a *mayara*, tied to a female until she grew tired of him. He had fun, enjoyed the company of a female, then moved on when she wanted something more serious. Now he was with a female he wanted to stay with and she could drop him at any time.

His uncle poked him with his cane. Mat groaned, pushing the wooden stick away. "What was that for?"

"Don't growl at your commander," his uncle ordered. "You know better."

"He's feeling prickly because he's thinking with his prick," Alchan cut in. "I'm willing to ignore it for now."

"I'm not," Leshaun snapped. "He knows better."

"Wait. I can't growl at Alchan but you can get snappy with him?" Matesh spread his arms in a confused gesture. "Really? I thought we were past these double standards, *bodrya*. Alchan knows I would never challenge his authority."

"See? Your boy is fine." Alchan yawned. "And has a point."

Leshaun just continued to glare down at him. Mat bared his teeth in response. In the pits, he'd been older than Mave and Rain, the experienced male they could lean on. Now he felt like a boy, and it annoyed him. He didn't need to be treated like this. The only comfort was that Leshaun treated everyone like this, constantly giving them all a hard time.

"Varon says we should do something with her when we get off the boat. Take her out, let her experience the city before we move on to the village," Nevyn suggested for his mute lover.

"He means we should get her drunk and see if she relaxes. Varon, that doesn't sound like you." Luykas groaned. "That sounds like a terrible idea."

"Because it is, but we normally go out when we get back into Olost. No reason to rush back to the village just because we have her."

Mat looked over to Alchan, frowning. He was confused until he realized what Alchan's game was. He was worried about her fitting in with the other Andinna, so he was willing to do anything to put it off. The Company already had a hard time in the main village, and it only grew worse in the more remote communities. Having Mave was going to make things tense. He didn't want to deal with it yet.

Matesh was thankful for Alchan's avoidance. It meant he had time to get her more comfortable with him and being together. He wanted to hear her say the words, the acknowledgment that he was part of her *mayara* and she could rely on him. He wanted that security before they made it to the village. Before he had to deal with other females and she was introduced to nicer males who would see her for what she was: a beautiful Andinna female with a body to die for and the pure Andinna soul she tried to hide.

"Fine." Luykas moved to stand up. Mat watched the white-winged male walk closer to him and his uncle. "Speaking of things. Why haven't you pushed her into blood magic training? We had a deal."

"I decided her Andena was more important. We'll begin with her on blood magic later. She's making no attempts to use it and she's focused on her communication situation. I'd like to not distract and confuse her." Leshaun shrugged. "Deal with it."

"She won't speak to me unless it's a lesson and she hasn't needed one of those from me since she stole all my Common and Elvasi books to work on by herself. The sooner she understands some of the rules of blood magic, the sooner I think she'll be more understanding about the blood bond-"

"Don't rush her training to fix your problem, Luykas," Leshaun ordered. "You made that decision, and now you have to live with it."

Luykas looked down at Mat. He just shrugged in response to the stare. The mutt's problem wasn't his. He didn't make Luykas' life easier, and no one was stupid enough to ask him to.

I'm not giving up her bed every night to make you feel better, Luykas. Figure out how to deal with it or get used to your hand.

He wasn't going to say that out loud, but he knew Luykas got the message from his inaction and silence. Grunting, the mutt walked away, heading inside.

"You should be nicer to him…" Rain finally said quietly, breaking the silence over the company.

"He saved her life and I'm grateful, really, but that doesn't mean I have to cater to his every need. He's uncomfortable. He needs to stop being uncomfortable. We're Andinna. We have sex because it's nice and it eases the temper when other outlets wouldn't be acceptable. His being an accidental third party isn't my problem." Mat refused to back down.

"You don't need to fuck her every night," Zayden muttered. "He's not the only one losing sleep."

Mat reached out and slammed a hand onto Zayden's wing, causing his friend to curse and pull the wing away. While he didn't like his friend telling him to quit, he felt a warm pride that he was still pleasing her so well every night.

"Mat's right," Nevyn commented lightly. "It's not his responsibility to make sure those blood-bonded are comfortable. That's up to Luykas and Mave. If she's shutting him out, he needs to talk to her or deal with it, not expect her *bodanra* to fix it by stepping away. He should know better."

"Thank you." Mat was grateful someone saw his side of things.

"It's not like Varon and I lose any sleep. We're busy too. You two just make more noise." Nevyn grinned his way. "Speaking of, I'm bored. Varon, want to head in?"

Mat heard the mute stand up and knew exactly where those two were headed. He watched as they passed, Nevyn throwing an arm over his lover's shoulders and curling a wing over him to block the sun. They didn't separate until they had to get through the door.

"Those two are like rabbits," Zayden muttered.

"Not really. They ain't poppin' out children all the time," Bryn said, yawning himself. "I'm so ready to get off this ship. Anyone want to play some cards?"

"Nope." Matesh got up, beginning his escape. Cards with Bryn was like giving money away. The rogue was the best with cards in the Company and knew how to swindle them.

"Copper only," Alchan ordered. "Seriously, Bryn. You can't steal everyone's money."

"I ain't stealin' nothin'. Y'all just need to get better at cards." Bryn chuckled. "Anyone?"

"I'm in."

Matesh began to chuckle himself as he ducked inside. Zayden was going to be pissy later when he had no small currency left. Well, the fool knew what he was signing up for. If Bryn was the best at cards in the Company, Mat's old friend was the worst.

"Nephew, I feel like she went to hide in your bedroom," Leshaun said behind him, coming inside as well.

"How's she doing, really? Is she going as slow as she claims?" He worried, but she hated when he talked about her Andena and how she was doing now. It was why he just didn't bring it up anymore.

"She's doing better than she thinks, but she has no confidence in it. Go, help her. Your *amanra* needs you." Leshaun smiled at him. "Take some books from my cabin. I think you might reach her better than me right now."

"Do you like her?" he asked softly. "You've always been worried about the sort of females I used to..." It became another one of those moments he felt like a boy, but this time he was asking for it.

"I think she's everything we prize in females. A strong temper that can attract strong males. We like our women when they push us around. It's in our nature. She's a warrior, something I know had been a sticking point for you. Many of our free females are warriors when it's called for, but not by nature, because many of our most fearsome women were lost or are still in hiding. She is a warrior in soul and that's something you've always wanted. A female who will fight with you, and let you be the warrior you are."

"You didn't answer the question." He wasn't letting his uncle get away this time.

"I like her, but I worry. She's everything we prize in females, and yet so very different than any female I've ever known." Leshaun considered him. Mat felt like he was being judged. "You can't treat her like every other female, Mat. Remember that and I think you two will be happy for a very long time, even as she continues to build her *mayara*. Forget that, and I think she'll hurt you and I won't like her very much anymore. It'll be your fault, too." With that, his uncle patted his shoulder and walked around him, heading into the dining area.

Mat stored that piece of advice, promising himself he wouldn't forget it. He headed for his uncle's cabin, slipping inside and stealing two books he knew well. Both were legends and religious histories, things every Andinna learned young from their parents and local priests. Things that would only help her in the long run to understand their people. He hurried out with them and towards their shared cabin.

Once he got to the door, he leaned against it, thinking about her. She would be curled up on the spare bed, head over a book, her hair falling over her face in a way that made her mysterious and self-conscious.

He opened the door slowly and found her exactly as he thought he would.

"Hey, Mave," he called. "You ran off earlier. Everyone was looking forward to seeing you for training." It was a white lie he knew none of them would deny. The Company knew the game of trying to make a freed slave more comfortable. They might not be looking forward to spending time with her, but he knew none of them were averse to it either, except maybe Alchan. That was between Mave and Alchan.

She blinked twice before really registering he was there. He waited, not wanting to encroach into her personal space until she invited him. What he did in their private cabin wasn't what he did in public because he knew she didn't appreciate the attention.

"I didn't want to train with everyone," she muttered, not looking up from her own book. "Tell your uncle I'm sorry. I'm not up for more lessons today."

"He wanted me to see how you're doing, that's all. Anything you need help with?" He glanced at the page she was on and saw she was working with her Elvasi writing. "Were those giving you trouble? Or maybe I can do your lesson today…"

"What?" she looked up, frowning. "You want to do my lesson?"

He showed her the books, hoping she didn't get angry. "I figured I could help you with Andena today." Another thing he brought to her other than his body. Another piece of worth he could have that wasn't just sex. Another reason for her to keep him. He knew why his uncle suggested this now. It was helping him too.

"And what do you suggest as a lesson?"

"What does Leshaun make you do?"

"Recite it out loud for him. In Common and in Andena. I hate it." She curled her lip at the books and he looked down to see if he had grabbed the Common version as well. He hadn't, so he went with another idea.

"You've memorized the glyphs, right?"

"I've been trying," she answered. "Why?"

"Have you tried just…reading?" He wondered if his uncle was right and she was moving along. "If you know the glyphs, you should be able to just read."

"I can't pronounce half the words right!" She growled and shoved her Elvasi book away off her lap.

"I'm not asking you to pronounce them," he said quickly. "Just read them out in Common."

"What?" She frowned at him again.

He took a deep breath. "Just read it and tell me what it says in Common. That's all. If you get stuck, we can work it out. You've got a small book here, right? Your alphabets are written in it. And glyphs.

We can keep adding to it and you can keep studying the book." He looked over her face. "Get your book. Read for a little while. Write the glyphs you don't know, then together we'll work them out."

She nodded slowly. He knew this was a different lesson than she got from his uncle, but he didn't want to force her into thinking about pronunciations. He just wanted to prove to her that she did know something. He knew she would have trouble, but he also knew that she wasn't going to be completely helpless.

He watched her get to work, reading out in very broken-sounding Common what she was mentally translating. It was something.

"Good, keep going," he ordered softly, grabbing her weapons from the chest in the room. He pulled them out and began to sharpen them, taking care of them for her while she worked. He only stopped to correct her when she was completely wrong and had her write down what made her stumble so they could go back to it when he felt she had enough to go over.

It felt like ages, but finally, he was done with the swords and put them aside.

"What do you have?" he asked, moving closer to her again.

"They're ones I don't know yet. I've been collecting them. One of them has a root I know, but I don't know the other piece of it." She gestured at it. "Andena is weird. Some glyphs are sounds to form a word. Some glyphs are the entire word, or some obscure thing. I don't know how you keep it all straight."

"We live for thousands of years and spend the first hundred of them becoming fluent in the language. We have time." He could see the frustration in her eyes. She was a female who was used to seeing an obstacle and blowing past it or living to learn with it not impeding her. This was hard for her, no matter how fast she was picking it up, and she didn't like it. She couldn't brute force it.

"I don't have time."

"Yeah, you do. Come on, let's teach you some new words. Just me and you. You haven't let me help you with Andena yet." He smiled as he scooted closer. She groaned, but made space for him. He noticed she didn't put up much of a fight. Like every time he sat next to her like this, he wrapped a wing over her, making sure there were no distractions.

"I just wish I could do this faster."

"You don't give yourself enough credit. From what my uncle says, you're learning quickly."

"Everyone is speaking Andena and I don't understand, and it's frustrating because I feel so…" She swallowed. "Alone."

He moved some hair from her face and leaned in to kiss her temple, avoiding her horn. He felt so guilty for his uncle's little trick that he knew he needed to tell her. Not yet, though. If he undermined his uncle's plan, she would get pissed off at all of them instead of pushing herself to jump in and take her place the way she should. He wanted so badly to see her become a closer member of the Company. He'd thought they were doing well, but she had slowly locked herself away again, creating that emotional distance he had seen in her when they met. Now it wasn't about survival. Now he knew she was protecting her insecurities from the other Andinna, males she had all her problems exposed to.

And here she was, telling him how she felt.

"*Na al Sema, ut vahne,*" he whispered.

"I don't know what that means!" She pulled away from him. "Why is everyone always talking in Andena when I don't know what you're saying? It's not helping!"

He swallowed and reached to her, not letting her jump away. He knew the problem now. Really knew it. She was hearing Andena and writing herself off as being unable to understand it. He knew better. After three weeks on the ship, she knew more than she thought she did, but she was trying to protect herself by hiding. "Mave, stop. Stop avoiding the language. Listen. You know some of this."

"I am listening!"

"No, you aren't." She snarled and he growled back. "You know what I said, at least most of it. I can explain the rest. It's not a problem, but stop believing you don't know any of it. Now, listen." He went slower this time. "*Na al Sema, ut vahne.* You know what part of that means. Think about it. Listen to it. *Na al Sema, ut vahne.*"

Finally, a small light entered her eyes, but the insecurity was there in her posture. She had an idea, but no idea whether she was right or wrong. Because of that, he knew she would rather remain silent. Mave hated being wrong.

"Tell me," he crooned, trying to ease it out of her.

"By the Skies..." She worked over what he said to her. Finally, he knew she actually heard him and was paying attention. She had it.

"By the Skies, you are strong," he murmured. "We have no word for 'are'. If someone is something, we just say 'you strong' or 'you weak' or whatever you need. *Et* is 'me' or 'I,' while *ut* is 'you.'"

"What is kind?" she asked softly. He watched how her face softened as she asked the question.

"*Nola,*" he answered.

"*Ut nola.*"

He could only respond with a grin, kissing her slowly. "I would rather be called many things other than kind."

"Don't make me learn annoying or arrogant in Andena yet." She chuckled. "Thank you for that important lesson."

"Hm..." He considered for a moment telling her, then decided she could go ask anyone else. He wasn't giving her the keys to yelling at him in three languages. She was fairly good at yelling at him in two and his Elvasi was terrible, so he barely understood when she used it. "Keep reading. Tell me when you need anything. And stop forgetting that you *have* learned, Mave. This is hard, yeah, but it's not impossible. You are picking things up. You are."

He watched her go back into the book, writing out glyphs she had a hard time with and comparing them to a list of ones she knew already, the basics. She would ask him something, like what word could possibly be made out of the glyphs for blood and life.

"Birth," he answered. "Birth is a combination of blood and life."

"Oh. That seems..."

"Obvious? Yeah, our language seems really complicated, but it's not."

"It's hard to guess that, but then you say it and it seems so obvious," she agreed. "This is going to take me years to figure out, isn't it?"

"Yeah, and that's okay. There's still things I need to learn in Elvasi. The only reason I'm this good at Common is because we work a lot in Olost. But when we were in Anden? Well, let's say I didn't make my uncle proud with my education."

She considered him and he stayed seated under her weighty stare, refusing to run from any judgement she had. He did lower his eyes, after a moment. He got the response he wanted, an elbow to the side. He chuckled, leaning back and stretching out a little as she continued her work.

Honestly, I could watch her do this for a century and I don't think I would get tired of it.

The thought hit him like a punch to the gut. He wanted the century of watching her become perfect with Andena, learning every single little thing they had in their language.

And he wanted more. He wanted her in every part of his life. He just needed to make that happen.

4

BRYNEC

"Good mornin'," Brynec said as Mave sat next to him for breakfast *again*. Every morning, she sat down right there next to him and every morning, he tried to talk to her. He'd been glad - Skies, more than glad - to help her the day before with her wings, the first time she'd really spent any time with him since the first few days on board.

"Good morning," she replied.

"How're you?" he asked, hoping for more. Yesterday, she had run off on him after the wing workout, and he still wasn't sure how to stop it from happening again. They had been having a good time and she was so happy over her progress.

She eyed him before turning away quickly. "Good."

"So, I'm in charge of yer wings now. With ya moving into exercises, ya need someone with ya at all times. And that's me." He knew the sooner he laid that out on the table for her, the more time she would have to adjust to the new reality.

He watched her face morph into something akin to dread. He knew she hated to be touched. He had learned that very quickly when they met, but that couldn't stand in the way of her learning to fly. He and Leshaun were the best to help, and Leshaun was too old to be doing the physical work she needed done.

"Oh. Well." She moved uncomfortably in her seat and he just watched. "They're sore from yesterday."

"I bet they are," he replied, wondering why the conversation seemed to be moving like molasses. "Today we're stretching in the morning, working them in the afternoon, then stretching them before letting you sleep."

"Okay. And how long will I need to do this before going to the next step?"

"The next step would be some very short-range gliding and that could be months. Focus on this now." An older voice said it before Bryn had the chance to.

Bryn looked away from her to see Leshaun walk in, eyeing him. Probably wanted to yell that Bryn wasn't speaking Andena like everyone else walking in. He hated that damned idea. He didn't like how dejected she looked when the entire Company started off in Andena. It made her look lost.

"Well, eat up," Bryn ordered her, grinning. "Then we can go work."

"Months." She sighed heavily, looking away from him.

"You know, if you work extra hard at it and we keep your wings healthy, it could be even faster. It's just about how hard you push yourself." Bryn wanted to give her some hope. He watched her touch the new scar on her neck, her eyes focused on some distant place, and knew exactly where she was mentally. No one else in the Company understood like he did. He might not have been in the pits with her like Matesh and Rain, but he was the one who knew what hundreds of years of slavery did to someone. "Mave, ain't nobody going to stop ya from flyin' except ya now."

His comment startled her enough that she jumped. "I'm going to eat on the deck," she mumbled quickly, grabbing her plate.

Matesh was speechless as she launched out of her seat and left the dining area before anyone really could think to stop her. "What did you say to her?" he demanded. "Bryn, seriously, what was that?"

"I got it," he answered, grabbing his own plate and standing up. He had pricked Matesh's protective side with her running off like that. He followed her out to the deck, sitting next to her on a large crate, staring out over the sea. "Why ya run?" he asked gently. "Was it what I said? It's true, Mave. The Empire ain't comin' back to put leather around yer wings or a collar around yer neck. And yer makin' progress."

"I feel lost," she whispered. He watched her eyes, a light blue-grey that he could have sworn were more grey inside but now more blue. She had that type of eyes, where they changed with the light. "I don't know what I'm doing, Brynec. Matesh keeps saying, 'Oh everything will be fine,' but I have no idea where to go from here or what I'm doing. I'm…lost."

"I was too, when I finally convinced them to let me join. Didn't know up from down, and they wanted me flying in a year."

"Everyone didn't hate you," she muttered.

"Excuse me?" Bryn jerked back. "No one here hates ya, Mave."

She didn't respond. If she were another Andinna, he would have poked her in the side to get her attention, but she wasn't another Andinna. She'd gut him for it.

"There ain't no hate here," he repeated. "Where do ya get that impression?"

"Why else would they all speak in Andena when I can't understand or join in?" she asked, a demanding note in her tone that made him wince. "I know I'm a damned outcast, an *ensam*. I get that. I just thought this would be different."

"It's not about hating ya," he quickly said, unable to not answer her. She was an insanely dominant female. She didn't ask. She stated and it got done. He wondered what sort of fools were going to fall for her. He liked her, but she was nearly too strong for him. A lot of huge males like Matesh would adore her. Those were probably the sorts of males she would end up with. They would all love a female who was snappy, fierce, and dangerous, able to toss even the biggest Andinna males around. "Maybe it's about trying to help ya."

"What?" she frowned.

"Did ya ever think that they're using it so you get used to it? I don't like it, but the group had the idea and-" *Please, don't be mad at me.*

"They're...doing it on purpose?" she hissed out. Bryn swallowed the fear and nodded. "To help me?"

"Aye."

"They could have said something!" She turned to look at the door inside, and Bryn continued nodding slowly. He agreed. As it was, he was going to get in trouble for outing the plan, but he was tired of watching it. When Bryn had joined the Company, he already knew Andena, but it hadn't mattered. They made the effort to talk to him, make sure he was okay.

Aside from Matesh and Rainev, only he really was trying to talk to her. *Not that she makes it easy.*

"Matesh says I should just start asking for them to repeat it in Common, to explain but..." She shook her head. "That's..."

That wounds her pride and makes her feel even more alone. I can see how that idea wouldn't work for her.

"I'll make ya a deal," Bryn said quickly, realizing this was his chance. "We're going to come out here and work on yer wings every day, three times a day, just like planned."

"Okay."

"And while they all talk in Andena, I'm going to translate for ya. Explain things, if yer too scared to ask."

"And what do you get out of it?" she asked, now eyeing him with such suspicion that he was worried she would pass up on his offer.

"Uh..." He hadn't gotten that far. He just wanted to help. He wanted to pass forward the great things the Company had given him. It was the Andinna way of things, to pass forward good deeds like that. "It's best for the Company to get along, and by doing this, I help ya and ya become more helpful to the Company." He shrugged. "I mean...Two prior slaves, me and ya, both fucked over by pointed-ear bastards for just havin' wings and horns, and tails. Why wouldn't I want to help ya? Maybe I feel a little bad for bein' a gladiator too, seeing what the others did to ya. I don't know. Not really. I just know I want to help ya."

He laid it all out there and hoped. She didn't give him many chances to speak with her. He never really talked that much to new people, but something about her made him want her approval.

Damn being an Andinna male sometimes. It's because she's a dominant female. Of course I want her approval.

"You're a strange male, Bryn," she commented, still watching him.

"I've been called worse," he conceded. There were worse things she could have said to him. "Strange isn't an insult, though. Neither is different." He pointed at her plate. "Eat yer breakfast, then we'll get to work on yer wings."

She didn't respond to him, focusing on her food. He ate quickly as well, hoping today was the day any sort of progress would be made. He was glad she didn't run when he got too serious or personal. That seemed to be the sticking point. She had so many walls to climb over, and that deterred everyone. He felt like he'd made it over one.

He took their plates in when she was done and hustled back out to start on her wings before the Company came out to waste time doing nothing. Other than her strict training and lesson regiment, no one had much to do on the ship.

"So, they're sore from yesterday, aye?" he asked, running a hand over her right wing. He didn't miss how her tail twitched with anxiety, probably from being touched. Her tail didn't reflexively move as much as others, so he needed to watch it with extra care. If it was bouncing around, he knew she was being pushed too hard. He pulled his hand back until she responded.

"Yes, but I still want to work them out today again."

"I'm going to start, okay?" he asked, just to make sure.

"Okay." He watched her tense up as she answered and knew she was going to make his work difficult.

He nodded and began to rub out the muscles of her wings, starting at the main joint. He was taller than her, which made his job a bit easier. She was an average height for a female, and even as a shorter male himself, he had her in height. It made him think more about her time in the pits with dozens of other Andinna males, all her enemies. They all probably had her in height and weight, and yet she spent nearly a thousand years putting them down and winning.

"Relax, little miss," he murmured, working slowly. "I ain't going to stab ya in the back or nothing. Just focus on how good this feels for yer wings. Pretend I'm Rain or Mat."

When he was at her right shoulder, he continued to work on the muscles in her back as she stood patiently, looking out on the ocean. He could remember all the places he had knots in his back when he was learning to fly again. She relaxed by little degrees until he wondered if she were real or putty, swaying a little from the breeze around them. It was the most relaxed he'd ever seen her.

A small noise escaped her mouth, which he smartly ignored. He figured it would be rude to comment on the small moan of pleasure, since it wasn't for him to hear. It really just told him he was doing a good job, and that wasn't something he could ignore. Something male and satisfied filled him, then a shred of annoyance. *Andinna males serve, and here I am, servin'. Should have known my fuckin' instincts would love this.*

He wanted to scoff at his male brain for wanting to knead a little harder to see if he could elicit the noise again. He resisted the temptation. He wasn't her male and he wasn't interested in becoming her male. He just wanted to help, since he was one of the only males who could.

"Tell me about everyone," she ordered. He wondered if she meant to ask, but it came out like an order. Another sign of a dominant female who knew her place and knew his, even if she truly didn't realize what she was doing. "I feel like everyone knows everything about me, but I don't know anything about…any of you."

"Ya know a lot about Rainev and Matesh," he countered.

"That's different. We were in the pits together."

"Why don't ya ask 'em?" He was curious. "I'm positive Rain would tell ya everythin' you want to know." He snorted. "Matesh would probably like to talk to ya about anythin' else. Or not talk at all."

The look he got from her should have stripped the flesh and muscle from his bones. "Is there a problem with Matesh and I?"

"No, but ya haven't answered my question." He quickly backtracked and refocused on what she brought up instead of teasing her about the big male more.

"I don't want to rely on Mat for everything," she admitted softly, turning away from him again. "I don't want him to be my crutch, and he's already helping me with so much."

"Ah. And Rain?" he asked softly.

"He's been withdrawn, and I don't want to bother him. He probably wants to spend time with his father-"

He had to cut her off there, laughing as he waved a hand for her to stop. "Mave, Rain hates spendin' time with his father. Yer right that he's been withdrawn, but that's somethin' different."

"Either way, I don't want to bother either of them." She shrugged. "Can I start my extensions?"

"Aye, but nothin' else." He backed away and watched her large, perfect black wings extend. When he was a slave, his wings had gotten scarred from accidental injuries. Like most Andinna who saw battle, his wings had a myriad of thin cuts and slices, even a couple of very small holes. Her wings? Perfect. As if they never saw a day of hardship. She held them in tight like he did, a habit neither of them would ever break from centuries of the bonds, but she had protected hers more. He was always impressed when he saw them, considering she had a warrior's scars on her body.

"So, tell me about them," she ordered again.

"Fine. You know Luykas and Alchan. Half brothers through their father. They're equally dominant, but ya will notice one is easier to deal with."

"Luykas," she responded. "He's easier. Alchan is a challenger."

"Good instincts. If ya need something personal, go to Luykas. If you need something dead, go to Alchan. If you need both, do like

Leshaun and Zayden did to get the rescue mission in the Empire, and play both of 'em. Don't think you can outsmart either of 'em, though. When they put their heads together, they're strategy and logistics geniuses." Bryn shrugged and walked in front of her. He didn't need to stay behind her, and he wanted to talk to her face. It also gave him the position to see if anyone else walked out on the deck. "Ya know a lot about 'em and don't even realize it. Yer father was training 'em from before the War and during it. I mean, I don't know too much about 'em either past that. They're closed-lipped about the time before meeting yer father. Aye, ya don't know as much as us, but not much less either."

"Okay. What about...Nevyn and Varon? They don't really talk to me."

Bryn chuckled, nodding. "They don't really talk to most new people. Ya got to approach them first. They're open and friendly, but they never make the first step."

"Why not?" she frowned and he watched her try and figure it out. "Males in the pits never thought two men together was bad. Is it different on the outside? What does that mean for Rain?"

"Ya've jumped to the wrong conclusion," Bryn said, waving a hand to stop her again. "There's nothing wrong with 'em in the eyes of other Andinna. Really, they're very good together and everyone else is jealous. They've been together longer than most of us have been alive."

"Then why do they never make the first move? Why do I need to go out of my way to meet them?"

Bryn tried to find a good way to explain it. It was complicated and very Andinna and he had found it ridiculous when Nevyn had explained it to him. "They don't want to give you the impression they want ya."

"What?"

"Two males together oftentimes look for a female together, but Nevyn and Varon...don't want a female. So they aren't going to approach ya, so ya don't get that impression. If ya approach them and offer friendship, they'll absolutely take it, but they won't make the first move and they won't accept more than friendship. Plus, they've worked with a lot of rescued slaves before and they think not everyone should be trying to get in yer face all the time."

"There's so much I don't understand," she mumbled.

"Aye, but then not many people understand Nevyn and Varon. A lot of females have tried to either get them as the pair or get between them, not realizin' they're blood-bonded and never leaving each other." Bryn chuckled. "They both like females, but they're that in love with each other. Not unacceptable in our culture, but not too common either. Normally a male pair will find a female who ends up in the center, but neither of 'em will ever let a female become that. They have eyes and hearts only for each other."

"You know a lot about them."

"They're my closest friends," he admitted. "I spend more time with 'em than anyone else. Varon is a priest, and a good one. Helps ease my soul when I need it. Nevyn is just fun. He's a good guy."

"They sound good," she murmured. He watched her intently, wondering what she was thinking about. "A priest…"

"You'll have to sit down with 'em to ask about all of that." He didn't want to get into it. Varon was a particular type of priest and Bryn felt that if he explained it, he would ruin her impression of the mute male. "But, there ya go. Nevyn and Varon."

"You said they were blood-bonded?"

He had wondered if she was going to catch that. He nodded, waiting to see if she would say any more, but instead, she looked away from him, getting that distant look where he could tell she was thinking of something and wouldn't share those thoughts. She had some obvious tells. He could probably swindle her out of a lot of money in cards, if he ever convinced her to play.

"How do yer wings feel?" he finally asked.

"Better, thank you."

"I'll massage 'em out like that every mornin', to make sure you don't get too stiff and pull anything now that we're trying to build the muscle." He kept his gaze on her face, wondering where to go from here. "Is there anythin' else ya want from me? We can play some cards and hang out. Take a day off."

"Um." She shook her head. "I was going to go read, but thank you for the offer." He watched her take a step back from him. He didn't try to stop her this time, just letting her go.

The conversation they'd just had was the most progress he'd seen from her in weeks. He just wanted to help her, and it felt like talking to a skittish rabbit. It was really hard to see the Champion when she acted like that. He could relate, but it had been a long time since he was in her shoes.

"Varon," he mumbled to himself. Varon always had these sorts of answers.

Bryn headed inside long enough after her so he wouldn't run into her. Not for his space, but so she knew he wasn't following her around. He had a tendency to walk quietly and spook people, and he knew that wouldn't end well with her. It made him careful about how he crept around the ship when he couldn't sleep. He knew she was working out on the deck more often than not, but he made sure she never knew he was out there too, trying not to panic about being locked on the ship.

"Bryn," Nevyn said plainly when he found himself at the couple's door. "You look like you need something."

"Varon's advice," he answered. "Y'all ain't busy, right?"

"We always got time for you," Nevyn reminded him kindly, pulling the door open wide. "Get in here. This is about Mave, isn't it?"

"It is. I'm trying to get her to open up and I don't understand. I'm doing everythin' right. I'm kind, unassumin', gentle." He walked in while he spoke and Nevyn shut them in, giving him the privacy he wanted for the conversation.

Something snapped in front of his face. He blinked and saw Varon's hand there. He followed the hand as it moved and the mute began to sign.

"You're male. There's nothing you can do except give her time."

He frowned. "She's not scared of cocks, Varon. She's more than capable of cuttin' 'em off when it suits her, I bet. She doesn't like bein' touched, but then, neither do I, or nearly any freed slave."

Varon shook his head and sighed, giving Nevyn a forlorn look. Nevyn chuckled, shrugging. Varon huffed, his eyes narrowing. Nevyn rolled his eyes a bit at Varon's behavior before sighing himself, nodding slowly. Bryn was always mystified by their completely silent interactions. In those small gestures, those two had an entire conversation and came to a resolution.

"She's not scared of us," Nevyn agreed. "She's wary. I mean, there's a reason Varon recommended you try to get to know her instead of offering his own very safe presence. You know how it feels to have no trust in fellow Andinna and see your kind as the enemy. But you're male and she's female."

"She trusts Mat and Rain," Bryn retorted.

"Hm. She's fucking Matesh and Rainev isn't a threat to her." Nevyn raised an eyebrow. "But you? An unattached male showing an interest while she's in a new place, dealing with so many new things, surrounded in tight spaces by males who have her in height and weight? She's not carrying steel. We're threats. She's naturally wary and trying to find the safest ways to do things."

"I'm not interested in her like that. None of us are except Matesh. I'm...She doesn't need to be an outcast. No one let me be an outcast when I first joined. Ya all spoke to me and helped me find my feet." Bryn didn't understand where Nevyn was going with. "And I know you don't want her thinkin' ya will join her *mayara* or anythin', but-"

"Don't go there. We're not getting in the middle of this because she's got Luykas breathing down her neck with a blood bond neither of them should have." Nevyn's voice grew taut and pissed-off. Bryn looked down, wincing as he remembered Nevyn and Varon *hated* the idea of Luykas and Mave's blood bond. Nevyn took a deep breath before continuing in a much calmer tone. "We're not getting in the middle of a new Andinna relationship that is trying to grow stronger by the day. Matesh is trying to settle his place with her, all of that young male insecurity involved, and if too many of us start taking her time, he'll get pissy and vulnerable. We're not getting in the middle of this for more reasons than just making sure she doesn't want to fuck us. Actually, it's one of the smallest worries I have right now. We're way too old for her and she doesn't trust males enough to deal with more than one in her bed, I think."

"Something she'll need to work past," Varon signed from his spot on the bedding on the floor. *"She's a female, and eventually she'll find a second male, probably more. I have a feeling she won't be like her mother and have only one lover."*

"Another good point, love." Nevyn softened, smiling at the priest. "You know more about these things than me. Personally, I like your idea of getting her drunk."

"That was your idea, not mine," Varon signed, then threw a pillow from the floor and hit Nevyn in the chest with it.

Bryn began to laugh, enjoying their easiness. "Really, Nevyn? You passed that off as Varon's idea?" he tried to ask. He was glad Nevyn could even understand him.

"Of course. They wouldn't listen to me if it was my suggestion. Mind you, only Kian and Leshaun are older than me, but I still get no respect from anyone."

"You might if you acted your age more often."

Bryn continued to laugh, bending over as Nevyn sputtered from Varon's silent insult. Nevyn was well-respected when it came to combat and he offered solid advice when it was needed, but he also believed in getting rowdy and crazy every so often. He could also tell a good joke. He wasn't always the most serious male, and that worked against him sometimes. He didn't stop laughing until someone gently touched his shoulder. He looked up to see Varon had gotten up and walked closer.

"Do you need anything?" Varon signed. *"Seeing her, dealing with her, I know it's bringing up bad memories for you."*

"I'm fine. Promise." Bryn swallowed. "The ship...I think that's the problem." He sighed. He didn't want the conversation on him so he shifted it quickly, aiming it on a younger male who really did need some help. He could figure out Mave later. "She mentioned Rain's been withdrawn. I've noticed it myself. Do ya have any idea on that?"

"I do, just like I think you have an idea of what's going on there. But I think this is one of those things no one should speak of, not yet. Wait for him to come to you."

"Love..." Nevyn sounded wary. "His father..."

"Is why Varon thinks no one should get into it yet," Bryn explained before Nevyn could go further. "It's why I haven't tried talkin' to him, because we're on this ship and his father could overhear. Not his *baba's* business, not yet. Has he gone to ya?"

Varon didn't answer, just turned away to break Bryn's line of sight on his hands. It was a sign that Varon was trying to keep something to himself, a tell that was to stop other tells. Bryn leaned on his back between his wings. They had suspicions, dark ones. Things that could happen to a small male in a world of anger, where control was for the powerful and the weak were expected to get on their knees.

"Do ya think he'll need ya?" Bryn asked softly. "Like I did."

With that Varon turned back around, smiling sadly. *"I think they'll both need me eventually. When that time will be is for them to decide."*

"Even Mave?"

Varon just nodded. Bryn didn't understand how Mave would ever end up needing the spiritual guidance Varon offered, but he didn't doubt it either. When Varon believed someone needed healing and guidance, he was always right. It was just about the timing after that. It had taken Bryn a decade to accept Varon's offer, Nevyn coaxing him into it. Hundreds of years later, when the nightmares were their worst, he still went to Varon and Nevyn, who let him slide into their room and bed for the comfort of Andinna he could truly trust.

He hoped, for their sake, that Mave and Rain both realized they needed it faster than he did, especially Rain. Bryn had let that sort of pain fester in himself before and it had nearly cost him everything.

"So, what are you going to do?" Nevyn asked, pulling him out of his thoughts.

"I was thinking we could play some cards. I have an afternoon workout with her. Then evening stretches. I can use both of those to get her talking to me, right? I've made a deal with her that I would translate Andena when people use it. I'm hoping that helps her."

"Just keep doing what you're doing." Varon shrugged. *"You are making progress. Not as fast as you'd like, but sometimes these things just go slow. It's admirable that you've decided you want to help her. Don't rush it."*

Don't rush it. He wasn't trying to rush it. He just needed to know that he was helping at all.

5

MAVE

Mave was excited for her afternoon training in a way she couldn't describe. Matesh noticed, chuckling at her as she put away her books. "What did Bryn do to make you act like this?" he asked curiously, considering her.

"He's going to translate Andena for me when you all use it," she explained. "Plus, I get to work out my wings now. Every day just brings me a day closer to flying. I'm good at physical work. Why wouldn't I be excited?"

"He's going to translate for you?" Matesh's smile turned to a frown in a second. "I could do that for you. Why didn't you ask me to help if you wanted that? I would have."

She could hear how he was wounded, but didn't really understand why. Certainly he should have been happy she was bothering someone else to help her. He did enough for her. She could chase him away by being needy and desperate for his help, and she didn't want that. "He offered and I said yes? It's not a big deal. You'll be working out with the Company and he'll be over with me, so it makes sense."

He nodded, looking thoughtful and somewhat pained. She didn't know what else to say. She hadn't thought this would offend him. When she opened her mouth to say more, he shook his head.

"I'm fine. You're right. This will help you in the long run." He tried to offer her an easy smile again, but she could see it was a little strained. She didn't understand. What if she asked Rain instead? Would he be okay with that? He stood there, nudging a pillow into a particular spot and didn't stop until he seemed satisfied. "All right. Let's get out there."

She didn't say anything, just leaving the room as she tried to figure out why that exchange hadn't gone the way she thought it would. Matesh was supposed to be the male she understood, and now he was acting strange.

She didn't slow until she was on the deck, and even then, she was to the side trying to stay out of the way of the males who were already beginning to stretch. Brynec was waiting for her near the rail, waving.

"Ya ready? I was thinkin' of what exercise I want ya doing today." Brynec grinned, motioning for her to come closer.

"And what will that be?"

"Ya will extend yer wings, flap them twice, then bring them back in. Repeat. Ten times. But first, extension stretches. Get to it. Ya can do those without anyone needin' to monitor ya now."

She took a deep breath, listening to the training happening behind her begin. She went through the extension stretches with ease now, feeling looser than she ever had before. Whatever Brynec had done in the morning was the cause of how good her wings and back felt. He had magic in his hands, she was sure of it.

"*Sita!*" Alchan snapped.

She tilted her head at Bryn, who narrowed his eyes on the Company.

"Means…submit, or submissive. In this case, submit. Alchan's pretty pissed at someone if he's tellin' them to drop their eyes." Bryn continued to watch, but she didn't turn around. She didn't want to seem like someone who needed to watch drama. She wanted to, desperately, but she resisted. "Something happen between you and Matesh?"

"What?" She had no idea where the question came from.

"Nothing. Male things, I bet," Bryn muttered, shaking his head. He refocused on her. "Get to work. They're talking about Mat being in a bit of a mood. He eyed Alchan hard enough that Alchan got pissed." Bryn snorted. "Not hard to do, mind ya. Alchan despises eye contact. He won't get snarly with a female for it most of the time, but he won't submit even if it gets him killed. Another male? The other male is asking to get his ass whooped. The only males I've seen get away with it have been Luykas and Leshaun. He won't fight with 'em, but he has to really try not to. Leshaun for his age, and Luykas because he's family. Everyone else is fair game."

"What's his problem?" she asked. "He's an ass."

"He's a *bedru* - a male too dominant by nature - and nothin' he can do about it. Every male in his father's bloodline had been one and every male will be. Quirk of his bloodline."

"Luykas isn't," she retorted. She filed the new word away. A *bedru*. She would need to ask for more information about that later. She had never heard the term before. "He lowers his eyes."

"Aye, but Luykas is half-Elvasi. Calmer people. Luykas is dominant enough to be a *bedru*, but he doesn't have the temperament that makes *bedru* males such a pain in the ass." Brynec eyed her carefully. "They're dangerous, possessive, and solitary males. They're everything we don't want in our males anymore. They will keep a female, regardless of how she feels about being alone with a male, and kill any other male who attempts to join with her. Some make it work, but many don't and will never join a *mayara* because they can't control it."

"What are you trying to say?" she asked. He was obviously trying to teach her something, but she felt like she was missing some key point.

"He's just like that?" Bryn shrugged. "They're like…a throwback. To how we were when we first were scrawlin' on cave walls. Males like Alchan are the reason our society became completely matriarchal and gave females all the power. To protect ourselves from killin' off our own people. Mind ya, we should have always been that way, since the royal family always was. We made mistakes as a young race."

"You want me to be careful around him," she mumbled, realizing what Bryn was saying.

"Everyone should be careful around Alchan. He dislikes other Andinna in general, and aye, he especially doesn't like really dominant ones like you." Bryn snorted again, shaking his head. "Get to yer exercises."

"So there's no chance Alchan will ever like me." Something in her felt defeated before it ever got to fight. She began to extend her wings, pushing through the exercise. Physical work always cleared the mind.

"No…" Bryn was thoughtful. "Not that bad. I would just focus on ya finding a way to be comfortable in the Company without worrying about him. Ya two will always butt horns, even if you become friends, 'cause it's both of yer natures. I wouldn't say yer enemies either. He doesn't know how to deal with dominant females without it becoming a fight and ya don't know how to deal with males like him." He shrugged after that. "We Andinna are weird compared to other races."

"And here I am, more weird than most…" She curled a lip at the words. She knew where she stood.

"Actually, ya aren't. If anythin', yer pretty normal past the stuff like not knowin' Andena or much else. Needin' to learn doesn't make you weird. Just means you got to catch up."

"Explain," she demanded, wondering what he meant by that.

"Mave, Andinna love dominant, strong females. Even when ya aren't warriors, ya females are always orderin' the rest of us around. Ya do it, like just now. Ya don't think to ask, ya just demand an explanation. Something in you says it's yer place to expect a male to drop his eyes. Now, other races would say we males are weak, but it takes strong males to handle strong females, to support and serve females with strong personalities and dominant natures. Plus, who's going to say someone like Mat is weak? Or even Rain? He's small for an

Andinna male because he's a *raki*, but he's bigger than most humans, Elvasi, and clan members." Bryn reached out and patted her shoulder. "Yer not weird. Yer pretty normal, really. Ya just don't know it yet. Ya haven't seen much to go by to know how it all works."

"*Raki* means mutt," she muttered, showing him she knew what word he'd used but hadn't explained. She didn't know what else to say about the rest. *Andinna females are expected to be dominant and strong? He's right. I need to see more before I'll be able to come to terms with that. I've never even met another female in her prime, and the one old female I knew didn't speak to me nearly at all.*

"Keep goin' on with your exercises," he suggested, looking away from her with a smile. "Anythin' else you want to know?"

"What are they talking about now?" she asked softly as she went through the cycle for the third time. Her curiosity was piqued now and it felt like there was no sating it. He was giving her all sorts of information she hadn't expected. Leshaun was worried about her formal education, and Matesh helped him, but Bryn? Bryn was giving her so much more now.

"What do ya hear?" he asked back.

"Um…" she listened in and heard a few keywords she knew. Evening, uncle, nephew. "Something to do at night with…Leshaun and Matesh, at least?"

"They're talkin' about an idea they have for when we get into port. It's a surprise for ya, so I'm not goin' to ruin it." He grinned at that. "Sometimes it's nice you don't know the language yet. We can do these sorts of things."

She reached out to smack his chest, much like she did to Matesh and Rain when she was annoyed. Bryn was laughing, jumping away, and she ended up missing. Something felt easier between them, and she was quickly forgetting all the reservations she had built over three weeks of avoiding him. It felt like those first easy moments of meeting him, when he gave her the copper star and then the gold sun. It felt good.

"Finish yer exercises," he ordered her again, chuckling.

"Of course." She composed herself and went back to it. She needed seven more cycles. Each one burned a bit more than the last, but they all felt good. When her wings were fully extended, she grew accustomed to the wind hitting them, letting her feel how sensitive they were to the air. When she flapped them, she felt powerful, like she could take herself off the ground and reach the skies.

Soon. I'll fly soon. I might not succeed at anything else, but I will learn to fly.

"All right, ya hit ten. Stretch them a couple more times, then yer done for the day." Bryn was leaning on the rail, and she watched him yawn. "I'm going to nap before the evenin'. I'll be givin' ya another full back massage before ya lie on them. Hopefully, ya won't be as stiff startin' tomorrow."

She was excited for that full back message. *His hands are magic, I'm certain of it.*

When she was done, she left him to head inside while he joined the rest of the Company. Before she got inside, someone called out for her, making her turn. It was Zayden, and he was walking fast in her direction. His eyes locked on hers and she bared her teeth. Just like that, his eyes dropped, a momentary defeat, before coming back up in a more peaceful manner, less challenging.

"If you see my son, tell him to get his ass up here for training. He knows better than to skip."

"If I see him, I'll let him know you want him up here. What he decides to do is on him. He is an adult." She turned away from the angry father, rolling her eyes. He was always making demands on Rain to be somewhere or do something. She wasn't sure if it was because he was strict or what, but it was annoying.

But his request made her curious. Why wasn't Rain at the afternoon training? She frowned and went towards the cabin she knew he shared. She peeked inside but didn't see him. Shaking her head, she went deeper into the ship, even checking the sailors' sleep bay.

She didn't find him until she was at the bottom of the ship in the cargo hold.

"Rain?" she called, seeing the tops of his deep blue wings.

"Yeah, Mave?" he called back. She could hear something shake in his voice. It made her step faster. She didn't want to say anything until she was seated next to him, wrapping her arms around him. Even then, she wasn't sure what to say. "What do you need, *illo amyr*?" He wiped his face, pulling away from her.

"You didn't show up for afternoon training. Your father asked me to come find you-"

The string of curses in both Common and Andena surprised her. "Why can't he just let me have a few days off? It's not like we're required to be there right now. Alchan and Luykas don't care since we're not getting back to work the moment we get on dry land."

"Rain. Why were you down here?" She didn't care about the drama between him and his father, but she knew this had little to do with it. She and Zayden kept a wide berth. He was a cranky shit and she just didn't have the patience for it. But she would always worry about Rain.

"I haven't been sleeping," he admitted. "I came down here to try and nap where no one could find me immediately."

"Why haven't you been sleeping?" She knew the answer. They hadn't spoken of that awful day since they were running out of the Empire. She hadn't wanted to bug him about it, and she knew he was trying to hide the leftover pain. Countless times, she had seen this. There had been a time when it was her. Where she had wallowed in the pain. She grew past it, but it had been hard and lonely.

"I keep closing my eyes and…seeing them," he whispered.

"They're dead." She had made sure of it. She could remember how they fell, cleaved open and bleeding, the life drained from their eyes. She could remember every single one of them and how they died. "They're not going to come after you again."

"They haunt me, and I don't know how to make them stop." His words shook, so she pulled him close to her again. Gingerly, she opened her wings and wrapped them over them, rocking slightly as he curled closer, his wings held so tight to his back that they weren't in the way. She wrapped the tip of her tail around his and pulled them both closer to their legs.

"You should talk to someone," she said gently. "I wished for a long time to have someone to talk to. Matesh would listen. Or me." She had never told anyone that she had wished for it, but she had. Every night. Every private moment. Then she would bury it again.

"I'll get over it," he mumbled. "I'll be okay."

"Rain, I'm worried about you. Please don't think you have to do this all by yourself."

That made him pull away, shaking his head. She opened her wings so he could leave. "You did it by yourself. You were strong enough to do it. I'm not some weak little boy who needs to be coddled."

She jerked her head back at the animosity of his words. They hurt in a way she didn't expect. "I have never considered you a weak little boy," she snapped back. "I've seen you fight off males with centuries more experience than you. I know defeating a gryphon in combat without aid or the ability to fly is only possible by a true warrior. I know you're not a boy."

"But I'm still weak enough to need someone's help with this." He was growling now and she didn't know who he was really mad at. Her, his father, himself.

"I did it alone because I had no one. You have people," she reminded him. "Rain, I just wanted to check on you. You don't need to tell me anything. I thought offering you some comfort would help." Now she was backtracking, hoping he would calm down. She hadn't wanted to upset Matesh *and* Rain in the same day. This had started as such a good day.

"Well, I don't need to be coddled," he snarled. Then he turned and stormed out, leaving her reeling and confused. Her heart felt like it was going to break as she listened to her *illi bodyr* stomp up the stairs.

She sat down on a crate, unable to move.

What did I do wrong?

All she had wanted to do was help. She knew how bad the hurt was. How it took hold of the heart and crushed it. She was over it, for the most part, but seeing him in that much pain? She felt herself being dragged back into the dark, a dark she had left behind long before she met Mat and Rain. Truly alone, truly vulnerable and violated. Dark times in her life, very dark.

It all came flooding back, as she remembered the pain in his eyes. The way he had looked when she and Mat had gotten to him.

She had once been the same. No one had come for her. She just thought he would like someone to talk to about it. She understood, she really did. She had never shared it with anyone, but she would have shared it with him to help him.

Mave didn't move until she heard someone else coming into the cargo hold. She looked back towards the door and saw Brynec, who was obviously confused by her presence there as well.

"Well, little miss, I thought I wouldn't see ya until later tonight."

"Are you down here for your nap?" she asked at the same time. They both stopped talking for a moment until Bryn sat down next to her.

"Aye. I find it hard to sleep in enclosed spaces. This is the biggest place on the ship and no one will bother me down here. Alchan and Luykas don't like when I sleep outside." He nudged her with an elbow. "Why are ya down here?"

"I found Rain down here," she answered. "And he…got mad at me. So I stayed down here."

"What's goin' on with him? If ya don't mind tellin' me. I can ask him, if I need to."

She looked at him, wondering where that came from. No one except Zayden had openly asked what was going on with Rain yet and she hadn't expected it from Brynec. He was the last person she had expected it from, really. Maybe Alchan or Leshaun. Or even Varon, being a priest. But Brynec the rogue, the other prior gladiator?

"Why?" She tried to hide the hostility, but was unable. He was another gladiator. In that moment, while the darkness touched the back of her mind, trying to drown her, he was the enemy.

"I think I can help him too," he answered.

"Excuse me?" She pulled back from him, shocked out of her temper. It came back harder, bringing a snarl from her lips. She wasn't going to let some other gladiator near her little brother. "You? How? I know what happened and I'm doing everything I can to-"

"Ya aren't male," Bryn cut in. "I am. I'm not a *raki*, and I'm not *as* small as him, but I'm on the smaller side of Andinna males, Mave. I was a gladiator, too. Livin' with bigger males. Aye, I think I can help in ways you can't, because I'm male."

She blinked, swallowing her idiocy. Of course. "You too." The rage faded. The darkness, the memories, they didn't, but something eased in her.

"Aye, me too." Bryn looked away after that. "Like nearly everyone who lives in that world."

"Yeah," she sighed out, nodding. "I didn't even think of that. I'm sorry."

"Tell me more about the argument? I'd like to know before I try to talk to him what to expect."

"He doesn't want help. He feels it makes him weak," she explained. Something continued to shift in her. Suddenly, Bryn wasn't just any other gladiator like Seventy-Two or the monsters she was used to, the ones who made her a monster in return. He was a gladiator like her and Rain. Someone who had to fight a bit harder to be safe. Someone who understood what it meant to be the target in hell.

Something in her trusted him a bit more, knowing what sort of darkness he held in his past as well. He understood.

"Of course he does," Bryn said, groaning. "And his *bodra*, the *kuk*, isn't helping."

"Did you just call Zayden an ass?" she asked without thinking. She'd heard *kuk* before and was nearly certain that's what it meant.

"Of course. What else is he?" Bryn shook his head. "He's overprotective. He loved Summer, ya need to understand. Rain is all he has left of her, and he won't live a full life span. Zayden wants to keep his boy alive as long as he can. Can't blame him, but it's probably not helpin' Rain's head."

"No, I don't think it is," she agreed. "I made him so mad when all I wanted to do was help, Bryn. He's hurting and I don't know how to help if he won't accept my comfort. I'm not even good at comforting. I've never really done it before. I've never had anyone to comfort and I want to help him." She was rambling now, saying more in the span of those moments than she had in weeks to anyone. It felt like floodgates were opening. "I failed to protect him the pits, Bryn. I failed him and Matesh. We got there right before, but I don't think it was soon enough. They had beat him so bad-"

"You didn't fail him then," Bryn cut in again. "Ya didn't fail him."

"I did. My first family in a thousand years, and he got hurt when I should have been there to protect him, and now I can't help him. He doesn't want my help." Her chest began to heave as it all settled in. She'd spent weeks thinking she was okay, but seeing Rain in that state, seeing him so angry that he stormed out - it all crashed into the fragile wall she had built around that day. Around the vulnerability she felt over losing his love. She didn't want to lose her *illi bodyr* because she had failed.

"I'll talk to him. I've been where he is. No worries. Ya just tell Matesh that I know now so he doesn't cleave my head off my shoulders. I like the big brute, so I don't want to gut him for anything stupid like being attacked for talking to Rain about something sensitive."

She couldn't stop a small hiccup of a laugh. "He loves Rain," she mumbled. She didn't know why she said it, since Bryn probably knew even better than her, having known them for centuries to her short two months or so.

"Aye, I know. He's been that way with Rain since the boy was born. There's a reason Rain calls him uncle."

"He doesn't call you uncle," she noted, suddenly thinking about it. "Why not?"

"I wasn't...that involved in raisin' him, like Matesh and Luykas. Varon and Nevyn both really enjoyed it, since they won't ever have kids, but it's not my thing. But I'll talk to him about this, I promise ya.

He doesn't have to do this alone like he thinks he does. Maybe hearing that from another male might help him."

"Thank you," she murmured, grateful he found her down in the cargo hold when he had. She couldn't have taken this to Matesh, knowing her lover would take it to Zayden, but she hadn't wanted to deal with it alone, not knowing what to do. "And...thank you for telling me about you." She felt like she needed to recognize that.

"If ya need to talk, just let me know," he told her kindly in return. "I'm male, cock and all, but I'm sure I can understand some of what ya went through."

She swallowed, considering that. She hadn't thought about her own nightmares in a long time. Now they were being scratched, itching for her to spill them to the disarmingly charming Andinna with sky blue eyes.

And what would I say? I lost my virginity on show? That I was given by the Empress to her lover to be beaten and taken for the first time?

No...he doesn't need that sort of baggage from me. He can help Rain.

"Thanks for the offer," she replied. She stood up, feeling stiff and awkward now, and stepped away. "I'm going to head up. You came down here to sleep. Thank you for talking to me and...keep me updated on Rain? Please?"

"Aye, of course." He stood up, sweeping dust off himself. She turned and left the room before anything else could get brought up.

Nightmares. She had been doing really well for the last few weeks on the ship, pretending she could just remain focused on the future. Now it itched. Seeing Rain falling apart, hearing Bryn once lived in similar circumstances and had lived through the very things she had tried to protect Rain from.

The day had taken a dark turn on her and she wasn't sure where to go with it, so she went to her shared room with Matesh. He was lying on the bed and she didn't say anything as she lay next to him. Without thinking, she touched her tail to his, causing him to roll so they could stare at each other.

"I gave Bryn permission to talk to Rain about what happened," she told him. Something appeared on Mat's face that she couldn't identify and made her feel the need to explain. "Apparently-"

"You don't need to explain. I know Bryn's story and he should be able to help Rain. What happened?"

"Rain yelled at me," she whispered.

Hurt flashed in his eyes. That she could understand. She rolled closer to him and put her head on his chest.

"He yelled at me too, when he came upstairs. He took off for a fly after that in his wyvern form. If Bryn can't talk some sense into him, we'll have to tell his father."

She shook her head. "It's not our secret to tell, Mat. I can't expose him like that. I barely said anything to Bryn. He guessed, but neither of us really ever said the words."

"Well, we'll see how this plays out. Let's take our minds off it. Want to practice Andena?"

"Sure," she mumbled. "Can we just…talk to each other? I'm not in the mood to read."

"Yeah, we can do that," Matesh answered.

6

MAVE

That evening, Mave didn't say anything when Bryn walked out from below deck with Rain beside him. She didn't want to pry, no matter how much she worried. It wasn't her business what was said between them, if there was anything said at all.

"He wants some time to figure out what to do, to process it, and he feels like no one is giving him the time he needs. He just wants to be left alone for a little while. I'm giving him my room to get away from his father. I barely use it." Bryn didn't look at her directly as he spoke, seeming distracted.

"Thank you. I didn't…want to ask." She twisted her hands together, uncomfortable. *I've never done any of this. Until I met Mat and Rain, I never dealt with this sort of thing. No one wanted to be my friend and I didn't want any of them.*

"Ya care for him. In lonely worlds like the ones we've been in, that's important." Bryn's words were gentle. Her heart thumped hard at the truth in them. She hadn't given him enough credit over the last few weeks. "Let's get started on this."

"Did he tell you exactly what happened?" She turned away from him, spreading her wings to a more natural relaxed position so he could work on them.

"No. We never really talked. I found him when he came back in, told him I saw he was strugglin' with somethin'." Bryn started touching her, those swift and steady hands kneading into her muscles. "He doesn't know as much about me as the rest of the Company, but he ain't stupid either. He said he wanted some space and that was it."

The conversation dropped quickly after that. Mave wasn't sure what to say and she could tell Bryn was distant with her now. She wanted to pull him back into a conversation, like a desperate need to know more about this other gladiator, this other slave with a scar.

"Why do you cover the scar?" she asked, staring out over the water. She was glad she didn't have to look him in the face for the question. She didn't hide hers, but then, she hid none of her scars. She didn't see why she should.

"I was teased for it. Then it became useful, the scarf. The scarf can cover much of my face when I need it to."

"But what's the point? You're Andinna, the horns give that away. The wings. The tail." She was frowning now, trying to puzzle out his reasoning.

"It just feels safer." He paused on a knot in her left wing. "I do some very illegal things for the Company, and there's plenty of Andinna roaming around Olost. Not mercenaries, but there's some rare trade caravans and some who just need to roam a little. I don't want people to think it's me."

"Really?" She gasped, turning to look more closely at him. "What sort of illegal things are we talking about?"

"Nothing too serious, really. Every so often, there's some uppity human that wants all non-humans out of Olost. We deal with them. Well, *I* deal with them. It's been a hundred years since the last one. The Free Cities of Olost are as free as they claim because they know that the longer-lived races there keep it that way. Take Captain Sen. He's a pirate, sure, but as long as Olost accepts him, his kind, a mutt, he'll protect Olost ships and warn them of Elvasi forces if they come too close." Bryn pulled on her wing, an indication she needed to turn back around so he could continue working. She obliged the request, letting him deliver attention to a particular knot in her left wing.

He killed people, important people, to help maintain the reputation of Olost being a place for the free and anyone who needed a home.

If there ever was a good reason to kill, that would be one. I like that. I've killed for less, much less.

"Now, my turn for a question," he murmured, rubbing a little harder as his hands moved to her shoulders. His hands brought that annoying little sound from her, but she couldn't stop it. Her muscles had never felt like this before and it was because he was doing this that she even knew they could be this relaxed. "Who was the first person ya killed?"

"A guard," she answered. After a pause, she decided to finish the story. The very short story. "I was ninety-seven. He tried to rape me."

"Temper snapped, aye?" Bryn's question was sad.

"Yeah. I was thrown in the Colosseum after that."

"Did he succeed?" Bryn's words were taut. His grip tightened, but she didn't mind it as he pushed his fingers to her flesh, forcing the tightness of her own muscles to abate.

"No."

"Good job," he whispered. His hands were bordering on painful now. "I hate the Elvasi. I hate that we had to work with one of them to get ya out."

In her mind, that Elvasi's face flashed. Trevan, the guard who showed an unexpected kindness. She knew he was dead now. There was no way he survived that night.

And Dave. Her human. She should have been kinder to him.

Her heart hurt for a moment, tightening.

"Who was the first person you killed?" She didn't want to think about her past anymore. She had spent all afternoon thinking about her former life.

"My first owner. He succeeded, but only once. I got him back after that. He put my collar on me, so before he bled out, I cut off his hands." Bryn's hands left her shoulders. "Sorry-"

She reached back and grabbed his wrist with a hand, wrapping her tail around one of his ankles at the same time. "Don't go. You're the only person who *knows*. I won't judge you for any of it, if you don't judge me." By the end of her request, her voice shook. Matesh and Rain were her saviors, the first two Andinna to show her any real kindness and acceptance, but even with them, she felt like a monster sometimes. The female Andinna that butchered her own people trying to survive in hell. They would listen, but she wondered if they ever really understood. They did by the end, but they had only been in the hell of the pits for a few weeks.

Bryn made her feel different, she realized. He made her feel like she wasn't so alone in the world. He knew. He understood. He was male, sure, but he had lived the same pains.

"We were the small ones," she whispered. "We had to become deadlier than any of them if we wanted to make it through the day."

"Aye, we did," he agreed. "What else would you like to know? I'll tell ya anythin'."

"I don't sound like a fool, right?" she asked, with a hint of desperation.

"Nah, Mave, ya don't sound like a fool. I understand, I do. It's hard, not havin' anyone who really understands." He stepped closer to her again, and she released his wrist for him to continue rubbing her back. "I thought I was crazy when I got freed. I wanted to talk about all of it, but I thought I didn't need to. It festered in me, festered for a long time. Ya think yer too strong to need to talk about it. It all happened a long time ago, right? Never going to happen again, right? So why do ya need to talk about it?" He chuckled dryly. "I understand better than anyone else on this boat, little miss."

"Do you ever feel lost?" she asked. "I do. I don't know what I'm doing. What is freedom? Where do I go and what do I do? Am I ever going to learn everything?"

"Ya joined us, so you'll go where Alchan and Luykas tell us to go.

Ya will do what they tell ya to do, except on your off time, like here on the ship. Ya will have Matesh, who can help guide ya through meetin' and livin' with our people. Ya will have Rain, who is yer family now. And if ya lose those two, the rest of the Company will pick up the slack, because yer one of us now. Freedom ain't scary, it's just big." He sighed. "But aye, in the beginnin', I felt lost and alone. I had a world I knew and suddenly had a world I never dreamed off."

"I'm sorry I avoided you for most of the trip." She swallowed. "I've been…distrustful of everyone and focusing on other things."

"A bit of distrust is warranted. Ya don't know any of us. That'll change in time, but we expected it. And you have a point. Leshaun has been riding ya hard to learn, to catch up on everything. Plus, I think you've been riding yerself too hard."

"You tried to tell me that trust is something the Company offers, and I haven't…done very well with it." She didn't want to admit how hard she was being on herself with her lessons. If it was that obvious, then she didn't need to give him the satisfaction of admitting to it.

"We trust ya to do what the Company expects. Follow orders, kill when necessary. Don't die. But that's Company trust. Ya can expect us to do the same. When it comes to violence, we'll be at yer back, no matter who. That includes Alchan and Luykas. We expect ya to be at our backs." He patted her back gently. "Ya speak of a different trust. We never expected ya to open up with all yer secrets on day one. That takes time. It'll come though, because ya will learn to trust us with those too."

She heard what he said, and nodded. There was a deep need in her to admit one secret, to show him that the trust was building thanks to their shared backgrounds. She needed one person who really understood her and she had a feeling it was the lean male in front of her. Already, she was considering him in a different light.

"I hated the other Andinna more than the Elvasi," she admitted softly. "The Elvasi, I understood. Their cruelty was easy to deal with. The Andinna…"

"Ya don't need to tell me," he cut in. "I might hate the Elvasi a lot more, but I know what the Andinna are capable of when pushed too hard by the cruelty in their own lives."

"Maybe next time I'll say more," she said, chuckling darkly. "I've never voiced a lot of this. When Matesh and Rain showed up, I was in charge of the pits and these are all distant memories. No one could stand against me on the sands, and no one would attempt to hurt me in the pits. I should have known the games would give them a chance to strike."

"They still are distant memories, but they've festered. Ya ever think that the hurts they gave you are the reason yer havin' a hard time here?"

"I know that's why," she answered. "I'm not foolish. I know that's my problem. I need to keep reminding myself that males who are free are like Matesh and Rain, not…"

"And me. I'm not like those males in the pits."

She turned to him and wanted to say he was once one of those males in the pits but couldn't bring herself to say it. He'd once admitted to disliking her from a distance, while he was still a slave, but they had never met. He had never been in Elliar, in her Colosseum. But the way he said it, she knew he was saying he never treated other Andinna the way she was treated.

He was saying he was once treated the same way she was.

"No, you aren't like those males in the pits either," she agreed softly. He visibly relaxed, as if her judgement really mattered.

"Would ya like to play some cards and keep talkin'?" he asked, seeming nervous.

"I would," she agreed, smiling a little. "Dining area?"

"Aye, it should be quiet down there by now."

Together, they walked inside and found only Alchan and Luykas sitting in the dining area. She nearly turned around to leave again, but Bryn just stopped and looked at her, a questioning look on his face.

She shrugged. She knew she needed to start getting more acquainted with everyone and there wasn't a massive group, which always made her feel lonely.

It was just Alchan and Luykas.

"You two should be heading to sleep," Luykas noted as they drew closer.

"We're goin' to play some cards and talk. We just got done with her evenin' stretch." Bryn slid into a seat, leaning back nonchalantly. She took a seat across from him. "No money."

"Of course, she doesn't have any for you to swindle from her," Alchan muttered. The comment made both Luykas and Bryn chuckle, but Mave wasn't sure what was so funny.

"Does Bryn swindle many people?" she asked, looking between them.

"Everyone," Luykas explained. "He takes everyone to task playing cards. Don't expect him to go easy on you."

"Aye, but think, I'm the best person to teach her this." Bryn grinned, turning it on her. It was boyish in an attractive way, not a youthful Rain sort of way. She hadn't been expecting it, not after everything they had just talked about. "What are ya two plottin'?"

"What we need to get done in port." Alchan looked at her thoughtfully. "Want to hear about it? This will end up being important to you as well."

"I would. Thank you." She tried her best to not meet his eyes and make a scene but failed. Luykas sighed as Alchan's lip twitched, revealing a canine as they stared each other down.

"Stop it, both of you. There's no need for it."

Mave tore her eyes away first, realizing the mutt was right. There was no reason for her and Alchan to get into it, none at all. She mumbled a quick apology, looking down at the papers between them.

"Sorry." Alchan had a bite to him, but he said it. "Mave, maybe it's time to explain-"

"I already explained to her what ya are," Bryn cut in. "Ya two need to work it out now."

"Ah, the curse of our family," Luykas said in a pained way.

"Moving on," Alchan growled. "We're planning what we need to do when we hit port. We'll be entering Olost through Namur, a port city in Southern Olost."

"Namur is the home to the most pirates in Olost," Bryn added nonchalantly. "Captain Sen lives there when he isn't on a boat."

"It's also the closest port city to home." Luykas sighed. "So, a lot of Southern Olost is mountainous and just a bit colder than the rest of the continent. It's the furthest from Anden we could get, but it's…as close to home as we could get."

"And that's where the village of Andinna is?" she asked.

"One of them, the biggest. Well, we filled up those mountains, really. You'll see. It might as well be the Anden of Olost." Luykas gave her a small smile. "You'll like it there I think."

"Back to what we're doing in Namur," Alchan said quickly. "We need to supply for the two week trip to the mountains. We need to grab gifts for back home as well. We can't return to them without supplies for winter; they'll throw a damned fit."

"We've got time for another job before winter, so there's no reason to worry about stocking up just yet for that." Luykas groaned. "We're going to winter there this year, Bryn. Be ready for that. You're good at numbers, so when the time comes, I'm going to need you to look over what sort of job we'll need to take before the first snow to make sure we're good."

"Ah, and when were ya going to tell the rest of the Company?" Bryn pulled out a deck of cards, smiling. "I have no problem, but ya know Matesh is going to be put out by it. He hates wintering there."

"He'll live," Alchan growled. "If I have to deal with it, so can he."

"Why would Matesh have a problem? And why are we wintering there if people don't like it?" She leaned forward, wanting to know more.

"Matesh will have to tell you why," Luykas said at the exact same time Bryn also gave an answer.

"Matty," was all the rogue said, with an ominous note. She curled a lip. She hated that nickname for Mat and she remembered the origin of it. A previous lover. "Think about it later, little miss. No reason to get possessive right now."

She schooled her face, feeling the warmth of embarrassment heat her cheeks.

"We're wintering in the village partly so you can meet other Andinna," Luykas explained. "Also, we need the break from working all the time. We don't winter with them every year, but sometimes we just need to settle for a few seasons. After the adventure we just had, we'll do one more job before winter hits so we have the finances covered, then settle in."

"There's a lot of reasons we need to winter there this year." Alchan waved at her. "You'll see. You'll fit in there, I bet. There's a lot of females like you that you'll fall in with."

"Thanks for the confidence in the matter," she retorted. "You make it sound like it's a bad thing."

"It's not," he conceded. "If Bryn explained to you what I am, then you should know I'm the strange one in this case. A *bedru* like me? I just don't fit. I can't kneel to the females in charge, which throws off everything in our society. It makes me a bit of an *ensam* with females. Males are fine. We have our own pecking orders outside of what you females do." He bared his teeth in a bad smile. "Look at it this way, Mave. A normal Andinna finds how dominant you females can be to be the most attractive thing they've ever experienced. I don't find it appealing at all. I have an urge to be in your place, controlling, owning, and the strongest. It's a curse on the family Luykas and I were born to, and a blight on Andinna society."

"Well, maybe I should talk to other Andinna about this." She turned away from him, looking back to Bryn for help. She didn't know how to go on from here.

"Let me teach ya how to play cards," he said nonchalantly, saving her. "We can save all of that for later."

Quietly, Bryn told her about the cards. She had learned some of this from Zayden already, but it was nice getting even more information now. He explained Andinna poker, even dealing Luykas in while the brothers worked on their plans.

She tried to pay attention to both and ended up losing every hand to Bryn, as she struggled to keep up. Finally, Bryn just started laughing, taking her hand and playing for both of them as he tried to explain better. She stopped listening to Alchan and Luykas bicker about what inns were the best to stay at, what shops were the best for raw materials, and other things she had never really considered before. She wanted to know what Bryn was trying to teach her.

"I'm heading to bed," Alchan finally declared, shaking his head. "Bryn, get Luykas to figure out this mess. I have a suspicion he wants to spend more money than we have."

"He always does," Bryn replied, chuckling. "Aye, I'll deal with it. Luykas, give me all of that and play with Mave while I clean up this mess ya've probably made."

Mave looked at the mutt warily. He seemed frustrated, shoving all the papers to Bryn. When he caught her staring, something changed. He dropped the frustration and focused on her with the sort of expression that made her feel like he was sizing her up for a duel.

"I think I'll just go get some sleep," she said quickly, putting her cards down. She didn't want to have Luykas' attention, not even for a second. The double heartbeat in her chest became apparent as she stood up. Her body didn't like the idea her mind had, leaving when Luykas was finally this close. She had gotten so good at ignoring it over the last three weeks and now it was too obvious, like the day she first noticed it.

"Wait," Luykas said with a begging note. "We haven't talked or-"

"There's nothing to talk about," she replied quickly. She was nearly away from the table when something wrapped around her ankle. Looking down, she found Bryn's tail.

"Stay, please. I won't be long." He nodded his head back to her seat. "We were having fun."

"I can tell you more about your family, if you don't want to talk about the blood bond," Luykas suggested. "Please. I don't like being avoided, not by you."

She slowly sat back down under the weight of both their requests. "Tell me about them," she ordered. He put talking about her family on the table, and she was going to take that opportunity.

He knows exactly what to say to get to me. Prick.

"Where do I start? Do you want to know about your father? What about your mother? There's also both your brothers." Luykas waited for her answer with such an anxious expression she wasn't sure how to handle it.

"My mother," she answered with a tentative beat of excitement in her chest.

"She was a warrior like the rest of your family. She and your father met as grunts, common soldiers, when they were stationioned in the same war group, a *svamor*." Luykas chuckled, looking away from her. He seemed lost in memories for a second. "They told everyone that they fell in love right off the bat, but she made your father work for it, and work hard. She was incredibly dominant like you and only the best males ever had a chance with her. Or that's what everyone would say, anyway. Kelsiana Lorren, second in our military only to your father. He ran most of the military, but your mother? She was in charge of tactical *svamors* that would do all sorts of madness. Her warriors were called the *somaro*, or the elite warriors. Once, we found a camp of Elvasi penetrating the mountains, and she had us blow a cliff up and crash it on them. No survivors. She was a genius in her own right."

"Why wasn't she completely in charge if we're matriarchal?" She was suddenly very glad she'd stuck around.

"She didn't want it." Luykas shrugged. "She just didn't want it," he repeated softer. "Sometimes, Alchan and I will wonder to ourselves how the War would have gone differently. We were winning, but it was taking so long, and the Elvasi just kept throwing short-lived humans at our mountains. They were developing more ways to kill us."

"And what would you have changed, to help us win instead of lose?" She knew what she thought.

My mother should have never had me. None of this would have happened.

"Keeping you in the camp with everyone else. Thousands of soldiers would have protected you better than a safe house. At the time, we agreed with your father and mother. Plus, your capture was just one piece of the nightmare that the end of the War was. There were better ways to handle the situation, but your father had just lost his blood-bonded *amanra*, and you were taken. The Empress planned her schemes well."

"So…what did you and Alchan decide?" She noticed that he hadn't changed his answer.

"That trying to change the past is futile, and we shouldn't try. We can only make do with what we have. The War is over, our people are enslaved, and the few of us free? We just need to survive the next winter."

He finally says something I can relate to, and it's the most fatalistic thing I've ever heard. Do I sound like that to other people?

"What about my brothers?" she asked, trying not to think too hard about the end of the War. She knew her place in that chain of events.

"They were good males. Hertesh was the older one. He was…" Luykas frowned. "Somewhere around two thousand when he died. Seanev, the younger one, was in his fourteen hundreds. They were like older brothers to me. They were so excited about you, by the way. They couldn't wait to teach you everything they knew, including how to make your parents upset." Luykas coughed, thumping his own chest with a fist. "They made Alchan and I promise to help protect you, to pass on the big brother affection they had given us. Sadly, we all failed in the end."

She looked away at that, not knowing what to say. Who failed? Her? Her mother? Them? Everyone?

Or maybe they were all just victims of the cunning bitch who ruled the Elvasi.

She knew better than to dive too far into the past. All day now, she had been haunted by her past. First thanks to Rain, then Bryn. Now Luykas, going back even further, to things she couldn't even remember.

"I think I will get some sleep," she declared. "I'm tired. Thank you for talking to me, though. I appreciate it."

"Any time," Luykas said, standing. "I mean that. I'm more than willing to tell you…everything I know about them, and more." He looked down and tapped his fingers on the table before saying more. "I just want to talk to you. There's no reason we should be making this blood bond harder on ourselves."

"You did this," she reminded him, reaching out to poke the scar on his forearm, the one matching her own. It was a scar she would never lose, and a constant reminder of the soft second heartbeat in her chest. Normally, it was so faint that she had to concentrate to notice it. "Don't forget that."

With that, she turned and left the room, finally done with everything for the night. The day felt like it had been too long, too full of things. Less than three weeks on the ship and she was ready to get off it. Now she knew why the sailors muttered about cabin fever.

She nestled next to Matesh where he lay, already asleep. She hadn't realized she was back to the room so late. He groaned and she sighed as the emerald eyes opened to see her.

"Done hanging out with Bryn?" he asked.

"I am. Sorry for waking you," she whispered. "Go back to sleep."

He wrapped an arm around her, cuddling up with a possessiveness she normally didn't feel from him.

7

RAINEV

Rain sat quietly, hoping no one found him again. He just needed to be alone. Why couldn't anyone understand that?
Well, Bryn understands. Thank the Skies for him.

Without Bryn, Rain would have never gotten a space where he didn't have his father breathing down his neck, trying to figure out what was wrong. Rain couldn't bring himself to tell his father or anyone else. And he was trying not to be angry with whoever told Bryn what was going on. He couldn't believe Mave, Matesh, or Luykas would betray him like that, even if it got him a private place to hide in for the rest of the trip.

A soft knock at the door made him snarl and Bryn's head poked in.

"Just checkin' on ya," the calm young rogue said.

"Who told you?" Rain demanded immediately. It had been on his mind since Bryn had come to him.

"No one, not really. Mave said ya were withdrawn, how she failed ya, but she never gave me any details. I won't make assumptions about yer plight, but I think I know what's riding ya. Ya just stay in here until yer ready to deal with people. No pressure."

"They didn't rape me," he growled.

"Good." Bryn watched him, narrowing his eyes. "So-"

"But Mave and Matesh had to save me." Rain looked away, covering his face. "I need to get stronger so I don't need to be saved, Bryn, but I don't know how."

"Ask for help," Bryn answered. Without saying anything more, he closed the door, leaving Rain in the dark silence again. Rain stared at the door in shock that he was left there with such simple advice. That was it? Ask for help?

Rain shook his head. Asking for help would be admitting that his father was right. He was too weak, too young, and too vulnerable to be in the Company with everyone else. This had been his first mission, and look at what happened. Look at what those other gladiators did to him.

Rain curled up, resting his head on his knees.

He just kept thinking about it. Was there anyone in the Company who would help him? He could talk to Varon and Nevyn, but he knew the priest would make it a big deal and want to help in ways that Rain wasn't sure he could handle. Varon was a priest of their love, fertility, sex, art, and music goddess, after all. He was a strange male. Nevyn would only point him to Varon, which didn't help.

Luykas wanted him to talk it out with his father. Mave just wanted to cuddle and coddle him. Matesh was just being an annoying uncle, also thinking he should tell his father. He didn't really see how telling his father would help, so Rain refused to.

That left fewer options. Brynec, Kian, and Alchan. Kian was off the table. He would just tell Zayden immediately, and there'd be no stopping him. Bryn was the one who told him to ask for help, and Rain knew Bryn had lived through similar things. They never told Rain the graphic details, but he could talk to the rogue at least. When he was ready.

I'm not ready yet.

And he could ask Alchan to make him strong. Alchan wouldn't question it, since it was the only thing he really did when they were in the main village. He took it as his personal responsibility that the villages were trained to protect themselves, even if he always claimed to hate being there. Rain could easily convince Alchan for private tutoring.

Rain wouldn't be able to get Alchan alone until they made it to the village. That was a problem, since the closer to Olost they got, the more he dreaded going back to the main Andinna village. He had an on-and off-again lover there. A lover that would think he was still okay, but Rain couldn't even begin to think of sex anymore without his stomach flipping in uncomfortable ways. He couldn't think about that lover who liked to be a bit dominant with him, and Rain had once liked it.

And there was his father. He couldn't let his father get in his way, which meant he couldn't know that he went to Alchan for training, not yet.

The plan began to form. First he would go to Alchan. He would learn to be stronger without needing his wyvern side, the ferocious beast clawing at his chest to kill everything that scared him. If that didn't help him, he would talk to Bryn. That worked.

8

MAVE

"Bryn, how'd I do today?" she asked, panting. "I lost count." The sun was hot enough that she needed to lean on the rail, sweat dripping down her body.

"Ya did over thirty. I'm almost worried yer pushin' too hard." Bryn stepped closer, looking over her face with some concern. "We've only been exercisin' yer wings for less than a week. Ya okay?"

"I like physical exercise," she answered. "This is nothing." It wasn't, not to her. She had pushed her body further than this for centuries. If anything, it felt good to be working a part of the body that she had been forced to neglect for so long. "Just tell me if you're worried I'm going to do any damage."

"Nah, I don't think there will be any damage," Bryn said, now eyeing her wings. "But I think if ya push too hard, ya might get too sore and have to sit out for a couple of days. I bet that would piss ya off."

"I won't go that hard." Or she would try not to. *I make no promises.* She wiped her face off and turned to look at the males training. Her eyes drifted to Matesh first and she drank that sight in. These males were always shirtless, only preferring to wear their leathers, which hugged muscular thighs. The entire look suited Mat in ways that pleased her.

"Ya stare any harder and people might begin to think yer in love with him," Bryn teased. "Are ya?"

Mave coughed at the suddenness of the comment, heat flooding her face. When all she could summon was a stammering response, Bryn just laughed, throwing his head back like it was the best joke he'd ever heard.

"I don't know," she answered, finally finding the resolve to say anything. "I've never…been in love."

"Ah, I didn't mean to touch a sore spot then." He gave her an apologetic smile. "He likes ya a lot and ya obviously like him. It's fun to watch for the rest of us."

"Is it?" She frowned, wondering what they were all watching that was so interesting.

"Hm. He's doing everything ya could expect from an Andinna male. He's puffin' his chest out, helping ya with every little thing, always tryin' to spend the most time with ya. It'll calm down eventually, but we're all havin' a good time watching the beginnin' stages." Bryn chuckled. "I mean, now that yer talkin' to me and not staring at him, he's staring over here, wondering how he lost your attention. He might even get a little jealous of the time ya spend with me, but a proper Andinna male will never voice it, knowing it's not his place."

She turned back to see Bryn was right. Mat smiled at her and she couldn't resist one herself as she met emerald green eyes across the deck. Without warning, Mat crumpled over, wheezing. The males training all began to laugh as Leshaun held up his cane and pointed it at her.

"Stop distracting him," the old male ordered her. She couldn't even get insulted or angry. It had been so sudden that she was laughing along with everyone else.

"*Bodrya*. Why?" Matesh coughed out. She could see he was still smiling, and something about the entire scene warmed her, but not in a physical way. It was like some ice chip on her heart melted.

"Staring at females gets males killed," Leshaun explained. "And so does staring at males, Mave!"

She laughed harder, covering her face. Never in her long life had she ever stared at someone to the point of distraction. She was better than that, but the accusation made her feel normal. She also had a sneaking suspicion that she really could stare at Matesh to the point of injury. He was a fine-looking male and she finally had time to appreciate it.

She was still giggling as the other Andinna on the deck quieted and went back to work. Sailors had even stopped to watch what happened, which was unusual. For the entire trip, the human sailors had kept to their own, leaving the Andinna a wide berth unless they were on cooking or cleaning duty.

She turned back to Brynec and noticed he was watching her with a bemused expression.

"What?" she asked, the humor dying.

"Ya have a nice laugh," he answered, shrugging. "I was tryin' to remember if I ever heard ya laugh so much."

"I…" She wasn't sure what to say. It was a common occurrence, really. Years of silence had left her unprepared for comments like that.

"Now I'm tryin' to figure out how I can make it happen again. Laughin' is good for the soul. Eases some of the tension, relieves some of the stress. Ya should laugh more, I think." He turned as he spoke. "I'm goin' in to think about this. Want to come in and play cards?"

"No…" She waved at him. "I'll see you at dinner, I guess. Then evening stretches?"

"Ya don't need me for the stretches, but aye, I'll be there." Bryn smiled over his shoulder at her and then went inside.

She was enjoying the sun too much to go inside. She leaned on the rail again, looking out at the ocean. She loved the look of it. Endless blue, so different from the dirty, dark tunnels of the pits or the white walls of Elliar. A few seabirds flew high above them, diving down to grab fish. A sign that they were drawing closer to Olost with every breath they took. So close to shore, to a new land, to her freedom.

When the ocean bored her, she turned back to the training males. This time, she looked at all of them, much like she had watched the other gladiators. It felt different, though.

I'm not watching them like I need to protect myself.

No, instead she was just drinking them in. Cut, firm bodies. Fine males with clear, dark ink swirling and cutting across their bodies, except the odd white that Luykas had. All of them were in their prime except Leshaun, who wasn't working out with the younger males. Like her, he was just watching.

They fascinated her, truly.

Nevyn and Varon, with their dark colors and how they moved, like they were in sync. She watched them spar as a pair against Alchan and Luykas, moving so fluidly she was certain they could read each other's minds. She saw that they even kept their tails hooked with each other at the tips, as if they wanted to be one body in a deadly dance against two opponents. They didn't let Alchan or Luykas between them, forcing the other pair to split up and lose their rhythm.

They won easily, forcing Luykas and Alchan to admit defeat, everyone laughing and shaking hands at the exciting spar. She admired that. In the pits, even sparring partners could be cruel to each other, trying to one up and do better, even injure each other. The difference was startling. The comradery was something she wasn't used to, though she had been getting close with Rain and Mat.

After that, she saw Matesh and Zayden pairing off. Matesh was taller, but Zayden was a broad male, packed with muscle and dangerous in his own right. She could see he had a temper as fiery as the sun, snarling and attacking, not allowing Mat a break to breathe.

"What do you see?" Leshaun asked her, walking closer.

"Zayden fights like he's going to die and take everyone down with him," she replied, not surprised by Leshaun finally coming to see her. The way he fought was something she felt like she might have in common with the grouchy father.

"Yes, he's like that. Always has been, since he was boy. He named Rainev for it."

"Here I thought Rain was named for the…rain," she muttered. "Let me guess. An Andena term I'm missing?"

"The *rai*," Leshaun explained. "The *rai* is our passion, the fierceness of what we feel. Or, as everyone says, our temper. Temper is the most common way it presents itself. Many don't use *rai* anymore."

"*Rai*," she said in a softly, hushed way, testing the word out for herself. "And he made it into Rainev."

"Yes, but to know more, you would need to talk to Zayden."

"Of course." She snorted. "He and I don't do much talking."

"You don't talk to many. I'm glad to see you talking to Brynec now. He's a sound choice of a friend, even if he is…morally grey." Leshaun tapped his cane on the deck thoughtfully. "I'm glad to see you out at all for more than just your own exercises. I know I'm tough on your education, but I also feel like this is important."

"I'm tough on myself. I don't like not knowing."

He looked down at her, silent for a moment. She wondered what those half-blind eyes saw in her. Leshaun was tough, but also kind. Caring, but stern. He wasn't afraid to whack someone with his cane, no matter who they were, but he was also patient with her mistakes.

"*Ala non lerani eni vorha.*"

"No…running…mountain." She frowned. "That's all I got."

"It roughly translates to 'there is no sprinting up a mountain.' It means you need to pace yourself. Yes, work hard, but don't fault yourself for not making as much ground as you want in a single day. It's a long journey to the peak and moving too fast one day may only slow you down later in the trip." He gave her a small, weary smile. "You didn't know any of those words when you came on the ship."

"Fitting. I'll remember that, thank you." She crossed her arms over her chest. She went back to watching the males. Rainev was now sparring with Luykas, growling as he over-extended to get past Luykas' defenses. It was a foolish mistake, driven by emotions and anger. She sighed, shaking her head as Luykas disarmed him. No one said anything or laughed this time. It was becoming more apparent every day that Rain was losing his patience with being on the ship. And that he was finding his temper harder to control.

"Go inside," Luykas ordered him. It wasn't harsh, but it wasn't forgiving either. There was no room in Luykas' tone that meant it could be disobeyed. Rain didn't say anything, tossing his wooden practice sword to Matesh and storming inside.

"To be young and upset," Leshaun said, sighing.

"Yeah…" She had once been there. To control herself in the pits, she had locked it all away. While Rain was battling the new sensations of pain, she was trying to keep hers from flooding back up. Repressing it for so many centuries was beginning to take its toll, her tight hold on the reins of her emotions slipping more often as she found less real need to hold them. She hoped he worked it out. She hoped he found what he needed to heal and not become like her.

"Would you like to spar, Mave?" Matesh called out.

"I'm out of practice," she called back.

"Liar!" Matesh grinned, holding up the wooden sword Rain left. She knew a challenge when she saw one and stepped closer, leaving Leshaun behind, the old male chuckling. As she grew closer, everyone stopped and began to watch her. She took the offered sword and backed away again, spinning it in her hand, testing its weight.

"Who wants to call winner?" Matesh asked.

"I will," Luykas answered. "Three hits or a fatal blow is the winner. Ready?"

She focused on Mat, blocking out the rest of the Company and the sailors around her. Even Captain Sen was saying something from his wheel along the lines of 'Let's see this female knock his ass around.'

"Go!" Luykas ordered.

Mave dove forward fast, dodging Matesh's first swing as he misjudged the speed of her attack. She slammed the wooden sword into his gut, pushing him back hard enough he lost his footing.

"Out of practice, she says," Nevyn mumbled. "*Voek. Al amov Andinna vahne.*" Alchan laughed at that, but Matesh growled softly.

That was all she needed to know about whatever *voek* and *amov* meant.

Take the chance, Mave. Call him out and ask for an answer. You can do this. An insult is an insult in any language.

"I didn't catch all of that," she said. "Care to explain?"

Nevyn's eyes went wide as what she said settled in. Varon began to sign wildly to someone.

"Please. I knew half of it. Let's hear it. Particularly *voek* and *amov*." She waved the wooden short sword at him, beckoning a response. She couldn't back down now. She declared her own ignorance, and now she would need an answer or they would always use Andena to talk about her.

"*Voek* is damn," Nevyn said, groaning afterwards. "*Amov* is…the Andena equivalent to bitch. If you wanted to call me that, it would be *bodov*. Basically, I said 'Damn. The bitch Andinna is strong.'"

"And what did I ever do to get called a bitch by you?" She shut down. She locked away the hurt and anger at his explanation. She knew what she was doing as Matesh cursed, standing up to step in front of her.

"It's not so much insulting as just the way we talk. He just wanted to call you a female," he tried to explain. "Nevyn didn't mean anything by it, not against you anyway. He was more making fun of me."

"I didn't," the male agreed. "You haven't done anything. It just rolled off my tongue when you said you were out of practice and then you did that. Matesh is the beefiest male here, and you landed him on his ass. Male was beaten by a bitch, that's all."

She tried to pull the walls back down and relax, but it was hard. He hadn't meant anything by it. She kept repeating that to herself.

"Keep practicing with us?" Matesh asked softly. "Please?"

"Of course," she murmured, giving him a tight smile. As she turned away from Nevyn and the small crowd around him, she made her hands relax. She took a deep breath.

"Hey." She glanced back at the male, wondering what he wanted now. "Good work with that, by the way. You surprised me with that move, that's all."

"Thanks. I was told you're good. Care to spar?" She threw the proverbial gauntlet.

Nevyn grinned at that. "What's on the line? I accidentally insulted you, so maybe we should put a bet on this."

"I want to know how you and Varon worked so well together. If I win, you'll tell me."

"Hm. I would have told you anyway, but then again, knowledge is power. If I win, I want to teach you how to use different blades and we're tossing those ugly Elvasi short swords into the sea."

"I would have wanted to learn anyway," she responded, smiling. "But you are the resident master everyone talks about."

"Everyone, out of the way," Nevyn ordered, walking forward. "Live steel. Three bloods. Nothing fatal."

"Good terms." She handed off her wooden sword to Matesh, who made no complaint. A sword was held out to her after that, a gladius she knew well. Nevyn was using a wicked blade with a curve at the end. It was similar to a scimitar and made her interested. She had never seen anything like it.

"Go," Luykas called, his tone more tense this time.

Nevyn didn't charge her and since she didn't know him, she didn't make the first move either. Andinna and sailors began to back away further, leaving them a large circle. They paced around, keeping their bodies towards the other, waiting for an opening.

"How long have you been a warrior?" she asked, hoping the conversation would give a distraction and give her the opening she wanted.

"I've been a soldier since I was two hundred," Nevyn told her nonchalantly, not missing a beat. "Thirty-three hundred years of weapons. It's all I know."

She raised an eyebrow. He was in his thirty-five hundreds then. He had centuries of experience on her. She would take him seriously, more seriously than she took many of the older gladiators. He seemed confident in a way that she recognized. This was a warrior who still fought on real battlefields, not on sands for entertainment. She could see it in the way he moved, the way he kept the same watchful eye on her.

"Get on with it," someone called out.

They made the first step towards each other at the same time, and suddenly, steel was clashing, singing and sparking in the bright sun. She pulled her wings in as tight as she could, holding them out of her way. She spun, ducking an overhead swing. She sliced his thigh and jumped back, but didn't get the distance she wanted. He followed and thanks to his longer reach, he cut her upper arm once.

Before she could recover, he gave her a second cut across her ribs. She snarled, spinning again, this time using her tail to grab his leg. He was faster than her, and that annoyed her. A big male like him wasn't supposed to be so much faster than her.

Or as smart as he was.

He sliced her tail, making her stop moving.

"I win," he called. She dropped her sword in shock at the speed of her defeat, unable to really process how that just happened. He picked up and held it out for her. "I've seen you fight before, remember? I know what you like to do. You trip people up with spins, keeping your wings in, something most Andinna can't pull off. The problem is you have no formal training and you forgot to account that I do. I've also been in thousands more fights against all sorts of different peoples. You're very good, and anyone else in the Company would have a hard time. I won't."

"I take it this means you're going to start training me in a different weapon." She took her sword back, feeling stung from the loss, but also proud of his compliments.

"This." He held up the curved blade. "This is a *morok*. It's a weapon only we Andinna use. While we each tend to get weapons that suit us most, I make sure everyone is trained in our heritage. I think your style and the *morok* would do well together. And if you do well, maybe Varon and I will still tell you how we fight so well together."

"May I?" She nodded to the blade, hoping he would let her try it for a moment. He didn't answer, only held it out. She handed him her sword and took the *morok*. She spun it in her hand, testing its weight and balance. It was heavier at the tip than the gladius but she was satisfied with the way it felt. It had a force thanks to the weight, but it seemed sharp enough to slice through bone. She did a few practice swings, and when she enjoyed those, she couldn't stop a small smile.

"I think she's in love. Mat, you need to get better at cuddling or my sword is going to replace yours." Nevyn snorted. Matesh groaned.

Males are always so cocky. At least he seems to be a good sport. Two can play at that game.

She began to chuckle, still swinging the sword a little. She glanced over at the male, raising an eyebrow. Casually, with purpose, she looked him over. Standing behind Nevyn, Varon was grinning, his shoulders shaking with silent laughter. Nevyn spread his arms, welcoming the inspection.

"There she goes with the 'I'm going to eat people' face again," Zayden muttered.

She held Nevyn's sword back out to him. "I like the blade, but it's a bit on the small side like the gladius. I like my males to have bigger swords than mine." She delivered it with a straight face and got the reaction she was looking for.

Nevyn's jaw dropped, obviously shocked she had come back with a sly insult. Varon gasped, looking shocked and amused, maybe even a little impressed. Alchan and Luykas were both coughing, leaning on each other for support and covering their faces to hide laughter, proving how alike they really were. Matesh and Zayden began to laugh, the sailors joining them. She looked past her opponent to see Leshaun smiling across the deck. He inclined his head to her and she felt like she did something right.

The males continued to tease each other as she walked back to the older male. Matesh followed her, wrapping an arm around her shoulders. She was glad that he felt comfortable enough to touch her like that in public, and even more glad she felt comfortable when he did it. It all made her feel like she was finding her place.

"I think you'll fit right in with time," Leshaun said, still smiling.

"Thank you. So, what's next?" She felt strangely ready for anything.

9

LUYKAS

Luykas had to grit his teeth and bear it. He watched her spar with Matesh and was a little annoyed at just how easily she could take him out. He knew they had trained together in the pits, and honestly expected more from Matesh. Then there was Nevyn, who made a comment and got called out.

But did she gut him like a fish? No. Instead she sparred with him too and then started making cock jokes like it was another day.

Something thumped him on the back as he watched the scene unfold. Mave and Matesh walked over to Leshaun, striking up a conversation with the old male. Luykas couldn't take his eyes off her, even though he wanted to. He *really* wanted to.

Another thump made him growl.

"Don't start that with me," Alchan snapped. "You're being very obvious with the whole 'I can't control the blood bond' thing right now."

"Fuck," Luykas muttered, turning around to see his brother. That put her behind him, completely out of sight.

Sadly, not out of mind.

His heart tugged and pulled with a force that was practically unbearable. In the weeks since he did that bit of nearly regrettable magic, he realized he had a serious problem. He thought he had blocked her from feeling the effects, and for the most part, he did. The blood bond, however, decided to have a sense of humor. It's what he deserved, really, for playing with the blood magic of their gods the way he did.

"It's not my fault," he growled, trying to rationalize what was happening to him.

"You did it, so yeah, it is." Alchan snorted. "Think you can make it inside?"

Luykas considered that. She was only fifteen, maybe twenty feet away. All he had to do was turn around and he'd be able to see her. Maybe going inside, where she wouldn't be so easy to watch, would help.

But something kept him pinned to his spot, resisting the idea of having her behind a wood wall. He could hear her talk and laugh, attempting some broken, beginners' Andena with Leshaun and Matesh. Such a change in such a short time. He knew it had to do with the close quarters of the ship and the time they were required to spend together. He couldn't discount Brynec's attentions on her. He seemed to relax her while they worked on her wings. Luykas wished he was the one who had volunteered for that job. It would give him the ability to just be next to her.

Regrettable that when he wanted to ease the bond in any way he could think of, she refused to get near him.

"Come inside, Luykas," Alchan ordered. "Come inside and try to stop thinking about her just for a minute. You need to step away."

"I can't," he snapped, wincing as he realized he'd yelled that. He hoped she hadn't heard him.

Suddenly, Varon was in front of him, cutting between him and his brother. Alchan stepped back, looking offended at the sudden intrusion of the mute. Varon searched Luykas' face intently before grabbing his shoulders. With a swift yank, Varon had him moving towards the door and Luykas didn't fight it, knowing it was the best chance he had of going inside and getting some distance. Nevyn opened it for them, glaring at Luykas like he'd committed the great sin of hitting on Varon or something. He wasn't really sure why Nevyn was so pissed off.

They were in the dining area when Alchan finally caught up.

"Excuse me you two, but my brother and I were having a conversation. You can't drag him off."

"Oh, we know, and we're joining it. It's about time Luykas gets a fucking piece of my damned mind." Nevyn's response was strained, as the male tried to hold back weeks' worth of anger. Luykas had known this was coming. Weeks of dancing around the nasty business of an argument with two of the older members of the company. Two people who firmly held on to every tradition they could, every edict from the gods the Andinna had.

Luykas had been hoping it would wait until they were off the boat.

They didn't stop moving until they were down in the cargo hold, the most private place on the ship.

"What the hell? I'm tryin' to sleep down here!" Bryn exclaimed, seeing all of them walk in. Luykas looked up from his feet and watched the rogue's eyes go wide. "Aye…I'll go."

"Good idea," he agreed. He wished he could.

Within seconds, Bryn was gone, hauling ass up the stairs towards the deck. Luykas wished he could follow. The direction Bryn was going was towards her. His heart felt like it was being yanked from his chest. He collapsed on the floor the moment Varon let him go. He hadn't been expecting the sudden lack of support. He didn't bother getting up, leaning on a crate and looking up at the other males.

"You need to chill out," Nevyn growled, leaning down to say it right in his face. "She didn't ask for the blood bond. She didn't ask for you to be like this or the shit she's probably feeling. Varon and I don't behave like you when we're apart. Get over it."

"He's been getting…night sweats," Alchan said, maybe trying to buy him some sympathy. "If she's awake, he is. He-"

"Hold on," Nevyn cut him off. They all turned to Varon, knowing Nevyn wanted his priest lover to chime in.

Varon watched Luykas with thought as his hands began to move, spelling out words in Andena. *"What did you do? The magic you put in the bond. What exactly did you weave in that blasted spell?"*

"I blocked as much as I could. She doesn't get the same thing as the rest of us. She feels the slight pull, but she's not getting-"

"Slight pull?" Nevyn snarled. "You're acting like it's a thousand times worse than normal and she thinks of it as a *slight pull*? That's what your damned magic did?"

"She can barely feel my heartbeat under hers." Luykas needed to explain. "I couldn't let her go into a full blood bond, I couldn't. She knows what she feels is…dampened. She doesn't know I'm feeling this strongly. I can't find the time to tell her because she won't speak to me." He had told them this before, but this time he knew he was in for it.

Nevyn's nostrils flared in barely contained frustration and rage. Luykas had known that if he pissed anyone off, it would have been these two. Together and blood-bonded since before he was born, or close to it, they were also devout.

"The feelings have rebounded. You are feeling the effects of both of you, aren't you?" Varon's hands were moving fast now. *"You know, if you had ever listened to me, you would have known that our gods love to meddle. They aren't cruel, but they keep their hands in our lives as best they can, even if they can only do small things. What you did was offensive, no matter the reason, and this is what you deserve. There's no saving you."*

"Varon…" Nevyn leaned towards his lover. "What if there is? I hate it and she doesn't deserve it, but he's one of our bosses. Is there anything we can do to help?"

"He would need to convince Mave to let him remove the spell. Good luck with that. She hates you. I can't say I blame her, and shit, it might not even work." Varon shook his head. *"She's going to have two males in her* mayara *before winter and here you are, getting in the way. She's a female who deserves males who deserve her. You don't, and yet you have the blood*

bond I'm certain Mat would kill for. You went too far this time, Luykas, and you need to deal with those consequences."

"Two?" Alchan asked innocently.

Luykas wanted to roll his eyes. He thought it was obvious. It galled him, but he knew that was the blood bond. The bond was screaming for him to get closer to her and find a way to stay next to her. He was certain it wasn't all because of the blood bond, but the bond was making it much more extreme.

"Brynec. He's enamored and hasn't realized it," Varon answered, still signing so fast Luykas was having a hard time deciphering it. *"And I'll be damned, Luykas, if you get in his way."*

Message received. The priest will have my balls if I fuck up Bryn's shot.

"Here, here," Nevyn agreed, grinning. "Those two are made for each other. Give them the first mission, watch it happen. It'll be fun." Nevyn sounded more innocent, but with a smirk showing off a canine, the soldier was just as serious as his lover.

And so will Nevyn. They'll each take one and probably wear them like those fucking human friendship necklaces.

"With how new Matesh is to her, do you really think she'll take a second so quickly? She could be like her mother and stick to the one." Alchan was trying his best to be pragmatic. They all knew that wasn't the case.

"No, she's going to have a large *mayara*. We're certain of it." Nevyn shook his head at Alchan's suggestion. "As for Bryn and Matesh, they offer her different things."

"You think too much about this," Luykas muttered. "This is why Alchan never wanted females in the Company."

"I'm lover to a priest of Amanora. You know her. Our goddess of love, fertility, and the arts. Of course I think a lot about the ways of love." Nevyn said it in a way that made it seem very obvious that he put a lot of his time into it. "And Varon can't come out right and say it, so I do. Plus, this isn't why Alchan didn't want females in the Company. He didn't want them here because they challenge him in a way none of us will. Females change the dominance dynamics." Nevyn shrugged. "I can't blame you for that, Alchan."

"I didn't think you would. She's here now though, and there's no other good options. She's in the Company." Alchan grumbled, sitting down on a crate. "So, now that you've yelled at him…you really don't have any way to help him?"

"Nevyn is nicer than me. I don't even want to help him. I just wanted to yell at him," Varon signed, ending with a shrug and look of disinterest. *"Thirty-four hundred years on this earth and flying these skies, and yet, I can still be surprised by the absolute arrogance of the Elvasi. It's always worse when they toy with things they don't understand."*

Luykas felt the sting of that rebuke. It hit him in a nasty way, making his shame into an anger that was pure Andinna. A snarl escaped him, echoing in the cargo hold as the others remained silent. Nevyn took a step back from him. Varon didn't seem affected, which pissed him off more.

"Take that back," he demanded.

Varon shook his head, his hands moving. *"No. Sometimes you need to be reminded that you carry two natures. I don't think the Elvasi in you is bad, just that it has its faults. The Andinna aren't perfect, but we also don't pretend to be."*

Luykas looked away, the growl in his chest refusing to stop. It rumbled, an indignant anger directed at the truthfulness of those words. He'd been able to stop this lecture from Leshaun, but then, Leshaun was an old soldier first. Varon was a priest, with all the training the Andinna had to offer at looking into the soul of a person and picking them apart. He was a soldier second, and only because he fell in love with Nevyn. His heart belonged to Nevyn, but his soul belonged to his goddess and always would.

"Ah, you've upset him, love." Nevyn sighed. "Luykas, we're pissy because we know how important blood bonds are. We know better than anyone. Most don't blood bond at all and very few keep it up like we do. We know all the ins and outs of it in ways others will never comprehend."

"And I know the educational version," he said, agreeing with Nevyn. "I know. I knew that when I did it, but I had nothing else."

"It doesn't matter to the gods why you did it. Just that you did and then fucked with it." Nevyn shrugged. "At least she's a great fighter. She's an outstanding addition to the Company, no matter the reason she had to join."

"You kicked her ass," Alchan reminded him, snorting. "She can't be that good. She's efficient, and better than most foot soldiers, but she's no *somaro* like you and Varon were."

Luykas wanted to agree with his brother but kept his mouth shut. *She's not an elite warrior, but I have a feeling Nevyn wants to make her into one.*

"She could be. Look at who her parents were." Nevyn went back to a smirk. "You should actually be jealous, Alchan."

And I was right. Luykas wanted to grin. Nevyn was an easy man to know. He loved Varon and didn't tolerate others disrespecting that. He respected the gods and Andinna tradition. Lastly? He loved war. He loved the fight, the battle, and he was always on the lookout to train others who had that same spark.

"Why?" Alchan looked disgusted with the idea.

"When you were a thousand years old, you couldn't land first hit on me. She did. Stung a bit. I wasn't expecting it. I corrected quickly, but she's obviously talented."

"Fine. She's good." Alchan groaned. "I don't really care. I'm not sure why I even came down here. If I wanted to talk more about her, I would have gone to see Matesh. He can't shut up."

"You just have a stick up your ass. Get laid." Nevyn chuckled. "You might be easier around her."

"You offering?" Alchan asked, raising an eyebrow. "I'm more than willing at this point."

"No. Varon and I aren't into your type of bedroom activities. You *bedru* males have a weird definition of fun." Nevyn wrinkled his nose. "There's a male in port right? Someone you like to go see?"

"Yeah, and I plan on it." Alchan sighed. "I wish there was an *ahren* anywhere in Olost."

"I've never met one," Nevyn commented, almost a little sadly. Varon shook his head as well.

Luykas didn't offer a comment. Most of the *bedru* issues of his Andinna bloodline were mellowed out or missing thanks to his Elvasi half. He didn't need to find an *ahren* female to tolerate him. Then again, he wasn't like Alchan in most bedroom ways. Luykas very much preferred females of really any type while Alchan would never really give a damn what was in his bed as long as it wasn't more dominant than him and didn't challenge him all the time.

"They've always been rare, and that's just the way it is. You could try and tolerate it like some other bedru *males I've met,"* Varon signed slowly. Luykas was honestly glad to have the topic change to Alchan's sex life. It meant he wasn't being hounded for the blood bond and Mave. *"I knew several who made deals with less dominant females that they loved. Time shares where only he can have her at certain points and her other husbands couldn't come around. They have two homes, two beds where he doesn't have to mix with the others and the female doesn't have to banish him from her* mayara*."*

"You know why I don't want a female unless it's an *ahren*." Alchan chuckled darkly. "It's not just about me being a *bedru*, Varon. You know that. There can't be other males."

"Your situation is more complicated than most, I will give you that. We've talked about this before and will again one day." Varon spread his hands in a defeated gesture. *"I still think I'm right."*

"About?" Luykas was missing something. He didn't know what Varon was mentioning and he wanted to.

"He thinks I should find a submissive male that's willing to be more…permanent than most of my liaisons. Someone who might like what I can give them, whatever the hell that is." Alchan shook his head. "I travel too much, Varon. Finding someone who can handle what I am, handle my traveling, and promise not to take anyone else to their bed is a near impossibility."

"Near." Nevyn emphasized that word.

"Could work," Luykas commented lightly. "Nevyn has a point. There could be a nice male out there for you." Luykas knew it was a desperate wish, and it didn't change that Alchan had other pressures weighing on him that Luykas didn't. Luykas wanted to be there for his brother more, but this was one way in which their lives were worlds apart.

"Of course you would consider it. This is why I don't talk to you about my sex life." Alchan glared, swinging his tail out to hit Luykas in the thigh. His wings tensed and opened slightly, a subconscious intimidation move. "Stop pondering and trying to find a way to play matchmaker. You have enough of your own problems."

"Yeah…" Luykas rubbed his thigh, shaking his head. Even at the mention of his problems, he focused on the beat of his heart and its loud echo underneath. At least he could have a normal conversation, which meant she wasn't getting into bed with anyone. In fact, she felt a bit warm. He focused a little more. She was still on the deck in the sun, getting hotter by the second. He wondered why she didn't go inside when she was obviously uncomfortable.

"We've lost him," Alchan muttered. "See? This is what I've been putting up with. He just fades away as he feels things that aren't happening to him."

"I remember the early days of our blood bond," Nevyn said, looking towards Varon, smiling. "I would just live in it, loving how much I could feel you."

Varon's answering smile was bright and loving. Then his hands began to move. Luykas felt the insane urge to break those fingers as they signed out what Varon was thinking. *"Yes, and I loved it. It was a welcome closeness. I can't imagine how hard it is to deal with when it's a completely unwanted addition to an already hard life."* The lovers kissed after that, Nevyn giving a very satisfied male growl.

"He's really mean to you," Alchan muttered, leaning down to say it softly to Luykas.

"I've noticed," Luykas bit out. "I'm going to dock their pay so we can afford extra supplies. Bryn says we can't, but I really think I can make it work."

"That's harsh," Nevyn retorted. "But if you do dock our pay, give that female her first paycheck. I'd say she deserves it, being tied to a male she doesn't want."

Luykas growled louder, but Nevyn didn't back down. Age and experience made the warrior the winner of the argument. With Varon backing him up, Luykas had no chance.

"Sometimes I wonder who runs the Company..." Alchan waved the couple away. "Get out of here before one of us tries to kill one of you."

"You're both fine leaders, don't worry. I would never challenge your decisions on the battlefield. You're trained for that and I'm not." Nevyn grinned. "For everything else? Well, let's just say I keep having to remind myself how young you two actually are." With that, Nevyn threw his arm over Varon's shoulders. They left together in a way Luykas had seen a thousand or more times before.

"Eighteen hundred years old and we're young. Can you believe that? We brought these males together and at every opportunity, they give us shit for something or another." Luykas snorted. "No one would ever guess if they saw us like this that we're trained in tactical warfare, raised to lead armies full of Andinna like Nevyn."

"We're not exactly models of Andinna life and culture," his brother reminded him. "We made the Ivory Shadows because we couldn't bring ourselves to settle."

"We couldn't accept losing," he corrected softly. "We thought we were too smart to have lost the War. We were misfits with minds and ability, and yet, we lost. We let Javon move the army into a bad place and didn't speak our minds about it, and..."

"Yeah..." Alchan sighed. "And it's not like we're out saving our people now."

"We're just trying to keep the few free ones alive now." Luykas ran a hand through the black hair between his horns. "Does it feel like it gets harder every year?"

"Feels more tiring every year. I hated this mission, but it was at least exciting. Like those few couple of centuries when we first founded the Company. Felt good to be an Andinna in Myrsten, fighting through those Elvasi soldiers. Like we mattered for a moment." Alchan looked down at his hands.

Luykas swallowed the feelings. He knew what Alchan was talking about. They worked for money now, raiding storehouses, catching bounties for Olost's city states. Anything to make the money to pay their warriors or feed their people. Anything to survive another year.

And sometimes they got to piss the Empire off doing it. Sometimes.

"I'm going up," Alchan said finally, standing. "Not in the mood to mope."

"I am," he mumbled.

"Then stay down here and mope." Alchan kicked his boot as he walked by. Luykas chuckled, watching his normal, pureblood brother walk out.

Luykas let his thoughts take him. From Mave to the state of the Company, he knew they needed to make a change for the better or every year was going to get worse. When they made it to port, he was going to need a mission ready for them to hit, and one that didn't involve a contract or a paycheck.

They needed something like the good old days. They needed some glory in their lives, like rescuing Matesh and Rain just gave them, like freeing Mave gave them, but better-paying.

10

MAVE

The ship rocked as a wave slammed into it. Mave stumbled and fell into a wall, unable to hold onto anything. The jarring impact made her slip and her knees hit the wood.

"Shit!" someone snapped. "There's always a damned storm right before we reach this fucking port." Someone grabbed her elbow. "Let me help you up!"

She looked up and saw Nevyn there. She reached out and took his other hand as the ship rocked to the other side, sending them to the other wall. It ended up with her body against his in a way that she really didn't want to think about.

Why couldn't he have been Matesh? My male would have loved this. Nevyn probably just finds this weird.

"Sorry!" she yelled over the sound of rain and thunder. The waves sounded like they were monsters threatening to sink them.

"It's fine!" He didn't seem too bothered with the way she was now pressed up against him. "Get to your room and hide out!"

"Okay!" She nodded and looked down the hall. Her cabin was four doors away.

Everything had been fine. Captain Sen had just been telling them how they were only a few days from port when the skies began to darken. It hit them faster than she could have reckoned possible. From the sound of it, this sort of thing was common in the region and the sailors were always ready for it. That didn't settle her nerves.

Nevyn stayed with her the entire way down the dangerous hall, and even opened her door. She thought he was being courteous but then he shoved her in. She landed on her bed of blankets and mattresses as the ship tilted again, causing her and the entire bundle of fabrics and linen to slide into another wall. The door slammed shut and she was left alone in the small cabin as the world went mad.

She had been fine on the ship for the entire trip. She hadn't gotten seasick or anything. She hadn't felt unsafe. From what others had told her, she had been handling the sea well for being landlocked her entire life.

Now she felt all of those things. Her stomach turned and she feared for her life and the lives of everyone else. Where was Matesh? He had forced her in first, saying he needed to find his uncle. She understood that, but she had no idea if he was safe now and she couldn't trust her own legs.

"I put Mave in her cabin!" Nevyn roared beyond the door. It sounded distant, nearly drowned out by the waves. "Rain, with me!"

"Good!" someone screamed back. She didn't even have a chance to think about who that might have been as the ship rocked and sent her back into a wall.

Suddenly her door flew open again and someone came tumbling in. She hoped it was Matesh, but the body that hit hers wasn't as big as she was used to.

Looking up, she saw Brynec, his face pale.

"Mat needed to stay with his uncle!" he said loudly to her. "Rain and Zayden with Varon and Nevyn!"

"Why are you here?" she asked, holding on to him like her life depended on it.

"No one can be left alone. If someone gets hurt from the tossin' around, we need to have others on hand to help." He was so close to her now that she realized neither of them had to yell over the sounds of the waves.

She nodded. The reasoning was sound. Suddenly one more body came through the door. This one she recognized and knew immediately. White wings told her the ivory Andinna was there. Her chest told her it was Luykas before he even opened the door, but she didn't have the chance to consider that.

"Alchan went to see Mat and Leshaun and stay with them," Luykas told them, his words nearly not loud enough. He had an air of calm that neither of them did. "So I'm left here with you two. Bryn, did you get tossed on top of her?"

She realized at that moment how the waves had left her and Bryn. He was over her, his hands braced next to her head. Their bodies were pressed together like the most intimate of lovers. He pushed away first.

"Aye. Sorry, Mave." He fell backwards, landing on one of her stripped bed frames. She stayed in her floor bed. Luykas shut them in together and moved to the other frame.

"Matesh do all of this?" Luykas asked politely, waving down to her mattresses, pillows, and blankets.

"He did. It's easier-"

"For you to cuddle on the floor. Yes, I know his reasoning." Luykas chuckled. She glared. The white-winged Andinna know-it-all. The sorcerer mutt. The gold-eyed Elvasi. In that moment, he was all of them and she disliked the calm attitude he had. "Andinna like bed floors. Varon and Nevyn do it all the time, no matter where we stay or how big the beds are."

"Maybe now isn't the time to educate her on bedroom tradition," Bryn said, leaning back. "Fuckin' boats. Fuckin' storms. Fuckin' travelin'."

"Are you okay?" she asked. She didn't like how pale he was. She probably didn't look much better.

"Aye. Just hate this." He leaned over, his wings bent awkwardly out of his back, and put his head between his legs. His tail's tip hooked with hers and she immediately knew it was a comforting gesture. "Luykas doesn't let anythin' bother him, the freak."

"I'm used to this and it's never really scared me. It's like flying during a storm, which we might have to do if the ship goes down. The biggest worry then is lightning." Luykas shrugged. "You'll get used to this, Mave. Bryn's fear is personal."

"Aye! Don't call me out," Bryn snarled from his spot. She realized she was in a cabin, sitting between two of the worst males she could be with. Bryn, who was having a hard time, even rougher than her, and Luykas, who seemed to be completely unfazed and couldn't keep his mouth shut. Bryn looked at her, those sky blue eyes glassed over. "I'll tell ya why when we get on shore. When I have dry land under my feet."

"Why don't we all try to get some sleep?" she asked, hoping she could close her eyes and this would all be over when she woke.

"We need to be awake in case anything happens. We can either sit here in silence for hours or find something to talk about. Your choice." Luykas' gold eyes were pinning her to the spot now, obviously wanting her to offer them the suggestion.

"Talk," Bryn answered for her. "Talk about anythin' except important shit. Can't focus on important shit right now."

"I was asking Mave," the mutt clarified.

"He's right," she cut in, before the males could start riding their tempers. "Talk about anything. I don't care."

"When we get to port, we're going to start planning our next job. We're going to pass through the village to drop off Rain and check in, ask what they need before winter. You'll be able to meet several of the Andinna there. We won't be there long, maybe a few weeks." Luykas was so calm, so nonchalant, speaking just loud enough that she could hear him. He wasn't even trying. "Enough time to recharge our batteries."

"Aye, tell her the mission we've talked about." Bryn heaved after saying that.

"We're going to raid some Elvasi merchant's storehouse. He's a known supplier to Empire loyalists in Olost. It's a small faction that is dedicated to getting Olost to bend the knee to the Empress. We need to give them a hard time. It's been too long since we bothered them, since they aren't much of a problem unless we catch them supplying hunters. No one in Olost wants to join the bitch." Luykas grinned. "But we need to remind Olost we're only in their nation to survive, not take over, and this helps."

"And we get to mess with the Empire," Bryn added, looking up. She didn't like how he looked, moving closer.

"Bryn, come down here," she ordered. "It's easier down here and more comfortable." She was getting to the point where she was beginning to feel normal. She couldn't ignore the tossing of the ship, but it was easier than trying to stand and then getting flung.

Bryn shook his head. "Can't. Ain't right." She didn't miss the darkening of his skin from a blush finally showing up on his pale, sick face.

"Maybe now I should tell her about Andinna bed traditions." Luykas chuckled. "We're going to stay up here because a male never gets into a family's bed unless he's been invited into her *mayara* and the other males know. Matesh made this bed for you and him because it's the best we can on this ship. We're not welcome."

"I thought females were in charge of the relationships," she retorted.

"Yes, but this is also Matesh's bed. If you want a separate space from him later, you can take whatever male you want to it, but you can't bring one to a shared bed, not unless that male is being brought into the *mayara*." Luykas sighed. He sounded like the conversation was tiresome.

"Ya could come to my bed but I ain't getting in yours," Bryn clarified. "If ya didn't share this one with Matesh, it would be okay if he didn't know I was in it. But ya do and I can't."

"Are beds really that important?" she demanded, looking between them. "It's comfortable down here. Brynec, you're sick. You need to come down here for your own health."

"You might not consider Matesh a member of your *mayara*, but we do. We're not getting into your bed, Mave. Drop it." Luykas' tone turned sharp and annoyed. "You're putting Bryn in a bad place with that sort of invitation, even if you don't mean to."

Mave looked away from the mutt, growling. It was her bed and Bryn wasn't feeling well. She trusted the male enough to let him down here. Why did any of this matter?

And she was stuck on what Luykas had said about her *mayara*. Was Matesh that close with her? Did she really want one of those strange female family units? Did she already have one and not know it? Was that possible?

Would that keep Matesh with her? Or would her saying he was just chase him away?

"Would he say yes?" she whispered to herself.

"Of course he would. I don't think you even need to ask. He already considers himself your first lover, the bedrock of your *mayara* and he acts like it." Luykas gave her an unwanted answer. She hadn't thought he could hear her.

"Do you need to have a word about everything?" she demanded, full of annoyance.

"You asked." Luykas shook his head, practically rolling his eyes. "Females."

She snarled at that. Bryn reached out and grabbed her shoulder, keeping her seated, she figured.

"Leave it," he said gently. "Luykas is annoyed he's in here with us two."

"I didn't ask him to be here!" she snapped waving a hand in Luykas' direction. "We could all die tonight and I'm stuck here with the male who…" She couldn't finish, her anger growing with every second.

"Aye, but this is what ya got for now. Ya two need to get along for this." Bryn let her go. "What will make ya feel easier?"

"If you came down here and got comfortable instead of being up there, sick and unsafe." She didn't care about the stupid tradition. There was no reason to be so stubborn, she figured. The damned male just needed to come down and she would deal with Matesh if he got angry.

Bryn looked away from her, mumbling something about Mat killing him. He left the empty frame and sat next to her stiffly on the mattresses on the floor. She grabbed a pillow and put it behind his back so he wasn't leaning on the hard wood.

"Females," Luykas muttered again. "I'm not going down there. This is a firestorm waiting to happen."

"I didn't ask you to and I sure as hell don't need your opinion on it anymore," she growled, still working to make sure Bryn would be okay. Bryn was tense, but she ignored it.

And once she was satisfied, she settled back, happy with herself. She was new to the idea of having so many other Andinna in her life that she could trust and care for. She wasn't sure how to do any of it right. This felt right, making sure Bryn was comfortable. This was something a friend could do for a friend.

"Tell me why this scares you so much," she asked softly, leaning close to him. "Does it have to do from a time you were a slave?"

Bryn nodded. "Mave..."

"I'm here to listen," she promised. *Please tell me. Please trust me. Please show me we're closer now than we were. I need to know I'm doing something right here.*

"Sometimes, very rarely, a slave would get in so much trouble that they would lock us in a tall thin cage where we had to stand and had no room to move. Then they would lower it into the bay, particularly during rough waters, a storm. They would leave just enough space that we could try to breathe. It happened to me once. I lived through it, but a lot of others don't. It's awful. It was a long time ago. Haven't liked water and shit since. Okay?" Bryn's explanation came fast and desperate. He was shaking now and she gently wrapped her arm around his shoulder.

"I don't like males because all of you have only wanted to hurt me. But here I am, on a ship with so many of you and needing to rely on you. If it weren't for Mat and Rain, this would have never happened. I would never trust any of you." She hoped her words meant something. "So...just let me help, okay? It's how I can give back."

"We're fucked up," Bryn mumbled.

"We are," she agreed.

"Thank ya." The words were so hushed, she nearly missed them. She just bumped her horns to his, hoping he knew what she was trying to say back.

Eventually, he stopped shaking. He relaxed next to her. She knew the moment he fell asleep and didn't wake him up. Instead, she watched Luykas, who watched them.

"I've never seen him sleep, not like that." Luykas nodded to Bryn. "Should wake him, in case anything happens, but it feels like the storm is already calming down."

"Is this how it normally happens? They hit hard and fast then disappear?"

"Every time. There was one trip that we were hit by three in fast succession. Bryn here nearly lost his mind. We had to tie him up and toss him in his own room."

"When was that?" she asked softly.

"The trip we accidentally picked him up on. He stowed away on the ship, a slave trying to get his own freedom. We found him pretty quickly and told him off, saying he didn't need to hide. If he could escape, he could have just run with us and we would have fed him sooner." Luykas chuckled. "He was a lot like you, actually. He didn't trust easily. Shied away from everyone who wanted to talk to him. Hated being touched and nearly stabbed Nevyn for it, scaring the shit out of the warrior."

"How did he change?"

"We didn't let him hide from us like we let you hide. We forced him to sit with us at meals and talk. We made him come outside and practice, learning he was a violent little gladiator."

"Little?" She snorted. He was a head taller than her, only going to his chin. She knew Luykas meant little to the other males, since Bryn was on the short side for one of them, but he was taller than any average female.

"Little to us." Luykas chuckled as he clarified. "It was Varon and Nevyn who saved him from himself in the end. Varon, really. That priest knows how to deal with the wounded and bleeding. He knows how to balm the soul."

"I haven't spoken much to them. What are they like?"

"As long as you don't try to get in the middle of their *bedyara*, they're amazing. They'll gut anyone who tries to break them up or join in on it, thinking the love extends past them. Makes things a little complicated because of what type of priest Varon is, but they make it work."

"And what type of priest is he?" She frowned, tilting her head. She knew what *bedyara* meant. It was a male-only committed family. She knew there was a female version as well. Rain had explained this to her before.

"You'll need to talk to him and Nevyn about that. I'm not the best person to explain gods and priests. I don't put all that much stock in them. Apparently, I should start." Something at the end of statement screamed bitter.

"I don't either." She could relate with him. "They've never done me any good."

"Oh?" He narrowed his eyes, watching her carefully. She knew he was judging her, trying to figure it out.

"I've prayed to them for a thousand years, and look at what it got me. You've done more for me than they ever have." She remembered her bitter, angry words. How she screamed at the gods for forcing her to hurt Matesh and Rain. How she would rather die than keep fighting if it meant hurting the two people she finally cared about.

She had asked the gods for so much. Freedom. Safety. Peace. None of it ever was granted. Finally, she had begged them to keep her new males safe and they had failed her one last time.

No, she would never love the Andinna gods. She couldn't bring herself to.

"The Andinna gods are..." Luykas trailed off, as if he was looking for the right word. "Stand-offish. They meddle, but not much. Again, something to talk to Varon about, not me. I've got two pantheons. The Elvasi gods have been silent for millennia and religion in the Empire is for show now. They don't put any stock in their own gods except for festivals and excuses to behave in certain ways."

"You talk as if they're real."

"To many, they are." Luykas shook his head. "And sometimes, I wonder myself. Not like they're walking the earth, but sometimes..." He didn't continue on that topic, pointing at Bryn. "Back to that one. He's a good male. Quiet, which is understandable, but reliable and trustworthy, and smarter than any of us could have known. We never would have known any of that about him if it wasn't for Varon really helping him make it past some large hurdles."

"Sounds like everyone took much more of an active role in Brynec's freedom than mine," she muttered.

"You're harder to deal with. First, you're female, and in our culture, that makes you our better. We have to tread carefully or we'll find ourselves with a female that can and will rip our balls off. You might not understand them, but you feel the instincts to dominate and rule, like nearly every other female of our people." Luykas laughed like he had some private joke. "Second, you're you. Maevana Lorren. Your parents' names were so well known that our people knew them second only to our Queen and the royal family." He leaned forward, his face too close to hers. "That ties into the last one. You have a reputation Bryn didn't. You're the Champion of the Colosseum, and while you aren't there anymore, the legend of you has reached Olost and the free Andinna. We never thought you were real. We had never seen you. Imagine what it's like to deal with someone who is so infamous that people would tell their children scary stories about them."

She swallowed. That did change everything.

"Then add in that you don't know...anything. We're teaching you things children are raised with. This bed thing...no other female would ever offer her bed to a male for any reason like this, not her *mayara* bed anyway. Not the bed her other males made for her."

"Fine, so I'm more difficult than Bryn. I get it." *Of course I am. Why would I expect anything to be easy just because it was for someone else?*

"You don't make it easy, that's for sure. You scare the shit out of the sailors, too. That's why they don't talk to you or any of the Andinna when you're around. No one, and I mean no one, sees female Andinna anymore. They're all in hiding in our villages. They don't go out and put big fucking males on their asses. They know we defer to our females and that's it. Now there is one and the humans don't know what the hell to do."

"I didn't realize I was such a...disturbance." She said the words tightly, trying to contain the hurt in them.

"That one isn't on you. It's just the circumstances of what's going on." Luykas sighed, looking down. "And I didn't make this easy for you either. For that, I'm sorry."

"Excuse me?"

"The blood bond. I had to do something, and that was all I had. And before that...I'm normally not this bad at helping people, you must understand. You've thrown me for a loop just by existing, and forgive me...but I'm willing to do anything to make sure you live."

"I don't understand why." She needed to. "You could have let me die, and no one would hate you for it...well, Mat and Rain would hopefully miss me, but it's not like I'm irreplaceable-"

"But you are. You are irreplaceable."

She didn't have a response and she didn't understand why he would say that. She didn't think she was. She was just the sole survivor of a family that used to be important. She was the reason her people were enslaved. If anything, that was a good reason to let her die. Not that she wasn't grateful to be alive, but at the cost he'd put on them?

She just wasn't sure she was worth that.

Sitting next to Bryn, knowing where his pain came from, she hoped she could prove she was, even if it felt like an impossible task.

11

MAVE

A sailor poked his head in, startling Mave and Luykas. They had been silent for the remainder of the storm, not sure what else to talk about.

"Storm's over. Seas are calming down. Ya can go about yer days." The sailor closed the door again, leaving them with the news.

"Well, this was fun." Luykas jumped up. "Thanks for tolerating my presence in your space, Mave."

She jumped up as well, leaving Bryn where he was. He'd fallen into such a deep sleep, she wasn't sure she could wake him. She ignored Luykas, going for her door. She reached for the handle at the same time as the mutt, their hands touching.

For just a second, her world was two worlds. Her body was flooded with guilt and confusion that wasn't hers. It was full of an undeniable need to touch, to be near someone. Him.

She snarled, shoving him back from her.

"Don't touch me," she snapped.

"It was an accident," he pleaded. "I didn't think you would go for the door knob."

"Well, don't do it again," she growled. She shoved the door open, storming out and running into a massive chest. Instantly, she calmed down as she recognized Mat's scent. That spiciness she had never experienced before meeting him.

"Something wrong?" he asked quickly.

"No," she answered. "Luykas and I accidentally touched and it upset me for a moment. I'm glad you're okay."

"I'm glad you are too. I'm sorry for not being here, but my uncle-"

"No, I understand," she said quickly. "Leshaun needs his nephew to help him. He's your family."

"Let's get some rest. The storm was awful." Matesh leaned down and kissed her slowly. "I want you." His words were sensual. She let him back her up to their room, ignoring how Luykas walked away quickly. She wanted to forget that mutt and have her male. She was glad he was okay and wanted to show him.

They stopped at the door when Matesh tensed.

"Why is Bryn in our bed?" he asked, an edge to his words that made her realize very quickly that he needed an explanation or someone was going to end up hurt. She knew how males could ride their tempers. She had never expected it from something like this.

"He was ill. I told him to lie down where he was more comfortable. I told him to, Matesh. He and Luykas tried to tell me he shouldn't, but I didn't want him sick and uncomfortable. I got him to fall asleep during the storm." She said the words sternly, enunciating every word.

Matesh's nostrils flared. She could see barely restrained fury in his emerald eyes. "It's our bed, Mave," he growled. "Ours."

"I know, but-"

"He's not *yours*," Mat snapped. "He's not *mayara* and he doesn't belong there."

"And are you *mayara*?" she asked softly, pulling his face to hers, hoping to distract him. "Are you?"

"Of course I am." His chest rumbled with the words.

"I wanted to help him, and if you want to stay with me, you would understand that," she said quickly. "Please, Mat. They warned me this wouldn't go over well, they did. Be mad at me, not Bryn."

"I'm not…" Mat growled again. "I'm not mad." He pulled away. "I'm frustrated."

"Why?" she asked.

"Because you should have listened to them. They know why this is a problem." He turned away and walked away. "I'll stay with my uncle for the night."

"Mat!" She called out, watching him walk down the hall. She stood there in shock for a long time, just not understanding why that had happened. She didn't know why this was such a big deal. Bryn was just sleeping and they were all friends. Why couldn't he see she was just trying to do something nice? It took a lot for her to do these sorts of things, and he just threw it in her face and didn't listen.

Feeling burned, she went back into her room and shut the door. She didn't go to her bed to sleep. She grabbed a book of Andena from her chest and worked her frustration out translating the glyphs on her own.

Maybe somewhere in one of the passages there would be a reason the fucking bed was so important.

"Where am I?" Bryn mumbled, startling her out of her concentration. It felt like hours later, and she had no idea how long she had been struggling and forcing herself to read the Andena, but she knew it had been too long. She should have tried to sleep long before he woke up.

"In my room," she answered. "How are you feeling?"

"Better," he said, opening his eyes. "Where's Luykas?"

"He left. The storm ended. We let you sleep through it, since there were two of us to keep an eye on things." She smiled down at him. "I'm glad you're feeling better."

"The storm ended and you didn't wake me?" He snapped to attention now. "Where's Matesh?"

She swallowed. "He's staying with Leshaun."

"Shit," Bryn growled. "He's goin' to kill me." He scrambled to stand, pushing off the blanket she'd put on his legs.

"He's not angry with you," she whispered, looking down at her book. Bryn stopped once he was on his feet. She saw his hands grab her book and she let him pull it away. "He's angry with me."

"Ah...We should have explained the bed thing better, but the storm..." Bryn sat next to her. "Male Andinna...we build these beds for our females. The bed is made by the males of a *mayara* to show they can do something wonderful for the female by giving her this soft place to lay her head. And for us. The *mayara* bed is the one place where we feel secure in our place with our female and the other males. It's a place of great trust. No one is a threat to the other. We all are there for her. I'm not in your *mayara*, Mave. I'm a threat in Mat's most trusted place. I could be here, convincing you to throw him out and take me. I would never, but that's what he feels."

She listened, taking that in. She should have listened. It would have been like if she found a strange male in her room in the pits. She would have never felt safe again. She also would have killed the intruder.

"I'm sorry," she murmured. "I wanted to do something nice. I didn't think..."

"You didn't really know," he reminded her. "Which is our fault, really. This is something we should have explained ages ago, or made Mat explain. It would have stopped these sorts of misunderstandings. I shouldn't have given in, either. I made that mistake. I'll need to apologize to him."

"Will he...leave me for this?" She felt that worry now.

"No," Bryn promised. "He won't leave ya for this. He'll probably beat me up in training once or twice, though, if I don't hurry up and tell him it was just an accident and it won't happen again. I'm not going to be allowed in this room again, or any room ya stay in now. He's not going to allow it."

"I don't see why-"

"It's his job to protect ya," Bryn said quickly, cutting her off. "From everyone and everythin'. This is the place ya should be the most safe, and yet there was a male in yer bed that he didn't know. We're instinctual people, Mave. We rubbed all of his instincts wrong and he's probably tryin' to not kill anyone. If he hadn't shown any control, he would have come in here to kill me. He's probably with his uncle to make space and get over it." Bryn sighed. "It's not just Matesh. Any male ya ever bring into yer *mayara* will act this way. Well, any of the official males, yer *bodanras*. Rain, who is yer brother in the eyes of the Andinna now, is *mayara*, but he won't step up to fight unless your *bodanras* aren't available. He'll defer to them."

"Why is this so complicated?" she asked, trying to work it out in her mind and failing.

"I think ya need to see it. When we get to the village, ya will understand a bit more. We're spendin' some time there for the mission, then winterin' there, and ya will be completely immersed in how females run things and how the males have their own places, with their own power and rights." Bryn patted her thigh tentatively. "I'm goin' to go see him now. Ya should wait here. Make him come to this ground and show him it's safe again. If that's what ya want."

"Okay," she agreed. "I'm sorry."

"Yer learnin', and we're failin' at catchin' you up. This is as much Mat's fault as it is mine or yers." Bryn stood up and when he reached the door, he turned back to her. "Mave…thank ya. I haven't slept like that in a long time."

"Of course. You've helped me a lot, and…"

"Ya don't owe me, but I get it." He smiled and walked out, leaving her to her thoughts.

She went back down into the bed, feeling like it was more important now. For weeks it had just been a bed. Now it felt like a gift. Why hadn't Matesh told her any of this? Why hadn't he told her that this was special?

She picked up a blanket and held it to her chest. She thought about the bed she shared with her mother, all the furs and pillows. It had been cozy and wonderful. Had her father made that bed for them?

The door opened with a creak.

Here we go. Time for me to realize just how bad of a mistake this is.

"Mave…" Mat sounded strained. "Bryn came to see me."

"I know," she answered, still looking at the blanket she held, her fingers rubbing the soft fabric. She figured it was the fanciest thing on the ship. "Where did you get this one?"

"I asked Sen for it, knowing he would have the nicest stuff on the ship. He isn't one of us, but he knew what I was after."

Oh. Oh, that's so nice of him. I've never had something so fine and I didn't even notice.

"I'm sorry," she whispered, pulling it up to her face. "I just wanted to do something nice for him and he was hurting. He…understands me in a lot of ways, and he's kind to me when he doesn't have to be. He's another gladiator and he's *kind*."

"I know." He walked closer and she heard the door shut. "And I'm sorry. Leshaun hit me with his cane a few times, telling me that I needed to remember you don't understand. He had to order me to do something I should have already been doing."

"Oh?"

"Teaching you about how our relationships really work." He took the blanket from her, then tilted her chin up to look at him. It made her feel small. She was taller than every other race on the ship, but her large male made her feel small. "I've been coasting, thinking you'll just be okay. You're learning Andena and you're opening up with the Company, and I thought it was fine. I was doing these things for you and you weren't noticing. Then you started talking to Bryn a lot and I…" He sighed. "I messed up too. I forgot you had no idea what signals I was trying to send you. When you asked if I was in your *mayara*, I realized how much I messed up and knew I needed to step back."

She leaned in to kiss him, and he obliged. Her heart began to speed up, realizing he wanted the same thing. Then he pulled away.

"This is why I'm so bad at this. You're a damned distraction," he said.

She couldn't stop a laugh. "So are you," she retorted. "So, tell me all these things I don't know. Bryn…explained more about the bed."

"Yeah, he caught me up on that. Leshaun took that as another chance to hit me with his cane, too."

"If I had known it was such a big deal, I would have given Bryn a pillow and blanket and left him on one of the frames. But I couldn't just leave him with nothing."

"I know," he whispered. "Oh, I know, lover. I knew when you explained it. I was there in the pits with you. I know how the other males treated you. I know that Bryn's kindness touched you and you wanted to do something for him. You're like that. You did it with Rain and me." He kissed her again. "Ask anything you like. I'll answer all of it."

"In the morning," she murmured against his lips. He growled in pleasure at her obvious invitation. "So…we're a *mayara* now."

"Hm, we have been, but I'm glad you finally realized it." He chuckled, kissing her deeper. It was forceful enough that she lay back and he crawled over her. He moved off her lips, kissing her jawline and down her neck. "You own me," he said against her skin.

"Oh," she gasped as his tail slid between her legs, rubbing over her sensitive core.

"And things like this will happen again, but don't worry…" He pushed her pants down. "I'm always willing to get over myself and help you."

"And I'm willing to learn," she promised softly. No other males in the bed. She could make that happen.

"Ask me something," he demanded softly, kissing down her stomach.

"Why do you buckle my shirt in the morning?" She relented and did what he wanted. "Just trying to be helpful, or is that important too?"

"It's important, because it's a male's responsibility to help his female get ready for the day. During times of war, a female's *mayara* will help her ready by making her armor perfect. We clean your blades, we clean your gear. We dress you. Then you lead us, because it's bred into what you are and what we are." He nibbled on her thigh between sentences, breathing on her flesh, promising something wonderful.

"Why do you do that?" She felt one of his fingers graze over that nub of sensitive flesh. "Serve."

"There's fewer females than males. We're matriarchal, and a male must prove his worth. We need to, we have a drive to. Just because I'm *mayara* now doesn't mean you can't banish me. For every day that I want to be with you, I'll work for it. There's hundreds of other males who would want to be in my place, and you could want one of them alongside me, which would be fine." He bit harder on her thigh, almost aggressively. She moaned, tensing under the bite as he sank a finger into her. At her soft cry of pleasure, he released her. "Or you could replace me if another male does everything I do. Generally, males of a *mayara* all offer different things, in a sense. But if there was a male like me who did what I could do better and claimed your heart? You wouldn't need me anymore."

"I would never," she answered as he kissed back up her, his finger still buried in her body, rubbing gently against her inner walls.

"There are females who do. Building the perfect family. And relationships end sometimes. It happens, and it breaks hearts, but it happens." Matesh kissed her. "So we males work to keep it alive. A female needs to have a life outside her men, though. She can't be expected to bend over backwards for all of us, not when we ask females to have multiple males thanks to our population. So we do. We work that hard and we make her think we're worth it."

"That's...romantic and strange," she admitted softly. "I'm not sure how to handle that level of devotion."

"You've been handling it for weeks without even knowing it." He chuckled, sliding a second finger into her. "And you can't say you don't like it," he teased, nipping her earlobe now.

He has a point. I love this.

"Can we talk about it more in the morning?" she asked, hoping he would just continue the part she loved the most. How his hands were on her.

"I was having fun," he said with more of that teasing, arrogant note. "But I know what you want."

"You're very good at it," she murmured, smiling a little.

"Oh, I know," he crooned, pulling his fingers out of her. While he undid his breeches, his tail rubbed against her, driving her further up. She ran her hands over his chest and reached behind him, touching the very sensitive spot where wings and flesh met. He moaned, grinding his tail harder against her. "You have to stop that."

"Do I?" she asked, now teasing him. He growled in response, pulling out of her reach. She rolled over onto her stomach, a more comfortable position. "Is this what you want?" she asked, raising her ass up for him to see it. Her tail was to the side, not blocking the view. Since she and Mat had gotten together, they had tried a number of things. He revealed once that one way he loved a woman was from behind.

For hurting him earlier, she had moved into the position he wanted the most.

"Well, you won't be able to taunt me from this angle and ruin this faster than I want," he answered, leaning over to press against her. She let her wings lie flat, out of his way. His hands were on either side of her head. His tail pulled hers out of his way completely. His weight held her down.

But it was Matesh and she trusted him. There was something primal about the position, something that made her want to buck and fight, just to see if he would win. She could ask about that later as well.

I'll need to start keeping a better list of things to ask about.

When he went to knee her thighs open since she hadn't yet for him, she resisted. It made him snarl.

"Mave, that's a game you aren't ready for yet," he warned. "I promise you, you aren't ready for that yet."

"Oh?" She looked over her shoulder at him, wondering why.

He bent his arms to growl near her ear. "Well, here's something you need to know, then. When you let a *mayara* male begin, expect him to finish. Expect him to fight for it."

"You won't stop if I wanted you to?" she asked, suddenly slightly afraid.

He pressed against her harder. "Do you want me to? Because you need to be very clear, if that's the case. I will, if you need it. I'll back off." His words made it sound like the task would be difficult, but he held such conviction that she believed him. She could also now hear his temper, that passion, the *rai*. She had pushed him in too many ways. Bryn in the bed to this.

"No."

"Then you're trying to play a game. You want me to prove I'm strong enough to have you. To protect you. It's a...test, a proving thing for us. You and I haven't done that yet, and I'm not doing it tonight. You...you've been through too much for that game."

She eased her legs open, realizing she knew what he was talking about. She had wanted to test him. She wanted a male who could win against her. She had always admired how strong he was and wanted more of it.

"You need a female friend," he said, his cock now pressed against her. "Do you still want me?" he asked softly, but not gently.

He needs this now. Sex eases the temper and he's having such a hard time. Why is this so damned attractive, to have him like this, pushed so far that he's barely holding back?

"Yes," she murmured. The moment the word left her mouth, he slammed home in one quick thrust that left her dazed and screaming.

Something changed once he was buried in her. She saw his fingers curl into the fabrics under them.

"Mat? Are you okay?" She didn't miss how he stopped or how tense his body was now. She could feel him vibrating, barely restrained. He needed to continue, she knew it. Why did he stop?

"I've been holding back my temper all night while we talked," he whispered harshly in her ear, their horns knocking together. "And you nearly set me off with that little trick, trying to keep your legs closed. Do you want me rough? I can do that for you, or I can hold back. Tell me, lover, so I know where to go from here."

My instincts were right. "Rough," she gasped. "Don't hold back. I want all of you."

"Thank you." The words were barely audible.

He didn't hold back, just like she asked, giving her all of the temper she had accidentally pulled out of him. He slammed into her like it was the last time they would ever have each other. Her fingers curled into the blankets, and she bit down on a pillow, screaming as he rode her hard. He didn't let up as their bodies slammed together. She knew this was part of her education, handling her male when she upset him. It was a blessing she loved when he was rough and powerful.

He was using her body, she realized. Oh, she was getting what she wanted out of it, but he was more focused on his cock going into her than her. He didn't care how rough it was, as long as he was in her.

Why do I love this so much?

She was nearly at her peak when he stopped, buried in her, but not finishing.

"Promise me something."

"What?" She whimpered at his hard cock in her, not moving anymore. She tried to move, to keep it going, but his weight held her.

"No male comes to this bed for the first time without me here, even if I know about them. I need to know you're safe with others. I need to know they'll take care of you, Mave. I have to."

"I promise!" She barely heard what he said, but damn, she wanted him to continue.

He went back to it immediately, now a bit slower, more controlled. She felt the shift in his mood as something settled in him. He was no longer using her body to work out his temper, but really with her. One of his hands shifted, touching hers with his fingers. She hooked her index finger with his, enjoying the small connection, a sign they were in this together again.

Now he was driving her further up and not just himself. The way he rolled his hips, the angle he was driving into her…She didn't last much longer, losing herself to the pleasure, and the world faded away.

Her climax was strong enough that he growled, driving faster again as her core tried to hold him.

Finally, he buried himself once more, snarling as he came in her.

When he pulled out, he fell next to her, breathing hard like her.

"Come here?" he asked softly, lying on his back, much calmer than he had been. She moved to lay her head on his chest. His fingers toyed in her hair. "Thank you for that."

"You needed it," she murmured, kissing the large chest underneath her. "I could tell somehow. You know anything about that?"

"Yeah, you definitely need some female friends," he said, chuckling. "Ah, I'm still really sorry about not telling you so much about how we do things. I just-"

She pushed up and kissed him before he could say more. Was she plagued by the idea of knowing nothing about her own people? Yes, but there was no changing it now. There was no reason to keep beating anyone up for it.

She just wanted to keep moving forward. Any day now, their feet would be back on dry land. She couldn't wait.

ZAYDEN

"Rain!" Zayden called out. He was watching his son walk away from him again. "Please talk to me."

"*Baba*, I'm not in the mood to talk. I'm sorry." Rain turned back to him, shaking his head.

"You haven't spoken to me in a week. We just spent hours locked up thanks to the storm, and you ignored me the entire time. Please." Zayden's heart felt like it was being crushed.

"I'm just really tired of how nosy you are and I need some space. Can you just respect that?" Rain's words became a snarling anger at the end, making Zayden pull back. They were standing in the cramped hall of the ship and others were trying to get around them. "Damn the Skies, *bodra*, you need to leave me alone, please."

"What happened that made you like this?" he asked, not sure where his happy son had gone. The weeks on the ship, his son kept growing darker, more secluded and private. He knew Rain hadn't been sleeping well. He knew his boy was even snapping at Matesh, something he never expected.

"None of your business," Rain snapped.

That did it. Zayden snarled his frustration and anger at that. "I'm your father. It sure is my fucking business."

"No, it's not!" Rain roared.

"Break it up!" Luykas called. "Get the hell out of everyone's way, you two. Make space and leave each other alone."

"He's my fucking son, not yours," Zayden growled back at their mutt leader. "Stay out of it."

"I'd rather have Luykas at this point," Rain said bitterly. Rain turned away and stomped off, leaving Zayden in the way. Someone nudged his back but he couldn't move for a moment.

"Zayden?" Luykas whispered gently. "Hey, it's not-"

"Don't touch me," he growled. He shook off Luykas' hand on his shoulder, still growling and grumbling as pain settled in his chest.

Zayden walked out onto the deck, ignoring the mumbles of the males behind him. Mave and Matesh hadn't been in the group, which told him a lot about what was going on there. He was feeling itchy and pissed off, and the storm hadn't helped that.

No, he was really pissed by the general disregard his son was treating him with now. Moving out of the room, avoiding him and everyone else. The time he yelled at Matesh over Rain during training was a real kick to everyone's balls, and now this? Zayden wasn't sure what to do. He knew it had something to do with the pits, the slavery his boy was forced to endure, but no one was telling him anything, especially not the two Andinna who were there with Rain.

I never thought Matesh would keep secrets from me about Rainev. He's my son, damn it all. Why can't I reach him?

And since he hadn't seen Mave or Matesh, he knew it wasn't a good time to go find them and start beating them for answers.

A shadow fell over him, stopping the red glow of their moon. Zayden gritted his teeth, frustrated with the intrusion.

"You okay?" Nevyn asked casually.

Zayden bared his teeth at the warrior in front of him, blocking his view.

"Want to tell me why my son is avoiding me?" he asked as the warrior stared down at him. "Or are you going to call me an ass like everyone else on this blasted ship?" That was happening more and more. He would try to talk to Rain and someone would say he was being a pushy ass. He really hated it when it came from Matesh, his oldest and closest friend. Everyone else could go jump off the boat and drown, but Matesh? That was too much for him.

"Both," Nevyn answered, moving to sit on the crate next to him. "These freak storms. I hate this area, but it's the closest port to home."

"Nice change of topic." Zayden groaned, rubbing his face. Nevyn was at least a good person to talk to about this. He and Varon took a very active role in Rain's life. They knew him well. Maybe they would be willing to help him get his son back to normal. "He moved out of our room, Nevyn. What am I doing wrong?"

"You're riding his ass when he needs space and time to think," Nevyn answered. "And you're being an ass about it."

Zayden growled. "I'm his father, and-"

"And you're overprotective, which probably won't change any time soon, but it's the problem. He's three hundred and twelve years old, Zayden. At that age, every Andinna on this ship was an adult and treated like one. You're treating him like he's still a boy."

Zayden should have known Nevyn wouldn't help him. None of them understood how it was, to have a son who felt like he could take on the world, shift into a massive beast, and yet...

"He's not going to outlive me," he mumbled, looking away. "And you know, I think it's reasonable to want him to have a happy life, doing safe things, so that his life doesn't get cut shorter than it already is."

"He's all you have left of Summer, too." Nevyn sighed. "We all know why you're upset, but you need to let him deal with this on his own."

"I want to help him!" Zayden took a deep breath, trying to contain his indignation and fury. This was one Andinna he couldn't get rowdy with. Nevyn would have his ass on the deck in seconds.

"He doesn't want your help!" Nevyn growled back, growing angry with him. "If you haven't noticed that, then you've gone blind and deaf."

"Then what do I do?" Zayden demanded. "Ignore him back? He's my son, Nevyn, and he's in pain."

"There's no right answer," Nevyn admitted, looking away from him. Zayden turned back to the ocean as well. "Only Mave and Matesh were in the pits with him, and they won't tell anyone. I'm pretty sure they're trying to let Rain gather the courage to say something himself, when he's ready."

"They should tell me," Zayden muttered. "I'm his father, and-"

"He's an adult. They're trying to keep his trust and respect him like one. Again, stop trying to think of him as a boy. It's not going to fix this situation." Nevyn chuckled dryly. "If it helps, I get it. Varon is the one who had to talk me down from dragging Rain to speak with him. He thinks Rainev needs to come to it in his own time and find the person he can speak to. I've been trying not to be like you. I'm older, and the *rai* doesn't ride me like it rides you."

"Is everyone talking about my boy now?" Zayden snorted. "So I'm not fucked in the head. There *is* something wrong. I haven't fabricated this in my head?"

"Of course there is!" Nevyn threw his arms up. "But we can't force him to tell us and fix it for him, Zayden! You know Varon and I love him. You know that. You know I would move mountains for him. You know Varon would give him whatever help he needs if it's called for. But there's a difference between knowing there's something wrong and behaving like you are."

Zayden leaned over, putting his face in his hands. "I don't know another way."

"Why don't you try just offering him support quietly? Prove to him you're listening. Give him the space he wants." Nevyn patted his thigh. "I just wanted to come out here and say that."

"It hurts to be blown off by my only family," Zayden admitted. "I've done nothing but love that boy, and…"

"I'm sorry, Zayden, I am. But you need to leave him be. I think that's the healthiest thing for your relationship with him at this point. Treat him like an adult. Let him make mistakes and get hurt."

"He shouldn't be getting hurt!" Zayden snapped. "He should be living a really happy life away from all of this!"

"It's not the life he wanted."

"He won't live as long as us…" Zayden repeated from earlier, always thinking about it.

"Which is why it's all the more important that you let him grow up and experience all the things the rest of us adults get to experience. Like falling in love and getting our hearts broken. Learning a new skill and getting hurt." Nevyn patted his thigh. "Your parents obviously didn't hold you back. Don't hold your son back."

"I can't promise anything," he muttered. He didn't know if he could control the raging fear in his chest at the idea of Rain being hurt. Nevyn was right, the *rai* always rode him hard. He'd always been that Andinna, with the fierce temper and the deep feelings.

And the day he held Rain for the first time, he realized that nothing could ever dim that passion. He had never known such depth to his feelings.

Now he was being asked to step back. Didn't they know how hard that was?

"I'm not asking for a promise. I'm asking you to try. For Rainev's sake and for the Company's sake. Luykas and Alchan are losing their patience with your behavior. They see Rain as an adult and a member of the Company. He doesn't deserve to be hounded, and they don't deserve your pissy shit when Rain demands what you rightfully owe him."

Zayden winced. He shouldn't have gotten pissy with Luykas below deck. "Who sent you to come yell at me?" he asked.

"Varon and Luykas. Rain is hiding in Bryn's room, and we're all going to let him."

"Okay." Zayden didn't argue. If that's what they wanted, then he would give it to them. He would try his damnedest to leave his son alone. It hurt like hell, but he would try. He couldn't imagine life without Rain or the Company.

And if I get my dumb ass kicked out, Rain will still be out there trying to play soldier with the rest of them.

He needed to behave and be protective from afar for a moment. He could handle that.

Nevyn walked off after that, leaving him alone with the red moon. He continued to watch it as it moved through the clear sky. The freak storms in the area always left the night sky like this, completely clear, not a cloud in sight. It was a good thing, since he could hear Sen talking to a sailor about their route. The storm had pushed them closer to their destination, which was a blessing. Sometimes, the storms continued to push ships away from port and it would drag the trip out by weeks, until everyone was going mad from it.

Zayden didn't know how long he was sitting out there, but he knew it was too long when he heard the light footsteps of the only female on board. For who she was, he always figured she would stomp around. She didn't. She walked lightly, as if always on her toes, ready for action.

I guess that makes more sense than her having a heavy step.

He turned to see her standing in the night, awash in the moon's red glow. She held two short swords and began to work through the steps of an invisible fight. They all knew she would come out onto the deck long before they woke up and did so nearly every morning. He had never been around to witness it before.

Seeing her train was like watching a dance. She flowed from attack to attack, into a block. He watched the sweat form on her, making her skin shine. He thought about watching her take down the mounted horsemen. She had done it with very little help from him. All her insecurity, and he'd been thinking about how unimpressive she was. Then she did that and left him in shock.

She knows what's wrong with my son. As his big sister, she has to.

He didn't ask, though. He didn't break her concentration, because he didn't want to be rude. He'd spent weeks wrapped up only in what was going on with Rain and ignoring her. He felt a little guilty for it now. He never asked Matesh how the pits were and made sure his oldest friend was okay. He never checked in with this female to see if she was doing well.

She stopped and looked over at him. He didn't budge from the stare for a moment, then respectfully dropped his eyes. She was more dominant than him and it was something he'd missed that first night of knowing her. She fell into following orders well and he hadn't thought about it. The weeks on the ship made him realize she would expect his deference.

Another reason I'm not going to bother her about Rain. Would rather fight with Matesh over it. Or anyone else, really.

"Why are you still awake?" she asked. He could tell she was actively trying to make small talk. The question was awkward and forced, but it was there nonetheless. All that power and skill, but simple conversational skill was evasive to her.

For some reason, he could nearly relate to that.

He shrugged. "Your little brother is a prick and I want to strangle him."

She frowned at him. "He's your son…"

"No, I love my son, and he's a wonderful young male who listens to me. Your little brother ignores me, yells at me, and is much darker than my son." He needed to say it. "My son was taken by the Empire and I didn't get him back."

He watched hurt flash over her face before she did that thing he hated. He'd seen it before. They all had. Her face became blank as walls came up and locked away whatever was going on underneath. Nothing about her body gave away a single piece of her emotion.

"The pit changes people," she said calmly. "I'm sorry that the experience changed Rain in the way that it did."

"I know you are," he said, accepting the apology. "Doesn't change that something in the hellhole you lived in was so fucked up that it's really hurt my boy. But here you are…" He bit back his last comment. He didn't want to piss her off.

"Here I am what?" she asked, stepping closer. He noticed a small slip in control, as a growl came out on the last word.

"Practicing your languages. Working out. Laughing. Fucking Matesh all the time. My son is missing and you're...doing anything else." He shouldn't have answered, but his anger at it all was now boiling over, seeing her there. Rain's *illo amyr*. She should be helping him more. If Rain wouldn't accept his help, then she should be there for his boy.

And it looked like she wasn't.

"He doesn't want my help," she said quietly, looking away from him. "I tried."

He narrowed his eyes on her. "Did you?"

"I tried to tell him what I went through..." She trailed off, shaking her head. "It doesn't matter. He didn't want to listen."

He was frowning now. "If not you, me, or Matesh, then who?"

"I don't know. Bryn?" She walked to him now, closing all the distance, and sat next to him. "I hate this too, you know. I'm...lost. I've never tried to help someone like him before. I've never wanted to help someone before. He's my first family, did you know that? I haven't heard anyone claim me as family since the day my mother died. Rain did. Rain saw me alone and decided I needed a family." She looked up to the moon. "And I can't help him now. I'm sorry for that."

Zayden listened and realized he was wrong about her. "I'm sorry too. We can mope together, I guess."

"It doesn't help that since becoming free he and Bryn have been very good at reminding me of everything I went through." She huffed, shaking her head. "It was a hard world to live in. You should be proud of Rain, though. You should be happy he's here at all."

"I am, but I'm not sure why-"

"He lived through it. He came out different, and that hurts and I know it. He came into the pits so bright, and I couldn't resist the young male who wouldn't stop talking to me...but at least he survived. Not many do."

"I know you're right," he conceded. "I'm not trying to argue with you." He also wondered how much of Rain's survival was really due to her. Did she save his son's life in every way she could? He had a feeling she did. He'd had the sneaking suspicion he owed her when he saved her from drowning. Now it was growing to a belief.

My son is alive because of this female. This awkward, out of place gladiator female. And here I am, accusing her of not caring for him. I'm a fucking idiot.

They sat in silence for a time after that. He was still uncomfortable with the female. He was always getting mixed signals from her. Insecurity and bold confidence. Peace and turmoil. It scratched at his temper a little, but he tried not to act on it.

"How is your Andena going?" he asked, tired of the silence.

"Slow, but everyone seems to be rather forgiving for it." She bared her teeth. "I want to learn faster, but it's not an easy language. It's so different from Common and Elvasi."

"Always feel comfortable asking us to explain something." Zayden didn't know where to go from there. He didn't find Andena hard at all, but then, he grew up with it as his first language.

The conversation died again. Skies, he was bad at talking to this female. He normally didn't talk to females at all. After Summer had passed on, he focused on Rain and ignored the females, falling out of practice.

Though, Matesh always says I'm bad at females. Summer had been nice to me, tolerating me, he claimed. The prick.

Finally, she got back up and began to train again, ignoring him. He watched the sky and wanted to take a deep breath of relief when the sun began to creep over the horizon.

And with it, a sliver of land to the north.

"LAND!" a sailor screamed from the bird's nest.

13

MAVE

"LAND!" A sailor screamed right as the dawn of a new day lightened the sky. Mave stumbled in the middle of a swing.

Did I hear that right?

"LAND!" the sailor called out again. "Captain, we're here!"

"Aye! I see it, boy!" Captain Sen hollered back, laughter in his voice.

Mave's heart began to race and she looked up to see where the sailor was pointing to. She raced in the direction of the sailor's pointing hand, squinting as she hit the rail, and there it was. On the horizon, there was land. Free land. A place where she could be Andinna and no one would put a collar on her neck.

Zayden came up next to her. She hadn't expected to share this moment with the cranky father, but then, she expected nothing that happened on this long trip, even the fact that she would be taking it.

In a sense, it was poetic. If it weren't for the sudden appearance of this male, she would never be here. She would be dead on the sands, her dying wish being that Rain and Mat could survive in the pits without her.

"Welcome to Olost," he said to her. "And you know, I don't think

I've ever said it, but…thank you for being there for my boy in the pits. Thank you for taking him and Mat in. Without you, I don't know if they would have made it through."

"Thank you," she whispered. "For bringing me this far."

"What?" He frowned at her, not understanding her reference. She grinned at the dawn, the land right there.

"You freed me that night. Thank you. I would have never seen this if you hadn't come." She couldn't stop the words from tumbling out of her mouth. "I would never be here if it weren't for you."

"Ah…well…" Zayden looked away, scratching the back of his neck. "You were with Matesh and Rainev…and well…"

She laughed, patting his shoulder, then turned back to Olost. In the beat of a few seconds, the deck was flooded with people. Arms wrapped around her waist and a large chest nestled between her wings on her back.

"We're here," Matesh whispered, holding her close.

"We are." She was unable to stop smiling, just watching them draw closer.

Around them, people were cheering. She could hear Alchan and Luykas try to direct the Company to get ready for things they needed to do in port, but no one was listening. She certainly wasn't. Dawn was right there, and by midday, their feet would be on solid ground. It had taken just over a month. Thirty-two days. She had counted, because it was the first thirty-two days free she ever had.

"How do you feel?" he asked softly, not loosening his grip.

"Excited." That was the first feeling. "Nervous." She had never walked free before, not in her living memory.

"No fear? Of course not," he said, chuckling.

"No fear," she confirmed, nodding. "Not right now." She had those moments of fearing it, but in that moment, there was none. She could only imagine what sort of new life she was about to have and she hoped he would stay with her through all of it. Something about confirming that they were in a real Andinna relationship made her less insecure.

"COMPANY! TO ME!" Alchan roared, the angry order going over the cheers. The Andinna quieted and the sailors scattered to get back to work. Mave sighed as Matesh let her go and took her hand instead.

"Come on, before he pops that vein in his forehead." Matesh was still in a good mood, even with Alchan roaring and stomping his feet on the deck. Mave followed dutifully, knowing this was her life now. Alchan and Luykas gave orders and she promised to follow them. If she wanted to remain in the Company, she had to, and the idea of being in the Company was all she had going forward. She didn't know what other job she could do.

They circled around the half-brothers. Alchan took the lead and began barking out instructions.

"When we get off the ship, the sailors are going to hold our things. Bryn, you're going to run out and get us an inn for one night. You understand? One night. Take Matesh and Mave with you and leave them there so she stays out of trouble."

"Why would I get into trouble?" she asked, cutting into the next part of his speech.

His eyes narrowed at her. She liked the amber color of them and wondered what they would look like plucked out of his face and threaded on a necklace. She was strongly considering it.

"It's not so much you looking for trouble as others causing it. Female Andinna don't leave our unofficial territory. There's too much risk of hunters grabbing them and selling them to the Empire for a quick payout. I don't want you out and about with only Matesh."

"Okay." She could agree to that, then; just as long as he didn't think she was going to go off and explore a place she'd never been to and get into fights by herself. She was tough, but she wasn't that stupid.

"You accepted that fairly easily," he noted, still watching her.

"No reason for me to argue. I'm not in the mood to get recaptured and sent back."

A couple of the males snorted, obviously trying not to laugh. Alchan finally looked away from her, and continued.

"Luykas, you and I will run out and set up supply pickups for tomorrow. We're also going to check on our horses, and let's hope they're in good shape to ride out quickly. I'm hoping we leave tomorrow. We'll probably need to see the bank to make all this happen. Bryn?"

"Aye, ya will. We have enough. I wrote down the numbers for Luykas."

"Thank you. When we're done with that, Luykas will meet you all at the inn. Varon, Nevyn, Rainev, and Zayden, once Bryn is back from the inn, he'll lead you and a few of the sailors in taking all our gear to the inn. Wait for Luykas, then you can all go out to drink and have a good time. Don't leave Mave alone out there, though, and stay together. Don't do anything stupid. We're only doing this tonight. I'm not in the mood to sit around this city."

She noticed he wouldn't be coming back with Luykas. She didn't like him enough to ask about it, but she was still curious. She considered the idea of asking someone else later why their leader would be allowed to disappear with no one, when it was obvious that the Company needed to stay in at least pairs.

"With that, everyone go pack up your cabins and clean up. We're not leaving this ship a mess for Captain Sen. He's been a real life-saver this mission." Alchan clapped and the males began to disperse. She followed Matesh back inside, only glancing back once to see Olost drawing closer. It was so exciting, but she knew they had a lot of work to do before getting off the ship.

IT TOOK A LONG TIME, but by the time they were docked, everything was on the deck. Mave waited for the ramp to drop. She was about to put her feet on free land. She wondered how it would change her. There was another good thing about this as well.

I'm so ready to be off this ship.

Mat stood patiently next to her. Together, they watched the sailors drop the ramp. A few of them started cheering again. Captain Sen was the first off the ship, meeting someone official looking at the bottom. A couple of seconds later, he looked back up to them and waved them down.

"You're free again! Get off my boat!" He was smiling. She watched Luykas and Alchan go first, then Bryn.

Mat nudged her gently. "Let's go," he said.

She nodded and silently made her way onto the ramp and walked down it. The moment her foot touched the pier, she felt like she could breathe easy. She'd done it. She made it to another continent. Olost, home of the Free Cities.

Her legs wobbled as they walked down the pier. Something seemed off, and Bryn was the one who noticed.

"Aye, ya still usin' yer sea legs. Don't worry, that'll wear off by the end of the day."

"Is that what's wrong?" she asked, wondering why her balance was off.

"Yeah. Your body adjusted while we were at sea. We're all going to be a bit off for a couple of hours, I bet." Matesh chuckled. "You get used to it."

"As long as it's not permanent," she mumbled, shaking her head. She didn't like the sensation.

They split off from Luykas and Alchan quickly. Mave took the time to walk a little slower than she normally did. She wanted to take in this new place.

Namur, one of the city states of Olost, one of those legendary free cities she had heard about. It smelled like the sea and fish, something she was used to now. Colors exploded everywhere, from the rich colors of people's clothing to the tarps of market stalls lining the streets. The cobble beneath her feet was even a pretty shade of blue and the buildings were clashing different colors of stones. It wasn't as tall as Elliar, but it had some size to it, going up a hill away from the coast, like it was growing over her.

It was the most different city she could probably see from what she knew. For all the white of Elliar, there was none here. Everything had color and it stood out. It was chaotic and beautiful.

Someone grabbed her elbow and shocked her.

"Mave, you need to keep up," Mat said to her, smiling. "Enjoying the sights?"

"I am," she answered. "It's really pretty here."

"It's very different than most places, that's for sure. It's considered the pirate city and with it, there's a lot of different cultures here, coming together to create what Namur is. They also say fashion is born here, thanks to the crazy creative people that are drawn to the wildness of the city."

"You pay attention to those types of things?" She couldn't believe it.

"Mave…I've been passing through Namur for a thousand years. Maybe it's because you've been stuck in one place, but yeah, I pay attention. Every Andinna does, especially those of us that travel. This city was very different a millennium ago. I've gotten to witness it blossom into this."

"What was it like? A thousand years ago, what did Namur look like?"

"It was a dreary port city that did mostly fishing. It's come a long way." Matesh grinned. "Come on. Bryn's already decided on the inn he wants us to stay in for the night. We just need to get there and get settled in."

"Aye, yeah, and we need to hurry. They might not have rooms and if they don't, we'll need to check other places." Bryn was ahead of both of them. Mave realized they were towering over everyone else. Humans went to her chin, for the most part, and the two males she was with? They towered over everyone like dark specters.

She walked faster for them, still trying to drink in the city. They were only going to be there for the night. She wanted to experience as much of it as possible. She even had to resist stopping and looking in shop windows at rich gowns so different from the ones she had seen in Elliar.

When they arrived at the inn, Mave stopped a moment to read the sign before being pulled inside. Hornbuckle Inn and Tavern, in Common. There was another language underneath she didn't understand. It wasn't Elvasi, Common, or Andinna. Inside, there were fires going, even though it was summer. People sat at tables and behind the bar in the back was a dwarf. She wasn't expecting that.

"Togi!" Bryn called out. "Have space for the Company tonight?"

The dwarf looked over the three of them and gave them a grin. "Always! You know I love when y'all drop by! What do you need?" He looked over her the longest. "A female." There was an awe to his last word. She remembered what Luykas had said about females never traveling now. It sank home in that moment.

"New member of the Company, Togi," Matesh explained. "Mave, meet Togi. The Hornbuckle family, dwarves that once lived in Anden, are big supporters of ours. They're all over Olost now and run one of these places in each city. They will always welcome you if you need a place to lay your head."

"Nice to meet you," she greeted the male.

Togi extended a hand. She didn't have much experience with dwarves. The only one she had known was another slave, convicted to life in slavery for murdering his wife. She had never gotten along with him. She trusted Matesh and Bryn, though. She took the hand and shook with the dwarf, firm and steady.

"Nice to meet you as well!" he replied brightly, already having shaken off his shock at her appearance. "Now, Bryn, you know the entire Company is going to cost you…"

"Aye! Let's work out the details." Bryn chuckled and sat down at the bar. She watched him pull out a few pieces of paper and begin talking and pointing to different things with Togi. While they did business, she looked out at the other patrons. Many of them watched her back, some with wide eyes.

"There's a lot of people staring at me. It's because I'm female, isn't it?" She hoped it wasn't.

"It is. You'll get that a lot. I'm sorry. The Company tends to draw the eye already, since we're the biggest roaming group of Andinna around, but having a female is going to make it worse." Matesh sighed. "Leni, can we get drinks and settled in a booth while Bryn and Togi work things out?"

A female dwarf quickly agreed, nodding without a word, and Mat led her to a large booth that was obviously fit to handle wings and tails. It was made for Andinna. The table was even taller than others.

Drinks slid in front of them and she sipped hers carefully. She didn't think it would be poisoned, thanks to what Matesh said. No, she just had no idea what was in the cup.

"What is this?" She wasn't sure she liked the thick alcohol taste.

"Ale. It's standard fare for the dwarves and most taverns. Mead is more common for us Andinna to drink, but it can be seasonal, and wine is pretty expensive." Matesh took a long swallow of his drink. "You get used to it. It'll ease the nerves."

"And get me drunk," she reminded him.

"Yeah, well…how do you think it eases the nerves?" He grinned, showing off his canines. She chuckled, only sipping from her drink with care. She hadn't gotten drunk before and she wasn't sure she wanted to experience it yet.

She listened to the conversations around her, or tried to. Music was playing from a man with a violin. Others were chatting about the food or the weather. Nothing important or interesting, but it was all things she had never once talked about with someone, not in such an aimless way. The closest she had gotten to talking about aimless things in the pits was the time she defended the slop from Rain's criticism.

Of all the things I enjoyed. The slop.

She huffed at the thought. The spicy jerky and endless fish on the ship was better than it, and even the males had been complaining by halfway through the trip. She was told to expect even better food on land, and that excited her.

"Hey, we have rooms now," Bryn said, walking over and peeking into the booth. "Come on. Leni will show ya to yer room. I got ya two the biggest one."

"You didn't have to do that," Mat replied, standing up with a stretch.

"I did. Gift to Mave. Enjoy it. It's got that Elvasi internal pipe stuff." Bryn grinned.

Mave wasn't sure what her response should be, so she just smiled back. "Thank you."

The female dwarf, Leni, silently led them up some stairs in the back of the tavern area of the inn. They went to the top floor, three flights of stairs up, and she handed Mat a key before walking away.

"Is she always so quiet?" Mave asked, hoping it wasn't because of her.

"Leni? Yeah." Matesh sighed, unlocking the door. "She doesn't have a tongue, just so you know. Should have warned you."

"Oh!" Mave gasped. "That's awful."

"Isn't it? It was eight hundred years ago. Leni is a great lady. Togi's wife, by the way." Mat opened the door. "Come on. Go check out the place Bryn probably blew half his money on."

Mave tentatively entered the room and sucked in a breath. It was luxury personified, with rich fabrics in deep, saturated colors and thick rugs underneath the furniture in some sections. The floor was a deep red wood that was warm and inviting.

It was beautiful.

And in the middle? A huge bed, big enough for three Andinna or more, she was certain of it.

"He really was trying to give you something nice," Mat commented. She could notice the very small bite to it. "Go take a bath and test all of that out. Getting clean is going to be everyone's first priority."

"Don't care to join me?" she asked softly, turning back to him.

"Tell me if there's enough space and I absolutely will," he answered, grinning again. That had knocked the edge off him, like she had hoped.

She wandered into the other room, admiring the large tub and the strange faucets. She fiddled with them, curious. Water began to pour out and she looked under the tub, realizing she could open a vent and heat would come from a fireplace down below. It all seemed very ingenious and advanced.

Almost too much, really. She didn't really care about hot water or anything, just as long as she could bathe.

Then she saw all the bottles near the tub. Those she could figure out a bit easier. She had once been Shadra's slave handmaiden. Soaps and perfumes for the body. Shampoos and other liquids for the hair. She had never used any herself, but there had been a time when she helped Shadra with all of these things.

It should have been wonderful, to be a female playing with all of these items, she guessed. Honestly, they left a somewhat bad taste in her mouth. They only reminded her of that distant time in slavery before she was thrown to the pits. Where she went from struggling young female to hardened and dangerous warrior.

So long ago.

When the tub had enough water, she stepped in, grabbing a cloth to begin cleaning herself. Weeks of grime needed to go. It was the longest she had gone without bathing in centuries, that was certain.

The door opened and she saw Matesh standing in it, nude, waiting for her invitation.

"I think there's enough space, if we both stand," she murmured, gesturing for him to come closer.

He did, stepping in next to her. There was enough space. The tub was bigger than her old bathing pool. He didn't start cleaning himself, though. He grabbed another cloth and a bar of soap, lathering it up. She shivered when the washcloth ran over the inside of her right wing.

"Is this a thing too?" she asked, enjoying the feeling of him washing her wings.

"It is," he answered, kissing a clean area. "And when you're done,

I'll finish up. Would you like to help with my wings? I would appreciate it, but you don't have to."

She chuckled, letting him continue to scrub her wings. "Yes, I'll help you with your wings," she told him with a smile.

She used a fancy little bucket to scoop some water and begin on her hair, pouring it over her. She relented on using the shampoo for it when she realized just what sort of state her hair was in. How did Mat ever find her attractive on the ship?

She glanced back at him and saw why. *I didn't realize how dirty we both were. He's just as bad.*

They bathed slowly and with care. When she was done, she helped him get all the sea salt off his wings, watching how he got shivers as well from the touch.

There was an intimacy to it all, bathing like this with someone else. She enjoyed it, hoping they would get to do it again, and soon. Especially with the way Mat looked at her as they stepped out of the tub.

Heat simmered between them.

They didn't make it to the bed. Not the first time.

14

ALCHAN

Alchan walked quietly with Luykas, trying to enjoy being on solid land again. He couldn't find the excitement, but then, he never really could. Soon, he would be back with the other Andinna and all the problems he wanted to avoid would come back. All the responsibility and all the weight of it, threatening to crush him.

His brother knew why he was in a mood. Luykas didn't have the same problem, thanks to his Elvasi half.

"Are you going to be okay?" Luykas asked softly as they stepped into the Namur bank, or one of them. There were a few around the city, all regulated by the city's government.

"I'm going to get laid, and that might help," he answered honestly. "You know I don't like being…home."

"Yeah, I know, but even you need to put your feet up sometimes. You can't run yourself into the ground working." Luykas patted his back with brotherly affection.

I wish I could. It would be easier than dealing with everything else.

Alchan felt childish and bitter for the thought, but he was thrust into a terrible position at only eight hundred years old. At eighteen hundred, nothing was easier. He wasn't any better at the job, and he feared he never would be. The only thing he could really be grateful for in his life was the Company, the males who didn't treat him any differently. They respected him, most of the time, and they were his friends, also most of the time.

"How much are we pulling out of our savings?" he asked, wondering what he and Bryn had come up with.

"More than we really should, but this mission was hard and it didn't earn us anything. Things are going to be a little lean for us this winter, even with the raid."

Alchan sighed. They went through phases of too much money and not enough. Something would always happen that drained their finances, and it would take a few years to rebuild their savings in the different cities.

"Just Namur, right?" He didn't want them going broke in all the cities of Olost. Each city ran a self-contained banking system. They talked to each other, and you could withdraw coin from a different from a bank in Namur, but it was iffy business. Anything could go wrong. It was safer to keep savings evenly distributed between the cities and use what was available in each one.

"Yeah, just Namur, so it's not that bad. We could always take a quick trip to another city to get more if we need it." Luykas gave him an easy smile, and he took it as a good sign.

"If you sirs could come with me," a human said politely to them. Alchan almost smirked. Humans tended to serve them quickly and get them out of the bank as soon as possible. Maybe it was the fact that they were all probably twice the size of all of them, or that Andinna were very good at killing.

Luykas took the lead, while he trailed behind. He didn't like dealing with the banks or the money. He would rather be out there, planning an attack or an escape, getting into a fight and proving he was the best warrior in Olost. He wasn't, but he knew his Company was the best group of warriors the Andinna could offer. Their numbers used to be higher. A few retirements, several deaths, a couple of captures they couldn't save in time.

But they were still the best warriors on this continent, and he enjoyed testing their limits, making sure his males were still sharp.

And female. Let's not forget that new addition. I can't - she's never going to let me forget she's there. I just hope we make it out of this city without any incidents.

He wanted to hate her, he really did. A female who challenged him constantly, who called him out on his behavior. It was like he had one of the bitches from the villages with him all the time now.

She was right to do that, though. I was an intolerable prick when I first laid eyes on her. I've never been that rude to a female, even when I've wanted to be.

And now she knew what he was. That helped him, he guessed. She didn't seem to want to strangle him as bad and she hadn't back-talked his order to stay hidden while she only had Matesh. She quickly fell in line with his reasoning.

He was ignoring Luykas and the banker, only tuning in to the conversation when they told him to sign something. He ended up signing more pieces of paper than he wanted.

"Do you need to make a personal withdrawal?" Luykas asked him. "For…"

"Yes. I'll need fifty gold suns. Give me two hundred silver moons as well."

The banker jumped up, wide-eyed. Fifty gold suns was an amazing amount of money. Most humans, unless they were filthy rich merchants or politicians, would never see that sort of money.

"Don't blow it all in one place," Luykas teased with a huff, knowing full well Alchan intended to. Probably getting blown in the deal. "The silver?"

"I just wanted some pocket money as well." Alchan shrugged. "The gold goes to…you know, but I wanted some change in case I wanted to grab a bite to eat or anything."

"Copper would be better," his brother reminded him.

"Copper makes people think I'm poor." Alchan raised an eyebrow. He was the wealthiest person in the Company, though it wasn't because of his money management. "It would be dishonest."

"You are such a-"

"Your withdrawals, sirs," the banker interrupted, holding three large bags. Behind him, two others carried a small chest. "Fifty gold suns and two hundred silver moons for you, sir." He placed two bags in front of Alchan. "And…three hundred gold suns and four hundred silver moons in the chest."

"The last bag?" Alchan asked, frowning.

"You need to pay attention," his brother mumbled. "It's for…It's for Mave. She needs certain things. I'm not going to tell her I got this out for her, but you know if we go to the village without…"

"Yeah…" Alchan groaned. Females. He knew Mave probably didn't care about anything Luykas was thinking of, but the females back home? They would notice the absence and question the reason. "How much are you considering spending on her?"

"Not too much. A hundred silver."

Not too much, he says. Liar. He's trying to buy himself into her good graces. Alchan thought about that. *It's not going to work, but I'm going to laugh as he tries.*

They were escorted back out of the building, carrying way too much money. At least they would be blowing it all quickly.

"We're going to the nicer places," Alchan ordered. "We might get less, but I don't want to deal with low quality items in unsafe areas with this much." He didn't like that Luykas was carrying a small fortune. It would get them three carts of supplies that the village would store for them. It would all be for community use, because that's what the Andinna did, and it would show that the Company wasn't just a drain on resources when it passed through. Not that the Company was ever accused of that, but they never wanted it to happen.

"I can agree with that." Luykas nodded. "Thank goodness we didn't bring Bryn."

"He's wily, that one." Alchan chuckled. "He doesn't like when we force him to go to the nicer areas. Which inn did he choose, by the way?"

"Hornbuckle place, like he always does." Luykas began to chuckle as well. "Love those dwarves."

"Same." Alchan knew they would remind him of his responsibilities and his place, but they never made it seem too big, not like the Andinna in the mountains did.

The brothers walked shoulder to shoulder towards the rich district of Namur. The streets were cleaner as they went and so were the buildings, less bombarded by the sea salt and grime.

He let Luykas loose in the market and went to the stables run by an Elvasi mutt he knew well. "Han," he called out, walking into the main building. "You here?"

"Is that Alchan Andini I hear?"

Alchan wanted to wince at his last name. Dragon-child. The family last name. Thanks to his father's bloodline, he was given his father's last name and not his mother's, like Andinna custom normally pointed to. Luykas took the last name when he came to Anden from the Empire, since he had no other options.

"It is!" Alchan waited, looking over a few of the horses near the stable's entrance. None of them were the Company's.

The Elvasi mutt walked out grinning. The Empire despised mutts. The idea that one of their people would breed with another race was disgusting to them, so most ended up in Olost, free from the pressures of their long-lived side. This one, with his delicately pointed ears and dancing hazel eyes, was half-human and had worked with the Company for seven hundred years.

"It's good to see you alive. Rumors hit Namur that some of your men were captured. Then more rumors hit us just a few days ago that you did some crazy-ass shit right in Elliar. Legendary Champion of the Colosseum is now free. Empress Shadra is pissed off. Know anything about that?"

"I might," he answered, smiling. "It was fun. I hated every second of it, but Han, it was really fun shoving the middle finger at that bitch."

"I bet it was!" Han laughed, walking closer. Alchan dared to hug the male when it was offered. They were old friends now. Han was a rich merchant, normally the type Alchan avoided, but Han was too down to earth. He should despise the Elvasi heritage, but Alchan could also remember a time when the Elvasi weren't the enemy the way they were now. Han was evidence that the Empire was being pointed by a bitch, but their people weren't all that awful. Captain Sen was the same.

Off the top of his head, Alchan could think of nearly a dozen Elvasi or Elvasi mutts that weren't out to destroy his people.

"How are the horses?" he asked cautiously. They had been left in Namur for a long time. He hoped his gelding even recognized him.

"Good. I let Luykas' stallion mount a few mares for the breeding operation. Fine foals should come from those."

Alchan smiled as Han led him to a particular stable on the back end of the mutt's property. The Company's stable. Being long-lived meant they tried not to get too attached to their mounts. They didn't use horses for any travel, except when the distance was too far to fly or they couldn't for secrecy. They hired Han, who had the privilege of saying he bred the horses used by the Ivory Shadow Mercenary Company and had for seven hundred years. Before him, they were constantly buying new horses.

Alchan knew his gelding was a distant descendant of a stallion he once rode. That's how far back their breeding operation went.

"How many do you need from the herd?" Han asked.

"Keep the stallion, and give Luykas a spare gelding. He needs to keep breeding. Do we have any other stallions or do you need to get new stock?"

"I've got stock for the next three decades, don't worry about that." Han chuckled. "You know that."

"All right. Well…" Alchan began to explain their needs. Individual mounts for seven. Him, Luykas, Zayden, Rain, and Matesh, with spares, just in case. Three for carts of supplies. He figured Bryn, Varon, Nevyn, Leshaun, and Mave could handle those. He knew the female wasn't experienced with it, but it was safer than putting her on her own horse for now. Varon and Nevyn would just want to sit together. Han promised to get it all worked out and meet them the next day. It was a rush, but they could make it all work.

With that, Alchan took his leave and went to find his brother. Luykas was talking with a merchant in the square. They looked like they were concluding their business, which was good.

"Do you want to do her stuff now or tomorrow, right before we leave?" Alchan asked as he drew closer.

"Tomorrow. I'll need her to look at things, smell things. All of that."

"You don't really intend on making this all happen in one day, right?" Alchan frowned.

"No!" Luykas shook his head quickly. "Not at all. But she needs stones for the jewelry. There's a few females in the village who can make the final pieces - they just need the materials. And the fabrics. She can't wear leather all the time. She needs fabrics so they can make her a wardrobe for her downtime."

"Understandable." Alchan ran his hand over some fabric as his brother spoke. He was glad Luykas wasn't asking him to join in on this. He understood the need for all of it, but he wasn't the best person for the task. "Take Leshaun."

"Good idea, but I'll just talk to him. He knows the most about what females need. I want her alone…" Luykas snapped his fingers and pointed at him as he spoke. "The supplies…The merchant here says that Han will need to bring the carts over at dawn to load up."

"Run and let Han know who you picked. Three carts, right?"

"Yup."

After so many years, they were good at guessing these things. Alchan took the chest from Luykas, who jogged off to see Han. It wasn't too long before he was back and they were ready to leave the marketplace.

"Have fun tonight with the Company," he said before they made it back to the lower district.

"Of course. Let me take that. Be safe on your own. I'll send someone to get you in the morning."

"Thank you." Alchan waved as Luykas walked away.

Now it was time for him to deal with his own needs. He wished he could go out with the Company, but he needed this. He hated it, but he needed it.

He turned back into the richer district and went to a small townhome, well-maintained and pretty. It was unassuming and didn't stand out. He knocked twice and waited.

The door opened to reveal a tall Elvasi mutt with two tiny horns in his forehead. Somewhere, he had a tiny bit of Andinna in his bloodline, but not enough to make any difference. His parents continued to breed back to Elvasi instead of Andinna. He didn't get the wings and always said he didn't miss the need to fly. His horns, easily hidden by his hairstyle, were the only sign that he had even a drop of Andinna blood in his veins.

"Alchan…"

"Keyit," he replied. "Am I interrupting anything?"

"No…I'll send out a messenger to cancel my appointment tonight. Come in." The mutt opened the door further.

Alchan took the chance to look Keyit over as he stepped in, noting the somewhat revealing and transparent clothing he was wearing. It was shades of purple that complimented Keyit's brilliant brown eyes and his mahogany skin. It even went well with the thick, black hair that cascaded down his shoulders and back.

Alchan's mouth nearly watered, even though he normally didn't care for the fancy clothing.

"You were expecting someone. I know it wasn't me. I hope it's not a trouble."

"You're only going to be here tonight, I'm guessing?" Keyit closed them in.

Alchan walked behind him to a small sitting room. "Yeah." He normally booked a later day when he arrived in the city. It was rare that he just dropped in on the mutt. He waited patiently as Keyit wrote a note and ran it outside to send off.

Alchan untied the pouch of gold coins and dropped them on a small table. This was the part he hated. Keyit once told him he didn't have to pay. Even though he was mostly Elvasi, he understood that Alchan had no one else thanks to being a *bedru*. Alchan paid the escort, though, refusing to use him for free. Someone deserved something for being with him, even for an occasional night.

"Is the word still 'sun?'" he asked softly as Keyit walked back in.

"Yes it is," the male answered, shifting into a role Alchan knew well. Keyit spent centuries perfecting the act, something that would make Alchan let go of his tightly-reined control. "Sit down, sir, and I'll get you some wine."

Alchan growled. No one ordered him to do anything. It was part of the game. Keyit wanted Alchan to break past thecontrolled act he put on. Alchan would get nothing from this if he tried to hold back.

It wasn't that he hurt anyone, not purposefully. Alchan needed control. He needed to give orders and demand things. He pushed people to their limits and he made them like it as he got everything he wanted out of them.

That's why they had a word that would stop the game if it was needed. It was the one line Alchan would never cross. It was a signal he was doing something he would hate himself even more for. Many Andinna used them to protect their relationships when things became rough.

"Strip and get on your knees. I'll drink wine later."

He didn't care for fancy clothing.

15

MAVE

"They're back!" Matesh called. "Time to get out of bed."

Mave sighed, pushing her face into the pillow. A large hand ran over her ass. They spent the afternoon loving on each other. She felt like it was the best way to celebrate being off the ship after such a nice bath.

"Mave," he crooned. "I'm more than willing to stay here all night with you, but the guys want you to come down and have a good time with them."

She felt the bed press down and he moved over her. Oh, she could tell he was more than willing. She lifted her hips to tease him, eliciting a growl as she pushed his control.

I love that I can be this way with him.

It was a nice change of pace from the centuries of trying to have a quick fuck without getting killed. Or just being whored. For once, she enjoyed the bedroom and the male in it. She always came back to that thought when she was with him. He'd given her this ability to relax and trust.

"Mat!" Rain called. "Mave! Come on! We're done and want to start drinking!"

She groaned as Mat got off her. She pushed up from the bed and watched him get dressed quickly. "Let's go, *amanra*," he said patiently, smiling. "We can come back up here later tonight."

"We will be, that's certain." She swung her legs off the bed.

It only took a few moments to get presentable, and they walked out of the room to find Rain waiting on them. He looked nearly normal for the moment, smiling with a brightness she had missed.

"Hey, *illi bodyr*," she greeted him. "How are you feeling?"

"Better. The ship was getting too small for me." Rain shrugged. "Hoping to just have a good night. How are you?"

"Haven't felt this good in a very long time," she answered. "Or this clean."

Rain laughed, nodding. "We got everything here and went to the bathhouse next door. The ship was dirtier than the pits. I didn't think it was possible."

"Right?" She chuckled, wrapping an arm over his shoulders. They were the same height, so it was a little awkward, but she wanted to touch him, show him some real affection. She didn't want him to think she was going to hold his attitude on the ship against him. He deserved to be upset, and he would have to figure out how to handle it on his own.

Mat followed behind them, a large, silent observer. She glanced back at him once, only to find him smiling and looking down at her ass. She flicked her tail's tip near his face, making him look up, realizing he'd been caught.

They made it back down into the tavern area, where she saw that several tables had been pushed together and most of the Company was sitting around. She noticed that Alchan wasn't there and it reminded her that he had said something about it earlier in the day on the ship.

"Where is Alchan going to be tonight?" she pondered out loud, not really expecting an answer.

"With Keyit, probably." Matesh made it sound very casual and simple. "If we're only here for one night, he needs to work some shit out of his system."

"I like Keyit," Rain commented lightly. "He's a good male and was really nice when I saw him once. Offered me a drink and everything. Mave, he wouldn't be your type."

"Why would I care if he's my type?" She frowned, not understanding Rain's point.

"He's an escort in the rich district," Mat explained. "Alchan is one of his patrons. They're pretty open about it. Everyone in the Company has gone to pick Alchan up from his place at least once. Skies, most of us have gone at least a half a dozen times."

"What?" she snapped. Alchan hired a *whore*? Didn't he know what that sort of work did to someone? The toll it demanded on the soul or the body?

I thought I hated him already.

She didn't realize she was snarling until Mat put a hand gently over her mouth.

"Mave, Keyit loves his job. He does it because he wants to. This isn't like what you went through. He's trained in it because he wanted to be. There's a guild for it here, just like blacksmiths or tradesmen. It's an honest profession and makes Keyit rich."

Luykas walked over. "He's right, Mave. What goes on between Alchan and Keyit is between them. Keyit isn't being forced into it and he can always turn Alchan or anyone else away."

Mave tried to come to terms with that. She tried to hold back the snarls, knowing she was scaring the non-Andinna in the tavern. They were all staring at her. She pulled Mat's hand from her mouth when she was finally able to stop.

"Rain, you didn't hire him, right?" she asked, remembering what he'd said.

"No!" Rain laughed nervously. "No. Only Alchan sees him. I was in Namur with the Company before and went with Varon to get him. Met Keyit. He and Varon are actually good friends too."

She tried her best to process this and decided she would just ignore it. If someone *wanted* to whore, that was their business, not hers. She couldn't relate in any way. She didn't think she could handle meeting this Keyit, even if everyone liked him.

"Come sit down," Luykas ordered. "Have a drink. There's going to be some culture shock."

She already knew that, but never had she thought people would actually want to be *whores*. In the Empire, Elvasi whores were backstreet bitches with nothing else. They were the lowest of society. Being forced to whore in the Empire was a sign that the woman had no worth except her cunt, and it robbed her of any possibility of marriage. It's why the gladiators were whored the way they were. Slaves had no worth. She'd heard stories about Andinna slaves that were used by their owners even outside the pits. Guards and new gladiators would talk about it.

With that awful mental image, the idea of her new leader using someone paid for sex, she sat down and grabbed the first pint she could. She didn't like the taste of the ale but she took several swallows.

"That was mine," Nevyn said calmly, trying to take it back. When she bared her teeth, he moved his hand away, nodding. "I'll order another. Togi! We need more drinks!"

"Coming right up!"

Matesh sat down on her left, hooking his tail with hers. He pointed at Nevyn and Varon's tails, showing her they were the same.

"Our version of holding hands like the humans," he whispered to her.

"I like it," she replied. "Keeps my hands free."

"Exactly." He smiled, kissing her cheek. They were sitting close enough that their wings also touched. Of course, Nevyn was close enough on her other side that their wings were touching as well. That seemed to be something she needed to get used to since Nevyn didn't seem bothered at all or attempt to move.

"So, what sort of trouble should we get into tonight?" Matesh asked loudly, looking down the table at someone else. She followed his gaze and saw Zayden nursing a drink.

"Hopefully none," he answered, just as loud. "Luykas, anything we're not allowed to do?"

"Kill people," he answered mildly. "Like always."

She wasn't sure what to do. She was already sitting with all of them and drinking, but they had done that on the ship during meals. She continued to sip on her ale. Nevyn and Varon were doing that hand signaling to each other, with Nevyn chuckling every so often. Matesh struck up a conversation with Zayden and Luykas.

She saw Rain and Bryn chatting softly further away and across from her. She could interrupt them, but didn't want to and she wasn't going to talk to Luykas.

She tapped Nevyn's arm nervously.

"What are you two talking about?" she asked.

Nevyn turned and looked down at her. "Oh, we're talking about the time Matesh fell asleep outside when we got him drunk. Varon was telling me I shouldn't do the same thing to you. There's different dangers involved and everything." He was grinning as he said it.

"You would do that to me?" She leaned away from him, confused. Varon's head began to shake wildly, sending his black hair everywhere. He was one of the few males she had ever seen with such long, loose hair.

"No! See? Varon is looking out for you." Nevyn laughed. "It's a little hazing we do when one of the guys can't remember their limits with drink. We can handle a bit more alcohol than the other races, but that doesn't mean we can drink a tavern dry. Matesh and Zayden have both tried a few times. We don't leave them outside alone, either. Someone guards them to make sure nothing happens." Nevyn patted her arm. "No, we won't do that to you. Drink, relax, be merry. This is your first night in a free land."

Varon's hands began to move faster and Nevyn watched them with interest. When they were done, Varon stood up and extended a hand.

"He wants to be your first dance," Nevyn explained. "He's a great dancer, you should say yes."

"Oh…Okay." Mave took the hand cautiously and let Varon lift her up from her seat. She could fight battles and defeat any opponent she'd ever come against.

Dancing made her nervous.

Varon didn't pull her very close, not like she saw lords and ladies dance, keeping a proper distance between them. He positioned her hands on his shoulders, and put his on her waist. Then he began to rock to the beat.

She didn't say anything, just letting him sway her around the empty area in the middle of the tavern where other dancers were. He grabbed one of her hands and led her through an awkward spin, made even stranger thanks to her wings.

As the song continued, she noticed he was mouthing the words to the song.

"You do know how to speak," she said suddenly.

He nodded and said something, but no sound came out. She could tell he was talking and knew from the look on his face that something had happened. There was a story there. She didn't see any scars or disfiguration that would damage someone's voice and she could see a tongue in his mouth. So why couldn't he speak?

The song ended and he led her back to the table. Mat, who hadn't commented when she left, wrapped his arm around her waist, pulling her possessively back to him and further from Nevyn.

"Ah, jealous male. Sorry, Varon and I aren't *mayara* and seem to have insulted your male." Nevyn winked but she wasn't sure why.

"I'm not insulted," Mat countered. "I turned and she was gone. She wasn't holding my tail anymore."

"Are you okay?" she asked him, hoping she wasn't insulting him.

"I am." His cheeks turned red. She noticed two empty pints in front of him now. "Nevyn's right, and it's not something you need to worry about."

"Yeah. We males don't burden our females with our jealousy. Well, we're taught not to." Nevyn reached around her and thumped Mat. "You know we're not going to steal her from you, so calm down."

Matesh laughed, nodding. Then he kissed the back of her head. "Be careful with those two. They like to get people drunk and start parties. Nevyn's a bit of a prankster when he's in the mood."

"We've been giving you some space," Nevyn admitted. "I think tonight, you should hang with us and leave the lover. Come make friends."

She considered it, looking between the two males on either side of her. She knew what Matesh wanted, seeing his encouraging gaze. He wanted her to try talking and hanging out with Nevyn and Varon. It meant leaving the security of his side, knowing he wouldn't be there to back her up. It meant going out on her own with two males she had barely spoken to.

They're Company. Mat told me I can trust anyone in the Company and so have Bryn and Rain. This would be a good sign that I can.

"Okay. You have fun with Zayden." She patted his arm.

"Oh, I will." He grinned. "Nevyn, if you get her too drunk, give her back to me. Don't leave her in the street."

"No worries!" Nevyn jumped up. "Come on, female. We're going to show you the town."

She stood up slowly and followed Nevyn out of the tavern, Varon following behind them. She had no idea what she signed up for, but she was in it now.

"So, I was thinking that place down by the docks." Nevyn crossed his arms. "But I also have enough to take us up to the rich district. Love?" He looked at Varon, who began to sign. Once Varon was done, Nevyn grinned. "The docks it is. Mave, you like a good fight, right?"

"Who doesn't?" she asked, smiling.

"Well, this tavern by the docks has fights, normally between sailors in their off time. The thing is, when we show up, we get called out and go a few rounds. You up for that?" Nevyn looked like he was going to start jumping from excitement.

"Sure?" She had never seen anything like that before and this was going to be her first night in a free land. Fighting? It was at least something she knew.

They didn't need to weave through the crowd. It parted for them.

Nevyn took the lead, and she fell into the natural position behind him to the right, with Varon mirroring her on Nevyn's left. They were a unit, and thanks to their size, others got out of their way.

She could hear the tavern long before they arrived at it. The screams of men came from a run-down building near one of the piers. Nevyn gave three copper coins to a human at the door and walked in. The human waved Mave and Varon to follow. Varon grabbed her elbow preemptively and she realized why inside.

It was packed wall-to-wall with all sorts of people, cheering around a raised center ring. There was even a second floor. Tables were everywhere, but hardly anyone was sitting down. The top floor looked quieter, people watching over the balcony. Every so often, someone threw something up on the stage, like a loaf of bread.

"Oh!" She took it all in with wide eyes. Something about it felt like home, and yet it couldn't be more different. Something about it screamed the Colosseum, but there was no one dying in the ring. She saw the two fighters just punch and kick each other until one fell, his nose broken and bleeding. A human jumped on stage and declared the other fighter the winner.

"What do you think?" Nevyn yelled, trying to talk over the crowd.

"This looks interesting!" she said back, trying to be loud enough for him as well.

He led them further inside and they were able to claim a table on the second floor. Everyone in the tavern realized they were there at that point, many pointing, and a few even screaming Nevyn's name. He waved at them, grinning. Varon pulled out a chair for her and helped her sit down. She thanked him quietly, never having a male do that for her before. He just raised a hand, as if to tell her to stop. He sat next to her and began to sign in Nevyn's direction.

"He says he was raised to treat everyone like a…uh, I'm not saying that, Varon." Nevyn coughed before continuing. "He's polite. You don't need to thank him - it makes him feel weird. He just does what he does and you should get used to it."

"Well, okay." She nodded, pretending she understood anything. In reality, she had no idea what was going on. It didn't help that she had no idea how to understand the mute's way of communication or much about him at all, except that he was Nevyn's *bodanra* and a priest.

"Let's just get some drinks and watch some fights, eh?" Nevyn grinned, waving down someone. He put an order for ale, two pints for everyone at the table. "That should get us started!"

She took her first pint when it arrived and drank more. What had Matesh said? It would help her relax? She hoped so, because Nevyn was acting rowdy and Varon was doing nothing she could see to stop it. The mute was sipping on his drink, with a patient, loving expression as he watched Nevyn jump up and down, shouting at the fighters down below.

"Is he always like this?" she asked the mute. Varon only nodded in return. Then he snapped his fingers. He reached into his breeches' pocket and pulled out a little book. Then she saw a charcoal stick. He scribbled something down then slid it to her.

"I picked these up so I could talk to you. It'll be easier when I get you started learning the hand signs I use, but this is a good fix."

"Yes, this works. Thank you for writing in Common." She said her response out loud, not wanting to waste any of his paper. It was a small, bound book with blank pages. She could fit it in the palm of her hand and he wrote fairly small in it.

"Nevyn was raised to be a warrior. He's one of the best we've ever had as a race. Very talented and very skilled."

"I was beginning to realize that," she replied, looking up at the ecstatic male cheering.

Varon tapped her to get her attention again. *"He taught me to fight. He'll teach you to be just as good. But this? He thinks this is fun. I come to keep him out of trouble. He'll get into at least three fights in that ring tonight."*

She laughed at the words he'd written.

"What about you? Will you fight if someone challenges you?"

"Can they do that?" she asked.

"Everyone who comes here can be challenged. I'm quiet so only people scared of Nevyn fight me. They don't realize I'm nearly as dangerous. You? You'll get challengers, no doubt. You can deny, though. Or declare a Champion, someone to fight for you. Many women come to see men and declare male friends as their Champions."

She snorted. "I would never have someone else fight my battles. I am a Champion, Varon. I'll never use one."

He gave her an indulgent smile as he wrote the next part. *"No killing here. Remember that if you go to the ring."*

"I will," she promised.

He just nodded, closing up the book and sliding it back into his pocket. The charcoal stick disappeared next. He sipped on his ale again, watching his lover cheer and shout, even beginning to gamble on whatever fight was going on.

Mave just watched with him. She was already on her second pint, taking it back quickly as she settled in for the show going on down below. She could see it from her seat, since she was right next to the rail. Some burly human beat the shit out of a small, fast little one. He shoved his fists in the air, roaring when he was declared the winner.

"Who do you challenge?" someone called out. The big male pointed up to the second flood.

"I want one of the Andinna! I hear you're warriors!"

Mave smirked as Nevyn laughed, throwing his head back. "Human, are you sure?" the older male called back down. "I have over three thousand years of practice!"

"That means nothing!"

Nevyn's laugh died and a quieter smile came over his face. She watched him jump up, his wings expanding and catching the air. He went over the rail and landed squarely in the middle of the ring, shocking everyone. She could see the burly human stumble back, realizing just how *big* Nevyn really was.

She grinned towards Varon, who heaved a sigh of acceptance, giving an exaggerated shrug. He knew this was going to happen. It wasn't his scene, but it was his lover's scene, so he would be here, rooting him on. They both stood up to lean over the balcony. Neither of them screamed, but they watched intently as Nevyn began exchanging fast punches with the human. Nevyn looked like he was playing with a child, while the human began to breathe hard. She noticed he wasn't even using his tail to try and trip the human up. It was clean, physical strength versus physical strength.

Nevyn dodged a punch to his face and landed one in return on the human, sending him back, knocked unconscious.

People began to gasp and yell. Fights broke out as people lost their money and some gained money. Nevyn just jumped off the stage, his arms wide as if he were daring the world to try again. When he returned to the table, he swooped down to kiss Varon senseless. She raised an eyebrow at the display, only getting laughter in return.

"How's that?" he asked. "Think this might be a place you like?"

"I think it might be," she said, sitting down again. They had fresh drinks and she picked hers up, slamming it with his. They both swung back a swallow after that.

Something about the raucous crowd, the drinking, and the grins of the two Andinna agreed with her. She felt like she was having fun.

16

MATESH

Matesh wandered the streets looking for another tavern to drink at with Rainev, Zayden, Brynec, and Luykas. They left Leshaun for a quiet night at the Hornbuckles'. He was in a great mood, watching the moon rise higher over their heads, washing the world in its red glow. Everyone was laughing, glad to be on land. He missed Mave a little, but he had a good idea at where Nevyn and Varon took her. Nevyn always hit up that fighting place on the docks when he passed through. He didn't know how Mave would react to it, but it was an experience that she needed.

Just like learning about escorts. I didn't even consider how many things she hated were regularly accepted things in other parts of the world.

He also figured she needed to spend time with other members of the Company. He was happy to see her coming out of her tight shell. It was slow and he knew she had to work for it, but she was really trying.

"Mat, you in there?" Zayden asked, elbowing him.

"Yeah." Mat chuckled. "Have we picked a place?"

"We're here. You haven't been paying attention." Zayden pointed to the tavern, smiling. "Come on."

He followed the group inside. He noticed how Rain was sticking close to Bryn and not with him. He didn't blame the young male. Zayden was with him and the father-son duo weren't getting along.

"How are you and Rain?" he asked his closest friend, quiet enough where the rest of their group wouldn't hear.

"I've decided to give him the space he wants even if it kills me," Zayden replied, growling softly. "Trying. I'm trying to give him space."

"That's good. You know, in the pits, I realized just how much of an adult he is now. It was a real eye-opener, for sure. He was defending Mave from my affections like a grown Andinna male family member should. He wasn't discouraging the feelings, but he was protecting her best interests." Mat sighed, remembering their first day. "He's the one who decided to even try and sit with her. He couldn't stand the idea of a female alone the way she was. I was trying to find the biggest group and get us in good, make us safe. But Rain? He was a real male."

"Mave said similar," his friend replied. "Said Rain was the first family she ever had."

"He wasted no time in claiming her, that's certain." Mat shrugged. "It happened. We're out now. Just give him time to overcome it."

"As I said," Zayden growled the words, "I'm trying. Would help if anyone told me what happened, but I've realized that's not going to happen."

It wouldn't help, ildan. It wouldn't help at all.

Mat couldn't say those words. He knew it would only make the overprotective father a thousand times worse. He was just glad Zayden wasn't trying to ride Rain's ass their entire night out. His boy just needed to have some fun, like Mave did.

"It wasn't a good place, Zayden. He needs some normal. Skies, so do I."

Zayden eyed him. "You've never really talked about how it was for you."

Mat looked away. "Where do I start? I killed people in cold blood who couldn't fight back. They had me performing executions on our own people for things like stealing a loaf of bread from a merchant as they ran an errand for their master." Matesh tried his best to never think about it. He would rather stay focused on the future. Tomorrow. "I have Mave to help. I want to leave the pits behind."

"*Anvea et, oto ildan*," Zayden said, stepping into Mat's line of sight again. Mat wondered why he was asking for forgiveness. "I've been so focused on my son that I haven't remembered that my oldest friend was also there. You walked out with a female who has finally made you want to settle. You're helping form a *mayara*, and that's a gift." He sighed. "But I should have checked on you sooner. I shouldn't have seen that as a sign you were okay."

"I am okay, really. They were cruel males. I was bigger than most of them. They jumped me with numbers. What the Empress made me do on the sands if I wanted to keep my head? Someone else would have had to do it. Mave said she had done it before. She had known it was a hard thing to do. I hate that I did it, but there was nothing else. If I didn't do it, Rain and Mave would have been alone." Matesh took a deep breath. "It wasn't good death, Zayden. That's what stuck with me. Kristanya is probably ashamed of what I had to do out there." Their goddess of war and death was probably giving him the evil eye for the things he had done on the sands.

"Have you prayed?" he asked softly.

"No, not yet. I hope…" He swallowed some emotion. "Nothing."

"Pray to Kristanya. Whatever you might be hoping, I think will be helped by taking her talisman from Varon and having a few words between you." Zayden patted him on the shoulder. "I truly am sorry for everything you all went through. I'm just frustrated I can't help. Not you, not my son. I'm not even sure where to begin with Mave." Zayden snorted at the end. "That female. I'm not sure how you do it."

"She's a good female," he answered. "So it's not hard. It's just catching her up and teaching her all the things we grew up with and took for granted. That's not on her, though. Her lack of knowledge isn't her fault. It's those *lintis* in the pits." Mat bared his teeth at the memories. The shunning of her, the hate they had. The distance they were willing to go to *hurt* her, a female. The *best* female.

"Hey, you two!" Luykas called out. "Get over here and sit down!"

Matesh looked to their group, seeing they had claimed two tables to fit all of them. All the humans had backed away from them, and there were already drinks waiting on the table.

"We'll come back to this?" Mat asked his friend, hoping Zayden would want to talk more about it.

"Later. Not much to say, though. Try my suggestion and see if it helps you." Zayden thumped him on the shoulder. "Thank you for allowing me to be a shit friend for the last month. I'll do better."

"Ah, well, you've been worried about Rain. I was never going to hold it against you." Matesh grinned, feeling better. The slavery they endured hadn't just hurt him and Rain. It had hurt Zayden as well. His oldest friend had lost his son and Mat in one swift move.

They walked together to the tables and sat down, ready to drink and waste the night. Matesh chugged his first ale. The serious conversation had knocked him off his good buzz and he had to restart. It was a pain thanks to his size. He knew Zayden was going to have the same issue, seeing the male chugging his first drink back as well.

They tended to hop between taverns because of how much they needed to drink. It wasn't hard for a group of Andinna to drink a bar dry if they never moved on.

He watched as Rain's face grew flushed over the evening. The deep blue of his tatua made him more interesting to the humans, who tried to talk to him when he walked out to take a piss. Mat stood up, wondering if his adopted nephew needed any back up. Rain just casually avoided the humans, leaving without getting caught up in any conversation about why he was blue or smaller than the others.

"Thank the Skies he can turn into a wyvern if they give him too much trouble," Bryn muttered, smiling. He threw a wink at Mat.

"You caught me watching?" Mat chuckled, taking a drink of his fifth ale.

"Not caught, also guilty. I was watchin' too." Bryn lifted his drink in a silent salute as Rain came walking back in. "Rain's interestin', so I can't blame the humans. He looks different than the rest of us, by a long shot."

"Also makes him a target."

"Aye, it does." Bryn sipped now on his drink.

Matesh realized he needed to handle his business as well. It sucked, since he knew if he left his drink, someone was going to finish it for him. He would need to get a fresh one when he came back in. He also saw an opportunity he couldn't pass up.

"Want to step out with me?" he asked the rogue casually as he stood up. "I got to go."

Bryn eyed him. They both knew this was going to be a talk. Mat had more words he needed to say to the rogue and he knew the rogue probably had more to say to him. With Mave not around, they needed to take the chance they had.

Silently, Brynec stood up and followed him. Once they were outside, Mat turned into a small alley and undid his breeches. Bryn was next to him doing the same. They finished up quickly but didn't bother going back in.

"You like her?" he asked, leaning on the wall, watching the rogue toy with the thick scarf he always wore around his neck.

"She's nice. Ya know I didn't mean anythin' with the bed, though. It's not like that." Bryn shrugged. "I like talkin' to her and she understands what I went through. I understand what she went through, even though I wasn't there."

"You sure it's not like that?" Mat didn't want to sound jealous or possessive. Instead, he was trying to explain something else.

For over a week now, he had watched Bryn gently care for her and her wings. He saw the excitement in her eyes about it, and how they would talk while they exercised. He brightened her day. Mat tried not to be jealous because it wasn't his place. Male Andinna couldn't and would never purposefully burden a female with something petty like jealousy. They needed to handle it between them, the males. They needed to make the terms and take them to the female, to show they could handle these problems without needing her to waste her precious time on their nonsense.

"It can be like that," he said softly, leaning closer to the rogue. "I'm okay with it. I would…fully support you bidding for a place in the bed." He watched Bryn's eyes widen a little. "She likes you, probably a lot more than she realizes. Take it from me. When we were in the pits, everything was so…withdrawn, but it simmered there between us. I didn't think it would be so strong on her end, but when we got on the ship, she showed me just how deep it was. She's surprising like that."

"I'm not the type of male who gets with a female like her," Bryn countered. "She's goin' to be attracted to a bunch of big males like ya and everyone knows it. I'm not even goin' to consider the idea-"

"You should consider it. Whatever that excuse was doesn't matter, Bryn. If you like her…you should let her know. You should make a claim and see what she does." Mat growled, trying to control his own feelings. "I don't want to be the reason it never happens. I knew I was getting jealous on the ship. My reaction to the bed thing probably scared the shit out of her. I don't want her thinking that she can't have anyone else."

"What reaction?" Bryn frowned at him. "What did you do?"

"I might have taken my temper out on her in bed. She said she liked it, and knew I needed it. You know…when you're with someone in bed and things get a little rough, and-"

"Aye, yeah. Kian's talked about that before. So have Nevyn and Varon. Sometimes things get rowdy in bed."

"She tried to play that game with me, too." Mat sighed. Oh, he so wished they had played that night. He would love to have her fight him like that in bed. Love it.

She can't yet, though. She needs more time and distance from the pits. If things went too wrong, one of us would end up gutted.

"Oh." Bryn's eyebrows shot up. "And?"

"I stopped it. Warned her. She knew what she was doing, but I don't think she really realized what would happen if it went too far." He rubbed his face. He hadn't expected to be talking about his sex life with Bryn, of all people. Bryn tended to stick close to Nevyn and Varon, while Mat hung with Rain and Zayden. The Company was a large family, but they all had their smaller groups. "Look, just know I'm saying I won't kill you if this goes down. If it goes down the right way."

"Ya will kill me if you find me in the *mayara* bed, Mat. Don't lie." Bryn crossed his arms. "Not like I'll ever be there again," he added quickly, kicking a rock and looking away.

"She and I made a promise. She can't bring a new male unless I'm there." Mat grinned sheepishly.

Bryn coughed, looking up in even more shock than earlier. "You got her to agree to that?"

"She probably wasn't thinking about exactly what I meant." Mat knew his primal need to get the promise had driven him to ask at the worst time for her. She probably hadn't been thinking about anything except his cock buried into her. Actually, he was fairly certain of it.

"Well, that will be fun…when another big male like you joins her *mayara*." Bryn smiled tightly. "She won't want me, so I'm not entertaining this, Mat."

He groaned as the rogue walked away. He thought he was doing something right, telling Bryn he could try. It looked like his suspicions were off-base, but he didn't think they were. He really thought he'd been on the right track, but if that's what Bryn wanted to say, he probably would never find out the truth. Bryn was great at secrets, great at hiding.

Mat almost felt like this was his fault. His jealousy on the ship, his rage over the bed thing. He'd tried his damnedest to hide the jealousy, but then he went and got possessive when she danced with Varon, of all people. Varon, the most non-threatening member of the Company. The priest and the warrior would never try for Mave. They never wanted anyone to come between them. Varon just wanted to give her that first dance, since Varon loved doing those artsy, frilly things.

I can't let my shit stop her from being with other males. It's not right. I need Bryn to admit his feelings for her. I need her to know it's okay.

He just didn't want to lose his place. He was her first male. He wanted to be her most important and her longest. Part of him wanted to be her only. It was a stupid want. It was an improper want. It wasn't very Andinna of him and it surely didn't make him a good male, like he wanted to be for her.

He needed to keep working at making sure she knew she was okay to explore those possible feelings for other males and that males were okay to make advances on her if she welcomed them. He had to make sure he wasn't ruining a possibly wonderful future for her.

17

MAVE

Mave was laughing as Nevyn took out his third opponent. She was six drinks in and feeling it. She was feeling it a lot, a warm buzz filling her body.

"I'm not super-drunk, am I?" she asked Varon. He held up a hand with some of his fingers out, and she knew it was a dizzy test. The lenasti used to do it when one of them took a particularly bad hit to the head. "There's three," she answered, knowing what he intended. He nodded. "So, not that drunk yet?"

Now he pulled out his little blank book and began to scribble some words. He practically rolled his eyes. *"No, not too drunk yet. I'll cut you off when I feel like you're going too far. Don't worry so much. Just enjoy. Just feel."*

"Okay, okay." She held up a hand, shooing his little book away. She wasn't sure she was capable of worrying too much. She had never felt so *good*. This feeling was like being carried away on clouds, nestled in warm blankets. She enjoyed it far too much, really.

"And the Andinna takes another down!" someone yelled out, causing a round of screaming cheers. She joined them, clapping.

"Go Nevyn!" she called. She really enjoyed the friendly feeling of the fighters down below. Everyone was there for a piece of fun and their pride. They were fighting Nevyn because it was fun, not because they hated him. He didn't knock anyone else out like he did the first guy. The next two had been a little more respectful in their challenges.

Nevyn jumped up, flapping his wings to get to the second floor this time. He landed on their table, nearly taking himself and the furniture down as he wobbled precariously on it.

"I win again!" he declared, spreading his arms wide. "Ha! The Andinna legacy remains strong!"

"I want to challenge the quiet one!" someone yelled out. "Maybe he's easier!"

There was laughter throughout the bar. Mave eyed Varon, who shrugged, jumping down without a blink. She shook her head in a bit of shock as Nevyn jumped next to her.

"Get him, love!" Nevyn roared. "You can do it!"

Varon waved a hand casually back at them.

"Does he speak at all?" someone asked near them.

"No. My male is a silent killer," Nevyn answered, grinning dangerously. When he looked back at her, he winked. He grew more ridiculous with every drink, and she couldn't help but follow him in the revelry.

"He's a good male," she agreed, patting his arm.

Nevyn threw the arm over her, pulling her closer. "Isn't he? Love him. And you? You're a good female. I like you. We'll need to train together more, I think. Too bad no one has challenged you to go down into the ring."

"I bet they're worried I'll declare you as my Champion." She couldn't help but laugh and tried to pull away from him, but he held her.

"You? You're the Champion of the Colosseum! What do you need me for? Plus, Mat would be your Champion, in a heartbeat. Nah, I think you're well covered." He rubbed a hand in her hair playfully. "It's almost a pity Varon and I don't want a female."

"Oh yeah, no thanks," she replied, pulling away more. "I have Mat."

"Oh, I wasn't offering. Just saying, if there was a female, you would be a good one. Let's watch this fight, though. You'll get to see my lover in action." Nevyn was still grinning as he pulled her back to him. She wasn't drunk enough to miss how he protectively wrapped a wing over her anyway.

They saw Varon's opponent square up to him and go for the first move as soon as someone declared the fight to start. Varon worked faster than Nevyn, sending the male over the edge of the ring into the crowd in one swift toss that left no question as to the strength the mute had.

"Oh, well, once again he ends it without a show." Nevyn chuckled as Varon quickly rejoined them, also jumping straight up to the second floor. "Love, people want action, drama."

Varon's hands moved quickly.

"Think of it like a play! You love theatre. Start treating it like that." Nevyn was desperately trying to get Varon to do something, but since she was missing half the conversation, she just sat down and watched the lovers have their strange conversation and didn't join in.

They continued to bicker in their weird way as more drinks were brought to them. Finally, they settled down and Varon looked at her, his hands moving.

"He's asking what we talked about while he was gone. He could hear bits and pieces," Nevyn explained.

"How?" she knew her jaw dropped with the question.

"He has really good hearing. Has since I met him. His eyesight is pretty amazing too. He's never missed a shot with his bow. That's not the point. Love, we were talking about how you're an amazing male, and Mave's not a bad female either. I threw out the idea that if we ever wanted a female, one like her wouldn't be so bad."

She could see Varon laugh, but it was so unusual not to hear it. He doubled over in his seat, his shoulders shaking hard. He pulled out his book and began to write something, trying to control himself. He pushed the book to her.

"I hope he didn't give you the wrong impression."

"Oh no. I'm not..." She shook her head. They were much older than her, even for Andinna standards. She figured someone had to be within a thousand years of her to be an option. That seemed acceptable, but they were well beyond that.

"See! I didn't make it weird for her!" Nevyn grinned innocently.

You most definitely did.

Varon signed quickly, pointing at her. Nevyn sighed heavily, defeated.

"He wants me to explain why." Nevyn groaned, leaning back in his seat. "We're afraid adding someone to our family will only hurt the new person. We'll never love a female as much as each other, which makes things complicated. A female is the center, as she should be, but we'll never treat her that way. It's unfair to her and mean of us. We sometimes have the occasional extra partner for a night or two, but we always make sure it's casual."

"You don't think there's anyone out there for you two?" She tilted her head. If she could find one male who wanted to be with her, they could find a female.

"We're positive and don't think it's a bad thing. Varon and I are... complete together. We don't want anyone else. Sometimes, it's fun to joke about the idea, to think 'if there is someone, I want him or her to be like whoever,' but we never feel like we need to go looking." Nevyn smiled lovingly at Varon. "No, if we only have each other until we're old and sore, that's okay. That's perfect, really."

She wanted someone to look at her the way they looked at each other. Would Mat ever gaze at her with so much love? She wanted him to. She wanted to believe she would only ever need her big male, the one who gave her more than she could have ever hoped for.

But she felt a nagging feeling in her chest that he wouldn't be her only. It made her a little sad and a bit scared. Did she not care for him enough because she thought she might have another lover one day?

"Are you okay?" Nevyn asked, looking over at her again.

"What does it mean if I want...more than Mat?" she asked softly.

"That you're a normal female. You care for him, he's yours and he will probably always be yours, but Andinna females have a want, a need to have a group of males. It's instinctual. Does wanting another mean you love the first one less? No, I've never seen that happen unless the first one was already fading or never really loved."

It wasn't Nevyn who reached out to her and patted her hand. It was Varon, who gave her a sympathetic smile. He signed something and Nevyn translated again.

"He says many young female Andinna go through this stage. It's always the strangest when you go from one to two, if there's a second possible. He says your upbringing would make the idea even stranger, but it's not wrong. He's saying…follow your heart. Our gods made us the way we are for a reason and we wouldn't be this way if we couldn't handle it."

She snorted at the mention of their gods, but didn't comment. While she didn't like that he brought up the gods, she also felt an ease to her sudden anxiety over the idea of wanting another male with her and Matesh. She didn't know who it would or could be, but she toyed with the idea and liked it. It felt right, even though it made her a little uncomfortable.

They went back to drinking as she let the conversation drop. Andinna relationships seemed so complicated. She was exposed to the Elvasi, who thought having multiple partners was dirty and disgraceful. She had never really thought about it at all. She had never wanted more than a quick fuck where she had control, not until Matesh.

"I want to fight the female!" a man suddenly screamed. "Rumor has it, they're in charge!"

She looked up from her glass, her buzz clouding her mind a little. Nevyn looked excited, grinning at her. He jumped up, waving at her to stand as well. Varon even stood up at the same time as her.

"Are you sure?" Nevyn called out in the direction of where the challenge came. "Our females are just as much warriors as the males and you're right, they are in charge!"

She looked over for whoever had said it but couldn't find anyone who seemed to be challenging her.

"Right here!" a male called out. She found him, jumping up to get into the ring. She narrowed her eyes on his pointed ears. He wasn't a mutt. He was pure Elvasi. She bared her teeth. "Come down here, and show us what you Andinna females are so infamous for! Your males always say we need to be scared, but my time in the Empire proved otherwise!"

Nevyn snarled at that. "You don't need to fight him. I could go down there and end his miserable existence."

"He doesn't know who I am," she countered softly. "He thinks all females are like the simpering slaves we've been forced to become in the Empire." She smiled. "He doesn't know what I am."

Varon nodded silently next to her. He gestured to the ring, almost inviting her to jump over the rail and land below. It would be the first time she ever tried something with her wings.

"Go for it," Nevyn encouraged. "We'll back you up if things get messy. Put that pointed-ear piece of shit back in his place." He chuckled. "In the fucking dirt."

She grabbed the rail and lifted her leg to rest on it. She pushed off, throwing her wings open at the top of her jump.

For the first time, she felt the power of them, catching the air, feeling the different small currents run over the sensitive leathery skin of them. She didn't dare to do more, letting them create enough drag that she landed without hurting herself in the ring.

It had been an exhilarating maneuver. One day, she knew she would jump off a cliffside and she wouldn't just have a controlled fall. She would fly.

But not tonight.

Tonight I'm going to beat the shit out of some Elvasi.

She straightened up, revealing she was just a bit taller than the male in front of her. She showed off the cut figure she worked so hard for, knowing everyone in the room was now watching her.

Thanks to her opponent, it all scratched at her memories, reminding her of when she was back in the Colosseum. Or in a bedroom she would be beaten in. She tried to ignore the feeling, even as it edged away her good buzz.

"Why do you look familiar up close?" he asked, frowning at her.

"Have you ever been to the Colosseum in Elliar?" she asked, spreading her hands in a small shrug.

He narrowed his eyes now. "You can't be. The Champion of the Colosseum? There's no way you escaped. That shit's a rumor-"

"Oh, it's not a rumor!" Nevyn called out, laughing. "You're about to fight the newest member of the Ivory Shadows Mercenary Company, you pointed-ear freak!"

The Elvasi glared at her companion for the insult then eyed her closer, sizing her up. "Still just a fucking Andinna slut slave."

"Oh? Did you have to force one of us underneath you in bed? Have fun forcing a slave to do what you wanted when you knew she couldn't fight back?" She bared her teeth. "You challenged me. Let's fight."

Someone called go and she charged, wrapping her tail around his ankle as she slammed a fist in his gut. When he doubled over, surprised and in pain from her assault, she yanked with her tail, sending him to his back. Then she backed off, hoping he would get back up so she could continue.

She fully intended to play with this male.

He was stupid enough to stand back up, charging her. She met him in the grapple, proving she carried just as much muscle mass as him. She slid a foot behind one of his and pulled it back to her, yanking the foot out from underneath him and sending him back to the floor of the ring.

"You wanted him in the dirt, Nevyn!" she called up, grinning. Now she felt good again. Years of listening to taunts like this Elvasi's and years of being able to do nothing about them. This male was a fool to think she would tolerate it.

"I did!" Nevyn's laugh could be heard over the cheers of the onlookers. "Tell me, Mave, if he were on the sands with you, what would you do?"

"Gut him or cut his fucking head off," she answered. "I would probably paint his blood on my face and revel in it, too, for the comments he made." She snarled in pleasure. The alcohol was probably ramping up her mood. The idea of painting more *tatua* on her face and body with her opponent's blood seemed like a very good idea. "How does that sound, Elvasi?"

The Elvasi stood back up slower this time, not jumping for her. He was furious and she was glad. She was winning. Then again, she had only recently met a male who could beat her and he was cheering for her from the balcony.

"Barbarian," the Elvasi muttered, spitting at her feet. "Women should know their place."

"You have Empress Shadra. Don't ever tell me that females are beneath you. We're obviously better." She scoffed at his insult, because it fell flat thanks to the years she spent with the cunning bitch that ran their damned Empire. Elvasi were more male-oriented, sure, but they still had the bitch running the place.

He kicked at her and she grabbed his foot, kicking out herself, aiming for his supporting leg. She let go of him as he began to fall back to the ring.

This time, she spat right in front of his face onto the floor of the ring. "Get better," she snapped.

Two thumps and a solid gust of wind told her Nevyn and Varon had landed.

"Serves you right, picking a fight with a female and then insulting her," Nevyn commented. "Do you want to stay?"

"No," she answered. "This was fun, but I think we should find somewhere else to drink. Somewhere a bit calmer."

"Good idea. Can't have three Andinna deep in the *rai*. People might start dying, starting with this one." Nevyn grinned. "Not like anyone would miss him."

She was laughing as she jumped out of the ring, both males following her. The crowd cleared a path so they could leave. Once outside, she took a deep breath of the fresh sea air.

"That was fun," she declared.

"Good. I was worried that Elvasi would ruin your mood." Nevyn had an arm thrown over Varon's shoulder, holding the other male as close to him as he could.

"No..." She smiled their way. "If anything, I think getting to beat on him improved it. Let's go keep drinking."

"Let's!" Nevyn threw a fist into the air and pointed down the cobble street. "I know a place. Maybe the rest of the Company is there or close by."

She let him and Varon take the lead and followed them back through the streets. They came across a large tavern and she followed them in.

"MAVE!" someone called out. She knew the voice and turned to a back corner of the room. Mat was jumping up from a table with a small stumble. It made several people laugh, including her. She didn't resist as he pulled her in for a kiss. "I missed you. Have fun with them?"

"I did! I got into a fight with some Elvasi scum and everything!" She continued to laugh as he pulled her to the table she saw most of the Company sitting around. "Can I get another drink? The fight killed my buzz."

"Fights do that." Mat nodded and grabbed a pint, holding it out for her. "That's my fresh one. You can have it. I should probably slow down anyway."

"Thank you," she murmured, kissing his cheek. One of his arms wrapped possessively around her, and she could feel the pleased male growl make his chest vibrate. There was a musician playing something, and he began to rock them to the beat. She sipped on her new drink as Nevyn and Varon began to regale Luykas, Bryn, and Zayden with their time at the docks. She nearly jumped when someone leaned on her other side and looked to find Rain leaning next to her. His face was redder than everyone else's, conflicting with his deep blue *tatua*.

"Hey, little brother," she said happily, smiling at him.

"Hey, big sister," he replied, continuing to lean on her. "I'm drunk."

"Are you? Should someone walk you back to the inn?" She chuckled, pulling away from Matesh to put her arm over Rain's shoulder.

"I'm a little buzzed, or I was. Trying to get back there."

"No, I don't want to go back yet." Rain had a lopsided smile. "This is nice. Makes it easy to pretend the pits…"

"I understand." She was feeling the same way. Here, with all of them, watching the Andinna laugh and tell stories, she felt like the pits were far away.

"It's like I was never there. It feels really good."

She couldn't relate to that. She was in the pits for so long that her current situation seemed surreal. She was drinking and partying with other Andinna, something she had never done before. She was on a different continent, one full of free people. One where most wouldn't assume she was a slave or treat her like one.

But she was glad that he could pretend the pits never happened for a night. Even though he was obviously drunk, she was glad it was giving him something he sorely needed.

"Go hang out with them," she ordered, nodding to Varon and Nevyn, who continued to tell the story of what happened down at the docks. He was finally at the Elvasi she fought, which had all of the males looking up at her, except Rain, who began to laugh.

"Yeah, *illo amyr*! You kicked some ass!" Rain pulled away, thumping her shoulder with a fist.

"He deserved it," she said, smiling. "Sit down before you fall down." Rain was wobbling precariously, like he was about to tip over.

Matesh reached out and grabbed him before it happened, helping her hold him up. "Sit down," her lover ordered.

Rain groaned but fell onto a stool like she wanted. She ruffled his hair and leaned to kiss the top of his head. When she straightened up, she caught several of the Company watching her intently.

She turned back to Mat and finished her drink off, brushing off the looks. "Another?" she asked.

"Of course," he murmured. "Then we should all get out of here and find another tavern."

"Good idea," Luykas agreed loudly.

She took the new drink in hand when Mat brought it to her. They paid for everything and she made sure the pint was included. She was stealing their glass. She was drinking as they walked out the door.

They walked as a massive, dark group, making humans jump out of the way, something she was beginning to really enjoy. She didn't end up tripping over someone, and in the Empire, that would have led to her getting spit on or beaten.

"There they are!" someone shouted. "That bitch is the one!"

"Looks like we have trouble!" Nevyn shouted, a laugh in his voice. "Come on, little Elvasi. You want to play?"

"Nevyn, we're trying not to get arrested tonight!" Luykas snapped.

Mave turned to see who it was and grinned when her gaze landed on the Elvasi she had fought before. She bared her teeth, ready for a fight.

"We can take 'em." Bryn sounded bloodthirsty. She glanced over at him, seeing he had a dagger drawn now and was testing its edge. There was a look in his eyes that made her a little scared for whoever was going to be on the other end of that sharp edge. It also made her appreciate the rogue, in a perverse way. "They really think they can cause us trouble in Olost?"

"He picked the fight with me," she added. "He doesn't get to cry foul now."

"Shut up, slut. You should be collared and beaten," one of the Elvasi, obviously drunk, taunted her.

She lifted her chin, hoping the red moon cast enough light to show off the white scar around her neck. "Been there, done that, survived. Find a better threat." She snarled viciously, which was echoed by several males around her. She wanted blood, if it came to it. She wasn't going to allow Elvasi scum to talk down to her again. She was a free female and she was damned well going to stay that way.

"Let us go," Luykas warned. "If you piss her off, we're all going to kill you at the snap of her fingers."

"Like you fucking can!" another Elvasi yelled. "You lost the War!"

That made Luykas snarl, his wings expanding out to make him look more threatening. She realized somewhere along the way, she had done the same, puffing her wings out. Her tail flicked around with agitation. They had scratched her Andinna temper and she was too buzzed and warm to control her reaction.

The two groups stood there posturing for a long time, humans and mutts stopping to see what was wrong. Guards began to show up, stepping between the two factions.

"Don't make this a scene. Namur doesn't care about the damned War - move along!" the guard ordered, pointing the Elvasi to turn away. Another guard appeared in front of the Andinna, pointing them to move along as well.

"Luykas, get your warriors and keep walking." The guard sounded somewhat desperate for them to start moving.

"You heard him. No arrests tonight," Luykas snapped. He looked directly at her. "Bring it down. Please pull it back, Mave. I need you to, if I want any of the guys to listen to me."

She bared her teeth and looked at the others. Matesh was glaring and snarling towards the Elvasi, along with Rain and Zayden behind him. Varon and Nevyn had their tails hooked, like the time they were sparring with the brothers. Bryn just waited, shifting further into the shadows of the buildings around them, as if he was ready to sneak around and begin the slaughter.

She took a deep breath, seeing that the Elvasi were beginning to move away. She reached out and touched Matesh first, forcing him to turn and look at her. She locked away the anger as best she could, pulling her wings back into her tight, most comfortable position. She forced her tail to stop whipping around, waiting to grab someone.

"Let's get back to the inn. I'm tired." She wasn't, but she knew it was probably safer than wandering the streets.

He looked over her face. "Okay," he agreed softly.

"All right!" Luykas hollered over the growing crowd. "Company, move out!"

They stepped off in unison. For the first time in her life, she realized she had been in charge of something. They had reacted to her anger, her fury. Luykas had needed her to calm down before he could get the males moving on.

She didn't ask Matesh about it. No, she figured the best person to ask would be the one who didn't react like the others: Luykas.

Not tonight. We'll have a few more drinks at Hornbuckle's, than I'll hit the bed.

That sounded like such a good idea that it was exactly what she did, making sure to drag Matesh upstairs with her later in the evening. The Elvasi were forgotten before her head hit a pillow.

18

MAVE

Mave nearly forgot where she was when she woke up. It took her several moments to realize she wasn't on the ship, nor was she in the pits.

"Olost," she whispered to herself, smiling. Free land. She considered the possibilities for a moment, looking down at Mat's sleeping form. She could go do *anything.* No one would stop her. She would need to be careful, of course, since she could get lost or something.

The only thing stopping her from going out was her. She could see outside that the sun was up and Mat's snore told her he would still be out for a little while.

I can stay close by.

She slid out of the bed quietly, pulling on her breeches and fought to get her shirt on without him. Once she managed to get dressed, she slipped out of the room and downstairs, enjoying the quiet of the tavern now. There was no one downstairs she could see, and the one dwarf behind the bar didn't speak to her, only went about his business as if she wasn't there.

She was nearly at the door when someone coughed. "Mave."

She stopped, sighing heavily. Right outside was sunshine and a quiet street lit by the dawn. Behind her, she knew, was Luykas. She hadn't realized he was awake and the bond was just saying he was nearby. She figured he was in a room, not downstairs with her.

"Sneaking out?" he asked causally. She heard him step closer.

"I was hoping to go outside and just look around. I'll stay close." She looked over her shoulder at him.

"I need to take you out today. Would you like to go now?" He stepped up next to her. "There's some things we need to pick up for you before going to the village. This is the best time to do it. The shops will just be opening and you'll be able to explore the city with some backup."

She considered him warily. "Can anyone else take me?"

"If you want to wake up Matesh after you got him very drunk last night. Even then, this is Company coin so I would go with you anyway." Luykas showed her a pouch in his palm.

"And what could I possibly need?" she demanded, crossing her arms. "Why can't I just go out there and wander around?"

"You need fabrics for clothing that some of the free Andinna will be able to sew for you. You'll need stones for jewelry. You'll learn more about those when we get to the village, but let's say that if you make no attempt at getting them, some may have a serious issue with you." Luykas shrugged. "You need things, including new armor. You can't wear hand-me down leather armor or the beat-up shit you wore in the pits forever."

She nodded slowly. He was right about the clothing, at least. She had nothing that was quality. She never had anything fancy before. Everything nice she had ever worn was forced on her by the Empress and she didn't get, or want, to keep any of those things.

Why is there so damned much I need? It seems excessive for a race everyone calls barbarians. Jewels and pretty stones? Why do we need jewelry?

"Lead the way," she said, defeated. She wasn't going to reject this. These were important things she was going to need and if he was willing to pay for them, that was just better for her. She had no coin, except one she wasn't willing to spend.

"Don't make this sound so awful," he muttered, shaking his head as if her reluctance to spend time with him was somehow insulting.

She bared her teeth. "We're bonded, but that doesn't mean I need to like you or be your friend. Remember? I was only asked to follow orders."

He bared his teeth back this time, showing off that he also had Andinna canines. Funny, she figured he picked up nothing from his Elvasi side, but his hair covered his ears and she never paid enough attention to him to find out.

"Is there anything Elvasi about you except your attitude?" she asked.

He must have known what she was asking, because he pushed back the hair that covered the tops of his ears. Sure enough, there was a less pronounced Elvasi point. It wasn't very noticeable and she knew at a distance, she wouldn't be able to tell. "There's a few things about me that are Elvasi," he answered. "My coloring, for one. Andinna don't normally get as dark as my skin nor get gold eyes like mine. Alchan and I got rare eye colors between the two races."

"I noticed that," she replied. "His amber, your gold."

"Yup." Luykas fixed his hair, covering his ears up again. "So yeah, there's some Elvasi in me, but I really did take a lot from my father. Other mutts tend to be more evenly split. Some things will always carry over - the ears, the horns, the wings, and the tails. But the coloring? It can get a bit crazy."

"You've met others?" she asked, looking over at him. She never had; it was illegal for the Elvasi to breed outside their race, and it was punishable to have children with the Andinna. She figured it might happen, but she had never seen them in the pits and that had been the extent of her world.

"You know what the Elvasi do to their slaves." He nodded sadly. "Yeah, I've met others. Some of them don't like me because I look so much like Alchan. Some just hate themselves. Some bend more Elvasi, some bend more Andinna."

She wasn't paying attention to where they were headed as he

spoke. When he stopped, she looked around and noticed they were in a much nicer area than she saw the previous day.

"Where are we?" she asked, looking around at the clean market square with merchants setting up their wares. There were a dozen shops as well, with fancy things in the windows.

"Rich district." He pointed to a jewelry shop. "We're going there first."

"Why?"

"The stones and jewelry I was talking about. So, Andinna wear certain jewelry for certain things - festivals, events, rituals and the like. Many just wear them normally. As we get closer to the village, you'll see the other males begin to put some on as they feel more comfortable. We can whip some things up for you and get some others that we can have the experts in the village create for you. We just need to take them the supplies."

"And I need these things." She wasn't sure she cared much for jewelry. *It's just so...feminine.* It screamed Elvasi to her, too: fine jewels and nice pretty things. Like the shampoo, it felt reminiscent of times in her life she didn't like to think about and actively tried not to.

"You do." He waved her to keep following him, and the owner of the shop got the door open right as they arrived. They strolled in and Luykas began to explain what they were looking for. "Precious stones, but nothing too outrageous. I don't need diamonds, rubies, sapphires, or emeralds." He turned back to her, considering. "Turquoise might be a good color for her."

"Oh yes, light blues would work well for her." The jeweler was also looking her over, staring particularly close to her face. "Do you have a preference, lady?"

"No." She tried not to curl a lip at being called a *lady*. He was probably trying to be nice to a customer, even one in hand-me-down, dirty clothing.

"Let's keep this simple, Ferris." Luykas sighed. "If you have bracelets, the bangles, I would like to take a look."

"Precious metals or leather?"

"I'm here." Luykas raised an eyebrow. "Precious metals."

Mave stood behind Luykas as he followed Ferris through the displays, pointing at different objects. She didn't really know what she was supposed to be looking at, so she didn't try. She didn't care about any of this.

"Will you be in the city long enough to have these sized?"

"No. I'm going to ask a jeweler back home to size them. We're leaving later today. Mave, come here and try these out for me."

Mave held back a groan, moving closer to see what Luykas had selected. A combination of silver and gold bracelets, pretty bands of varying widths and design were laid out. He picked one up and held it out.

"Females often wear several of these on each wrist," he explained. "When they're looking to dress up, anyway. Nice events, really."

"So do the Elvasi," she muttered, eyeing the bracelet.

"They stole the fashion from the Andinna. The Elvasi are more into delicate things while the Andinna like hardier items. A simple chain bracelet will break if exposed to the rough lifestyle of our people." He continued to hold it out. "So, try it on."

She grabbed the gold band and forced her hand through it. It was a very tight fit, and she wasn't sure if she would be able to remove it. Anxiety and fear ran through her. She struggled with it for a moment before it finally popped off and she handed it back to Luykas.

"No, thank you," she said politely, handing it back to him.

"Mave?" Luykas frowned at her but she wasn't paying attention to him anymore. She walked right out of the building, not looking back. When she was outside again, she took a deep breath.

I'm not there. That wasn't a manacle. There were no chains.

"Mave?" Luykas called out again, stepping out of the stop behind her. "What was that?"

"Do I have to wear those?" She wouldn't be able to do it.

"Uh…No, but you might be teased. You can wear leather too, if that's more your style. The gold and silver is just a sign of wealth.

Females of any race like pretty things. Males get those for their females as gifts-"

"I'll wear leather," she told him. "I can cut leather off."

"Oh..."

She couldn't see him, so wasn't prepared when a hand landed on her shoulder, a finger just grazing her skin. In that simple touch, she was flooded by Luykas' feelings. Regret. Sorrow. A strange need for her forgiveness.

"It's okay," she said, pulling away. "When I couldn't get it back off, I was worried it might be like..."

"The collar. We'll get you leather." He pulled further away again. "I'm going to pick up some stones, though. There's other things you can do."

"Like?" she asked.

"We wear things that hang from our horns. We don't fight in them, but they're fashionable when everyone is hanging around the village. There's also simple necklaces some of the other Andinna can make you, ones that won't feel like the collar. Then we can go to fabrics. That should be easier. You can just pick out what you like." Luykas left her outside when he was done talking. She leaned on the building, watching the crowd begin to grow. A woman walked with a young boy as they picked up vegetables at a stall and the young boy pointed at Mave. She froze, wondering what the boy would have to say. He just waved, smiling innocently. The mother looked in her direction, wondering what her son was doing. The mother smiled as well, waving.

Mave just waved back, unsure why. It felt like the right thing to do. She shifted, turning away to avoid more of the strange interaction. When Luykas walked back out, she didn't bring it up.

"What were you waving at?" he asked lightly.

Of course he's going to bring it up. He must have seen it through the window.

"Some...child waved at me. I waved back."

"Was this child human? They like waving at us because we're big and different." Luykas chuckled, holding out a pouch. "This is yours now. Take good care of it."

"What's in it?" She took the pouch, noticing it had some weight in her palm. She could hear things knocking around inside.

"Stones. Gems." Luykas sniffed, looking around. "You might not really understand why, not yet, but one day you will." He rubbed his hands together, looking nervous. "You know, I was nearly a hundred when I began to learn anything about being an Andinna. I didn't understand either. Not at first."

She pulled the pouch to her chest. "And?"

"Your father, on the way back to Anden with me, stopped to see some dwarves and their wares. Onyx was the stone he picked out for me, along with some others, but mostly onyx." Luykas reached out, drawing closer to her than she really wanted him to. "Because you have his eyes, I picked out some of the colors he used to wear. Light blues, for the most part. Some touches of grey and silver. I threw in some orange, though. It's Matesh's favorite color and the contrast with your eyes…" He continued talking, but she stopped hearing it.

Truthfully, she had stopped listening after he told her how her father did this for him. A touch of jealousy filled her, nuzzling beside the confusion and appreciation. She was confused by why she needed any of it. He explained, but she wasn't getting it. Appreciation that he even considered it and paid for it.

Jealousy that once, he spent this sort of time with the male she should have been raised by.

"How does this normally happen?" she asked, cutting into what he was saying.

"What?" Luykas frowned. They were still standing in front of the jewelry shop, not moving on to their next destination.

"How do Andinna normally get these?" She held up the pouch, indicating what she meant.

"Ah…The parents will choose a few pieces here and there as the child grows older. Some for the child to wear, some to start an adult collection. It's normally necklaces for young children. Horn decorations start when they're going into that awful puberty time. After they turn fifty, normally. Bracelets, those are normally for adults only. Well, the ones that are gold or silver, sometimes jade. The precious metals are kept for adults. Leather is for someone who works hard and doesn't want to ruin fine things or younger Andinna." He opened the bag and pulled out one silver bangle of a bracelet. "You don't like them right now, and that's understandable, but I got one, just in case. You'll notice, this one is not completely enclosed." He turned it over to show how it didn't create a perfect circle. "So it has a lot of give to put on and remove." He dropped it back in the bag, taking a deep breath. "Let's go get the rest of this done."

She wasn't able to find something to say before he started walking away, leaving her to nearly scramble to keep up. He pushed through the crowd, not waiting for them to make space. She was still stuck on how her father did all of this for him and now he was doing it for her. That meant something, she knew it.

And then she thought of it for longer.

"Did you know Andena when my father took you to Anden?" she asked suddenly, as loudly as she could so she knew he would hear her over the bustle of the crowing market crowd.

He turned slowly, shaking his head. "No. He had to teach me on the road, and it took me a long time to become proficient at it."

"You were like me." She felt so stupid for not putting it together sooner. He was exactly like her. He was raised by the Elvasi - he was kept by them. He was taken by her father to go be with his other people.

"Yes and no," he replied. "I fit with the Elvasi...a little. General Lorren found out about me when rumors started circulating around my area, about the white-winged Andinna youth with a temper. You see, I had no idea why I was acting the way I was. My mother kept me in complete isolation from the Andinna. I never saw one until your father showed up. It clicked in an instant for me." Luykas sighed, waving her to keep following him. As they walked, he continued to explain. "My mother was also on the cusp of getting married and her new husband couldn't know about me, couldn't know that I was hers. General Lorren used that against her." Luykas snorted. "Not like she loved her new husband, but it didn't matter."

"Luykas, you don't need to tell me this if you don't want to," she said, cutting in. He was getting personal, very personal.

"I want to. Honestly, I've messed up every chance with you, but you need to really understand why this means a lot to me." Luykas took a deep breath, running a hand through his black hair. "Your father gave me everything, including a place with our people. He taught me how to be Andinna. He introduced me to my own brother and the other half of my family. He made me feel less alone in the world. Without him, I would have nothing." He looked away from her. "And if I can pay him back by helping you…"

"So this isn't about me…"

"It is!" Luykas groaned. "This is what we do, Mave. We're brought into the community by another Andinna. We continue those communities by showing that kindness to another to bring them in. He taught me that. He also taught me how to slaughter my enemies, but we're a strange race." His lips twitched into a small smirk. "We build bonds that can handle the stress and pain of war and death. We're like that. So it's about all those things your father taught me and now…I can pass them on to you. I couldn't do any of this on the ship, so I waited for us to get here to Namur."

"What do you want?" she asked softly.

"I want you to accept my apology and the gifts I'm trying to give you. I'm an ass and an idiot. Would groveling work?" Luykas sounded sincere. Too sincere. Like he would actually drop to his knees and grovel right there in the street, with everyone watching. "I screwed up with the blood bond, Mave. I know I did. I know I messed up with the spell to get you to sleep. I shouldn't have done that to you. I'm *sorry*. I just want to do the rest of this right because you deserve better than I gave you to start with."

"Fine!" She didn't know what to do with his behavior. "Fine, I forgive you!" She backed away from him a couple of steps.

"Do you mean it?" He seemed shocked, leaning away from her as if she had just spit venom at him.

"Yeah, sure," she muttered, feeling unsettled by him.

They let an uncomfortable silence settle for a moment over them, ignoring the crowds of people who had to go around them in the street. She was angry at a few mistakes, one in particular that would last a very long time. She would probably always be angry over it, until it faded and she no longer had to deal with it. Even if it had saved her from the Empress, it angered her. It had already been a pain trying to reconcile those two feelings. Grateful and angry. In the end, she had just avoided him.

But hearing his story about her father and realizing he was once exactly where she was? That changed her perspective just enough to forgive him, even a little.

"It's going to be hard," she told him. "Being nice to you. That will be hard. The bond wants-"

"I know what the bond wants all too well. I'm just...tired of this animosity, Mave. I'm tired of seeing you and getting bared teeth like this morning. I'm trying so hard to make up for what I did. It's not perfect, but I just want a chance to do more things like this for you." He sighed, looking defeated, and tapped the pouch in her palm. "Will you allow me to help you now? It's all I want. It's all I've ever wanted."

She knew he had a point. The two nights she spoke to him weren't bad ones. He told her a lot about her family once, while Bryn worked on Company things for him, and then there was the storm. He'd called her difficult, and she realized that she was being difficult just for him. She was more than willing to wait for Leshaun, Matesh, Bryn or anyone else to explain something. She wasn't giving Luykas the chance. But she found it very hard to let go of how he bonded them together. It felt like a perverse ownership he had on her now. She could barely handle it, which was why she avoided it so much.

"I'll try," she promised. "I'll try to be nicer and not push you away when you're trying to help." He held a wealth of knowledge she wanted, mostly about her family. She needed to get over herself if she wanted that knowledge. "So...fabrics now."

"Yeah. That should be a lot easier. Just pick colors and textures you like. I'll get some choices for winter gear. You'll need more gear thanks to the climate here. It gets a lot colder than Elliar."

He led her to other stalls, and together, they picked out things. She had no idea what would be made out of any of the colors she picked. She just went with her gut. If a color looked nice, she picked it out. Luykas picked a similar color in the wools for winter clothing.

They were heading back to the inn with what felt like a mountain of things. Looking back on the morning, she realized Luykas hadn't been bad company. She was the one who had made the trip difficult, and once she decided to try and deal with him, everything went smoothly.

I'll make this work. This is just another thing I can learn to do. If he can grovel this much, I can at least honestly try.

RAINEV

Rainev woke up in his shared room with Bryn. The rogue had been kind enough to give his father his own room and let Rain hide with him. They had talked about it the night before, Bryn understanding his need to have a quiet place.

And Zayden was never quiet. His father didn't know the meaning of the word. He was a grumpy, chattering ass who wanted everything the way he wanted it. He was overbearing and annoying, refusing to treat Rain with any amount of respect.

"Stop growlin'. Too early in the morning for that."

He stopped, pulling back his anger.

Bryn looked up from his spot. He slept sitting on the bed, as if he was too uncomfortable to lie down and relax. "Ya need to calm down. Ya can't let the anger fester. Ya need to let it go." Bryn slid off his bed and began grabbing his clothes off the floor. "What has ya so angry this early?"

"I was thinking about my *bodra*," he answered.

"Ah. He was really good last night. Gave ya lots of space and didn't bother ya. Why ya mad at him when he did good?" Bryn frowned his way and Rain could only give an angry groan.

"It's not going to last long. I know Nevyn talked to him and so has, like, everyone else. I just want him to see me as an adult. I am one!"

"Ya are, but I don't think that's why you're really angry," the rogue countered. "He left ya alone yesterday and he probably will today. So why ya mad?"

Rain didn't answer this time, jumping out of his bed. He was dressed faster than Bryn and walked out, leaving the rogue. He didn't know why, that was the problem. Bryn was right, too. He should have been happy his father gave him some space to have a good time the night before. And he had a good time. Enough alcohol, and he could pretend it was like any other time he drank with the Company, just with Mave now.

He went downstairs, hoping to get breakfast, and saw Mave and Luykas walk in carrying so much stuff in their arms, he was worried for a moment that they would be buried. He ran to them as Luykas began to list to one side.

"Whoa!" Rain reached up, grabbing several packages off the top so Luykas could see better. "What did you do? Are these supplies?"

"No, these are for Mave," the other mutt explained. "Stuff so she can have some real clothes when we get settled in for the winter. A while off, since the Company needs to get a mission done before that, but that's no reason not to prepare."

Rain looked at Mave as she put her load down on a table. She seemed relaxed, at ease in a way he didn't expect.

"You went shopping with Luykas?" he asked, leaning closer to her. "Really?"

She sighed, moving packages around for seemingly no reason. "Yeah. I woke up wanting to explore. He said he needed to pick some things up for me. It happened."

"He's not dead or bleeding," Rain muttered, looking back at the half-Elvasi leader.

"No, he's not," she agreed. She was eyeing him now too. "We'll talk more about it later, I think."

"I'm going up to get the rest of the Company. Coya, is breakfast ready?" Luykas watched them back now, like a hawk ready to swoop and take prey. Or maybe it was more like the rabbit? He knew they were going to talk about him the moment he left the room.

"Aye," the quiet dwarf said with a grunt from behind the bar. Rain raised an eyebrow. He'd never heard Coya speak before.

"All right. You two have fun." Luykas strolled out quickly, not looking back.

"He's a brave male," Mave said immediately. "Leaving like that."

"So, what happened?" he demanded.

"Nothing. He explained that…well…" Mave threw her hands up. "He's not as hard to get along with as I thought. The only person being mean was me. I'll admit that."

"Yeah, and?" Rain waited for more. "What all did you get? Was it just clothing?"

"No." She rubbed her palms together before nervously getting a pouch off her belt. She opened it and showed him the contents. It was jewelry. Fancy stones and a silver bangle bracelet. "He got me these."

"Oh…" Rain swallowed. He knew what those meant. They were the start to a jewelry collection every Andinna had, regardless of sex. "You didn't have any of those before. I didn't even think to get them. I'm sorry."

"It's not…it's not that big of a deal," she promised, closing the pouch. "He wanted to do it for me because…well, my father did it for him, when he was taken to Anden."

Rain couldn't miss how her hands shook just a little. This was affecting her probably more than she wanted to recognize.

"That's really cool, though," Rain jumped in, smiling. "That your *bodra* helped him and now he's helping you. That's like…everything we Andinna are about. Passing the good deeds to the next of our community. It's how we build the bonds we do."

"He said similar," she murmured, nodding. "And it made me realize that he made some mistakes, but I was the one making it difficult. I still hate the blood bond, Rain. I hate it, but…he's trying to be kind. I should accept that kindness, right? I should forgive him."

"Forgiveness is important to our people," Rain reminded her. "Remember that first thing we told you? When you and Mat were really…"

"I remember." He could see the struggle in her eyes. He could see that she felt bad, but she was still feeling all the hurt of the blood bond, the pain of it, the hate she had for it. She wanted to get over it and be a good Andinna, but she couldn't resolve her own problems.

Why haven't I been helping her? I promised her I would.

He knew the answer. He was too wrapped up in his own pain. He didn't know why he was being haunted by what happened in the pits, and he wanted it to stop. He'd wanted everyone to leave him alone on the ship and now he was seeing the consequences of it. He was missing out on helping his big sister with her problems. He wasn't being a very good Andinna, either.

"Hey…" Rain reached out to touch her shoulder. He was impressed when she didn't jump as his hand rested on her. "Do you want to hang out with me today? We haven't spent a lot of time together. Last night was fun. Today is going to be busy, but it would be nice."

"I want to see more of the city before we leave it," she admitted. "Think we can find more errands to run?"

"Yeah, I'm sure we can find something that need to be done." Rain grinned. This was good. He could pretend to be normal for her. Not his father or really anyone else, but for her.

She eyed him, as if she could read his mind, but didn't say anything further. Was his grin not good enough? He wondered what was giving him away. Something had to be.

"Hey, you two!" Luykas called out, walking back in. "Done with whatever gossiping conversation you were having?"

"Yeah," Rain answered, looking away from her. "Is there anything else that's going to need to get done today?"

"Let me think…Han is bringing our horses and carts. They'll be loaded already for our trip. He's stopping by the merchants with our orders before heading this way." Luykas sighed. "I do need someone to pick up Alchan. Not right now - it'll piss him off. Too early in the morning and he needs all the time he can get, but when Han arrives, someone needs to pick him up from Keyit's."

"No thank you," Mave said with a bite.

Rain winced, remembering how she had reacted to the idea of Alchan seeing an escort the night before. She wouldn't be going on that particular errand any time soon.

"I'll go alone, then. It's not a far walk and the daylight will make it safer," Rain offered himself up for the task. He would need to get Alchan alone to talk to anyway. This seemed like as good a time as any. "Mave, we can hang out later. Maybe we can ride on the same cart. I can teach you to work the reins."

"Sounds like a good idea. What are we going to do until then?" She looked around, waving at her new items. "Is there somewhere we can put this?"

"Nah, we're going to leave it out until we have a cart to load it on." Luykas fell into a chair, looking between them. "Going to tell me what you said about me?"

"No," Rain said, chuckling. "You'll just have to live with never knowing, *bodrya*."

"I'm wounded," Luykas replied dramatically, holding a hand over his chest. "My *ildar bodyra* doesn't care about my feelings anymore. What have I done?"

"*Ildar?*" Mave looked between them, frowning.

"Adopted." Rain shrugged. "Sometimes we make the distinction, sometimes we don't. Not that it changes anything. An adopted relationship to us is just as important as a blood relation."

"That's right!" Luykas smiled, pointing at Rain. "The only difference is how the relationship is treated with others. I'm his adopted uncle and respected as such, but I'm not Zayden's brother nor treated that way. You know that by now. You and Rain are siblings, but-"

"No one considers Zayden and me family," she finished. "Yes. I just didn't know the word." Rain tried not to chuckle at how she rolled her eyes. This was a lesson she had already figured out or had someone explain, then.

"You know that counts romantically, right?" Rain wanted to keep going though. This was something he could help explain. "Like, it's not weird that you're with Mat, who's my adopted uncle-"

"I never found it weird," she said suddenly. "There's not blood shared. I'm not a heathen, thinking this is incestual or anything." She was beginning to get snarly. "Bryn! Tell me you have cards for us to play during breakfast. These two are driving me mad."

Rain looked over his shoulder to see the rogue at the bottom of the stairs.

"Aye. I'll save ya." Bryn sounded tired, yawning as he drew closer. He pulled his pack of cards from his pocket. They weren't as nice as the set Luykas made his father, but they were decent and better for everyday play.

"Thank you," she said with a note of gratefulness that Rain hadn't been expecting. He'd known they were spending more time together, but that was a tone he normally heard when she was talking to Matesh.

Is Bryn trying for mayara? *Does she want him there?*

Rain didn't ask about it. He would need to see how it played out. It wasn't a bad thing, though Matesh was probably climbing up the walls seeing it.

Sure enough, when Mat walked in, Rain watched as the big male pressed against Mave's side as she talked to Bryn about a rule she didn't understand very well. He didn't cut into the conversation, but he made sure his presence was known by her and Bryn, both of whom looked up at him. Bryn's glance was patient, male to male and full of understanding.

Rain was glad to see her branching out, and a little jealous himself. *It's my fault. She tried to talk to me and I yelled at her. I avoided everyone. She needs more than two friends, and she doesn't need a little brother who's mean to her.*

He needed to fix himself. He needed to get stronger and get over what happened to him. He knew if he started training harder, became a better warrior, he would feel more secure.

He firmly believed in it. He had nothing else to hold on to.

When Han showed up with carts and their supplies, everyone was awake and ready to go. The only thing they needed to go was send someone for Alchan.

Rain was out of the tavern and on the way before anyone could volunteer to go with him. He would have enjoyed making the quick walk with Mave, having the backup, but he didn't want any of the others. He could do this on his own.

Or so he thought.

As he walked quickly through the streets, he looked over his shoulder, feeling edgy. He found himself looking at dark alleyways, hoping no one was waiting in them.

When someone bumped into him on accident? He snarled, snapping at the small human. The female screeched as he just walked faster.

Sweat formed on his palms.

He didn't like being alone like this. He felt vulnerable. The crowds were loud.

Cheers. The crowds filling the streets were like the cheering crowd of the Colosseum.

The dark alleyways were like the dark place he was yanked. He'd been bleeding and in pain. He had needed to get to Matesh and Mave.

He rubbed his palms on his breeches, breathing shallow air, hoping his heart would slow down. He kept putting one foot in front of the other.

It wasn't dark on the street. The bright sun was overhead and he had nothing to worry about. There was no danger on the streets of Namur for a full grown male Andinna, not during broad daylight.

When he saw Keyit's townhome, he nearly ran. He stumbled up the steps, hitting a boot on one of the steps. He knocked as hard as he could. He needed to get in before someone came up behind him.

The door opened and Rain resisted pushing inside. He saw Keyit, who gave him a friendly smile. Friendly. That was something. It wasn't a cruel sneer, at least.

"Rainev, good to see you." Keyit's warm smile and soft voice relaxed him. He walked in when the door opened wider, an invitation. "He's upstairs, freshening up. I'll let him know you're here."

Rain could only nod and walk to the sitting room. He fell onto a couch, breathing harder, his pulse still racing. Rubbing his face, he could hear Keyit's voice upstairs, but not what was said. He heard the growl Alchan returned with.

He heard Keyit's cry of pleasure.

"Of course he's going another round," Rain mumbled, shaking his head a little. The idea of sex made his stomach twist into knots, flipping up and down in his gut like the storm had done to it.

It continued. Furniture could be heard bouncing against a wall, probably a dresser or something.

Skies, Alchan. Don't break the guy.

Everyone had known Alchan needed this. Rain hadn't expected it to be continuing well into the afternoon.

The finishing cry Keyit gave and Alchan's snarling crescendo ended, leaving a very empty silence in its place.

Rain waited, not even trying to be patient, his tail flicking with annoyance that his talk with Alchan was waiting now for the male to clean up.

Alchan walked down moments later, straightening his breeches. Like Rain, he was shirtless. Rain couldn't ignore the bruising fingerprints on Alchan's arms, or the bite marks on his chest. They were marks Matesh had nearly every morning when he convinced Mave to have a quickie before breakfast. Normally, the signs of love making healed during the following sleep.

"Have a good night?" Alchan asked him casually. "No one get arrested?"

"Yeah, we had fun. Had a run-in with some Elvasi. I don't know the full story there." Rain stood up, looking down from his leader's eyes in respect before continuing. "We're ready to go."

"I figured that," Alchan said, still adjusting his pants and playing with the strings, tucking them so they didn't come undone later. "You okay, Rainev?"

"Yeah. Why?"

"You've been acting strange. I try not to bother any of you about the small stuff, but that doesn't mean I don't notice."

Rain swallowed. Alchan was the last person anyone wanted really asking about things, and the purebred knew it. They preferred if Luykas was in their business. "I'm fine."

"Sure," Alchan snorted, shaking his head. He didn't press further, waving Rain to follow him out. "Until next time, Keyit!" he called back before shutting the door on the townhome.

Rain never liked being alone with Alchan, and he suddenly remembered why. The big male was a silent, imposing force, with an air of superiority that made Rain feel small and insignificant. Where Luykas had taken an active role with Rain as he grew up, Alchan never spent more than a few days in Rain's presence. He'd avoided Rain until he'd gone through his first *tatua* ritual, always saying he didn't like kids. The two-hundred-and-fifty-plus years since then? Alchan was an aloof leader with an overbearing attitude. Rain almost didn't join the Company because Alchan petrified him.

But Rain had something he needed to ask.

"Um, sir, I was-"

"Sir?" Alchan jerked to a stop, looking disgusted as he looked down to Rain's level. "What? Come on, none of you call me sir."

"Alchan…I was wondering-"

"Shit, that reminds me to tell Mave my title. She doesn't know yet, does she?"

"Uh, no, but-"

"That's going to be strange. She needs to know before we get back to the village. I'll find a good time to say something." Alchan shrugged. "What were you saying?"

Rain bit back a smart remark as his boss realized he was trying to speak. It would only get him in trouble. Making smart comments to

Alchan was a good way to get fired or lose body parts, depending on his mood and how badly you pissed him off.

"I wanted to ask if there was any way I could get some private training."

Alchan studied him, those amber eyes narrowing slightly. "Why? Luykas handled your training, with your father, Leshaun, and Matesh. Nevyn steps in when he thinks it's necessary. Why do you need me?"

"I think my *bodra* holds me back because he's trying to protect me. I want to start using my wyvern more. I think I can be a stronger asset to the Company than just a hand with a sword. I think if you're the one training me, no one is going to step in and try to stop me. Plus, you're you." Those were the excuses Rain had lined up for over a week now. Those were the reasons he hoped would sway Alchan to giving up his private time to deal with some mutt, the son of one of his men. Rain held no belief that Alchan truly saw him as a warrior, one of the Company males. This would be a chance to prove he was.

It would be a chance for Rain to get strong enough that he didn't feel so uneasy in his own skin.

"Okay. When we're back at the village, we'll start your training up. We'll see where you stand at the end of winter. You're sitting out the next mission, aren't you?" Alchan kept walking, but his amber eyes stayed on Rain.

Rain suddenly didn't want to take time off in the village. He should go on the next mission.

"I mean, it's a good idea for you. Taking time off is important for warriors, especially younger ones. You don't know how hard this life can stress you until you're in it," Alchan continued. "Mave...dumping her in a village and not leaving Luykas is a terrible idea, no matter how much I want to. Matesh is never going to slow down, and now he's got his cock so deep between her legs I'm scared I'll never have my warrior back." Alchan growled.

Rain opened and closed his mouth a few times as the rant kicked off.

"Good for him, but it couldn't be more inconvenient. Javon's daughter? Really, Matesh?" Alchan grumbled. "Luykas really wants us to coddle her, get her up to speed, make sure everything is okay. He's so fucking guilt-ridden by it, I'm worried he's going to get himself killed. Am I guilty? Yeah, I am. I don't like how we fucking left her in the capital and ignored the rumors and the whispers. But I have more important things to deal with. I'll help her now, but I need her to be a good warrior first. I don't need her to be my damned friend and offer me some forgiveness for my soul like Luykas."

"You don't like her, do you?" Rain wasn't sure why he asked the question. He shouldn't have. It wasn't his place to ask the question. He wasn't close or a confidant to Alchan, but it was Mave, his big sister.

"It's not about liking or disliking her," Alchan answered, his anger seemingly deflating as he stopped in the street. This was why they let Alchan go off and meet with escorts while the Company partied. It helped him take the edge off for a little while. He could back off his dominant anger and indignation faster. "I should have told her who I am sooner, so she knew why she can't buck up and dominate me. That's the problem. She came at an inconvenient time and she's dominant enough to roll me if I'm not on my guard, and that's not good for anyone, especially the Company." Alchan waved a hand around at Rain. "You're young. You'll learn one day that sometimes we have to do things we hate in order to survive. Sometimes we have to hurt people and break promises to continue helping the majority."

Rain nodded slowly. It sounded like Alchan was referring to something he didn't know about. There was something forlorn and sad, with a touch of bitter anger. That was a mix of emotions he'd never seen from their leader before. It showed a line of weakness the male didn't often show.

"Let's go," Alchan ordered, turning.

Rain took a deep breath, trying to control his shock. That was the first time he'd ever seen the leader vulnerable. Alchan had totally run over that conversation as well, not giving him much of a chance to say anything. Add to that, he'd basically ordered Rain to stay in the village for the next mission. His agreement with the plan was for sure going to keep Rain out of the action.

Rain could only hold onto one thing from that entire conversation. He'd gotten Alchan to agree to train him privately. That step was taken care of.

20

MAVE

"We're ready to go! Where's Rain and Alchan?" Nevyn called out from his cart, sitting next to Varon. Mave looked back from her seat, raising an eyebrow. There was no reason to yell. It wasn't evening yet. From her understanding, they were on schedule.

"Right here, you fucking prick!" Alchan growled from the back of their large caravan. She had to stand up to see him. "Sit down!" he roared. "You'll break a fucking wing like that."

"He's talking to you, Mave," Matesh said, pulling on her tail with his. "Come on."

"I thought him going to see that…" She tried her best not to be condescending or rude. "Escort. That's what he's called?"

"Yes, escort," Mat patiently agreed.

"Well, I thought it was supposed to calm him down." She sat down slowly, making sure she didn't lose her balance on the rickety wood cart.

"We'll see if it worked soon. You shouldn't stand on the cart, though. I would have stopped you if I knew you were planning on it.

He's serious - you can fall and seriously hurt yourself." Mat smiled tightly. "Please don't pick any fights with him."

She shrugged. "Sure." She wasn't in the mood to pick any fights today.

"Matesh, get on your horse," Alchan ordered as he walked by. "Brynec, help Mave with the cart."

"What?" Mave frowned, watching Mat jump up and off the cart.

"Bryn doesn't like to ride." Mat patted her thigh before going to get a large mare. "I'll ride right here, don't worry. It's just the way of things."

Bryn was suddenly next to her, grabbing the leather leaders. "Aye, he's not goin' to go far from ya." Bryn chuckled. "Are we ready to get movin', Alchan?"

"Yeah, you can start pulling out!" Alchan swung up on his own horse. Mave grabbed onto a wooden bit of the cart as it lurched into action with the click of Bryn's teeth. "Company! Stay together!"

She was almost mystified. They had all been wandering around, killing time. Then he showed up and it was like a whip had cracked. They jumped into position and things took off. They had fallen in without a second of hesitation, rolling with his commands with an easiness that defied what she thought of Andinna. Not even Luykas prodding them all day had gotten them moving so quickly.

Mave tried to get comfortable, shifting on the barely-padded bench at the front of the cart until she felt the best way to sit on it. It wasn't made for Andinna, that was certain. Her wings didn't have a good place to sit comfortably, and her tail was jammed against the back. The bench wasn't deep enough for her entire ass to fit on either.

"We're not even out of the city and I hate this," she muttered. "Bryn?"

"Aye, the carts aren't the best. Probably all Han had, not ready for us to just show up." Bryn looked over at her. "Try sitting more sideways. It'll give ya some space."

She adjusted and sure enough, it gave her tail some space to fall off the bench. One of her wings felt better for it too. The problem? She had to press her legs up to Bryn's. He'd been standoffish with her all morning, even during cards at breakfast. He wasn't as friendly.

"Are we going to continue my exercises on this trip?" she asked, trying for something light and casual. She didn't think she succeeded.

"If ya want. I mean, ya should always stretch in the morning and evening, but if ya want to exercise in the evenings, we can do that." Bryn just kept looking forward now. He ignored how their legs were touching, something she knew was probably making him uncomfortable too. "Or Matesh can help ya…"

"No, you're better at the wing things than I am." Matesh chuckled. "If you really need me to, I will, but I'm not a good judge of these things. I'm the idiot that had her trying to extend right after we cut the bonds off them."

"Ah, shit. That's right," Bryn mumbled, sighing with something that made her think he was defeated.

Did he not want to spend time with her anymore? That was the vibe she was getting, which made her worried. He was her friend, one of her few. Was it because they were on land now? Was it because of the trouble she brought onto the Company the night before? How the Elvasi nearly started a brawl with them in the street because of her?

"Hey. Look what I found!" Rain's laughing voice cut into her thoughts as it rang over the Company and the crowd. "Our bounties went up!"

"Damn it," Bryn snapped. "How much?"

"A thousand gold suns for each of us," Rain answered, riding over to their cart.

"Let me see those!" Alchan called out from the front. "Grab as many as you can."

"Is this something to worry about?" she asked Bryn as Rain rode off again. Bryn continued to hold one of the posters. There weren't any faces on it. Just that the Empire was offering a hefty reward for the capture of any members of the Ivory Shadow Mercenary

Company, one thousand gold suns a head. Wanted dead or alive, but preferred alive.

"Nah. They've always been around. No one ever comes after us, though." Bryn chuckled. "This is our highest bounty yet. That says something. The thing is? Not many loyal to the Empire here, and the Elvasi hunters who capture Andinna tend to go after the ones who are alone or in smaller groups. Ten or more full grown male Andinna? You need a small army to take us down."

"Or luck," Matesh offered. "They got lucky to catch Rain and I."

"Aye, we can't let that happen again." Bryn hummed a small tune, almost a happy thing, like he thought the new bounties were funny.

"You seemed more surprised when Rain found them," she pointed out, confused by his mood.

"There's no individual posters yet, which changes things." Bryn chuckled, shrugging. "I was worried he found individual ones, since those…they get people targeted in a bad way. At least with Company bounties, they only know we're in the Company if we're in the group. They aren't going to fight the group."

"Bryn's right. We'll worry more if Alchan's face shows up on a poster, or his name. Really, any of us. That changes the game." Mat smiled her way. "There's nothing to worry about. Like he said, small army. There isn't a small army of Empire Elvasi in Olost. They'll be hard-pressed to take any of us, no matter how much money they'll make."

"And you aren't worried about anyone else trying?" She took the poster and continued to look it over.

"Humans? Shifters? No. Short-lived people don't play those games with us. They leave the Andinna and Elvasi feud to us. They try their best not to get involved. Keeps them alive longer." Matesh began to laugh. "Not like they live all that long."

"It's why they're so protective," Bryn said, as if it was a joke. "Only get a century, at the best, you defend that century!"

"Right? I couldn't imagine. Seems like such a short time to do all the important things. Travel, find love, have kids. All the adult things. It just seems so rushed." Matesh snorted. "I couldn't handle it."

"Aye, me neither," Bryn agreed, nodding wisely.

Mave didn't have a comment. If she were short-lived, her pain and suffering in the pits at the hand of the Empress and the other Andinna would have ended a long time ago. She would have never been there. She would have had a life.

At least she was getting one now. That counted for something. She just hoped whatever life she was building could wash away the thousand years of pain. Things that should have broken a thousand men and women were piled on top of her.

She continued trying to ignore them as best she could. She shouldered them for so long; she could continue to shoulder them. She was certain of it.

The entire conversation had led her mind to a dark place and she wasn't sure how to get out of it. As they left the city, Bryn and Mat didn't notice her reserve as they continued to joke about something.

"So, that's how Mat ended up bedding a human and nearly getting her pregnant," Bryn said with a joyful laugh.

"What?" That yanked her right out of it. One minute she was lost in the memories, trying to keep them contained, and the next, a bubbling rage was forming in her chest. Her male had nearly bred a different female?

"Yeah! Did you miss the entire story?" Bryn frowned at her.

"Thank the Skies," Mat muttered. "Never again. Look, it was before I even knew Bryn. I was young and didn't know that humans didn't go through fertile times like we do. I figured she wasn't breeding at the time. Zayden told him the damned story, and now, like every other bad memory, he brings it up to piss me off."

"Okay." Mave shook her head. "No, I wasn't listening. Don't go having children with other females, Mat. I might rip your balls off for it. You don't have any children out there, right?"

"None that I know of. That was the only human I've ever been with. I've never fucked an Andinna female during her fertile time, so there really should be no reason to think I have young." Mat chuckled. "Please, don't rip my balls off. They belong to you."

"They better," she muttered. She trusted him, but there was some visceral feeling about the idea of him fathering young that weren't hers. It was madness, since she didn't intend on ever having children. Why would she ever bring young into this world? "How did you not know about humans and their breeding?" She knew. She'd had some of her humans explain over the years. They would talk about their wives, telling her about their children.

"There were no humans in Anden. The land was too tough for them. Andinna and a small population of dwarves were all we had, and you'll never catch an Andinna trying to breed a dwarf. There's a size problem. I'm not even sure it's possible." Matesh shrugged.

"Speakin' of fertile times..." Bryn scooted away from her. "Have ya two talked about that?"

Mave bit her tongue. No, they hadn't. She didn't want to.

"We will when we get to the village. Not like it's any of your business," Matesh replied, eyeing the rogue.

"Better me askin' than Varon or Leshaun." Bryn snorted, shaking his head. "You know if Varon brings it up, yer never getting away from it. He'll ride yer ass until he gets the information he wants."

Well, I know who I'm never talking to about it, then.

Mave didn't have a good experience with her fertile time. She'd only had one so far. She wasn't sure how normal that was, or how often she was supposed to have one. The only time she did have one had been over six hundred years ago, right after she'd gotten her private room in the pits. She could remember the bloody spotting she'd had, which had scared her, but she hid it.

I didn't know the males could smell it.

Her mind flashed to the moment she had walked into the chow hall late and all of them had looked up, nostrils flaring. One of them had whispered only one word.

Breeding. He'd said breeding like it was a prayer and a threat all rolled into one.

It had driven the male Andinna into a frenzy for nearly two weeks. In the end, she had to be locked into her own cell with food brought to her to keep her safe. It had been terrifying and awful. Every male in the pits had wanted her underneath him for those two weeks. Every male would have done everything he could to make it happen. Three guards died and she killed five gladiators before the Empress agreed to quarantine her.

No, she wasn't looking forward to having another. And now she was living with more males? They were nicer, friendlier and more trustworthy, but how was she to know they wouldn't react the same way?

If she never had another fertile time again, she wouldn't be sorry.

"We'll talk about it at the village," she agreed with her *bodanra*. She couldn't avoid it, but at least she could push it off for a time. She didn't think it was going to hit on the three week trip to the village.

The sun moved over their heads as they made slow progress away from the city. At sunset, she saw Alchan and Luykas bring their horses to a stop near a grove of trees.

"Let's camp here for the night!" Alchan called out. "Bryn and Matesh, walk her through how we bed down for the night. Leshaun, Nevyn, and Varon, you're in charge of dinner!"

The entire caravan came to a creeping stop and they all jumped off their respective mounts. Bryn helped Mave down from the cart, since she had nearly slipped earlier in the day when they were making a piss stop.

She didn't talk a lot as they walked her through getting out bedrolls, told her about watch order, and helped start up the campfire for the others to cook on. They wouldn't be eating great food for the evening, but it wouldn't be jerky either.

"Bryn? Want to do my wing exercises now?" she asked before he could walk away from her as they finished. He nodded silently, waving her to follow him.

They went out of earshot of the Company, but still in viewing distance. She didn't know why they were so far out, but she didn't mind it too much either. She could talk more comfortably without everyone listening in.

"Are you okay?" she asked first, as his hands touched her wings. She hadn't stretched enough over the last two days in the city, so she was a bit stiff.

"Aye. Just been thinkin'."

"About?" She felt nosy.

"Ya. Mat said some things last night that have me thinkin'." He rubbed into her wings as she extended them. "Ya can't do exercises tonight. Will need to wait 'til tomorrow."

"Okay..." She continued to stretch and wouldn't stop until he told her that she could. "What did Mat say?"

"He talked to me about what ya did about the bed thing. How ya tried to play with him. Hope ya don't mind." Bryn sighed. She had a feeling it wasn't the entire truth, but she accepted his answer without trying to get more out of him. "Ya know why the game might not be good for ya?"

"I have a guess," she answered.

"Ya play with a male, especially one in your *mayara*, and he'll force himself on ya. A lot of Andinna females do it on purpose, to give the males something to work for, test 'em. It's a game, and it makes everything exciting." Bryn rubbed a little harder. "Smart of Mat not to let it continue. Ya would have gutted him if you felt threatened, not understanding you started it."

"I wouldn't have," she objected, looking over her shoulder at him. "I wouldn't have hurt him."

"Ya would have. Ya sending all the signals that ya want it like that..." Bryn stopped touching her, pulling away. "A moment would have come where ya would have freaked yerself out and gone into survival mode."

"Why do you know this? You aren't female."

"Aye, I'm not female, but I am a male Andinna. I'm like Alchan. I'll stick my dick into anything, and I don't mind receiving from another male either. Sex is pleasurable and it relaxes our temper. When a male is playing the submissive one, we can get the other male to play the same game." Bryn chuckled at her silence. She could only wonder what her face looked like. She hadn't expected to hear any of that. "Yeah, ya heard me right. I've been with other males before. Both fuckin' and receivin'."

"I..." She shook her head. "There's nothing wrong with it. Do you like females? Or are you a *bedin* like Rain?"

"Hey, you know *bedin* now!" Brynec thumped her shoulder. Of course she did, since she heard Rain use it often enough. It just meant a male who only wanted other males. Her little brother had been kind enough to teach her the female version of the word as well, *ahin*. "Aye, I like females too. Don't really care who as long as I like 'em enough. They got to know how to get me up, though." He was grinning as he explained.

"It's not hard to get a male up," she said, looking down slowly. She was bold enough to stare until she got the reaction she wanted. A bulge was beginning to grow, but she didn't stare long enough to keep embarrassing him and see how big he got. When she went back up to his face, she shrugged. "It's easier than most things, really."

Bryn coughed, and he turned away from her while his face grew dark from a blush. "Well, I was just put in my place." He patted his chest, coughing a bit more before turning back around.

"So all of this is why you know how I would react with Matesh if I tried to play this game." She wasn't sure why they were calling it a game or playing. She didn't have another way to reference it, though.

"Aye. I nearly did it myself," Bryn said, sobering quickly. "Mave, ya want things that normal Andinna do and that's good, but those Andinna didn't live through what we did. To them, it's bedroom play. To us, it can quickly become our nightmares."

"And you've been thinking about this all day?" She frowned, unsure why he would worry about her bedroom so much.

"I was thinking how I got over it. I haven't had an incident in centuries." Bryn positioned her so he could go back to rubbing her wings. "I went to Varon. He walked me through it. We did it. He pushed, I resisted. When I began to freak out, he stopped and reminded me who he was. He gave me a word to stop it if it was truly too bad. Andinna, we do that. These types of games can get real dangerous. Males and females can get injured when one of the parties doesn't know how to hold back or one doesn't submit and stop in time." Bryn rubbed the tight knot in her left wing now. She hadn't realized it was there. It was the wing that was cramped on the cart all day. "He taught me how to trust the situation, in certain cases. It's not perfect. I don't receive from other males very often, so it's not somethin' I need to worry about too much."

"Are you saying I should go to Varon?" She curled a lip at the idea. She liked the priest, but he was with Nevyn. She wasn't attracted to him and they couldn't communicate well yet, either.

"No, but maybe ya should try it with Mat or a future member of yer *mayara* when yer ready. Just don't start playin' that game with 'em until ya have set some rules down. I'll tell Matesh to do the same, or ya can."

"You know, I'm glad I have you," she admitted softly. "You're the only person giving me this sort of advice."

"Ya need someone who understands," he replied. "I do."

"Do you want to talk about anything else?" She could only imagine what he was holding back.

"Where did ya go today? Ya went into yer head and missed a lot of Mat and I trying to talk to you. I noticed, and I'm pretty sure he did too." Bryn's hands nearly lulled her into relaxing until that question. "I told ya where I was, what I was thinkin' about. Turnabout is fair play."

"You know, nothing bothered me in the pits." She took a deep breath. "It's beginning to bother me. The old wounds feel like they're reopening, and I'm trying to hold them closed. I thought I was over all of it." She swallowed on some emotion. "Now I'm free, and what do I get? All these things keep coming back. I never let them drag me down when I was in the pits. Never. Why now?"

"Because ya finally have time to deal with them." Bryn's hands moved to her back and shoulders. "Ya finally have the space to deal with them. There ain't nothing wrong with looking back and realizing that ya were hurt. Yer life was awful. Maybe it's time to address it."

"Address what?" She scoffed. "I protected myself. I was the strongest Andinna in the pits, Bryn. What they did to me doesn't matter anymore. I'm free. They can't take that from me." For the first time in a very long time, tears threatened her eyes. She tried to keep it buried, but the conviction of her words didn't match the way her heart felt. "I wanted you to talk to Rain, not me. I don't want to give you all of this pain. This pain doesn't matter." She hadn't wanted to load him with her nightmares. "Sometimes, it feels like I'm drowning, just trying to keep my head above water. Not often, but…" Mave swallowed. The old pain would come rushing back without warning, and she would struggle in silence.

"It's like a bad storm that comes fast and out of nowhere." Bryn explained it so well. "It's fine. Ya can use my raft. Mat will always help ya. The Company will always help ya." He reached out again and this time, he didn't just grab her hand. He wrapped her into a hug. "Just like ya offered me stability during the storm. Ya just need to get better at tellin' others when ya need that help to stay afloat."

She tentatively wrapped her arms around him and eventually held him tightly. Her hands shook a little. "Thank you."

They held each other for a long time, as the sun continued to dip and the firelight was all they had.

"We should get back to the group," he finally said, gently pulling away. She could only nod, letting him go. "Ya know, it goes both ways."

"What does?" she asked softly.

"Ya think yer a burden, but yer not. Ya help me too." Bryn smiled and it was sweet. It was kind and gentle in ways she didn't understand. "When ya convinced me to sleep during the storm? It was the best sleep I had gotten the entire trip. It might be the best sleep I've gotten in the last decade. Thank ya for that."

He began to walk away at that, forcing her to move back to the group with him. She found a seat next to Mat, who didn't question why her evening stretches had taken so long. The Company, if anyone had been watching, could have seen what happened. None of them said anything, none of them teased or jeered or called her or Bryn weak for needing comfort.

She began to realize none of them ever would.

21

TREVAN

Trevan practiced against the dummy full of straw, knowing there was nothing else he could do except keep his training sharp. The sun beat down on him, every second draining his energy. It was only the afternoon training. He was still going to need to make it through dinner and the evening training.

And then I'll need to find a place to hide. It's been five days since they cornered me for a beating. They're probably getting antsy again.

Trevan didn't have much hope that he would be able to avoid them forever. Eventually, the Andinna were going to turn their sights back on him, but thankfully, they'd had new gladiators for the last couple of days to keep them preoccupied. He'd seen it as a guard. Newcomers were always hazed and harassed in the beginning. He just hoped one of them would end up causing more trouble and keeping the heat away from him for just a little longer.

As the only Elvasi in the pits as another slave, it was all he could hope for. A little more time.

He beat the wooden training sword into the dummy harder. At least he could heal nearly as fast as the Andinna. They took their healing sleep for granted. Elvasi had the same, but the Elvasi weren't made for war and combat the way the winged warriors were. He could heal much faster than a human, but bruises didn't always disappear overnight for him. He still had evidence of the last beating he'd gotten.

Why don't they just kill me?

Trevan asked himself that a lot. He knew the Empress was cruel. She wanted him to suffer. She wanted him to break under the weight of being a slave, unprotected from those who had all the right to hate him. He just wasn't sure why the Andinna hadn't killed him yet. Were they told not to? Were they toying with him? Were they hoping he would gain a shred of hope at surviving, then end him?

He had no hope of escaping. He had no hope it would end any time soon. He wasn't even sure why he was training so hard.

He leaned against the dummy at the end of his forms, out of ideas about what to do. The lenasti ignored him, yelling at the Andinna. The guards whispered at him, some cursing his name. They would beat him again soon, and he didn't have much of a chance at hiding from them. They could just order him to stay still and there wouldn't be much he could do about it.

He'd always thought the Champion had been alone in the pits, but looking back, he realized she had kept herself that way. The lenasti, the trainers, they had liked her a little. She was still a slave, but she was a well-behaved one, and the best gladiator in the pits. She brought them glory. The guards who had been around as long as him, they knew her as the one who didn't cause them trouble, unless they caused her trouble. It was amicable on their end.

He was alone. They all hated him. Andinna, Elvasi, it didn't matter. He couldn't even be well-behaved to get into anyone's good graces. He was a pariah, and they treated him as if he was the shit under their boots, something they were always trying to wipe clean, but couldn't.

"Everyone! Gather around!" a lenasti roared over the grunts and arguments of training. "The Empress has decided that monthly games shall proceed as normal. We've drawn up a schedule for two days from now."

Trevan straightened, wondering if he would be forced to fight. He didn't join the group of Andinna gathering around, staying behind them all. He knew if he got much closer and accidentally bumped one, it would start a brawl, one he would lose.

Truthfully, he wanted to get chosen. He couldn't fight back against the beatings, but maybe on the sands he could win once or twice and they would start leaving him alone. It was really the only hope he had. Maybe, in a couple of centuries, he would earn a room.

Maybe.

He only had one example of how an outcast could survive the pits, and it was her. Maevana. He'd never even said her name to her. She had always been the Champion to him, since before he even found himself a guard in the pits. He didn't know if how she did it would work for him, but he could try. He wasn't sure why in the end, since he was going to die sooner or later, but he was going to try.

The lenasti continued to call out numbers of fights and by the end, Trevan's number was never called. Not a single mention or reference to him.

No. I need to fight. I have to. If I never fight, they'll never know I can, and it'll always be a fucking shit-show down here.

The Andinna began to disperse and Trevan avoided them to go to the lenasti. The older Elvasi looked up from his parchment and glared. "What, slave?" There was a bitter, venomous anger in the question.

Trevan did as he'd learned over the last month. Keeping his eyes down, he swallowed the fear. "Sir, I wasn't chosen to fight?"

"No. Maybe next time."

"Sir-"

A crack echoed over the now silent training area. Trevan hissed as a whip sliced open his back.

"You heard him," another lenasti snapped. "Move along, slave."

Trevan bit back his own anger. He backed away, and once he was out of range of the whip, he turned and walked down the stairs into the dining area. Like many of the slaves, he had on only breeches, meaning every Andinna and other slave in the room could see the angry, bleeding line he probably had across his back now.

"I wonder if he thought he could whine to some other Elvasi," an Andinna commented to another. "Stupid pointed-ear bastard. That's what he gets."

"It's nice to see the Elvasi are bastards to their own people, too."

Laughter. Trevan's world was full of laughter. The cruel, mean kind. He took a bowl from a human slave. The short-lived slaves weren't nearly as cruel. He had the bowl filled with slop and went to the one place he could safely sit in the room.

Over the centuries, many had tried to claim the small table in the corner just to piss off the Champion. Now, none of them did. It was the only place he could sit. Once, they had claimed it was where she would watch them, spying on them for the Empress. Now, it was a place where they could all keep an eye on him.

He sat down quietly and began to eat quickly. He knew he was safe in the dining hall and had no intention of leaving when he was done with his food, but he knew if he didn't eat it fast enough, one of them would steal it. The guards didn't allow it between the Andinna, but there were no rules when it came to him.

The Andinna had free rein to do whatever they pleased to him, and there was no one and nothing to stop them.

Trevan finished his meal, and when the bell rang, he waited for the Andinna to go up into the training area first. He went up behind them and went back over to his training dummy, where none of them would bother him.

He noticed the lenasti were still ignoring him. They always did.

That's why they didn't choose me to fight. They're ignoring me. If I don't fight, I can't get killed, and my pain down here will only continue, probably just the way the Empress wants. It's all a part of the punishment.

With that realization, Trevan gritted his teeth. He beat into the dummy, working harder.

He had work to do. He had to find a way to change the game and get into the Colosseum so he could prove himself.

22

MAVE

They could see the mountains by the beginning of their thirteenth day on the road. They had been moving faster than planned. Alchan hadn't liked being on the road and moved them harder than he'd originally wanted to. She didn't mind.

"We're almost there," Alchan called out. "We're going to be in the village by tomorrow night. If all goes according to plan, we'll get a few weeks to rest before the mission."

Mave smiled. At least there was that. A small break from the road. A blessing, really.

The cart lurched into movement and the Company was back on its way for yet another day on the road.

Bryn sat next to her, his summer-sky-blue eyes on the road. For two weeks, they had been friendly, always on the cart next to each other, save the times when Mave practiced riding on Mat's horse. That had started a few days after the trip did. Every day in the afternoon, she rode the horse for a short time, learning the way of it. She could manage a little more every day. Between that, her Andena, and her wings, she felt like she could catch up faster than anyone thought she would.

When Mat rode around, handing out jerky for everyone, she chewed on it, not bothered anymore by the spice. She didn't have much of an appetite, though.

"Rain!" Alchan called out at the front of their caravan.

"Yes, sir?" Rain called back, standing on his cart and receiving a glare for it.

"Sit," Alchan snarled and quickly cut it off. "Later today, probably before we bed down, I want you to fly ahead. Get some rest now so you can fly all night. You're fast enough, I think you'll beat us to the village to let them know we're coming."

"Of course, sir." Rain smiled, nodding. He climbed into the back of the cart and bedded down. Mave wondered just how fast his wyvern actually was, but didn't want to bother anyone with the question.

"That's interesting," Mat commented. "Sending Rain instead of you, Bryn."

"Rain's fast as hell in his wyvern form," Bryn replied, chewing on his piece of jerky.

"Good point," Mat agreed. They continued riding, everyone quiet. Mave found herself staring at the mountains a lot. As they drew closer, she grew more excited. She felt like they were calling her. They had spent two weeks on roads near forests, farms, and through one tiny human village, but this…They were nearly to a place where she felt like she would feel at home. The flat lands didn't make her excited the way the mountains did.

It was late afternoon when the front group stopped. Mave stood up, curious to why.

"What's going on?" she asked, trying to see what stopped Alchan and Luykas in the front.

"Don't know," Mat said. "Let me go find out." He rode away, going towards the front.

It was Alchan who roared what was going on. "The road is blocked! Everyone off the road! We're going to bed down here for the night. You too, Rain. We're still too far out for me to send you along."

Mave sighed, jumping off the cart. Bryn was groaning to himself as he led the horses and cart off the road. She eyed the blockage at the front of their group as the rest of the carts got out of the way. It was like a storm had knocked down three trees in succession onto the road. Branches and other debris were everywhere. It would take the rest of the afternoon and evening to make the road clear enough to travel. At that point, they would be exhausted. She saw the wisdom of Alchan's order. They would need the rest after this.

"I can help," she offered as those on their own horses jumped down. Leshaun appeared next to her, using his cane. He was moving slower each day they were on the road, but the only complaints she heard from him were joking. He never asked anyone to slow down for him, just joked about old knees and a weak back.

"Are you sure? The big young men can handle it." His comment was mild, but she bared her teeth at it.

"I can help." She wasn't some simpering female. She was in the prime of her life and well built.

"We need all the hands we can get - these things are huge." Luykas smiled at her, nodding. "Matesh, you too."

"Yup." Matesh sighed and began to walk his horse off the road, grabbing the leads for Alchan's and Luykas' horses as well.

She moved to the trees, frowning. The size of them was impressive. They were thick enough to go to her waist on their sides the way they were.

"We'll clean up the small debris first," Alchan said, walking to stand beside her. "I want you on the branches while I get a group on the first tree."

"I can help with the trees," she said, narrowing her eyes at him.

"You can help with the next two. There's a lot of work to be done." He didn't seem to care about the way she was growling at him.

She started moving the large branches out of the road as most of the Company surrounded the tree. Rainev and Brynec were helping her and Leshaun was nowhere to be seen, likely with the carts and horses. The branches could have been small trees, if she didn't know any better. Most were bigger than every male in the Company.

"Skies, what kind of storm hit to knock these damned things down?" Rain groaned, pulling a branch off the road. She half-threw hers into the underbrush and out of the way.

"No idea. Ya would think the patrols from the village would have seen 'em and handled it." Bryn shook his head. "Lazy pigeons."

"Patrols? You mean the Andinna in the mountains?" She grabbed another branch, pulling it across the dirt. The males were now moving the tree out of the road. She could see all of them were getting red-faced from the exertion.

"Aye. They should be keeping the road safe and clear for us to come back. We're the only Andinna who ever leave the mountains regularly. They probably think we weren't coming back from the Empire." He chuckled darkly. "Alchan is going to give 'em hell for this when he gets the chance. Especially since we're bringin' a female back. All those males in the village are going to regret not makin' the trip easy on ya." He winked at her, making her shake her head at the antics.

"They're going to get really excited over you," Rain added, grinning. "You'll see. A new female that they haven't had to deal with for a few centuries? You're going to get all sorts of male attention."

"No thank you," she said softly, throwing another branch off the road. She didn't need or want any more male attention than she already had. She didn't even mean that in the sexual sense. She was constantly surrounded by males all the time, and it had been that way since she was thrown into the pits. Why would she want more? "Let's just get back to work." She didn't want to keep worrying about how life was going to be when they were in the village or the males she didn't know yet.

It was slow work. A lot of the smaller debris was easy, but plentiful. The large pieces began to get heavier. She and Bryn had to move one branch together as the Company finally moved on to the second large tree trunk.

"We're going to need more hands on this one," Luykas called out.

She smacked Rain's shoulder and pointed. Together, Bryn following behind, they went to help move the next tree with the Company.

"Where's Leshaun?" she asked, wrapping her arms around the tree as best she could.

"Setting up camp deeper in the woods. Bryn, how did the carts do getting out there?"

"There's enough clear space that they can get in and out. We didn't get them stuck. We found a campin' clearing. I'm pretty sure we've stopped here before."

"I wouldn't doubt it," Nevyn said, grunting.

She looked over to Mat, who was at the end. He was going to do most of the lifting at the front with Alchan so it didn't get caught on anything.

"On three," Alchan said down the line. "Three. Two. One. Move."

She growled as she half lifted and half pushed the tree with the Company. It was huge and heavy. One of the males near her snarled at the load. It felt so slow as they moved the tree together as a team. She was in the back and they were careful not to try and push too fast so they didn't throw off Alchan or Mat. Those two in the lead were careful not to try and pull too quickly and leave the rest of them trying to catch up and fumbling.

Finally, they were off the road and deep enough in the woods that they could slowly drop it. Mave was panting, like everyone else.

"Shit, there's one more?" Nevyn laughed, but it sounded pained.

"We can do it," she promised. She needed to lean over and put her hands on her knees. That had been harder than she expected. She realized quickly that she should have stretched before jumping in to do heavy lifting.

Stupid. Mave, the road and the calm are getting to you.

She wasn't sure why she was beating herself up. No one had stretched before doing this. It had been something she did for years, though. She liked to make sure her body was warmed up before this sort of training.

The problem was, her back was now hurting. It had a dull ache. The sun was beginning to dip as well, marking the start of evening. They had already been at this for a long time.

"Ya should sit the next one out," Bryn said, putting a hand on her shoulder.

"Why?" she demanded, looking up at him to see he seemed concerned.

"Muscles in yer wings are attached to yer back. Ya screw up yer back doing this and we'll get behind on yer wings." He bent over further. "Ya don't need to hurt yerself to help us."

"I can help," she said, not bothering to hide the bite to her words.

He sighed, pulling away with his hands up like he'd given up. She straightened up and winced. He must have noticed because he reached out and grabbed her shoulder again, rubbing it like he did when he massaged out her sore and stiff muscles.

"I told ya," he said softly, not bothering to hide the bite in his own words. "Ya don't see Leshaun over here hurting himself."

"Is this why Alchan had me on branches?" she asked.

The rogue nodded. "While ya strengthen your wings, ya need to be mindful of yer back. He knows this." He continued to rub her shoulders, now with both hands. She looked around to see most of the Company had wandered off. When she began to walk back out of the woods, Bryn held her back. "The last one is smaller. They don't need us. We'll get back on the small things when I'm sure ya didn't mess up anything back here yet."

"I don't need this." She was feeling a bit childish, needing him to continue to work those fingers and thumbs in her back. He hit the tender spot lower in her back and rubbed into it harder. She couldn't stop the betraying sound that came from her mouth.

He stopped this time. "Ya keep doing that," he said softly in her ear. "I'm goin' to need ya to stop."

"Sorry," she mumbled, looking back at him over her shoulder. "Can't help it."

"Should tell Matesh to do this," he muttered softly. "Speaking of."

She looked back towards the road and saw the males bringing the last tree into the woods. Rain wasn't helping them this time either, which meant he was probably working on the debris again. Mat looked up from his task and saw her. With a smile, he called for them to stop when they were deep enough into the woods. The tree was dropped and she saw how he took in the scene of her and Bryn. Bryn had gone suspiciously quiet and was working faster on her back than he normally did.

Mat's eyes flicked between them and an eyebrow went up. She wasn't sure what was going through his mind. Had she done something wrong again?

He sees Bryn helping me all the time. If he's upset this time, I might take his balls. I'm not in the mood for it.

"Did she hurt herself?" he asked Bryn as he got closer. She growled, mad he would immediately ask Bryn and not her.

Am I some fool who just hurts myself now and needs a male?

"Nah, just worked the muscles harder than they should have been. Doin' this before she's too sore for the rest of the evenin'. It'll help her tomorrow too. She won't be as sore as the rest of us."

"Thank you." Mat sounded genuinely pleased with Bryn's report and turned to her. "Trying to hurt yourself for us?" He was smart enough to put a teasing note into it, because her anger with him dissipated.

"I didn't think it was a problem. Stupidly didn't stretch." She tried not to let his stare make her break down and admit how guilty she was of doing this to herself.

"Luckily, Bryn knows all about this sort of thing. When you two are done, come eat dinner. Leshaun is probably already making something for everyone. I'll make sure there's enough left for you both." He had a strange smile as he kissed her cheek and walked away.

"What is with him?" she asked out loud to herself after he disappeared.

"He's comin' to terms with his place with ya and how I'm not a threat. He was dealin' with some jealousy issues on the ship. They're leavin'." Bryn pulled his hands away. "It's not like I'm out to steal ya from him, and he knows that."

"With hands like yours, you could," she said innocently, just trying to joke. She would never leave Matesh. Something about the big male was too tied up in her life now, and she didn't want to get rid of him. There was also no denying how those hands Bryn had tended to make her feel a lot better when he put them on her.

Bryn's face darkened as his eyelids dropped into a heavy stare. "Don't tease," he ordered softly. He stepped around her and walked away, leaving her alone in the trees as if she'd threatened him.

Frowning, she followed. She'd made jokes like that with the males in the Company before. She wouldn't have tried to make the joke if she knew it would bother him. She was just growing more comfortable with them by the day, and that feeling made her want to try her hand at humor.

This time, it had obviously not landed. Maybe it was because of the bed thing.

She wasn't sure, and by the time she made it back to camp, Bryn was up in a tree over them with a bowl and spoon, eating and ignoring the Company. Rain was beginning to come down as the sunlight disappeared. This wasn't their first wet night on the road, but she really wanted it to be the last.

"Did something happen?" Mat asked softly, handing her a bowl when she sat down beside him.

"I made a joke. I'll need to apologize for it later, it seems."

"What was the joke?" he asked gently, looking concerned.

"Doesn't matter." She took a bite of the stew. She closed her eyes as spices assaulted her. Damned Andinna food. Why did they always make it hurt so bad? She was beginning to miss the damned slop. "Leshaun went crazy with this one."

"It's a traditional recipe to fight the cold of the mountains," Mat explained, failing to hide a grin at her expense. "It's not so bad."

She glared at him until he was smart enough to drop his eyes and stop snickering. She refused to hold him when they made it to their bedrolls that night, just to be petty with him.

23

BRYNEC

Brynec watched the Company sleep from his vantage point in a tree as the rain began to pick up and pour on them. Varon and Nevyn were awake with him, his favorite two watch partners. They patrolled the perimeter while he kept an eye out. They kept each other in line of sight and the fire was still bright enough that Bryn could make out Varon's hand signs.

"*Of course I could hear them, love. I don't see why you want to know. You ask me for this every time. Stop being so nosy.*" Varon's hands were moving quickly enough to show he was annoyed with Nevyn's line of questioning.

"He hugged her. Bryn doesn't hug people, and you know it's not normal for her. You think it's going to happen? They deserve each other, I'm positive. Look at how friendly they've been over the last couple of weeks."

Bryn had to strain to hear Nevyn in Andena, but he could. Even though it was just barely a whisper, he was able to figure out what was being said.

"*I am too, but I'm not going to gossip their entire conversations to you.*" Varon threw his hands up when he was done.

"You should. I'm just saying. We don't keep secrets from each other." Nevyn was accusing, but not in a mean way. Bryn knew he was teasing Varon for trying to maintain Bryn's privacy.

I can't believe they're talkin' about me. Between them and Matesh...

Bryn shifted, turning away from his friends to look out over the road. He didn't want to be with Mave. He was positive that she would want other, bigger males. She liked the males like Matesh, and he wasn't going to try to compete with any of those. Plus, she probably didn't want someone who kept bringing up painful memories. He knew he pushed her, always trying to get her to talk about things. He was just trying to be helpful. He knew what it meant to have someone who could understand.

I don't have those sorts of feelings for her.

She was stunning, in that classic Andinna female way. He could admit that. He could watch her train with a sword all day and not think he was wasting time. He could imagine how she looked in those leather breeches when her back turned to him.

At the very idea, his cock got hard and his mouth watered, making him curse.

Maybe I am into her. Doesn't change the fact that she wouldn't want a skinny male like me. I'm not big like Matesh and she's too strong to have anythin' but big males like him.

Even as he tried to convince himself it would never happen, his mind assaulted him with images of what it would be like to trace her scars with his tongue. What she could possibly taste like. He'd been close enough now to know what she smelled like and knew he liked it. Like mountain earth, fresh from the rain. He wanted to live in the scent, sleep with it like he did on the ship.

"No," he snapped to himself. *I'm not anythin' more than physically attracted to her. I ain't entertainin' more than that. It's been weeks of just her. We'll get back to the village and I'll be able to get some space.*

"Bryn?"

He cursed silently to himself again, looking down. He hadn't realized that Nevyn and Varon were now on their patrol underneath him.

"Nothin'," he called down softly.

"All right," Nevyn said back, disbelieving.

He made sure they were gone before continuing his thoughts on the matter of the female sleeping on a bedroll next to her massive male. The big male that was strong enough to walk out of the pits like it barely happened, coming out with a pretty female and as the first member of a new *mayara*.

She wouldn't want a male like him because he was used. What good would she have of him? He wasn't the most dominant. He wasn't too strong. He was a rogue because it was the best way for him to learn to kill. He'd been too small, compared to the other gladiators he'd known, and he needed his own ways of winning. If that meant he shanked one of them before a fight, then that's what he would do. If that meant he found a poison to put on his blades without their owners knowing, he did that. He had to be cunning, since he couldn't overpower or dominate the others.

She was everything he wasn't. She was powerful and dangerous, with enough brute strength in her that even big males had to take a step back. She couldn't overpower them, being so much smaller, but she was still powerful. She didn't have to do the things he'd done to survive.

He would never be strong enough for her. It was wishful thinking to consider the idea of being with her, being a casual lover or a cherished member of her *mayara*. It didn't matter which. He would pick up the scraps if he could.

And she helped him sleep. He wondered if she knew the importance of that. How it had been so easy to fall asleep next to her during a storm that normally would have driven him mad. She had been warm and comfortable, offering him a shred of peace and a bed he didn't belong in.

He'd given in to her demand because he knew he'd never get another chance to be in that bed. He hadn't told Mat that. He wasn't an idiot. It would have given the big male grounds to take his head off and throw it overboard. He just wanted to experience that bed, just once. Looking back, he knew he was stupid, but he couldn't resist. Not at that moment, not feeling the way he had. The fear, the old memories flooding back, and a chance at the *mayara* bed even if it was chaste?

Oh no, he couldn't resist it. Not even for a moment. Luykas should have grabbed him and yanked him from it the moment he'd given in. Mave should have never offered.

I loved it there.

Bryn looked down at his hands, playing with a dagger he held without reason. He should have been sharpening it. He'd started before he caught Nevyn and Varon talking during their patrols.

There were other things to consider. She was still feeling out her place in the Company. She was about to be thrust into the new center of their culture. The main village was a learning experience for anyone who spent too much time away from their people. It took Bryn years to get used to the place. He couldn't even begin to imagine how she was going to react when they got there.

He tried to take his mind off it all by starting to sharpen his dagger again. There was nothing he could do about his growing attraction to Maevana Lorren.

Skies, even her damned name is beautiful. I wish she would use it.

Mave suited her in the idea that she was a gladiator, full of pain and anger, with the potential to hurt people. Maevana was the beautiful and perfect Andinna she could be. It was everything he found when she let him sleep in her *mayara* bed that Matesh made her.

He needed space from her, he decided. Thinking of her as a gladiator reminded him of all the bad things she had probably lived through, the darkness he saw in her eyes. He couldn't pressure her just because she was able to get his cock up. It was more difficult than she thought. He'd never risen so easy for anyone, but the way her eyes had trailed down, the confidence that she could do it? It had made his mind wander into a place where he imagined her freeing his cock and using it as she wanted.

He'd gotten hard instantly. Luckily, it wasn't too difficult for him to get it to stop. He just needed to remember his time in Myrsten and it went away quickly enough.

And then her comment today? How his hands could make her make *those* sounds? That damned little moan she made haunted him in his sleep every time she did it. He wanted more of it.

Space. He would never have her, so he needed space. He didn't want her to know how he was feeling and thinking it was her fault or her problem. Not after everything haunting her.

Lost in his thoughts again, he nearly missed them. Looking up to stare at the night scene of the road, he was surprised to see a group there. No one traveled Olost roads at night. No one who wasn't out looking for trouble, that was.

He didn't jump down immediately. Instead he went very still, except for his arm, sheathing his dagger slowly, hoping it didn't catch any light from the red moon. He slid gingerly off his perch and carefully went down the tree, hoping not to disturb anything.

He made it down without a sound, pulling his wings so tight against his back, he felt like they were bound again. He pulled his scarf over the bottom half of his face, creeping towards the group on the road. He didn't look back for Nevyn or Varon, knowing it would waste precious time. They could just be stupid travelers that hadn't bedded down, trying to get somewhere.

As he got closer, though, he realized his suspicions were right.

"You sure this is going to work?" one of the Elvasi asked, looking at another for reassurance.

"I don't see any lookouts. The trail leads into the woods. We'll catch them with their pants down in there." The arrogance of the Elvasi wasn't anything Bryn hadn't heard before. He turned back, creeping deeper into the grove back to the sleeping Company. He found Nevyn and Varon first, signing quickly.

"Elvasi on the road. Wake up the Company. They could come on us at any moment."

The lovers jumped into action immediately, one going for Alchan and Luykas and the other for Mave and Matesh. Bryn went for Rain and Zayden, nudging them gently. They didn't want too much noise or it would give away that they knew something was coming.

"Up. Elvasi," he signed to them as their eyes opened. He moved on to Leshaun nearby and gently shook the old male's shoulder. Out loud, he whispered, "Leshaun, take cover. We're about to have attackers."

"Okay. Is everyone-"

"You're last to rise. Go to the carts and horses. Be prepared to run if you need to. We're probably going to retreat if we can." Bryn didn't like ordering the older male to hide while they all fought, but not because he thought Leshaun should fight. He knew Leshaun disliked his old age. It was why he continued to run missions. Bryn was convinced, like most of the Company, that the old male needed to retire and take a safer role in a village. Maybe this would be it. Maybe these last few months would convince him to stay in the village with Rain for the next mission.

Leshaun moved as fast as his old bones were capable of. Bryn pulled a dagger to check it as Alchan came up beside him.

"How many?" Alchan signed.

"Roughly four dozen. Dark, and didn't want to waste time getting a head count." Bryn shoved the dagger away and signed the answer back.

"That's probably every fucking Elvasi in Namur. Every hunter wanting a piece of us. Think we can take them?" Alchan's question wasn't without cause. A group that size had given them casualties before.

Bryn snarled, knowing it wasn't possible to fight. They needed to move and run before the Elvasi entered the groves. "We can't take them." He was thirsty for Elvasi blood since they tried to start the brawl in Namur. Then again, Bryn was always thirsty for Elvasi blood.

But we can't do this. It's too dangerous.

It pissed Bryn off in a bad way. He wanted to kill all of them.

"Get in position to look out and let me know when they come any closer. Use the edge of the grove as the line of engagement. I'm going to mobilize everyone to get everything packed away. If we lose some bedrolls, we'll have to survive without them." Alchan turned away and began pointing Andinna to good spots and getting others moving to pack their things up. Bryn picked the sturdiest tree he could and went up high into its branches, hiding himself in the foliage.

They were going to turn the trap against the Elvasi, and the pointed-ear bastards weren't going to know what was happening.

24

MAVE

"Matesh. Mave. Get up," someone whispered.

She was awake instantly, wide-eyed and baring her teeth at the fool over her. She deflated when she realized it was Nevyn. The rain was the next thing she noticed. It was coming down at a rate that annoyed her. Was the storm so bad they had to move?

"What?" Matesh asked softly. "What's going on?"

"Bryn saw an Elvasi hunting party on the road. Looking for us. Get up, get armed. Wait for orders. Stay silent."

Mave's heart began to race. A hunting party. They were there to catch Andinna.

"Shit, we're so close to the mountains," Mat mumbled. "Come on."

He was up faster than her, and that had her scrambling. She grabbed her sword belt, getting it on quickly. She checked the blades, making sure they were ready. Not that it mattered. Ready and clean or not, they were getting used tonight.

"Mave, Mat, here!" Alchan ordered, waving them over. "Begin throwing everything in the carts. We have to move. They outnumber us by better than four to one."

She and Mat only nodded in return, remembering Nevyn's last order. Stay silent. There was no reason for them all to be talking and getting loud.

Without a pause to their steps, Mave and Mat began to grab bedrolls. They tossed them without direction or order into carts. Next they went for their eating supplies and food from the night before. They had left it all out for breakfast.

It was a mad dash, trying to stay quiet but also move quickly.

They didn't get very far before Alchan called them over again, making Mave realize how little time they had. This was happening now.

Time! We need time!

Her hopes for time fell on her gods' deaf ears, like always.

"Nevyn, Matesh, and Mave, I want you defending with Bryn and I. Varon, stay near everyone loading up the carts and offer cover fire. Hurry. Move. We might convince them to let us go, but if this turns bloody, I want all of you to ride out when you get the chance. There's no reason for all of us to die tonight. Rain, no shifting!"

"Why not?" Rain demanded. "I can kill all of them!"

"Because you'll kill all of us too, most likely, *and* destroy our supplies. We're fighting this the Andinna way. The wyvern is a last resort. Always. Never resort to that first." Luykas answered, with Alchan snarling in the background. "Plus, there's always the chance you lose control. We can't risk it."

If their position wasn't known before, it was now.

She moved swiftly as she pulled her swords, Mat on her heels. She looked to see Leshaun hiding by the carts, his sword drawn just in case as others continued to throw items into the backs of the carts. They were trying. They needed time to finish and leave with the supplies.

"Protection. Hard to see in the dark," Mat explained quickly. "In case he needs to run."

She didn't reply, nodding. She had wanted to make sure that was the case. It made Leshaun a bit of a target, since their supplies would be an easy thing for the Elvasi to attack to hurt them on their trip.

She hunkered down, Mat staying right next to her. Luckily, she had slept in her armor at the behest of her lover. Getting naked in the woods wasn't fun, he'd said. It had made sense, so she didn't.

"Trying to leave?" an Elvasi called out as they found half the Company packing up the site.

Alchan raised his *morok* to point at the Elvasi. "We're going. Don't test us, Elvasi. We'll go down, taking half or more of you with us. Just let us move on. We don't need mutually assured destruction."

"No, I think it's time you Andinna mercs were put in your place. You roam around Olost as if you're a free people. This isn't news, but you aren't. We're going to get rich off your heads."

"So be it." Their leader poured the water on the fire, plunging them all into darkness and smoke.

She was about to jump into action when she saw the black shape of Bryn fall first, so fast that it stunned her. His roar was impressive as well. It sounded like it came from a male three times his size.

She finally roared with the others as they jumped into the group of the Elvasi, their battle cries shattering the peace of the night, only a second after Bryn's. Thanks to Brynec, they were working with the upper hand, surprising the Elvasi, who definitely outnumbered them.

She gutted the first she could reach, kicking him back as he bled out. The goal was to do this quickly. They couldn't let any of these Elvasi walk away, not for trying to kill them.

She spun, sinking her sword deep into the chest of another. She yanked the blade out, turning to attack another, only for a curved sword tip to come out of the Elvasi's chest. She took the chance, scissoring her blades and cutting the male's head off to reveal Alchan on the other side as he pulled his sword from the body. He nodded with appreciation and she did the same back before turning back into the fray.

She pulled her left blade up to block a coming sword, aimed for her head. Steel sang, sending off sparks as she pushed it away and stabbed forward with her right gladius. She could see Nevyn using a *morok* in the dark, as well as Alchan.

Damn, I can't wait to learn that thing.

A head went flying with another roar. Blood sprayed over her as a body went down. She kicked out the leg of another Elvasi, sending him to the ground. Without hesitation, she slit his throat.

She turned to find another Elvasi, his sword over his head, ready to cut her down. In that moment, she was positive she was going to die. She didn't have time to bring her swords up to stop the blow. She wasn't that fast.

If my two options are dying or capture, I'll die. She saw no other answer.

The sword never came down as an arrow slammed into the Elvasi's eye. Mave looked over her shoulder to see Varon nocking another and taking another shot, killing an Elvasi coming for him. Then another. He didn't waste his arrows because he didn't miss.

With that, she kicked back another one running for her. With a swift slash, she opened his gut from right to left, watching his internal organs fall out. She wasted no time herself, going for one behind Matesh, saving him from a sword to the back as he fended off two at his front.

"Thanks," he said, seeing her come up beside him. She worked in tandem with him to kill the two before him. Once that was over, Matesh jumped into a group and began cutting more down.

Mave turned to see Leshaun fighting off two Elvasi as others who were supposed to be loading the carts fought off attackers. She began to run for him, knowing the older male was at a disadvantage, limping as he tried to push off the assault. The old male hadn't called for help, but that didn't mean he needed to fight alone.

The old fool! He's nearly blind! What is he thinking?

She saw how they pressed against him, saw how they were trying to cut him down, going for his legs. They were outnumbered in the fight. They should have known some were going to get around them to Leshaun.

She made it there at the same time as Rain, who jumped off a cart and landed on one of the attackers. She pulled Leshaun back, growling her fury at the Elvasi for going after their oldest member. She ran him through, feeling blood pump out onto her hands as she held the blade deep in the enemy's gut. She pulled it out slower, letting it drag and cause more damage.

The body dropped without any life in it. As it did, she spun on Leshaun and pointed for the cart.

"Stay down!" she ordered. "You can't get hurt!" Leshaun growled but backed away from her. She looked him over quickly then pointed at Rain. "Stay with him," she commanded. "Keep him from any harm."

Rain just nodded, agreeing with her with no backtalk. Just at that moment, Leshaun swayed and she barely grabbed him before he fell.

"Fuck!" She could feel the dark, growing spot of blood at the old male's side. "Mat! Rain, get Mat! Anyone!" She lowered Leshaun down slowly. "It's okay, Leshaun. I've got you."

"Go fight," the old male growled. "Go."

"No. Not until someone is here putting pressure on this." She felt around for the wound, realizing it was a deep gash. It didn't have to be fatal if they stopped the bleeding. She wasn't very good at sewing things up, though. She needed another pair of hands or a better medic.

"Let me see him," Zayden said quickly, moving next to her. "Rain, help me. Mave, go fight. We've got this."

"Are you sure?" she asked.

"They need you." Zayden nodded quickly. "Go."

She jumped up, her heart racing. She ran back for the rest of the Company and engaged with the first Elvasi she could. She took her rage out on him, roaring her battle cry as she kicked his chest, sending him falling back. She shoved one of her swords down into his chest, still roaring out that fury.

She took it all out on her enemies. If Leshaun died, it would be their fault. They slaughtered her people. They abused, maimed, and ruined her people. Her people, who finally accepted her, who finally gave her a place with her two swords and one skill. They respected her for what she could do. How she could kill.

These damned Elvasi weren't taking that away from her.

"Go! Rain, get us out of here! I need to treat Leshaun!" Zayden was roaring. Suddenly, screaming horses jumped into action and one of their carts began to move. Mave had no idea where the rest of their mounts went, probably bolting as the fighting started, but the cart horses had been trapped with them. Now two were being given the chance to run, so they did.

Mave watched for only a second as Rain directed the cart through the trees, Zayden trying to take care of Leshaun in the back. That second was something she shouldn't have taken. Something painful sliced through her wing. With a snarl, she turned and embedded her sword into the gut of yet another Elvasi.

Blood was everywhere now. It soaked the earth. It soaked her.

She felt alive.

With those three now gone, another roar rang through the night. Varon jumped into the fray, landing beside Nevyn. She could see them out of the corner of her eye, fighting in that deadly dance they had done on the ship. It was frighteningly good.

Luykas followed into the battle as well, no longer having anyone to direct to load the carts. The carts could be lost at this point. If Rain, Zayden, and Leshaun were the only ones to survive, then so be it. She knew this was their final stand, and they had been doing well so far.

But they were barely halfway through the Elvasi trying to take them dead or alive.

And some were going after those on the run.

She hoped Rain remembered everything she taught him.

"For the Andinna!" Alchan roared, lopping off a head.

All the Andinna roared with a renewed, last stand of fury. She couldn't resist the echo of her own, joining in.

She took another hit and pressed on. Then another. She knew she was bleeding from several spots now. Her thigh. Her left arm was feeling sluggish. She used her tail to yank down an Elvasi and stab him as he lay helpless.

They were cutting through their enemies, but their enemies were beginning to cut back. The remaining Elvasi began to circle the Andinna. They were all limping from injuries, hoping they could continue their standoff with the hunters.

I'll die before they take me. I'll kill Matesh and the rest of the Andinna if I have to. They won't take us. I won't let any of them be subjected to the horrors of slavery. Never again.

It was a silent promise to herself. It was the only promise she could make at that point.

25

ZAYDEN

Zayden tried to treat Leshaun on the ground, but it wasn't going to work with all of the chaos around him. He'd seen Mave over the bleeding older male, Rain there with her. He'd heard her call for help. He knew he was the one in the best position to respond.

"Stay with me, Leshaun," he ordered the old male who treated him like a son. "Mat can't lose you. I can't. Rain needs you too. Come on, stay with me."

Leshaun's words were hushed. Zayden couldn't make them out. He knew the male was inevitably being pulled into the healing sleep, even though combat happened all around them.

"Protect me as I get him into a cart!" Zayden cried out, ordering anyone around him for the help.

Luykas was immediately by his side, and so was Varon, still firing off arrows when he found a shot.

"Rain, get ready to take off with them!" Luykas cried out. Zayden nodded, forcing Leshaun up. Good, his son was going to get them out of there. The young needed to survive, mutt or not. He was glad Luykas knew that his son needed to live.

It was work and Zayden didn't want to injure Leshaun further. He got him into the cart as quickly and gingerly as he could. Right as he turned around, he had to kick back an Elvasi and jump in. Leshaun was bleeding out right in front of him.

"Go! Rain, get us out of here! I need to treat Leshaun!"

The cart lurched as the horses neighed and screamed, beginning to try and bolt. The fact that they hadn't yet was a testament to their training under Han. Zayden had already personally cut loose the mounts, leaving only the cart horses for them to deal with. The Company would need to survive, then worry about their rides. There was no point in protecting horses if they had no one to ride them.

Rain got them out of the grove, a bumpy and awful ride. Zayden pushed every piece of fabric he could get his hands on against the devastating wound on Leshaun's side. The bleeding wouldn't slow, which meant Zayden needed to sew him up with the blood in the way. An extra pair of hands would have been a blessing, but every other pair of hands was just trying to stay alive in their destroyed campsite and his son was getting them to safety.

"Don't stop for anything, Rain!" he called out, hoping his son could hear him. "Nothing!"

He found their medical kit. They kept one in every cart. It was the small preparations that mattered, because they never knew when something like this would happen. There was a needle and thread in it. Zayden knew Leshaun would kill him for this, but he began to sew, ignoring the roars of pain from the old male. He didn't try to stop Zayden, but he didn't much like it either.

It was slow, awful business and he looked up when he was halfway through, realizing they had company, and it wasn't their friends and family.

"Rain! Don't stop! We have Elvasi following hard!"

The Elvasi were on horses. They must have run for their own or stolen some from the Company. It didn't matter. The hunters were catching up, which meant this was now a run for their lives.

Zayden didn't think they would win. They couldn't abandon the cart, not with Leshaun down, and there was too much money invested into the supplies on board.

I just need Rain to try. I need to finish sewing up Leshaun.

He went back to it, keeping a close eye on the Elvasi as he worked.

But what he didn't expect was the cart to slow down right as he finished up.

"Rain, what are you doing?" he asked, screaming at the top of his lungs. "Keep us moving!"

"I've got this," his son snapped back, pulling them to a stop somehow. There was a fury to the words that made him concerned for his son.

Zayden kept his *morok* close, watching his blasted son roar and meet the riders. Zayden held onto his breath as he tried to keep Leshaun alive and his son risked his life to give him the time he needed.

Seeing his son in combat made Zayden realize how much he'd learned from the female in the pits. The way his boy moved, it defied everything that he'd been taught by the Company. The boldness of it was impressive. It was terrifying.

He cut down a horse, causing it to topple and crush the rider, ending one of the four threats.

Next, Rain shifted, roaring as a massive blue wyvern. His clothing disintegrated thanks to the explosive shift.

Zayden wasn't sure if he loved or hated the form.

Rain stomped and crushed another rider. He snapped his jaws, grabbing a horse and rider together, shaking viciously. He tossed the dead bodies probably fifty feet away in a bloody mess.

With the last one, he spit out those hell-hot flames, leaving the Elvasi and horse screaming for mercy. It caught a couple of trees on fire. They would be lucky with the storm, because Rain's flames were normally hot enough to start an uncontrollable forest fire.

And like that, his son protected them.

Zayden was even scared for his own life as the massive blue head of the wyvern turned to him.

He knew about the dual nature of the Clans of Zira. Summer had tried her hardest to explain to him that the beast was separate from the boy. That the wyvern was as much its own personality as it was his son. Now he could see it in the beast's eyes. His son was there, but not there. The wyvern was in charge of the body and mind.

The beast walked towards him, smoke erupting from its nostrils, twirling up into the night sky.

"Rainev," he whispered. "It's me. Your father. Your *baba*. Please, my boy. We're trying to protect Leshaun."

The wyvern snarled and jumped into the night, leaving him alone with the old male. Zayden knew his boy was out of control.

Zayden took a deep breath. He'd named his son for all the passion he'd felt on the young male's birth. Now he felt the name was apt in a different way. The wyvern, the *andinno*, the cousins of the Andinna. It encompassed all the same rage and passion as the Andinna. Their gods had made each of the two creatures in the same vein of passion and warlike tendencies they felt.

The wyvern was his son's *rai*. It was all the rage and anger his son was bottling up and trying to manage by himself.

"No wonder he wants to be alone," Zayden muttered, looking up to the sky, hoping to see his son. Rain was long gone. He had no idea when his boy would be back.

He didn't move to the driver's seat of the cart. He watched over Leshaun, hoping the Company would send someone for them on the side of the road. If he saw any Elvasi, he could only hope Rain came back to help. He couldn't go back to the Company. It would spell certain death to him and his charge.

Alone, Zayden waited.

26

MATESH

It was a madhouse.

Hell had broken loose after Rain left with Leshaun and Zayden and now, Mat found himself surrounded by Elvasi, with Alchan and Luykas at his back. Mave was deep in the mess, kicking one back as she gutted another. Right as the fight started, the Elvasi had the numbers to separate them easily.

"This is bad," he said, loud enough that he hoped his leaders would hear him over the clang of steel and the downpour.

"Obviously," Alchan snarled. "Let's push them out together. We need to get with the rest of the Company."

Mat nodded, following Alchan's lead as he pressed against one of the Elvasi. Mat and Luykas covered their leader's sides. Mat felt something slice over his thigh, but it was minor enough that it didn't bother him. Snarling, he shoved his broadsword into the Elvasi's gut and let the foe drop to the earth.

They broke through and went running for the rest of the Company. Nevyn was on his own and they got to him first, pulling him into their group. Mave was continuing to fight on her own, a monster with two swords.

"Mave, to us!" he called out, hoping she heard him. She didn't. She was so deep in her killing and rage that he wondered if anything would get her attention.

"Stand together!" Alchan roared, throwing his sword up. "We'll defeat them!"

Mat roared back in agreement, letting the energy for the fight take him. He loved fighting like this; it was why he became a soldier, a warrior for their people. Mave finally moved to his side, helping fight off two Elvasi trying to cut Alchan down from behind. He wasn't sure how she'd gotten to him, literally out of nowhere, but he was thankful. Nevyn jumped forward, snarling as he cut the head off another Elvasi.

Together, they worked at pushing back their foes. This had been coordinated, that was certain. He knew once it was done, if they weren't all dead, there was going to be a long discussion about it.

"Fuck," Luykas growled, burying his blade into the neck of an Elvasi, but not getting the clean kill. The Elvasi gurgled as he dropped to the ground.

The action slowed as the Elvasi must have realized they couldn't break through them.

"Give us the female and we'll leave the rest of you," one of the Elvasi said to Alchan.

Mat didn't like that. *Do they know who our leader is? I sure as fuck hope they don't.*

"You're a fool if you think I'm giving you one of my warriors," Alchan retorted.

Mave was tense next to him and he leaned to whisper in her ear, "We're not letting anyone have you, *amanra*. No one."

She nodded, remaining silent. He hoped she believed him. After everything, she should.

"Then we'll take all of you," the Elvasi said, sneering. "Nets!"

Mat was tense now. Not the fucking nets. He hated the fucking nets. And they were all together, right where someone could easily toss at them.

Suddenly, one came out of the trees. He jumped out of the way and into Alchan, who had to push his brother away for space so they didn't all get knocked over. Right at that moment, several of the Elvasi began to push their attack again. Mat defended himself, trying to get back to Mave's side as he realized they were focusing on her.

Why do they want her so bad?

He didn't understand, but he could see it. It was plain as day, even in the dark night with only the faint red glow of the moon behind the storm clouds.

She fought viciously as he worked to get back to her. What she couldn't do was dodge a net and fight multiple Elvasi at once. The net took her to the ground, weighted and tangling into her wings and horns.

It felt like time slowed down as she struggled to get it off her, Elvasi grabbing it and yanking her around. She swung wildly, trying to cut the net. He was moving too slow. They were trying to get control over her. Her tail whipped around, trying to stop them as she fought against the net, but it didn't help, only tangling up in it.

She looked over to him in the dark and rain. Lightning flashed.

For the first time since he'd met her, he saw real fear in her eyes.

"MAT!" she screamed as one of the Elvasi grabbed the net and began to drag. Everyone was fighting their own battles, including himself, with an Elvasi jumping in front of him. He didn't waste a second, kicking the foe away and running for her until an arrow hit his thigh, making him roar in pain.

He nearly dropped to the ground trying to get to her. The Elvasi dragging her away was smart enough to avoid her hands. She was trying to cut through the net and kill him but she was tangled completely up in it now.

He was nearly there when Bryn came out of the trees and landed on the one dragging her, shoving his daggers into the weak points of the Elvasi's armor. Mat had never been more pleased to see him.

"Where have you been?" Mat asked, standing over Mave as Bryn and he met more Elvasi.

"Killing the ones in the trees," he answered, a growl on his voice. "They can't have her. She's ours."

"No, they can't," he agreed, seeing how Bryn was far past civilized. He'd known the other male was beginning to like her more than he wanted to admit. Now it was on display. Bryn was there to defend his female. Their female. At least in Mat's mind.

Together, they fought off the Elvasi, cutting down each foe foolish enough to get close. It felt like dozens, even hundreds. It felt like the battlefields of old, during the War. When he had to jump away from Mave to kill one, Bryn was there over her, snarling viciously to stop anyone else from getting close. When Bryn had to advance on one of their enemies, he took over. She continued to cut herself out, panting with exertion. He could tell she was scared. Skies, he would be scared too if he'd been netted in the middle of a fight.

They weren't going to let the Elvasi have her.

Suddenly, all but Varon were surrounding her. He saw it was Alchan who grabbed the net on her and dragged her closer to one of the remaining carts. They moved with him. Mat stayed within feet of her, refusing to let any of the Elvasi near her. Varon jumped down from his perch on the cart, beginning to untie her. Once she was out, she roared, jumping back into the fight. Mat felt chills run down his spine at the sound.

27

MAVE

There were times when Mave knew she was afraid. The net had been one of those times. She hadn't let it paralyze her, but she couldn't deny the fear.

So she used it to her advantage.

They can't have me! NEVER AGAIN.

The promise roared and echoed in her head as soon as her blade connected with the flesh of one of the Elvasi. She roared as loud as she could, taking out all of her fear and rage on the monsters who tried to drag her away into the dark.

If it hadn't been for the Company, they would have taken me.

She was enraged with herself too, just for that. With each swing, she took it out on the Elvasi, cutting them open, clashing steel with steel as they danced and dueled in the storm, lightning, and the very faint glow of the red moon.

The dark didn't bother her. She knew how to fight in the dark, having protected herself in the dark pits for so long.

They won't live to regret this night!

She roared again, bringing both her blades down on one of the

Elvasi. Blood sprayed out of the wounds she opened up on each side of her foe's neck.

One was able to stop her assault, blocking her swing. He also used two blades and cut at her with his free short sword. She blocked it and delivered a swift kick to one of his knees, aiming low so she could put him into the mud. He fell, and screamed as she swung down, beheading him with a single, powerful strike.

On it went, her rage fueling her when her body began to grow weak. There were so many of them. Every time she felt like they were making progress, another wave of them appeared.

"Varon!" Nevyn roared. She turned to see the mute go still, a net over him. He didn't struggle as the Elvasi advanced on him. She pushed back the one she was fighting and ran for him, cutting off the Elvasi advance on him. He still wasn't moving or struggling against the net.

"Move," she ordered over her shoulder, keeping her body between him and the enemy.

"He's trying not to tangle in the net too bad," Nevyn said quickly, working to cut the net. Bryn and Matesh were at her side next, then Alchan and Luykas. They held off the Elvasi until Varon was free.

And so the fighting continued. Alchan screamed out for them to look for any Elvasi with nets and take them down first. She jumped behind the enemy front line and went for them, knowing they were the real threats. It was Alchan who followed her, snarling with a viciousness she respected.

"Stay close!" Luykas roared over the sounds of the battle and rain. She glanced back, his white standing out in the night. He was still with the others. She and Alchan were the only ones who could jump through the front line of Elvasi to get to their targets.

"Stay with me," he ordered.

She nodded, going back to back with him. They killed another Elvasi who had a net and looking for an opening to toss it. A body dropped next to them unexpectedly. "Good hit, Varon!" Once they slew another, Alchan nudged her, his tail grabbing hers. "Back to the group!"

She didn't respond, only followed his lead, backing away from their enemies. They were beginning to get circled now, able to see the Elvasi try to get around behind them.

Mave was panting as she dueled with another Elvasi. She was no longer fresh enough to give them quick kills. Now every member of the Company was struggling, trying to cut down another without going down. They were lucky that they were made for war and carnage while the Elvasi weren't, not in the same way. That was all they had going for them. Increased stamina, increased strength and size. They had advantages, but they were dwindling.

A roar echoed from a distance. Mave roared in return, like the males. The sound rejuvenated them for a moment.

She danced and dueled with her two opponents, exchanging sharp cuts as they were all beginning to make small mistakes.

We're dying.

It felt inevitable now.

But at least we're going to die.

The ground shook as another roar sounded off, much closer to them. The Elvasi in front of her stumbled in shock at the sound and she took the chance, cutting him open from shoulder to hip. She took a hit because of it though, as her second enemy landed a clear hit to her ribs, carving her open and cracking a few of her bones.

She hissed and stumbled at the pain of the blow. She bumped into Luykas, also on his last leg when it came to energy. He was sluggish in recovering from her accidental body check. The only good thing was that the contact wasn't skin to skin so the bond couldn't distract her.

Another roar, and something crashed to the ground.

Mave nearly cried as Rain landed in the grove behind the Elvasi.

Illi bodyr, *I love you so much right now.*

Wyvern-Rain snapped out, grabbing an Elvasi by his torso and tossing the fool into a tree. The Elvasi began to scream in fear, trying to run instead of fight. She took the chance to attack another one, cutting him down. She was too tired to give chase for any others, though.

Rain wasn't. She jumped out of the way as the wyvern barreled over them and grabbed another Elvasi, chomping down. He swatted at two more, sending them to die against trees from an impact that made bone crunch.

Only a few Elvasi made it out of the grove, all of them watching the retreat and the wyvern taking out whatever it could.

It quieted quickly, Mave leaning over and grabbing her side. Once again, Rain saved the day with his wyvern form. Damn, it was impressively strong. She was mystified by the power of it.

And she was so grateful to know Rain in that moment. For everything, even this.

With a roar, Rain stomped around, the rain falling on him and bouncing off. It was an impressive sight as the lightning struck and the massive deep blue head turned on them. Even in the rain, smoke began to trail out of his nose, small licks of fire ready to burn everything.

He took a step closer. She couldn't see anything of her little brother in the beast now. A snarl made her shake. She had defeated many enemies in her lifetime. The chimera was the most dangerous. She couldn't stop a wyvern from killing them.

"Rain. Shift back." Alchan's order were the first words any of them dared to speak.

Rain's wyvern bent and did as it was told. She watched bones rearrange and crunch into the young male she knew, who went to his knees on the blood-soaked dirt.

"I tried to control him. I tried to make sure he didn't destroy anything," Rain said quickly, panting. "It was hard. He wanted to set the whole damned forest on fire."

"You did good, young male. You did good," Alchan told him, leaning over to pat his shoulder. Mave could see an impressed light in their leader's eyes. He was probably already plotting how to continue to use Rain's wyvern form in the future.

She had a sneaking suspicion that even though Luykas and Zayden were against using the form, Alchan was more than willing to use it as much as he could. She had to fight a rush of protectiveness for her little brother. He was a warrior in the Company and Alchan was one of their leaders. She would have to trust them to make those decisions in the future.

"Where are your father and my uncle?" Mat demanded.

"I left them alone on the road. We had Elvasi chasing us and we weren't going to make it, so I took care of them. Then I came back here. Someone will need to tell them to come back so we can keep moving." Rain reported it like a good soldier. Mave's chest filled with pride.

"Who can fly?" Luykas asked loudly, looking around. She looked around as well. In the dark, she could see he was favoring a wing while the other had a small droop to it. Mat's wings were limp-looking and she touched one, wondering if she felt blood or water. They were all injured, it seemed.

Varon just jumped into the sky, leaving them in the grove.

"I guess he's doing it," Alchan muttered, looking up to where the mute had flown up. "I love it when you all take initiative and just get shit done."

They stood awkwardly after that, looking around at the dead in the dark. Mave was beginning to feel lightheaded, and she wasn't sure it was from blood loss. Something felt satisfied in her, as if she had just had the best meal of her life. Or the best sex. She felt supremely content and nearly happy, even though they had just been about to die.

She leaned on Mat, a small smile probably making her seem ridiculous. She watched Bryn begin to walk around the dead, searching their pockets. Without being asked, Nevyn and Alchan joined him. Luykas threw some pants to Rain, then they were all searching the dead except her and Mat.

Slowly, they got back to normal. Except her. She was feeling incredibly odd. Was it because she was happy to be alive and free still?

"Are you okay?" Mat asked her softly. "We need to treat everyone's injuries, like that one." He pointed to the slice on her ribs. She had practically forgotten about it, since it wasn't life threatening.

"She's blood-high," Bryn muttered, shaking his head. "Happens every so often - ya know that, Matesh. We Andinna love a good fight."

"You know, that makes sense." Mat chuckled, pulling her closer to him. She felt his absolutely straining-hard cock against her hip now. This was the second time she was covered in blood and so was he, and his cock wanted attention. "I'm pretty sure we all are."

"Is that what this was?" She waved around at the dead Elvasi. "A good fight? I never quite felt this way when I was a gladiator."

Bryn nodded. "Ya never fought a good fight as a gladiator. Those aren't good. They're tiresome. This…this was a good fight. We should have lost, but we proved ourselves to be better against a larger force in a real battle. Ya really never felt this way before?"

"Well, when I fought in the tavern that Nevyn and Varon took me to, sort of." She took a deep breath. Nevyn nodded to himself, as if he had done something right that night and this proved it.

"We're warrior people, Mave. Ya have to like being a warrior. We like the fight, the good fight. At least ya aren't male." He began to chuckle humorously.

"Why's that?"

"Ya don't get aroused by it. Well, maybe ya do, but not like us." He waved over the front of himself. "We do, if it really riles us up."

"Ah…I knew about that. Just didn't know why males were always so… male after killing someone." Trying not to look down at his cock, she waved a hand at what he was doing, still searching through the pockets of the dead. "You find anything yet?" She failed, her eyes sliding a bit to see the outline in the front of his breeches. For how lean he was, she hadn't expected the size she was greeted with. Her eyes flicked back up as fast as she could make them, which wasn't very quick.

He's not my type, but…

Didn't I just make a joke before dinner about his hands? What is wrong with me? Stop staring at him and taunting him, Mave. He's not your male.

"Aye. Have any of you found anything?" Bryn looked over to the other males, ignoring her blatant look. It wasn't the first time she had sized them up in that sort of way, but it was the first time she did it for the specific purpose of looking at the size of one of their cocks. She felt a little bad for it.

Even though she was thoroughly impressed by the one on her hip, thanks to Mat, and the one she just saw from Bryn, she knew she shouldn't be looking at any of them like that. Not with what they had just gone through. She worked harder to keep her eyes at chest level, at least, as they began talking about what was on the dead.

"Only some change on most of these," Nevyn said, rolling over another body. "We can take all their weapons and shit. There's no reason not to loot them."

"Aye." Bryn said, going back to turning out pockets of the dead. She helped, with Mat by her side.

They continued to work, Alchan glaring at them. When Varon came back with Zayden and Leshaun, he rushed to them, getting a report on Leshaun's injuries, but then came back, opening his mouth. She knew they were about to get told off. She could see it on his face.

"I want all of you tending your damned injuries!" Alchan snapped. "Worry about the dead in a minute."

"None of us are bleeding out," Mat said, sighing. She eyed him. His wings were limp, but in the dark, she couldn't tell where the blood was coming from on him. "We'll be fine."

"Look here, Matesh. When I say tend your-"

"I found somethin'," Bryn cut in, growling. "Forget the injuries for a minute, Alchan."

"What is it?" Mave didn't miss how Alchan's attention immediately went to Bryn without so much as a grumble. The *bedru's* complaints about their injuries dropped in a second.

Bryn pulled out one of his daggers and pinned something to a tree for them.

"Oh shit. Ten thousand gold suns." Alchan sounded sick.

"Never seen a bounty that high…" Nevyn was shaking his head.

Mave walked closer and found herself staring at a face she knew well.

Hers.

28

MAVE

Mave felt all of her blood leave her head. Staring back at her was her without her *tatua*. Underneath was a large bounty, one that defied reason.

The fear rushed back. The desperate plea began to echo in her mind again. The net and everything that came from it was on the forefront again. No longer was she pleased with how they handled the Elvasi.

Now she just wanted to fall to her knees and process this new piece of information.

No. No, she can't have me back.

"By the Skies," Luykas whispered. "Ten thousand gold suns for the return of Empress Shadra's property."

"They moved fast," Bryn said with a snarl. "The entire continent probably has this bounty now. Fucking Empire sorcery. This was an ambush to take her! To take all of us! We were going to make them fucking rich, just like they said!"

"Sorcery is right. She must have put the word out and had an artist make this up within days of our escape. This would have been circulating here for weeks now." Luykas reached out and touched the blood-stained parchment.

"And we paraded Mave through the streets," Nevyn added. "We confirmed who she was during our night out."

This is my fault. That realization slammed in her, making her desperately begin to find a way to fix it. She had to fix this.

"Fucking Skies!" Zayden exclaimed, looking the bounty poster over.

"What?" Alchan snapped suddenly, turning a glare on Nevyn. "You did what? Why didn't anyone fucking tell me earlier that you outed her identity back in Namur?"

"Varon and I took her to the docks for fights. We confirmed she was the Champion when some Elvasi piece of shit asked, saying he'd heard rumors. I don't remember the exact conversation - I was more excited for her to put him on his ass. She did, by the way. It led to more trouble later in the night." Nevyn groaned. "Fuck!"

"And it led to this!" Alchan roared. "They were here for her!"

Mave growled at their leader, who growled back.

"Not now, you two," Luykas snapped. "Alchan, find a better way to say it."

"It's not her fault - it's just that Nevyn should have known better. You all should have known better than to let people know she was the Champion. You should have known!" Alchan threw something, but she couldn't identify what it was. "Now we're going to be hunted down!"

"We need to hunt back," Bryn cut in. "We need to go after these sons of bitches! We can't run off to the village and hide! They're goin' to come after us. We need to show them we can fight back! We need them to think the bounty is too dangerous to go after!"

"I'm with Bryn." Matesh snarled. "They've never been stupid enough to come after us. We can't let this stand!"

"We're going to get ourselves killed if we start picking these sorts of fights in this shape," Alchan said, growling back. "And I'm in charge of this Company. The only person here who gets to back-talk me is Luykas."

Suddenly, it was an all-out argument. Mave watched as Bryn and Mat went against Alchan, yelling about how they needed to strike back and get the Elvasi for putting out the bounty. Nevyn tried pulling Bryn back, only to get snapped at.

Find a solution, Mave. This is your fault. You brought this on them.

Luykas stepped next to Mave, also watching. Rain and Zayden jumped in next, adding their voices to the fray. She could tell Rain was on her side, but Zayden was just trying to keep his son quiet. She could see Alchan was beginning to lose his patience, his face becoming red, causing an impressive contrast with his black tatua.

"What do you think?" the mutt asked calmly. "Do we go after them and get revenge for this, or do you think we should go to the village and keep our heads down? They're after you. I think it should be your call."

"Weren't you saying that the planned raid is against an Elvasi merchant who supports the Elvasi who do this sort of thing?" She was already thinking about it. She didn't know what her idea would be, but she could feel some inkling of an idea.

"I did." He offered no more information.

"What if we just follow the plan? We make a run by the village, a shorter one." She was beginning to feel the rage. Luykas was right. They were after her. They wanted her back in the Empire, back with the Empress. She tried to keep thinking about the plan forming in her head. "We will need to drop off Leshaun and Rain."

"He'll survive and is already in his healing sleep in the back of the cart. He'll heal slower, so you're right. He needs to go to the village." Luykas sounded genuinely concerned for the old male, but also hopeful.

"How far to the village from here?" She'd forgotten in the mess of things.

"Once we're in the mountains, it'll be quick. The village is close to the border." Luykas was simply giving her more information.

"Then we hit this merchant who funds these Elvasi. We hit hard. We ruin him. We kill him if we can. We fight back at a time that's safest, without being weighed down by all of this. We walk away with all of his goods." She waved to the carts of supplies. "Then we're in a win-win situation. Right? We're mercenaries and we need the supplies, but we hit harder than we planned, to prove we're not to be messed with." She would get the blood she craved. She wasn't going to be a victim to the Elvasi, not any more. They couldn't have her. She would kill every one of them in Olost if she had to.

I'm never going back.

"The guy we planned to hit might not be the one behind this," Luykas casually reminded her. He seemed so calm, so helpful. She nearly wanted to strangle him.

"So? All Elvasi are the enemy and we still need his supplies for winter, or so I've heard from you all." She didn't see a problem. Who cares where the Elvasi came from? If this one was funding their type of hunting, trying to capture her, attack the Company, and enslave their people, who cared?

The smile Luykas gave her was brilliant. Then he turned to the Company right as Alchan roared and went for Matesh. "ATTENTION ON ME!" Luykas roared at the top of his lungs.

In a second, Alchan was off Matesh, leaving her male on the ground, but unharmed. Everyone else snapped to attention.

With everyone silent, Luykas looked back at her. "Tell them your idea."

With a deep breath, she explained the reasoning she came to. She wasn't sure why Luykas was leaving it up to her, but as she spoke, she could see a light in his eyes, as if she was doing something right. Mat was watching her with a growing smile. Others were just nodding, hearing the reason of her words.

When she was done, it was Alchan who spoke first.

"Best idea anyone has had in over a fucking month," he muttered. "Everyone, get fucking moving. Treat injuries and let's get all of our horses back. Make sure they're okay. Claim the Elvasi horses if you can."

Andinna jumped into action, cleaning up the camp site. Alchan stomped towards her and Luykas. She raised her chin, ready to face him down.

Something soft passed over his face, though. "Your father would be proud of that," he said, nodding respectfully to her and extending a hand. She took it slowly. "He was always a level-headed man when it came to a problem as well."

"Thank you," she said, swallowing a lump of emotion she wasn't expecting. Pride?

"You know, Alchan, it sucks that it's Mave, but at least it isn't you." Nevyn walked over next, shrugging.

Alchan snarled, looking over his shoulder at the older male. "Don't go there."

"Why would it be worse for Alchan to be the one they're after?" She wanted an answer. Everyone began to shift around uncomfortably. She suddenly realized there was a secret, one they had been keeping from her this entire time. It pissed her off. "Tell me! I'm Company, so I deserve to know what everyone else does!"

"Tell her," Luykas said, cutting in again. "Alchan, it's time. Just tell her."

Alchan growled, looking her over. She waited, upset that after all of this, over a month knowing all of them, there was a big secret they were obviously keeping. One they all knew. Mat looked down from her and so did Rain.

They all know something.

"There's a rule in the Company that this is ignored. I'm one of the Company leaders first and foremost. I go by Alchan. I wanted to be treated normally. The guys, they all understand this. You need to as well."

"Okay?" She frowned, unsure as to what Alchan was talking about. Was this rule why they never told her? "What sort of thing could possibly-"

"My name is Alchan Andini and I'm the King of the Andinna. The *ruling* King. The Company is considered my royal guard in the eyes of the Andinna. That includes you now. I hadn't wanted to say anything until I was sure you were ready to hear it."

Mave was certain she didn't hear that right. Alchan still wore his standard, somewhat angry expression.

"What?" She barely got the word out. This wasn't the shock she was expecting right on the back of finding out she was the most wanted Andinna in the known world.

"The royal family is normally led by females, because we're matriarchal. I'm the sole pureblood survivor. At the time the War began, I was the grandson of the reigning Queen. My father was her oldest child, her son. I was sixth in line for the throne, thanks to being a male born from a male. I was considered one of the last options to ever inherit the throne. Now I'm all that's left."

Mave opened and closed her mouth more times than she could really count. She looked around at the Company. None of them seemed surprised.

None of them had acted like this grouch was a *king*. *The* King.

He was just Alchan, the *bedru* with a bad attitude that barked orders. She challenged him on a constant basis and they never got along.

She was challenging the fucking *King*. She was fighting with and against the fucking *King*.

He must have seen something that gave away what she was thinking because he snapped his fingers in her face. She bit back a snarl, realizing she couldn't do that to him. "Remember what I just said, Mave. Here in the Company, my title isn't important. I'm one of two leaders of the Ivory Shadows Mercenary Company and nothing more. I go by Alchan, and, *if* things are dangerous, sir. I don't acknowledge the title outside the mountains. There's no place for an Andinna king away from the Andinna. Everyone who sees me outside of the mountains that's not in the Company calls me sir, not sire." He sighed, turning away from her to stare at Luykas.

"I told you this would happen. Now she's going to be holding back."

"Mave?" Luykas walked closer to her. "Are you going to be okay with this? He's still just Alchan. The asshole you don't like."

"He's..." She tried to hold back a growl. She had bad experiences with royalty. That overrode her small fear and regret at her behavior. Suddenly, she was mad. She was expected to follow orders from another piece of royal shit. "No wonder you're an overbearing prick. You probably get everything you damned well could ever want thanks to having that sort of title to throw around."

"By the fucking Skies," Zayden mumbled. "She really didn't just say that, did she?"

"She did, *bodra*. She really did." Rain sounded downright fearful.

"She's a ballsy bitch," Nevyn added lightly, almost appreciating it.

Alchan glared and she held the gaze now. Fuck if he was the King. She had her fair share of experience dealing with royalty. If he expected her to fall in line with him because of his title, he had another thing fucking coming.

"You'll have to behead me if you think I'm going to play bitch," she continued. "I dare you to try."

It was Luykas who started to chuckle first, breaking out into a full-bellied laugh within a few seconds. Zayden was next, Rain following him, and Nevyn and Varon were at the front, snickering. Bryn and Mat were last, Mat hiding his face. Bryn pulled his scarf up but it didn't cover the sound.

Alchan dared to smirk. "Thank the Skies. I was worried you would become a supplicant when I need a warrior. For your information, Mave, I've never used my rank to get a damned thing. I trained at your father's knee so I could become a military commander. I worked my way up through the ranks of the army just like everyone else. Don't ever accuse me of that again."

"So you won't get pissy if I challenge you?" She knew now she was never going to be able to stop. King or not, she couldn't resist meeting his eyes and hoping he would one day back down. She wanted everyone to turn their eyes down to her, though. It wasn't an Alchan-specific problem.

"I'm always pissy when you challenge me." He scoffed but the smirk didn't leave. "But don't disobey an order - and that's from your Company commander, not the King. Here's the first order: get those ribs tended. Don't try to play tough. I hate it when you fuckers play tough and only get in worse shape. Ask any of them."

She watched him walk away, and once he was out of ear shot, she turned a glare on Mat.

"Why did no one tell me this earlier? He could have killed me."

"What's really bothering ya?" Bryn asked. "The fact that you've been challenging the King, or that you were once owned by the Empress and now work for the King?"

She wasn't really sure which was worse and she didn't like how observant Bryn was. She shouldn't be challenging a king, especially not this one. Even as she had been telling herself to be scared of him, to stop, she challenged him. She had no control over herself, that much was apparent.

"I don't know," she answered. "He's really not that bad?" She was trying to separate her idea of nobility and royalty from the grouchy, pissed-off *bedru* she had to deal with every day. His attitude made her worry he really was like the Elvasi, which only pissed her off. *How do I trust this asshole now? I know what royalty can do with their power.*

"Something you'll have to see for yourself," Mat said gently. "He's just Alchan here. Do you see any of us groveling? Skies, Bryn and I started a fight with him. Rain joined in. He's not having us beaten. I think he'll give us guard duty in the village over the winter. It's his favorite punishment and an easy one. Keeps us sharp when we're not on a mission."

She nodded, accepting that.

"I'll be fine," she finally said, everything weighing heavily on her mind. She would need time to process this. If it was something they ignored in the Company, she would need to see him with other Andinna. Was he domineering and mean? Did he use his position to get what he wanted out of others - sex, currency, or anything else? *I have to see. Until then, I'll withhold judgment.*

It was the best she could do with the new piece of information just thrust in her lap. Analyze it, wait, then act. She didn't survive a thousand years of the Empress by acting impulsively.

"Everyone, we're moving out after breakfast!" Alchan called out, sitting down on a log. The rain was still coming down on them, but it was slowing. While she had been learning about him, some of the Company had been rounding up their horses. She grabbed her own bowl of soup for breakfast and sat next to Mat, lost in thought as she ate.

29

LUYKAS

It had been a bloody night, evidenced by the scene at dawn as they ate breakfast and tended their wounds. Arrows stuck out of trees. Cuts across tree trunks marked where people had missed their attacks. The carts were generally okay, but Luykas' eyes fell to the puddle of blood that had come from someone. They had moved the bodies away from their things, towards the road, a warning for anyone foolish enough to try again. The dead were the best signal they had now.

Luykas hadn't been expecting to get harassed by Elvasi so quickly after they arrived back in Olost. He'd known it was going to happen eventually, but right before they made it back into the mountains? It was so fast. They had to be getting pushed hard by their backers to find more Andinna and capture them, to capture Mave.

There's no other reason. They've never been bold enough to put an ambush on the road for us like this. They had to be the reason the trees were down.

It reminded him of when they once actively tried to free slaves and the Empress would retaliate. It disturbed him on a deep, resounding level that he couldn't quite voice. Looking across camp at his brother, he knew Alchan felt the same. There was a tenseness to his brother, an anguish that couldn't be helped. Alchan was looking back on the mission they just did to save Matesh and Rainev, how they took Mave along, and was thinking about all the mistakes they had made.

And now, brother, we're going to go pick a fight with them again. We can't let this go unpunished. They need to know the Ivory Shadows aren't victims.

Then there was Mave. Luykas watched her now, seeing her help clean up as some of them ate. She was a solid warrior. She'd jumped into the fight without hesitation, as he and Alchan had expected of her. She hadn't disobeyed orders or deviated. When they had taken her down, she'd trusted them enough to call for help and have backup.

Seeing her work out the problem while the males argued? It was something her mother and father used to do. It was why those two had risen through the ranks to the power they had before the War. It wasn't a particularly difficult solution to come to, but he had wanted her to have the time to come to it on her own. He wanted to see if she had the mind for it.

"How do you feel about this?" Alchan asked, walking over. Together, they walked away from the Company for a private talk. They weren't followed. "I'm not liking how fast we were attacked. I don't like how big that bounty is."

"I was thinking the exact same thing."

"Freeing her changed everything, didn't it?" Alchan sighed. "You know I don't think this is her fault, right?"

"I do. You think it's mine." Luykas crossed his arms, waiting for his brother to confirm his suspicion. "Since I was the one who said we should free her in exchange for the human and Elvasi's help." He hadn't thought about those two in a long time, since they left the Empire that night. He knew they were both probably dead, and that was probably also a little of his fault.

"Just a little. Too late now, and we can't go back in time." Alchan eyed the Company as they loaded everything up. "She's a good addition, though. She probably saved Leshaun's life tonight, getting to him when she did. She, Zayden, and Rain are the reasons that old male is alive."

"I agree."

"Here I am, giving her some credit, and you aren't jumping for joy." His brother snorted. "She's not...so bad, I guess."

"What do you want me to say?" Luykas threw his arms up. "We both already knew she was a skilled warrior. We both already knew she would follow our orders if it came to it. She didn't ask for any of this either, Alchan." Luykas conceded one thing, though. "You're right about Nevyn. He should have kept her identity more secret in Namur. They shouldn't have bragged about it. He might not have taken her out fighting either. He gets rowdy in the fighting rings and with only Varon keeping him and Mave under control, something was bound to come of it."

"I'm glad you don't think I was out of line there." Alchan whistled. "Matesh, Brynec, come here."

"Well, all right then," Luykas mumbled, shaking his head. "You need to do this right now?"

"Yes. You really think I should put it off?"

"No, but..." Luykas groaned, turning away to not look at the two males about to have their asses handed to them. Those two knew better than to pick a fight with Alchan, their damned King, like that. Luykas wasn't in the mood to deal with it yet, but that didn't change the facts. "Let's get this done."

He didn't call Rain over. He must want to take that to Zayden for a discussion.

"You can soften it," Alchan told him. "But only a little."

Luykas snorted. He didn't really want to soften it, which was the problem. He normally played the good guy for the Company when Alchan needed to rail on them for something. Right now, he was feeling Alchan was going to go too soft on them, tired from the night. Luykas had an idea. Turning back around, he saw the two males in question were now closer; they came to a stop at attention in front of them.

"You two know what you did wrong?" he asked softly.

"Yes sir," they answered in unison.

"Good," Alchan growled. "When we settle in the village for winter, you'll be putting in three days a week on patrols each until the spring festival. Don't bitch about it or I'll make it the next three winters."

"Four days," Luykas cut in. It was only proper. They argued with a commanding officer, and that was ignoring who Alchan was, not taking into consideration they had argued, then *fought*, with their King.

"Three," Alchan repeated. "Three, because I don't want their female coming after me for not having any males."

"I'm not-" Bryn tried to back-talk and Luykas reached out, smacking his gut before he could finish.

"Now isn't the time," Luykas growled out. "You acted like she was your female, and now you're going to live with the consequences. But if you want four patrols a week, I'll make it happen behind Alchan's back."

"Yes sir," Bryn muttered, looking down.

"Get out of here, both of you," Alchan ordered. Once their warriors were gone, his brother turned on him. "I said you could soften the punishment, not make it worse. What was that, Luykas?"

"Sometimes, the Company needs to see you as the good guy," Luykas whispered back, knowing only Varon would hear him. He knew his brother wanted an explanation, and Luykas knew what he had done. It was a solid plan, in his mind. "Because you can't be the bad guy all the time, not in your position, especially not as we draw closer to the mountains. The other Andinna can't see you as a dictator who judges harshly and needs an *Elvasi mutt* to pull you back from hurting your people."

Alchan nodded slowly. "I see your reasoning. I don't like it, but I see it." Alchan sighed, rubbing the back of his neck. "I'm glad she's still got a bite to her now that she knows."

"You said you were worried and I thought you didn't need to be."

Luykas was sure not to add the classic 'I told you so' line, but it was there between his words.

"I hate it, but yeah. I can't trust you males to know when to fight against me. Look at today. Bryn and Mat knew we would have worked something out, but they picked a fight with me anyway."

"You were pretty upset." He wasn't going to let his brother live down his part in that.

"It was a gut reaction. I wasn't going to make a decision right at that moment." His brother shoved his hands into his pockets. "But having a dominant female around, one who isn't afraid to snap and snarl and be my equal, or close to it? It might make the other females and Andinna more comfortable with my position. I don't want her to change."

"You've been thinking a lot about this." Luykas was impressed.

"I bitch and complain a lot, but that doesn't mean I'm an idiot. I just like to vocalize my dislike for…everything." Alchan smirked. "Think they're ready to move out?"

With that, the conversation dropped. Luykas was still feeling impressed with Alchan as they got the Company moving. He was giving himself a balance. Luykas had no aspirations that his brother and Mave would ever get along, not really, but it was a start. Alchan wanted her to frustrate him, and Luykas had a sneaking suspicion Mave was never going to give a damn about the title Alchan carried around. She looked at him like being King made him the dirt under her boot, really.

"Has everyone eaten?" Luykas asked loudly. He saw Mave scarfing down several bites, her mouth stuffed. He didn't say anything, knowing she would never eat in front of them again if he did, but she still ate like a starving child. It was cute, in his opinion. He hated it, because of where it came from, but it was cute.

She waved a hand and dumped the rest of her bowl. There was very little left in it. He nodded to Alchan the moment she did that. A signal it was time.

"Move out!" Alchan roared. "Let's get on the road! I want us at the village as fast as possible!"

"The bodies?" Mave asked, seeming curious but not challenging. "Do we just leave them near the road?"

Alchan nodded. "That's exactly what we do. A very clear message to anyone else who wants to cause us trouble."

"Okay." Luykas wanted to laugh as the female shrugged. He watched her go back to Bryn on the cart, jumping up and taking her seat gingerly.

Something about her seemed a little different. Something seemed more confident, more secure. A little more like her parents, who were always so confident and secure in their decisions and how they walked through the world. He had seen her fear when the net was on her, but it was long gone now. Now there was a resolve in her eyes he'd seen when they were trying to escape.

Then there was Bryn next to her, which made him want to laugh. The male looked like he was doomed, trying to shrink and hide from his fate. He subtly shifted closer to her so their knees touched, breaking Mave out of whatever thoughts she had. She pulled her knee away, looking like she thought it was her fault they touched.

"He's so into her," Luykas muttered. Not like he could blame the lean rogue. Mave was something else, a female that demanded the attention of males, even without realizing it. He turned back to the tree and saw Bryn's dagger still holding the bounty there.

"Brynec, are you going to get this?" he asked mildly.

"No."

"Why not?"

"So whoever finds this knows why it happened," he growled out.

Luykas couldn't argue with that. They were going to get the Elvasi back for this. This was crossing an unspoken line they had maintained for a thousand years. No one tested the Company like this. They couldn't allow it to continue.

He swung onto his gelding and began the ride to the village with the rest of the Company.

30

MAVE

At midday, they were all still feeling the excitement of the night before. Mave listened to the males talk rapidly about their plans. The Elvasi thought they could take Mave back? Every one of them said the same thing. It was never going to happen. They would protect her to the death.

She couldn't help but think she truly belonged in those moments. They wanted to keep her, and they were going to fight with her to cripple the Elvasi organization in the area.

"So why has the Company never attacked this guy before?" she asked Bryn next to her. He refused to leave her side now. She needed to take a piss at one point, and he'd followed her with Mat. It had been the most uncomfortable thing she'd ever been through, at least in her recent freedom.

"We have." Bryn shrugged. "We've hit him a few times, actually, but different places he owns. He's easy to steal from. The thing is, hittin' too hard means the Elvasi hit back harder. Right now, we're willin' to take that risk, where we weren't before. They escalated, so we will."

"Oh." She nodded, absorbing what he said.

"We aren't lettin' 'em take you back, Mave. Not in our lifetimes." Bryn elbowed her. "You're Company and we fight for Company, remember?"

"I do," she promised. She still wasn't used to this idea of comradery. She was getting better with it every day.

Her mind kept going back to that moment the net hit her. She had been fighting the Elvasi, who were trying to capture or kill her. When their enemies had asked for her, she'd been shocked. When Alchan had denied them, she'd been pleased, glad that her cranky leader was loyal to her. It reinforced that she needed to be loyal to him, even without the added pressure of him being their King.

But all of that had been shadowed by the fear that took hold of her when the net hit her. The fucking net.

There were very few times in her life when she had experienced being netted and trapped. The nets used by the Elvasi were designed to get the Andinna tangled and stuck. They were weighted around the edges, making them heavy enough to knock someone down when they were thrown.

The first time in a net she could remember was when she tried to escape the pits and Elliar. The night she had tried to fly and failed. They had netted her then, and she had known in that moment that she had no hope of ever leaving.

That one had been the worst. They had beaten her. They had nearly torn off her wings. By the strange mercy of the Empress, she was spared, but it had been thanks to a loophole. She hadn't gotten off the ground. Her wings had been useless for her, so it wasn't a problem for her to keep them.

During the fight, she had been paralyzed for a moment by the fear, the old memories taking her back to that moment. She had screamed for the one male she knew she could trust. Matesh. She had hoped whatever they had was enough for him to risk everything to save her.

He'd come for her.

It had been enough for her to start trying to think of ways out.

Then Bryn had come for her. She looked at him from the corner of her eye. He'd charged up and protected her as well.

Then the Company had come. Every available male had put their bodies between her and capture. Alchan, of all the damned people, had been the one to pull her back closer to safety when she couldn't free herself.

The damned King of their people had protected and fought to keep *her*. Her, the reason they lost the War. The reason his entire family was dead and he was King and not one of his family. The reason they were all stuck in Olost and not in Anden, their home.

They had protected her.

She wasn't sure she could find the words to express to them what that had meant to her. She had been too shocked by the bounty to think of it afterwards.

But in the quiet morning the next day? She couldn't stop thinking about it. Did they know and just didn't want to say anything? Did they think she didn't care and had expected it of them? They had saved her from going back to her hell, and her throat closed up every time she thought about it. Even thinking about the prospect of their mission made her realize she was one of them, not some outsider. They were going to get back at these Elvasi for coming after her, a member of the Company.

It was quiet for the rest of the day, as the trip began to take its daily toll on them. The sun was dying, and the Company was exhausted. Mave knew how to trek on, having been this tired every day she lived in the pits. Was it frustrating? Of course, but she didn't complain even as others started.

Later in the day, Leshaun woke up and began bitching about how the cart hadn't stopped bouncing for hours. It was Rainev who was bold enough to tell him what had happened after he was hurt and while he was in his healing sleep, causing Leshaun to try and get up.

"They came after her? We're going to get them for it, right?" he asked, demanding an answer with that old male tone that everyone winced at.

"You need to heal, *bodyra*," Mat replied. "Please lie back down and relax. We'll explain more when we get to the village."

"Yeah, you've got it good," Nevyn said, teasing and annoyed at the same time. "You're back there all comfortable while we're the ones who haven't slept in a day. We haven't had the chance for the healing sleep yet."

Soon, the entire caravan was loud again, like it had been all through the night and most of the day.

"We're damned near there. All of you-" Alchan had started up on another evening of telling everyone to shut up when he was cut off.

"Well, I'll be damned!" a male voice called out. "The mercenaries are back!"

"Kian?" Mat said the name like a hushed prayer.

"Show yourself, you scoundrel!" Luykas called out.

Mave sat up, even daring to stand up when no one told her to stop. Walking out of the woods around them, ahead of the caravan, was a male Andinna. He wore only a pair of leather breeches and boots. She could see he was a pureblood, with the massive black wings and matching horns, tail, and *tatua*. He was as broad as Zayden, but nearly as tall as Matesh.

"That's Kian?" she asked Bryn, who whooped in excitement. Suddenly, she was flung back into her seat on the cart's front bench as it began to move again. The entire Company was pushing forward up the dirt road.

"Aye, that's Kian," Bryn finally answered her.

"Give me a status report! I've been sitting on my ass for weeks! We don't even hear rumors down here in the mountains." Kian jumped onto a cart and sat next to Nevyn, causing Mave to lose sight of him. "Why do you look like you're all limping from a fight?"

"We got Rain and Mat back from the Empire with no casualties other than Mat's horn," Nevyn told him loud enough for everyone to hear. "We also picked up a new member of the Company. We were attacked last night. The Elvasi set up an ambush. We'll explain all of it when we get to the village. It's a mess, *oto ildan*."

So, he's a friend of Nevyn, an old friend. If he's anything like Nevyn, I might get along with him.

"A new member? Who? And precious, perfect Mat broke a horn? He's probably still nursing his ego over it, I bet."

Mat groaned on his horse.

She couldn't see him, which meant he couldn't see her. She was dying to introduce herself to this new male. It was a strange change from when she was avoiding the Company when she met most of them.

"She's with Bryn on another cart. Take a look." Nevyn laughed as Kian stood up, causing Alchan to sputter and tell him to sit down. She could see him looking over the cart and his eyes fell on her. She dared to raise a hand and wave.

"Well, I'll be damned," Kian said with a grin. He jumped up, causing that cart to rock under the force, and flew back to her, Bryn, and Mat, landing next to the cart swiftly enough to spook their horses. "I'm Kian." He extended a hand up to her. "And you are?"

"Mave. I go by Mave," she answered, taking his hand in an Andinna handshake where they grabbed each other's elbows.

"And what's your story? How did they end up with three when they only intended to save two?" Kian looked her over curiously.

"Rain and I were thrown into the Colosseum in Elliar and met her in the pits with the other gladiators. It's a story, Kian," Mat answered, reaching down to pat Kian's shoulder. "How's the family?"

"Tired of having me around so much. They've been hoping you all survived so you can get me out of their hair. Nice break! The females will love you even more now, the poor things."

"I'm with Mave-" Mat wasn't able to finish as others began to break into the conversation.

"Pissing off your *amanra?*" Nevyn asked, laughing from his cart. Bryn pulled their cart up beside Nevyn and Varon's, leaving Rain and Zayden in the back. Mat and Kian were between them, looking between the two groups. Even Alchan and Luykas were looking back, waiting to hear what Kian had to say.

"Of course, but that's really all. The village is boring. Tell me more about how this mission happened." He quickly asked her something in Andena and she only caught a couple of words, like female.

"She doesn't know Andena well enough. You'll need to ask her in Common," Mat explained quickly. She tried not to feel a little embarrassed at the way Kian's eyebrows went up.

"And here I thought I should switch over to Andena, since we're in the mountains and she might know it better than Common. We don't use a lot of Common in the village, Mat."

"We're working on it," Luykas commented. "Just stick to Common for now."

Kian shrugged. "Well, I was saying maybe you should tell me everything, Mave. You're the new one and you seem to be in the middle of all of this."

"I had nothing to do with Mat and Rain showing up in the pits," she said, hoping he didn't have that sort of impression.

"No, I want to know how you met these assholes and ended up free with them." Kian smiled. "My *amanra* is going to be excited another female is coming to the village, especially a warrior. We haven't seen a new female join the community in over a century."

"Oh...well..." She tried to find a decent way to explain.

"Let's leave it for later tonight and I'll tell you everything. There's no reason to make her rehash it all when she had to live through the worst of it," Luykas cut in, saving her from the spotlight. "Let's talk about more pressing things. We're not settling in the village until later, Kian. You up for a mission?"

"I always am," Kian answered. "What's the job?"

"We were attacked last night, right on the border of the mountains, like Nevyn told you. That's where we learned something important. Mave here..." Alchan nodded to her. "She's ten thousand gold suns. Preferred alive."

Kian coughed, thumping his chest as the information processed. "And what's the mission, Alchan?"

"We're going to hit back. There's that merchant we've been eyeing for a few years, the one we've stolen from a few times. He helps fund anti-Andinna sentiment here in Olost and supplies the hunters. We're going to destroy him. No playing around this time. They tried to take Mave from us, nets and everything. We're going to raze them from the earth for it."

"I'm ready. You just say the word. What else is pressing?"

"We've got supplies for the village and we're going to winter there, so things need to start getting prepped now. Think you can run ahead and let them know we're close? We're bringing in wounded."

"Yeah. If you pick up speed, you'll be there before the evening meal ends. See you back at home." Kian took off without another word, suddenly serious, probably thanks to hearing about Leshaun's state. Mave watched him fly up higher, becoming a black dot, and race off, disappearing from view.

"He's interesting," she commented mildly.

"Kian is an old friend of Nevyn and Varon. Those three all joined the Company right as the War ended," Bryn explained. "He's also the only Company male with an *amanra* and the only member of a *mayara*. Was." He looked pointedly at Matesh.

"I'd caught that. He has a female. She has two other males, right?" She was pretty sure she hadn't heard that wrong whenever they brought up Kian.

"That's right. He's a lot like Nevyn, so he can get a little wild. Be careful drinking around him. He likes to take people down, drinking them under the table. He's normally the one who gets Mat so drunk that Nevyn can mess with him."

"I swear, Andinna turn three thousand and they go crazy," Mat said with a chuckle. "Well, Mave, you've officially met everyone in the Company. What do you think?"

"I think I need a pint," she answered. It caused Mat, Bryn, and several other males to begin laughing.

She was about to see her people free. Even if she hadn't met Kian, she could have used a drink to relax her just at that prospect.

And Kian's reaction to her? He hadn't questioned the idea of her being a new member of the Company. He'd just started a conversation, willing to get to know her. He didn't even balk at the idea of risking the Company in the effort to keep the Elvasi from coming after her. He was instantly for it.

She wasn't used to comradery, but she realized she enjoyed it.

31

ALCHAN

It was good to see Kian before they made it back to the village. Even on the back of an attack.

It also brought up some questions for him.

"Why do you think Kian was on patrol by himself? Think there's been some trouble? Other than the trouble we had?" He didn't like the idea of Elvasi so close to the mountains. That was a serious problem.

"I think he's been waiting on us every day because his wife hates having him around for too long," Luykas answered, laughing. "Come on. You know Senri. She loves her merc, but he gets on their nerves when he has nothing to do. Even if there was some other trouble, you didn't give him much of a chance to explain and he obviously didn't want to say on the road. He'll let us know when we get to the village while we're preparing for the mission."

"Maybe Mat is right. We Andinna turn three thousand and go crazy." Alchan huffed. Kian was the second oldest member of the Company. At thirty-eight hundred, the male was an experienced warrior, having served with Nevyn even before the male had met Varon. Long-time friends, much like Zayden and Mat, except neither of them was a grouch like the single father.

"No…" Luykas was still laughing. "I think they just don't take the world as seriously anymore because they're in their prime, they're settled, but also old. Eventually they'll turn into an old male like Leshaun, and you know, I would rather deal with their antics at this age."

"You think we take the world too seriously?" Alchan gritted his teeth. He had to take the damned world seriously. He didn't have much of a choice.

"I think you do, and it's not like they don't care. They just are better at enjoying life than you." Luykas shook his head, the laughter dying. "Calm down, my brother. Celebrate this moment, please. We're back on our turf. We've got everyone back together, even if it's just for a moment. We're *alive*, despite how hard the Elvasi have been trying to kill us recently."

Alchan sighed. His brother was right. This was a moment he should be celebrating. Other than Leshaun's unfortunate injury, they were walking away from their hardest mission in centuries alive and mostly intact, even freeing a female in the process. He was cranky with her, but he was privately happy they did it. Her reaction to his title had made him feel even more sure about her place in the Company, even if he publicly resisted it.

"How do you think he'll like her?"

"Well, he tried to talk to her the moment he realized she existed, so I think Kian isn't someone we have to worry about." Luykas gave Alchan a look. There would be some in the village that wouldn't like Mave. "I think his family won't be a worry either. You worried about anyone specific?"

"Not anyone specific," he answered. "I just don't want yet another Company warrior to find themselves on the fringes of our society, especially not a female. She needs a place. With how the females treat Nevyn and Varon, and how you and I have never really belonged here…I don't want to see her not find a place."

"For all your blustering, you do care," Luykas teased.

"I have to," Alchan snapped back. He was lucky they were far enough ahead of most of the Company that only Varon would be able to hear them. He was even luckier that Varon was great at keeping secrets. The things he'd probably heard Alchan and his brother talk about over the last thousand years would make many of the Company tuck tail and run. "Don't give me a hard time."

"Why not?" His brother began to chuckle, shaking his head. "You and she can barely be in the same room without a power struggle. You probably can't even be in the same mountains. We've discovered that over the last weeks."

Alchan stopped himself from reaching out and strangling his brother. He had a point. Alchan didn't have the easiest time with Mave, and she didn't have an easy time with him. It was just the way of things.

"You know that's never going to change, right? She and I will always be at each other's throats. It doesn't change the fact that I'm one of her commanding officers now. It doesn't change the fact that I'm her King." Alchan hated how much responsibility he had, but he didn't avoid it. "So yes, I'm going to care if our people decide to ostracize her. It would make her less happy, and morale is important for warriors constantly on the move like we can be."

"I just like teasing you, brother. I know you care and why." Luykas' fun attitude dropped and he took on a somber expression.

Alchan huffed. Already he could hear the chatter of the village. They were basically on top of it. He knew right around the bend, he would see it.

Here I go again.

As they rounded the bend silently, he took it in. Built into a cliffside, it had taken a century for the village to be livable. It had been a hard century, the Andinna scattered across the world, the Company fighting the Empire as much as it could, trying to free as many as they could. The Hornbuckles were smuggling their people as best they could to the freedom of Olost.

A long, hard century.

But through it all, somehow this village was built. The biggest one they had, the first of many. There were others, smaller homes and individuals living all throughout the mountains in southern Olost, but this was their hub. It was built close enough to Namur that a trip didn't seem too much of a problem if trading needed to happen. Alchan never liked how close it was to the edge of the mountains, but he understood the purpose.

On the ground beside the cliff were several large wood and stone buildings. Those were the community buildings for feasts, prayer, and other things he never participated in, including lodging for visitors and those who couldn't fly yet. Up the cliffside that shadowed the small area were wooden platforms and doors. Andinna built their homes into the mountains whenever they had the chance. There were homes on the ground level as well, and there was even a section for just the Company's living quarters, the single males at least. Many had their own places to live now. Zayden had been given a small ground-level home when he met Summer and had Rainev. They had moved a little higher when they had the chance and Summer was gone. Nevyn and Varon shared a small home much further up the cliffside. Luykas' was also high, as he preferred the space from the rest of the village, but still in it.

I need to see if they have space for Mave and Mat to have their own home, or have Luykas get on it.

Alchan saw the people coming out of their homes and the community buildings as word continued to spread of the arrival of the Company. It was always an affair. He never got to enter the village quietly without being bothered. He didn't even live in it. He only passed through to make sure the Company was settled. He lived on a different cliffside, by himself, how he liked it.

"Welcome home!" a female called out in Andena. "It's good to see the warriors have yet again returned from glory. Sire, it's good to see you are well."

Alchan held up a hand and waved silently, continuing to ride closer. Some cheered. Well, many cheered. They had sent Kian back to the village by himself, telling him to pass along what had happened and their return.

Alchan tried not to bristle at the title, either. He'd never liked it. Sire. Your Majesty. None of that ever suited him. His position in the royal family meant he had never been raised hearing it and it didn't suit him. He figured it never would.

He didn't stop moving forward until he was only a few steps in front of the lead female. An old female, she was roughly Leshaun's age, but Alchan never asked. She coordinated the entire village, was the tradition-keeper for festivals and many other things. There was a *mativa* for every major village and many of the smaller ones, many of whom looked to this old female for guidance.

She wore traditional garb: a long skirt of sorts with a slit running up the side, a cloth wrap belt around her hips. The shirt was loose, a very feminine look and something he hadn't expected. Dangling from her horns were several shiny and ancient stones on leather, gold, and silver bands. She had a somewhat ornate necklace as well, rich with color. It was the symbol of her position. Her arms were decorated in the bangle bracelets of their people, like many of the others had on.

For the most part, her look screamed that she had been spending her evening meal with her *mayara*. She had four old males who had been with her longer than most of the Company had been alive.

He swung himself off his horse, still silent. He extended a hand to the old female.

"It's good to see you as well, Jesvena," he finally said softly in Common. He kept his tone gentle, as to not be disrespectful. He might be King, but she was a female leader of the community. It made him internally growl and snarl, but he would never do it to her. He would try not to. They clashed occasionally, but they tried to keep it out of the public's view.

"Your Majesty." She took his elbow in their handshake, bowing to him in the same motion. "Was there success? Kian said you were going to save poor Rainev and Matesh. Were there any casualties on the mission?" She spoke in perfect Andena.

He knew Kian probably told her the answer to all of those questions, but he also knew she wanted more details from him. He didn't plan on giving her those yet, though. "We succeeded. We've brought glory to the Andinna and plan to continue to do so." He went with Common, knowing Mave would want to know everything he said. Everyone in the village would have to deal. He released her, turning to motion to his warriors, all dismounting as he had. They didn't move forward, standing behind him until he released them to go about their business on preparing for the mission. "We won't be staying long. I need healers for Leshaun. He took an injury on the road home. I'll also need preparations made for us to winter here. We've brought supplies to help lighten the load and will be bringing back more soon enough."

"Of course, Sire." Jesvena waved a hand. "You heard him. Help unload the carts. Bring the healers. Leshaun has been hurt. Find him and take him in."

All around him, the free Andinna jumped into action. He waited for Jesvena to be done pointing them around to continue. He had more for her.

"Is there anything else you need? Anything specific about the preparations?"

"We'll talk on it in a moment," he answered. "There's someone you need to meet." Jesvena raised an eyebrow. He took a deep breath and shouted, "Mave! Front and center!" He might as well make sure the old *mativa* before him knew Mave didn't know the language.

Many of the Andinna stopped and began to stare. Luykas slid closer to him.

"Can I release the rest of the Company?" his brother asked softly. "Before this becomes a scene?"

"Yeah, let them go. Everyone's going to want to bathe, I bet." Alchan tried not to sound dismissive, but he was just as tired as all of his warriors. He wanted a good night's sleep alone.

"Company! Fall out!" Luykas roared. Right as his brother began to walk away, Mave appeared by his side. To Jesvena's credit, the old female said nothing. She quietly took in Mave, studying her politely

He couldn't say much for any of the other free Andinna, rudely stopping and openly staring as if Mave had two heads. They stopped and stared as they unloaded the carts instead of getting their work done. Looking back, Alchan nearly groaned at the sight of Matesh protecting Mave's new personal items, hoarding them in the cart she had been riding with Bryn. He protectively held a small pouch Alchan knew carried the stones and gems that would begin Mave's collection of jewelry.

He watched his warriors for several moments as they broke up and went about their business, helping the free Andinna carry things into their stores, to give Mave and Jesvena time to handle their female shit. He didn't particularly care to witness the standard female dominance plays or get in the middle of them.

Finally, he could see out of the corner of his eye that Mave bared her teeth, but never dropped her eyes. She'd rolled the *mativa*, establishing herself higher than the leading female. That was something he knew was going to come back on him later.

Time to get this done. No more pretending to be distracted.

"Mave, this is the village's *mativa*, Jesvena." He didn't ask if she knew what a *mativa* was. He figured Leshaun covered that at some point in their studies.

"It's nice to meet you, tradition-keeper," Mave greeted, extending a hand. Alchan was glad his assumption was right.

He also silently prayed the old bat would accept the greeting, even if the Andena was broken and full of an Elliar accent most of them despised. It didn't help that Mave had obviously won the silent battle the females liked to have. He figured while Jesvena knew what just happened and why, Mave went instinctual and won out, even if it was disrespectful. She should have dropped her eyes to Jesvena's position out of respect, if not dominance. Sadly, this was Maevana Lorren and Alchan knew from experience that she didn't drop her eyes for anyone or anything.

Jesvena was slow to it, but eventually, she took Mave's hand.

"Greetings, Mave." Jesvena dismissed Mave after that, turning back to him. "A new female to join the community's ranks is always-"

"She's the newest member of the Company and will be treated as such." Alchan wasn't going to have Mave tangled up in the mess of the village politics. He wanted her to have a place, but he wanted it to be as a warrior. If his instincts were right, it would suit her better. He said it all in Common, even as Jesvena stayed in Andena. He wanted Mave to hear everything he said and understand it. She wouldn't understand yet why he did it, but she would one day. He wanted to show he was on her side from the start, even if he didn't always behave that way.

"Sire..." Jesvena looked over Mave again, who visibly bristled under the scrutiny. "While I understand your idea of her being a warrior, our numbers-"

"Matesh is a member of her *mayara*, and she shares a blood bond with Luykas. On top of that, she's been a warrior for at least nine hundred years. She's Company. You asked earlier what sort of preparations I need for the winter? She and Matesh need a home. Make sure it has room to grow as well, in case her family grows." Alchan leaned in closer, continuing in Common. "Don't test me on this, Jesvena."

He watched the old female bristle now. The females always had ideas and things they wanted. He wasn't in the mood for them. He should have expected this, honestly. Females were warriors, just like every Andinna, but since the War, they were hidden and locked away. They couldn't be risked, not if they wanted their race to survive.

Really, Jesvena was pissed that he was pulling rank on her. For a male to outrank a female? He lived in a difficult position. The *mativa* of a community was normally the most powerful Andinna of the area. They met in Councils that then reported regional issues to the ruling body. Normally, that was a Queen they could respect, a female like his grandmother or one of his aunts, who had spent centuries training to take the throne when it was one of their times.

Now they just had some *bedru* asshole always pissing them off.

"At least do me the respect of speaking in Andena," the old female snapped in Andena.

"He can't," Mave cut in. "I don't know the language well enough."

Alchan was shocked for a moment. She was sticking up for him now? "You caught enough of that?"

"I'm not fluent, but I know enough to catch some things," she reminded him, giving him a hard stare that had him raising his eyebrows. It was a challenge, but not one he was going to entertain, so he bit back his growl as she continued speaking. She eventually stopped, probably realizing they were at the same impasse they always were and turned back to Jesvena. "Why is it a problem I'm considered Company?"

"You're female, and we need to protect you," Jesvena said quickly, now in Common as well. Alchan knew the old female was trying to play nice to a female more dominant than her.

"I don't need protection." The bite, the indignation in her voice. Alchan wanted to snort in Jesvena's face. No, Maevana Lorren did not need protection and she would never let anyone put her to the side to be protected.

Someone gasped. Alchan took the moment to look around. They were being watched by nearly a third of the villagers now. His warriors were dispersed in there as well, looking for a way to step in if they needed to. They had come back when Alchan and Mave hadn't left as well. He felt a wave of pride seeing his warriors ready to step in, even if it meant getting into bad blood with the commoners.

"Every female who was in service to Elvasi needs time to heal. They probably had you doing menial tasks and-"

"I was a gladiator," Mave corrected. "I do well protecting myself and have for a very long time. I won't be kept in a nicer cage."

"Jes, you should have asked more about the rescue mission before making assumptions," Luykas said, coming to back him and Mave. "Now let my brother have his way. Mave won't follow you and stay with the community. She's chosen to join the King and me as a Company warrior."

Jesvena was so obviously unhappy that Alchan knew he would need to explain Luykas' meaning sooner rather than later.

"Mave, are you okay with getting this out there now? Who you are?" Alchan wouldn't announce it to the entire village without her approval. Luykas stiffened, and suddenly, Matesh was right there behind his female, ready to back her up if it was needed. The Company pushed out of the crowd, joining them. It was a clear sign they were going to stick with Mave, even if the other Andinna thought they were mad or disliked her. He stupidly realized he hadn't told Kian before sending the warrior off. Now, Kian stood in the crowd, holding a pint. He took a sip, meeting Alchan's gaze and raised an eyebrow.

Alchan tore his gaze away first, looking back at her, hoping for an answer sooner rather than later. She looked around, taking them all in as well. Alchan watched the wheels turn behind her eyes, calculating, analyzing. It was something he'd noticed about her long before. While she had started out skittish, she was observant, and it did her well. She was confident in battle, but when she wasn't confident, like the current situation, she was methodical, taking everything in before making any decisions.

"Go ahead," she finally answered.

"Everyone, I would like to introduce you to Maevana Lorren, daughter of the late General Javon Lorren and Kelsiana Lorren. Champion of the Colosseum. Freed slave of Empress Shadra. Newest warrior of the Ivory Shadows Mercenary Company." Alchan put every piece of detail he could into the title. They needed to know who she was from the get-go, or it would constantly come up and more pieces would slip out. If he wasn't clear right off the bat, it could sow distrust later.

"No," Jesvena snapped. "She can't be-"

"Look at her eyes, Jes." Luykas snapped his fingers in front of the old female's face. "Look at them. Did you ever know General Lorren? We did. Alchan and I knew her family."

Whispers were already breaking out. A legend. A scary story. A rumor.

Mave was all of those things, and they had brought her home, claimed her as his warrior. She beat Jesvena in a battle of will and now was an unknown force about to descend on their village. He wasn't going to tell her, but she was now technically in charge of the village. That was going to be something he would have to clear up on a later date. He didn't think she wanted to deal with all of the free Andinna.

Jesvena took a deep breath, pulling that Andinna temper back. Alchan was glad for it. He didn't want to put an old female in her place. He was the King and Mave was his warrior. What he said was law. He hated pulling rank, truly despised it, but he wasn't going to have his wishes ignored. He wasn't going to see his newest warrior swept away, thanks to what was between her legs or on her chest.

"Welcome, Maevana Lorren. May the blessing of the gods be upon you." Jesvena turned on her heel and walked away. The words had been respectful, but the disrespectful leave she took was aimed at Alchan.

"Disperse!" he roared at everyone around him. "Company, to me!"

They needed to talk about what just happened and he knew it wasn't over with Jesvena. That old pigeon was going to give him problems for years over this.

32

MAVE

Mave didn't move as Alchan roared for everyone to join them. The rest of the males were already close and came up in a circle, shielding them from the peering, curious eyes of the free Andinna villagers.

"We'll be here for two nights. Clean up tonight, get some real food, and find your places to settle in." Alchan sighed wearily. "We're all tired, I know it. I want you to look forward. We have a mission to carry out. We need to strike back at the Elvasi for their attack on the road. We need to make sure the scum understands that none of us are targets. We'll fight back and we'll crush them. Every time. We don't lose. In that effort, relax tomorrow. Recharge while you make preparations. Clean your gear, and patch it up. Think of why we're going on this mission, even though we've had it hard the last couple of months." He grinned. "We're mercenaries. We hunt bounties - we're not subject to them."

There were some pleased growls at their leader's words. There was even some chest thumping. She didn't partake in the maleness of it all, but she was feeling just as ready to strike back at the Elvasi. She didn't see a better way to start her new freedom with the Company. What was better than killing some of the pointed-ear bastards that made her life hell?

"Where will you be?" she asked him. "If we need you for something?"

"While in the village, everyone reports to me," Luykas explained. "Alchan doesn't stay here. When we're back from the mission, I'll show you the way to his home, in case of emergency, but it shouldn't be necessary for such a short stay."

She nodded, accepting the answer. That was all she needed to hear.

"Luykas, I want you and Kian to come see me," Alchan continued. "He needs to be caught up and we don't need the entire Company for that."

"Of course." Luykas nodded in acceptance.

Mave listened like the rest of the Company. They were waiting to be dismissed, and honestly, she had no idea what to do or where to go from here. She didn't understand what had just happened either. She knew *mativa* Jesvena was the leader of the village and everyone would follow the old female's lead. Leshaun had explained the community system of *mativa*, Council, then royal house to her. When he'd taught her that on the ship, she hadn't been expecting that Alchan was the head of the entire thing.

"Everyone, fall out and get clean." Alchan waved a hand, dismissing them. It was like a leash was taken off them.

"Can I see Senri with Mave while you're with Alchan?" Mat called out, grabbing her hand to pull her along to talk to Kian before he left.

"Why do you need my wife?" Kian asked back, ignoring how Luykas and Alchan were waiting on him. Nevyn and Varon stepped closer, nosy and wanting to listen in. She could tell by Nevyn's sly smile, he wanted to know everything.

"Mave needs some things set up before winter," Mat explained to him. Mave was still waiting for him to explain it to *her*. "Senri is the only female I really trust with it…"

Kian looked at his friends, the lovers. Luykas turned away from all of them, obviously about to laugh. When Kian turned back to her male and her, Mave had a sneaking suspicion he knew something she didn't. "Yeah, you can talk to Senri about it. She's probably not going to be too helpful. My wife is terrible at these things."

"Better than Allaina," Mat mumbled.

"Oh, I'm not getting into the middle of that." Kian shook his head.

"Let's leave Matesh to his mess and Mave. He'll sort it out or she'll have his balls." The mutt jerked his head towards their leader directing where to put the carts. She didn't know what he meant by the comment. She had yet to find a reason to get that mean with Mat. There had been a few times in the pits she threatened her male like that, but not any time recently.

I like his balls where they are.

"Fine. Let's go." Kian followed Luykas away, not bothering to say goodbye to anyone.

"Hey!" Nevyn yelled out. "We wanted to talk to him first!"

"Later," Luykas replied. Nevyn threw his hands up, looking at Varon for support. The mute just shrugged. A moment later, the couple waved at her and Mat, excusing themselves and launching into the air.

"Hold on for me?" Mat asked her. She didn't answer, just waving at him to do whatever he needed. She could stand and wait. She wasn't in any rush to dive into things alone.

Matesh jumped up and began to fly to a high platform, knocking on the door loud enough for her to hear it. She was beginning to realize a serious problem with the village. She couldn't fly. She couldn't live in one of the cliff-side homes or even visit anyone who did live in them. She pushed her hands into her breeches pockets, considering that. Over their trip to the village, she had kept working on her wings, but it would be months yet before she could fly, from Bryn's diagnosis. It was late summer and she was looking at midwinter before she was allowed to attempt feeling the wind beneath her wings.

Finally, Mat jumped back down, soaring low and gracefully landing. She always found it attractive to see him fly. Well, any Andinna male. It was perfection in her mind, the way their large bodies could cut through the air with a grace that defied how they appeared. After him, three more Andinna flew down swiftly, landing around him.

"Mave, let me introduce you to Kian's family. Senri, his *amanra*." He gestured respectfully to the female, even bowing slightly. She was just shorter than Mave, but built the same. Broader shoulders than Elvasi females, a robust muscular build that showed power. She was a pureblood Andinna with piercing orange eyes, and black *tatua* over her face and upper body, from what Mave could see. "These two are Willen and Gentrin. They're her other two *bodanras*, her husbands along with Kian." Mave looked them over too, but not as long. She had seen hundreds of male Andinna. Senri was her first female Andinna in her prime. She was something new.

Senri smiled kindly, walking closer. Those orange eyes warmed, glowing like an inviting fire. "It's a blessing to meet you, Mave."

"You as well," Mave replied, exchanging a quick Andinna handshake with her, locking into a battle of will. They were staring each other down, but it didn't feel like a war like it had with Jesvena.

"What do you and Matesh need of us? We're more than willing to help those new to freedom." Senri had a charm to her, but her eyes didn't drop, not for a long moment. She nodded respectfully when she finally gave in.

I can't bring myself to look down for them. Why do I keep challenging them? Why do they keep letting me?

"I was hoping I could get you three started on some things Mave is going to need. The Company purchased her fabric for a more appropriate off-time wardrobe, as well as stones for jewelries. I can pay-"

"No, no," Senri shook head. "I don't charge the Company for anything. You know that. You are Company now, right?" She looked over Mave. "Kian said something when he came back, but he didn't know too much. He declared Alchan tossed him away the second they were reunited. It was pitiful."

"He wanted someone to let the village know we were on the way and close. One of us was probably going to fly in if he hadn't shown up." Mat chuckled. "She's Company, our newest member and..." Mave nearly rolled her eyes at how Mat's chest pushed out, making him look even larger. The other two males began to chuckle, as if they knew where the display was coming from. "My *amanra*."

"Oh!" Senri's gasp practically echoed off the cliffside. "This is a story I really must hear. Come along. We'll sit down and talk. I'm going to assume you can't fly yet, Mave. Is that correct?"

"It is. I know it must look bad-"

"No slave can fly when they're recently freed. Don't worry. We'll get you in the air as fast as we can." Senri smiled. "We'll keep everything ground-level until then."

"They both stink from the road," Willen commented quietly. "Maybe we should take them to the springs with some small offerings of real food. They might like that. I'm sure everyone has cleared out, knowing most of the Company is headed there right now."

"Aye, Willen. Good idea." Gentrin elbowed the other male with a good-natured spirit that reminded her of Nevyn.

"That is a very sound idea. Gentrin, show them to the large spring. I bet every Company male is there now." Senri chuckled, shaking her head. "Mave, normally we females use a different one, a smaller one, but I expect you'll want to stay near some Andinna you know. The males aren't allowed at the female spring, but we're allowed at the male one."

"Why not?"

"Because if we let them there, we females would never have a private moment to ourselves and the spring would end up being a place where everyone would always be trying to fuck." Senri laughed. "Go on, you three. Willen and I will get food and catch up."

"Are you sure you want to go to the male spring, love?" Willen was still quiet.

"It's nothing I haven't seen from the Company before, or my own warriors." Senri snorted, turning on her heel and walking away. Willen sighed, looking desperately at Gentrin, who shook his head.

"Can't help you, my friend. She doesn't care about cock hanging around. You've been trying to make her for two thousand years and it's never going to work." Gentrin laughed to himself as Willen followed after his female, defeated by Gentrin's words. Turning to them, Gentrin looked them over. "It's good to see you alive, Matesh. Kian was worried about all of you, especially you and Rain. He was eaten up by the idea that the young ones were taken by the Empire."

"We're out now," was all Mat had to say. His tone made it sound like he wasn't up for any of that discussion.

With that, Mave found herself following the two males out of the village and up a trail. Gentrin informed her that they normally flew to the springs unless their wings were tired, which is why the trail even existed. She could hear the shouting and cheers of the males she knew well now. As they approached the deep, clean hot spring, she got an eyeful of male.

Bryn was reclining on a stone, waist-deep in water, looking relaxed and quite good. Rain was near him, underneath a small waterfall from a higher water source, letting the hot water run through his hair. Somehow, Nevyn and Varon had beat them to the spring as well. She was positive she had just seen them enter into one of the cliffside homes. They must have flown over here to get there faster.

Mat began to strip before her, along with Gentrin, who called out saying Senri was going to be there soon and that the males present needed to keep their cocks to themselves.

"Wait, Senri gets us a warning and Mave doesn't?" Nevyn asked, laughing. "What is this?"

"That's on Matesh to give that warning." Gentrin stepped into the hot water, wading closer to the other males.

Mat waited in the buff for her, nodding to the water. He had a smirk, as if he wasn't worried about anyone bothering her with their cocks. "You want to come in or do you want to wait and try the female spring later?"

"I'll come in," she answered. "I've been nude in front of a bunch of males before." What was really holding her back was the fact that she had never bathed safely with a group of males before. This screamed the community washing areas of the pits, and yet, there were only friendly smiles and easy conversations in the spring. It brought her back to this strange feeling of how she was free and she could trust these males in ways she could never trust the other gladiators.

With that, she pulled off her dirty, beaten leather armor and followed Mat into the steaming hot water. She hissed at the first touch of the heat then moaned as it sank into her bones. She couldn't resist finding the deepest area and sinking further in, letting it cover her shoulders. Mat stayed close to her, kissing her wet shoulder as a hand caressed her side.

The kissing moved to her neck and his hand roamed onto her ass, squeezing lightly. She turned and met his mouth in a slow kiss, but wasn't really thinking to take it any further. He was, his other hand creeping up her thigh. She could feel his cock pressed against her hip, begging for her attention.

"You're supposed to be bathing, you two!" Nevyn teased, splashing water at them. "No sex in the springs, remember?"

Mave shook her head as Mat growled at Nevyn. She would ride Mat later, but at that moment, she was just glad for how nice the water felt on her wings, how her muscles relaxed more with every passing second. It was heaven.

"None of that," she told her male. "Let's just enjoy this. I never let myself get so dirty until I met all of you." She was used to daily baths and wanted them back. She also wanted Elvasi blood. Therein lay her problem.

I should remember that life doesn't always give me what I want.

She nearly scoffed at herself. She had learned that lesson in the pits. Life had trade-offs. She was finally the member of a community, but she had lost the prestige and security she had built in the pits. She was finally free, but now she was a mercenary, a new one, and traveling meant she couldn't take the same bath, day in and day out. If she wanted Elvasi blood, she had to go out and find it, and that meant getting dirty.

Mat backed off without a verbal complaint, smiling that arrogant smile she found frustrating and sexy. He knew if he wanted to press the issue, he would get the attention he craved that she hadn't given him on the road. Not that he'd demanded it while they were on the road. Neither of them had pressed the issue.

She realized that at some point, he was going to beg for it while they were in the village. Needy male.

He's lucky I love that particular activity, too.

Zayden joined them a short time later, sinking into the water far from anyone else. He had been quiet the entire trip. He didn't bother Rain and he didn't talk to nearly anyone else.

Senri and Willen arrived last, slipping into the water slowly with plates of food. Mave's eyebrows went up at the amount. Were they trying to feed the entire Company?

"Snacks, everyone. Share so everyone has something to settle their stomachs." They put the food on a rocky outcropping in the middle of the spring. Mave didn't dive in yet, watching all the males scuffle over it. Senri finally sighed, reached between them, and stole an entire plate of what looked like meat cubes. She brought them to Mave and Mat and set them up on a rock behind them. "There. So you two don't need to fight with the rest of them."

"What is it?" Mave asked immediately, grabbing one of the raw-looking pieces. It was coated in some sort of seasoning and barely cooked, so juicy that it dripped into the spring. Mat just shoved one into his mouth, mumbling a thank you as Senri's males waded closer to them.

"Venison. Deer meat. We hunt here regularly, and maintain quality herds all over the mountains so the supply never dies off." Senri waved a hand at her. "Eat it."

Mave shoved it into her mouth, chewing slowly. The flavor was gamey and rich. The meat was tender and succulent. The juices, obviously some blood, mixed in with whatever seasonings were on it and the spice exploded in her mouth. She finished quickly, breathing hard to try and end the spice that had just exploded on her tongue.

"Shit. Should have warned you about the heat," Mat said apologetically.

She shook her head. "No. I knew it was going to be spicy. You all put this heat on everything. I'm just not completely used to it yet." She took another piece of the meat and ate it. "It's very delicious, though. Thank you." She directed the compliment at the female, who began to laugh.

"Oh, don't thank me. Willen just whipped those up thinking everyone here would enjoy it. I don't cook."

"Senri is in charge of the village's protection. A warrior like you, but she doesn't have Kian's roaming nature." Mat chuckled. "She hates cooking. She hated crafting. She would rather use all of those things than need to spend the time making them."

"Ah..." Mave ate another piece, nodding.

"Willen is the cook of my household. Gentrin is a blacksmith for the entire village, though most of his work is for the Company and my unit."

"Are females often in charge of protection?"

"Yes and no," Senri answered, giving Mave a curious look. "You don't know?"

"Uh..." Mave shook her head slowly.

"She doesn't know anything, our new little female," Nevyn called out. "You need to explain everything really clear for her."

"I was an *ensam* as a gladiator," Mave told her, hoping Senri wouldn't judge her for it. "I became a slave so young that I...don't really know anything. They're helping. I learn more every day."

It hurts less to admit each time I say it. That's something.

"Good. These males would have no excuse to leave you ignorant." Senri said it with a level of viciousness that Mave didn't really understand. "What kind of Andinna leave a female as an *ensam*? And what do you mean you were a gladiator?"

"You missed Alchan's announcement." Mat sighed.

"I'll tell her," Mave said quickly. Another female, one who was showing kindness already. Mave wanted to be the one to come forward and tell the story this time.

Senri's eyes went wide as Mave gave her the quick version of the tale. Who she was, why, and what she had been through. Only the barest of details of everything before meeting Mat and Rain. She told the story of the escape, noticing how Senri and her husbands were now watching avidly, not even touching the food. None of the Andinna in the spring were eating by the time she finished.

"Oh, you poor child," Senri whispered, reaching out. "Come here."

Mave wasn't sure how to feel as Senri wrapped her arms around Mave's waist, holding her close. She patted the female's back as she was held tightly. She hated being touched, but Senri didn't feel like a threat. The hug just made Mave uncomfortable.

"If you need anything, you let me know. I'm not good at many of the feminine things we Andinna do, but I can at least help guide you on the basics. I promise. You need a wardrobe? Willen, Gentrin, talk to some males you know about that. I don't want her in the hands of the other females until everything is prepared."

"Are the other females bad?" Mave asked, now worried.

"No, but they tend to make their own groups, little packs. I don't want to see you stuck in the middle of all of that, especially if you have Mat in your *mayara*." Senri gave Mat a look. "We all warned you that your behavior was going to come back on you."

Mave had no idea what *that* meant.

"Well, they'll deal. I never made any promises I couldn't keep and they all knew it." Mat was defensive. Mave narrowed her eyes. She had never seen Mat defensive before. He noticed her look and conceded without it needing to be a later conversation, continuing his explanation. "I...I had a lot of female attention that I enjoyed, but I never made any promises to join any *mayara*. There was no love in any of it, just sex."

"Until Allaina, who wanted him to leave the Company and stay with her. You almost joined hers until she gave you that ultimatum." It was Rain who said that, giving Mave another piece of the puzzle.

"She would do well to leave me alone," Mat growled back.

"Who's Allaina?" This was the second time Mave heard the female mentioned.

"Matty," Bryn called out. "The one who called him Matty."

Matesh snarled louder. She ran a hand over his thigh, realizing he wasn't happy with the line of discussion.

"We'll talk more about it later, if you want," she said quietly. She didn't want their first night in the village to be about old lovers. She didn't want to hear that awful nickname, either. It was so childish.

Senri and her males shared a silent look but didn't say anything about it. Instead, Senri began discussing who would make what for Mave. Mave decided this was the female she would trust her things with, like the stones. She couldn't carry those around for the mission.

They talked well into the night, until Mave could see the wrinkles on her fingers. Many were leaving now, jumping out of the water and grabbing their things before flying off, still in the nude. Mave didn't comment on that, shaking her head in silence at the sight. She couldn't stop herself from watching with Senri.

Especially Bryn. For some reason, she watched him intently when he rose out of the water. His lean form drew her eye, his *tatua* complimenting the way his muscles moved as he prowled out of the water. He had no fat on his body. He was nearly as scarred as her, too. She had never really noticed before how his body was marked with hundreds of years of violence, small white scars everywhere.

She couldn't help but take a look at him soft either. The cold night didn't seem to cause him any problems like she knew it did for many other males.

She tried to ignore a small bit of lust for the male. An errant thought ran through her mind, burning an image permanently there. Bryn's lean form between her legs, moving with the power of a bigger male, proving himself to be much more than he appeared.

When did I start looking at Bryn like that?

The image changed ever so slightly as Mat pressed up against her back, shifting her to sit on one of his thighs in the water. Mat was kissing her as Bryn sent her over the edge. That was now at the forefront of her mind.

She tried to banish the thought, continuing some conversation with Senri and her husbands. Mave had so many questions, but she didn't want to overload the female she had just met. After they dealt with the hunters, she would begin her interrogation. Senri would be able to tell her things the males couldn't. What had Mat said? She needed a female friend.

Finally, she rose out of the water with Mat, and together, they walked back to the village. Mave tried to banish the image. It left her feeling uncomfortable and strange, the idea of two males in her bed. It screamed of things she had once been forced to endure.

"We'll stay in the Company quarters for this visit," Mat said softly, directing her to a large, ground-level door. "We won't get much privacy because it's basically a barracks with small rooms, but it'll have to do until they set us up a home."

"That works," she responded, not really caring where they ended up sleeping, as long as it was comfortable. She was more tired than she had been in weeks. Arriving in the village had been exciting and exhausting, but she wasn't sure it was any different than she expected.

33

MAVE

The next day, Mave woke up in a small room with some simple blankets around her, alone. She quickly remembered where she was. The village, the strange incident with Jesvena, and meeting Senri.

One day to relax, then we're going Elvasi hunting.

Mave honestly couldn't wait. She didn't want to go out and travel more, but she knew they had to, and she couldn't say no to the idea of making sure they were never attacked like that again.

She rose and found clean, fresh clothing already waiting on her. Someone had come in and laid it out. She picked up the shirt, finding it was just a wrap and she didn't know how it worked. She dropped it and went for the bottoms instead, finding supple cloth breeches instead of the leather she had grown so accustomed to. She slid them on and went back to staring at the shirt, frowning.

Where's Matesh when I need him?

The folds and way it was designed made her think some of it was obvious but she really didn't understand. She tried a few different ways to put it on. Frustration began to brew and she dropped it again.

"I might as well go outside without it," she growled, staring at it on the floor. She looked to the door and wondered if there was anyone out there who could help her. She would need to apologize to Matesh later for it. She knew he loved helping her get ready in the morning. Normally, she thought it was a tad excessive, but this time, she really needed his help. "I really need to learn how to do this on my own..." She groaned, opening the door, not bothering to cover herself at all and look out to see who might want to help her.

She didn't see anyone immediately and stuck her head out further. At that point, she would even accept Luykas' help.

"Mave, what are ya doing with yer tits out?" Bryn asked as he rounded a corner. She jumped, turning to see him at the other end of the hall, in the direction she hadn't been paying attention to. His eyes dipped straight to her chest, making her have the obscene want to stick them out further. His summer-sky-blue eyes darkened, and she saw how his body tightened and tensed.

He likes them. She really enjoyed the idea of Bryn being attracted to her.

"I don't know how to put the damned shirt someone left me on," she said, explaining it calmly. "Get over the tits and come help me. Normally Mat is around when I wake up and does his thing helping me, but I have no idea where he is."

"Ah. I caught him taking yer armor out for cleanin'. He must have gotten someone to loan ya clothes. I was comin' to get ya. We have somewhere to be." Bryn's cheeks turned an amazing shade of pink as he turned away finally. She hadn't expected him to get embarrassed over some breasts, not when he had probably already seen them. Females had them, and there was nothing she could do about the size of hers. They had always been bigger than the Elvasi females she had seen. They were big enough that the other gladiators had liked making comments, even.

Maybe they only made comments because I had the only tits they ever saw. Doesn't matter. I need his damned help.

"Bryn. My tits are out. If you want them to stop being out, I need some help." She was growing more impatient by the second. He was also trying very hard not to look at said tits now, that much was clear. "If you won't, find someone who will explain how to put the damned thing on."

"I'm comin'," he muttered, looking down and away from her chest as he walked closer. She let him in the small room and he grabbed the shirt before she could. He lifted it, looked it over and nodded. "All right. So this is one that's designed for ya females to get on fast and without your males bothering you, or if you don't have any. You should get this pretty easily." He motioned for her to come closer. She stepped in front of him and paid attention to everything he did.

"Ya throw this over yer head." He showed her a loop that was sewn in. "Then ya take these two parts and wrap 'em around yer core, like so." He did it, showing her how the large piece of fabric split into two tails. She noticed how the fabric ended up laying naturally over her breasts, tight enough that they didn't fall out, but loose enough that she didn't feel cramped.

She also noticed how his knuckles accidentally grazed over her abdomen and ribs as he worked. Her mind brought up the vastly inappropriate image she had conjured the night before seeing him leave the spring. She wasn't able to focus again until he was done wrapping it and showed her the ending.

"Then ya tie 'em off or tuck 'em, yer choice." He tucked them in the front. In the end, it was the effect that she had a nice, thick shirt on, but it left her entire upper back exposed around her wings.

"This is what females wear?" she asked incredulously.

"Males wear 'em too, when we really need something to help against the cold. There was a time when Andinna females went shirtless too, but it was a long time ago, before we dealt with other races. The other races didn't appreciate it, and females ended up liking not havin' their tits do…things." Bryn shook his head. "Ya know. Tit things. Many females do go topless, in the hottest of summer months, as long as there are no humans or anythin' around."

"Moving around. Females don't like their breasts getting in the way." She could relate to that dislike. She got annoyed by it as well.

"Aye." Bryn stepped away from her. "Now, with that done, ya can go outside without feeling weird."

"Oh, I would have gone out without a top on if I had to." She didn't really care. Her body had been on display for the masses. It had been used and beaten in front of them. She had lived with males, and on the hottest days, they all stripped down. She normally kept bottoms of whatever she had on, just because it was a safety measure, but her tits? She didn't particularly care if those were on display anymore.

Bryn gave her an odd look and she didn't try to decipher it.

"I'll meet you outside," he said. He left first, almost running out. She sighed, following him. She didn't know if what she had just asked of him would hurt Mat or put him in a bad position. She walked down the hallway, ignored the main room of the community building, and went outside to breathe in the fresh mountain air. It was something she enjoyed on the roads. The air was thinner, and somehow nicer. It also didn't smell like fish like the ship and Namur. It didn't smell like old dirt or sweat like the pits.

The mountains had a freshness she wasn't used to.

Bryn was nowhere to be seen, so she idled at the door to the community building, unsure of where to go. Bryn had left her, even when he told her to follow. She tried not to be put out by it. It was a strange feeling, to have someone obviously run from her like that.

"Allaina, I need to get back inside. Please."

Mave's eyes found the source of Mat's voice, nearly thirty feet away, near a round building. Her male looked distressed and uncomfortable.

A female, wearing something like Mave was, ran a hand over his chest. "You got back and didn't come to see me. You were taken by the Empire. I was worried about you. What happened to your horn? They had looked so good and now…"

Mave bared her teeth at the touch and purr in her voice, but waited. This was Allaina. She wasn't going to get into the middle of Matesh's conversation, though. She wanted to see how he handled the female.

Mat shook his head. "No, I didn't come see you. Just like I haven't seen you when I've returned from missions for the last hundred years. We've been over for a long time, Allaina. I'm with someone now, so stop touching me." He pulled her hand off his chest by the wrist, but it wasn't rough. Mave wanted him to break the female's wrist, but he didn't. "It's serious, 'I'm in her *mayara'* sort of serious. Unless you have something important to tell me, I need to go."

"With someone? In her *mayara*? What did I miss yesterday while I was out hunting? I came back, was told you were here, and yet didn't see you. No one would even tell me where you were or what happened. They were surprisingly close-lipped about it with me."

Mave kept waiting, watching the interaction. Matesh was trying to step away from the female, his eyes down. He was tense and wanted to leave. She could see it even from the distance.

"With someone. You'll meet her eventually. She's a member of the Company. She knows how being a warrior is important to me because she's one too." Mat's tone was accusing as he ended that. "She's not telling me to stop being me."

"I wanted to keep you alive!" Allaina growled. "Alive, Matty! With me! With our family!"

"Your family. I never got along with your *bodanras*, and we both know that. They tolerated me as a casual lover. There's a lot of reasons why you and I were never going to work, Allaina. Drop it." Mat stepped further away from his old lover and towards the building Mave was standing in front of.

"I want to meet her," Allaina demanded. "A new female? She'll need friends. She'll need to submit to Jesvena if she hasn't yet. As *mativa*, Jesvena is in charge of all of us. We both know that. Maybe I can help her get in to a good position here-"

"I didn't submit to Jesvena," Mave called out. She didn't want anyone thinking she did. Or that she *should*. She watched Mat look up in shock, then a smile came over his face. She loved that smile. "Good morning, Mat."

"Mave," he crooned, walking closer. He was to her in ten steps and wrapped an arm around her waist. "The blue looks amazing on you. Senri offered that when I saw her at dawn. I was washing your armor, trying to get it done before you woke up."

"Thank you. Bryn had to teach me to put it on. I hope you don't mind." She wanted to clear that now. They were both ignoring the female slowly walking closer. Allaina could wait. She wasn't important anymore.

"I won't get pissy over it since it's my fault. I should have stayed and woken you up for first meal. My apologies, *amanra*." He kissed her to prove just how sorry he was. She was chuckling as he pulled back.

"I'm Allaina," the female greeted, finally close enough that Mave shouldn't ignore her. She could, if she wanted to be rude, and part of her really wanted to pretend like the greeting hadn't been extended. She turned on the female, meeting her eyes.

Allaina put up a fight, snarling with a viciousness that nearly had Mave ready to fight. Mave never dropped her eyes, and gave her nothing similar to that display. Not a single twitch of a muscle reacted to the threat Allaina just tried. The female stepped closer. They were the same height and now chest to chest. Allaina snarled again, narrowing her ruby-red eyes.

"Lower your eyes to the ground before I put them there," Mave said softly. "I don't submit to anyone and I never will. I'll kill you if I have to. I'm very good at it."

Allaina's nostrils flared in anger and then her eyes dropped. "You'll submit to someone eventually. You don't just get to show up in our village and take over."

"I don't plan on taking over, but I also don't plan on being underneath anyone. I'm a member of the Company. I follow the orders of Alchan and Luykas. I don't submit to an Andinna I've never met, and I never will. And don't think of trying to make me in the future." Mave made it clear as the day around them. If she needed to do this with every female she met, she would. She wouldn't submit to the males; she wouldn't submit to the females. She wasn't going to submit to anyone.

"Well, it's been a blessing to meet you," Allaina said with none of the politeness of Senri. She began to walk away without letting Mave respond or a handshake.

"That...well, I don't think it could have gone better, but it absolutely could have been worse. I'll be thankful that it wasn't." Mat sighed. "Allaina is in line to be the next *mativa* of the village. It's always gone to her head. Between her, Jesvena, and Senri, you've now proven more dominant than the three most influential females of the village."

"Is that a bad thing?" she asked, watching the beautiful female walk away. She hadn't wanted to admit it when the female was talking to Mat, but Allaina was pretty. Her shoulders were broad like every Andinna's, but her muscle didn't bulk up and look overly masculine. Her waist and hips created the illusion of an hourglass.

She was pretty, and Mave wanted to tear her ruby red-pink eyes out of her skull for it.

"No, but it'll make things interesting, for sure. Especially since Alchan declared you his and not the village's. Alchan doesn't submit to them either, so between the two of you, they're losing power. King and the most dominant female? It'll make things very interesting."

"This sounds much more complicated than I care for," she muttered.

"It is," he conceded. "Let's not worry about it. We only have today to relax and prep for the mission. Just think, tomorrow we'll be out of here again and killing some Elvasi."

She grinned. *Yeah, I can get behind that.*

"Hey, you two are finally both alive!" Nevyn dropped down next to them, but he wasn't smiling. He didn't exactly look excited to see them, only carrying some urgency. "Company meeting. Alchan wants to check in with us, make sure we're all healing now with a good night's sleep, then to talk about prep that needs to be done."

"Thanks," Mat said, sighing. "There goes the idea of relaxing."

"We've got Elvasi to kill," she said, grinning. "They did just attack us, Mat. We're going to get them for it."

"I love the way your female thinks." Nevyn was laughing as he jumped up and took off.

Mat sighed, taking her hand. "It's not just about them attacking us. They tried to take you."

She didn't have anything to say to that. It made her heart clench in an uncomfortable way.

Mat showed her the small trail to Alchan's home. Apparently, it was a different cliffside, one he claimed just for himself. There was a waterfall that came down the side of his mountain into a pool of his own, but not a hot spring. There was a platform, but it wasn't very high and even had some stairs to the door, nearly thirty feet up. She and Mat climbed up, and he let her in first.

It was the first time she had been in a mountainside home. She had heard about them from Leshaun during her lessons, but the community building was just a wood and stone structure. This was something very different.

The walls were carved from the mountain, and rough. She let her hand slide over one as she went further in. It was carved out large enough that her wings had ample room and Mat could get around her without needing to avoid her. The floors were also raw stone, smoothed and with rugs laid over the top.

She found the Company inside a large central room, waiting on her and Mat. She couldn't see anyone else missing. The males were mostly lounging on different pieces of low furniture, like bags with stuffing in them. They let their wings rest on the floor, along with their tails. She took it all in, ignoring the actual Andinna. She was more curious about the home. It was a little like the pits.

Yet so different. It was warm and dry. There was even a fire going, and it was only late summer. She wondered where the smoke went.

"Like my home?" Alchan asked her, obviously already annoyed with her.

"Could be nicer. There's not much color." She wasn't sure where the retort came from, but it had many of the males chuckling. "Not that I would know much about that. I grew up in the pits under the

Colosseum. Everything was dirt and stone there, with not a single shred of color."

"Hm. I'll take that into consideration." He wouldn't, his tone made that clear.

"You have jokes today?" Mat asked her softly, pulling her to sit down.

"I'm in a good mood," she answered, falling onto one of the giant cushions, letting her wings relax like the other males did. She saw Bryn standing in a corner behind Alchan and Luykas by himself, and he was watching her. Their eyes met for a moment and he quickly looked away. Her face betrayed her, heating up slightly. She wasn't sure where that reaction had come from, but she worked to control it.

"That's a first," Luykas said, staring at her oddly. "A good mood? Skies save us, we're all going to die." He finally broke out into a smile, snickering to himself.

"Does it have anything to do with putting Allaina underneath you?" Mat asked mildly.

"She what?" Alchan snapped. "Damn it."

"I'm not sure what's wrong with you now. Please tell me, *sire*." She narrowed her eyes at him until he growled.

"You can't roll every female here. Jesvena, Allaina. If you get Senri, you'll have outdone every female in the village. Those three rule."

She smiled, causing Luykas to laugh harder. Kian was the one who gave Alchan the bad news, though.

"Senri told me last night she was rolled. Didn't stand a chance." Kian began to chuckle. "Females."

"Since I've only just met other females, does anyone want to tell me why this is happening?" She tried to pose the question nonchalantly. The very few times she had experience with females before this, it was the old female in the castle in Elliar. Those interactions had been short and curt.

"You females instinctively try to make a pecking order. Dominance challenges, testing strength of mind and physical strength." Kian leaned closer. "Jesvena is dominant by nature and the will of her mind and her belief she can lead drove her to become a tradition-keeper and take over the area young. Allaina is much the same way and was chosen as an apprentice. Her training began years ago. Senri has no interest in those things and feels no need to challenge them, but she is a warrior and no other warrior that lives here permanently will ever challenge her. She'll put them on their ass. As a triad, they rule this village and its territory."

"Then you come in, a member of the Company, and put them all beneath you." Alchan sighed. She could see for just a moment the weight he bore on his shoulders and realized she should have recognized it sooner. There were rare days she had seen Shadra tired, and then she would quietly complain about the stress of ruling an Empire. Alchan was ruling a dying people without a real home. The stress of it was now starkly obvious. "We'll deal with it after the mission. Right now, we're going to stay focused on our newest problem."

"I told Alchan last night that attacks on you all coincide with an increased amount of Elvasi activities right outside the mountain." Kian stood up, holding a large scroll. "Now, they've never been bold enough to come into the mountains. The Elvasi know we rule here, even if we're outnumbered, but they'll pick off our hunters and patrols if we're not careful. We try to make sure our patrols are always well-manned enough to handle any trouble. Recently, Senri and I caught a scouting party coming into our territory. We killed them before they could report anything about our mountains back to their funders and other Elvasi."

"So the word went out that Mave has such a high bounty, and they kicked up, all looking for her." Luykas hummed, nodding thoughtfully. "We do need to attack them. Hiding isn't going to make this settle down."

"No, it won't," Alchan agreed. "How are everyone's injuries? Did you all get enough rest last night?"

A wave of confirmation ran through the Andinna in the room. A good night's rest and they were all healed. Being in their prime, it wasn't too much of a concern. Leshaun was the one who took the worst injury and would need to sit out to heal, thanks to his age. He wasn't even at the meeting.

"Good. I want you all handling your business today and preparing to go. We leave tomorrow at dawn, so there's plenty of time to plan this out. Make sure you eat, rest, make any plans you need before the winter. We're going to be on the move for another week to get to the location - be ready for that." Alchan smiled, a brutal thing showing off his canines. "And keep focused. We need to show these Elvasi that no one comes after one of ours."

Mave felt a flood of respect. She and Alchan didn't get along, but more than once now, he'd called her one of them. He wanted to fight for her, fight for the Company.

Walking out, she and Mat headed towards the village with a tail. Bryn hovered behind them, quietly walking when he could have flown. She looked back at him, causing him to look away.

"Let's do the horses together," Mat suggested, ignoring Bryn behind them. "The more familiar you are with them, the better."

"What about our gear?" she asked. She had blades to clean. Where was her armor? He'd gone to clean it, but she didn't know where he left it.

"I'll help her with the horses," Bryn said suddenly, stepping closer. "Ya can round up all of that and meet us in the stables."

Mat's eyes narrowed just a little at Bryn. She had no idea what he was thinking about, but he finally responded. "Yeah, that works. I'm going to take off."

"I'll walk back with her," Bryn promised.

Mave just raised an eyebrow. She knew the walk now. When had it been decided she needed an escort?

Mat swiftly kissed her cheek then jumped back and up into the air. Plants rustled around them as his powerful wings took him up into the air. She watched him disappear and turned on Bryn. "You said you would meet me outside earlier," she reminded him as he walked up to stand at her side.

"Varon got me pretty quickly to come over here. I figured one of the others would find ya."

She knew he was lying. From his entire posture, it screamed a lie. He didn't want to tell her why he wasn't outside to meet her. In the end, it didn't really matter, but she was still hurt by it. It felt like he brushed her off.

"Okay." She turned and started stomping down the trail back to the main village.

Bryn groaned, speeding up to keep pace with her. "Yer mad at me now. I understand. I did leave ya behind. I'm sorry."

"Apology accepted." It wasn't really, but she didn't exactly have the room to get pissy with him. He made his decision to go and it had all ended up fine.

"Thank ya." He moved closer to her side and stayed there for the entire walk back to the village and to the stables, pointing them out for her. Another one of the large wooden buildings in the village near the cliff-side, it blocked a view of an open field where several horses were running around, enjoying the morning.

"You didn't need to walk back with me," she finally said, staring out at the horses.

"Made Matesh feel better knowing you had someone instead of walking alone, and him letting me was a sign he trusts me with ya." Bryn shrugged. "It was something that needed to happen."

"I don't understand you males," she muttered, shaking her head. She continued to walk into the stables, finding the horses they had ridden in on and many more, including mules and donkeys for hauling. "We're just taking individual mounts for this, right? A few pack animals, too?" She wanted to work instead of fight with a headache over what males did between each other.

"Aye."

As they started working, he helped her with kind words and led her through preparation, always there. He never went ten feet from her. He hovered, and sometimes they would accidentally touch - and he would quickly jump away as if there was lightning between them.

As the day grew warmer, his shirt came off, revealing muscle she had seen already. She glanced at it a lot, seeing how the cut of his abdomen went down into his breeches, which he let ride very low. When he caught her looking, his face turned a little red and she turned away quickly.

"Let me get that," he offered, grabbing a saddle from her. She found herself staring at his chest again. She only nodded, letting him leave with it, her eyes falling down to see his ass in leather.

He's not my type. He's not my type. He's not my type.

Repeating it to herself didn't make the attraction she was feeling go away.

34

LUYKAS

Preparation to get out of the village and on the mission moved fast. Luykas oversaw all of it, knowing his brother was deep in thought and trusted him. The village, the Company, his title. Alchan needed the day to consider all of it without getting wrapped up in the little things, so Luykas played co-leader, his role. He wasn't royalty in the eyes of the Andinna, being a mutt, but his half-brother was the King and he was a co-founder of the Ivory Shadows alongside him. He demanded respect in his own right, even if he was always held at a distance like his brother. For different reasons, certainly, but held at a distance nonetheless.

He had a list of things he needed to do before they left, and he was half-avoiding all of them. He decided to try doing the easier stuff before confronting the hard part of his job.

"Do any of you need anything?" he asked in Andena, finding Nevyn, Varon, and Kian with Kian's family in the blacksmith's open building. Together, he knew all of their armor and weapons would be in great shape by the next morning.

"No, we're doing well," Kian answered, looking up to him, keeping to their native tongue. "What do you need, boss?"

"Something to do," he answered, sighing. "I left Alchan at his place, so let's try not to bother him until we're ready to go."

"Want to tell me even more about this new female?" Kian asked. He seemed nervous to even ask, which was out of character for the large, adult male. "I seem to still be a bit behind compared to the rest of you."

"You could try talking to her more." Nevyn was chuckling. "Never knew you to be nervous around a female, Kian."

"He better be nervous," Senri said, snapping. "If he ends up on her bad side, I'll have his damned hide. He knows it. There's finally a female in the Company to keep all of you in line."

Kian's nervousness was suddenly explained.

"Senri, be nice," Luykas chided softly, knowing if he was more aggressive, she would gut him. "Mave isn't an easy female to get a word in with, and she's hard to know in general. Alchan and I told you everything we honestly know, Kian. There's not much else. She's Maevana Lorren. She's the Champion, or rather, was. She's standoffish, but trying her best to get to know everyone, at her own pace. She's out of place and doesn't know too much about how to react to many situations we find normal. And she holds a mean grudge. She's not mean, mind you. Just don't get on her bad side once. It'll take ten good deeds to fix it." He knew that from experience.

"She's dominant, that's for sure." Senri sighed, shaking her head. "One day, and she's stirred up half the village. Allaina probably already hates her. Jesvena doesn't know what to do or say about it. Generally dominant females who don't want power put their eyes down anyway, just to maintain the status quo. She didn't."

Luykas groaned. He needed to take responsibility for this one. They all did, really. "Our fault. We've been so busy getting her up to speed with language, history, and everything else that some things have fallen behind. Hard for a bunch of males to really explain the inner workings of females. Mat's still trying to explain to her all the nuances of a *mayara* and relationships. I need to get on her ass over her blood magic and our bond, but she won't let me close enough to try and we've been busy. She only found out about Alchan right after we were attacked on the road."

"You were keeping Alchan's identity a secret from her?" Senri gasped, tossing down some tool she was using with all that female indignation he had seen before. "She's a Lorren! She should have known who Alchan was the moment they met!"

"Yeah, well, Alchan was putting it off, so that tied all of our hands," Nevyn said, jumping in to defend them. "Please, Senri-"

"No! I can't believe you males! You want her to trust you and you keep something like that from her? I'm amazed a female like her didn't gut one of you for it. Where's Alchan? *Bedru* and King or not, he needs this ass-chewing too."

"Wife of mine," Kian said, grabbing her before she could storm out. "No one gives the King an ass-chewing."

"Watch me!" she snapped.

"Mave beat you to it, but in a different way." Nevyn began to chuckle and Luykas quickly caught on to why. It led to him needing to smother some laughter. "She threatened him. It was impressive. She doesn't really care he's the King. If anything, she likes him less because of the title."

"Oh. That's good. She's more dominant than him, I think. He needs a real female to finally put his eyes down." Senri nodded, seeming satisfied. None of them burst her bubble that the battle of wills between Alchan and Mave was an ongoing issue. They were still challenging each other and Luykas honestly didn't know who would win one day.

The topic dropped as Kian continued to press for more information, something he could use to get to know Mave. Luykas had no advice, still trying to figure it out. He didn't want to give up the one secret they all knew worked, telling her about her family. That was something he wanted to use. He needed it.

"You know what, I'll go help her today. Senri, would you be appeased by that?" Kian leaned over his wife, smiling.

"Yes, I would. You're allowed to come back at dinner. I need you out of my hair for an afternoon." Senri waved him away, only giving him a dismissal in the form of a kiss on his cheek when he didn't move for her.

Kian grabbed Luykas on the way out, forcing them to leave everyone else behind.

"You're coming," he said.

"She's really riding you about this, isn't she?" Luykas looked over his shoulder to where Senri was left with the other males.

"She is." Kian sighed. "They spent one evening together and she's already protective in a way I can't describe. If I don't become Mave's friend and make sure she knows she has a place with my family, Senri will take my balls and feed them to gryphons."

"The problem?"

"I don't even know her, and getting to know her, as you say, will be hard." Kian shook his head. "I'll do it, though. I'll find a way to get in the good graces of the new female so Senri can have a new friend."

Luykas considered him. Then he gave up his best advice, even when he didn't want to. "We all figured out that she loves hearing about her family. If you have any stories about them, try and tell her some. She'll listen with bated breath, too curious to resist."

Kian crossed his arms, stopping to think about that. With a long hum, he nodded. "That would make sense, if she doesn't remember them very well."

"At all. She barely remembers them at all. Or her brothers, who I bet she saw even less of than her parents in the short time before the War ended."

"I remember the day her mother's fertile time started. Scared the shit out of everyone during a mission. We had to cut it short and get her back to camp." Kian snorted. "Then no one saw her or the General for days. Two years later, this little female was born and we never saw our commander again. She was sent away to hide. I should have known then it was a sign of bad things to come, not having her in the fight with us."

"They didn't want the War to stop them from having their lives either. You were with Senri back then. I bet you went home when her fertile time was coming closer." Luykas refused to fall into the belief that Mave's birth and everything after it was her fault. Or even her parents'. They had done what several others had done during the War, tried to keep moving forward and loving life.

"Took an entire year off, and we had an *oldura* make sure the timing was right, so I could be there for it." Kian smiled wistfully. "Didn't get lucky that time, but let's say it was the best vacation I had ever had. She's due for another in the next couple of years. Can't fucking wait."

"You see a future with kids?" he asked politely. He knew Kian desperately wanted a little boy or girl in the family.

"Of course! Senri has enough fertile times left to have at least one, maybe two, if we're lucky. Ah, it would be good to have another runt running around." Kian's smile stayed, now turning sad as they kept walking. "Maybe it'll ease the pain of losing the first."

Luykas had nothing to say about that. He knew saying something would only drag Kian down further. Out of all the older males, Kian was the one who used a grin and a laugh to cover a deep pain. At the beginning of the War, his family had one young son, about three hundred, who had wanted to be a warrior like Kian. He'd died in the first decade to a chance arrow during a skirmish. It had caused Senri to step back from the army, practically retiring from being a warrior until they had come to Olost, and Kian to fight even harder.

Finally, they were at the stables, and Kian's mood lightened again, covering that pain again, like he always did. "Well, I thought she was with Mat. Is Bryn another of her lovebirds?" Kian chuckled, nodding to the scene unfolding before them.

Luykas bit back a groan. He didn't like what he saw.

Bryn was shirtless, and Mave was just staring. Not even trying to hide it. When Bryn rose up from working on the shoes of one of the horses, she looked away. Bryn now stared at her, so obviously drinking in the sight of her that he was oblivious to them walking up. Then he grabbed a clay cup, put some water in it and handed it to her.

She took it so tentatively that Luykas nearly snarled just because of his own stupidity, wanting her to give him the look she was giving Bryn now. He wanted to be giving her the damned drink, now feeling stupid for not remembering to bring her some offering.

He must have had too much emotion on his face, because Kian was staring at him with curiosity.

"Are you okay? I hear some grumbling." Kian elbowed him. "Does someone here have a crush?"

"Yeah. Brynec," Luykas snapped. He did not look at Mave like that. He couldn't. Sure, they were in the right age distance for it to be normal. She was gorgeous and fierce. They had a blood bond, which now made his heart beat with such an intensity that he was concerned it would leave his chest. He was growing better at ignoring the signs from her every day.

Now it was too intense for him. Seeing her, wanting to be right next to her.

"Go bother her," he said quickly, stepping back. "I'm probably needed elsewhere."

"Are you sure?" Kian was so obviously trying not to laugh. "Oh, boss, you have problems. Aren't you blood-bonded with her?"

Luykas growled, taking off, leaving Kian's unsympathetic laughter behind.

He landed at his home, storming inside, trying to push the bond to the back of his mind again.

"Damn it!" he snarled. "Get out of my head!" He leaned on a wall, covering his face. The bond had nearly broken him during their fight with the Elvasi. He had seen her in that net and nearly lost it. They had nearly taken her. She would have gone so far from him if she'd been taken. Too far. The very idea of it had nearly driven him mad.

He'd never had to bury anything so quickly before. Seeing Mat and Bryn go to her side. Then his brother pulling her back to them, so they could keep her surrounded. Those things had brought him the shreds of peace he'd needed.

He wanted to tear out throats now. He'd come to his home to push the bond back down, but now he was absorbed in it. The undeniable need to be near her.

"I did this to myself," he said harshly, stumbling into his kitchen. "Fuck." His hands were shaking. She was too far away and he knew she was only a short flight away. It wasn't like this for others with the bond. They described it as a soft pull, but for him, it felt like his heart was being pulled out of his chest to go where it needed to be. "Fucking gods and their tricks." Why couldn't they just let him do it without this sort of backlash?

With some quick words, he started boiling water to make tea. A soothing brew would maybe help him. He still had so much to do for the day and couldn't be wound up with her on his mind like this. He needed to check on Leshaun and make sure Rain was going to be okay on his own in the village again.

As he worked in his kitchen, the bond faded. He distracted himself with other things he just had to do. Finally, he had a long sip of the finished tea and let it wash over him. It was made with a specific type of plant they had once harvested in Andena. Really, it was made for Andinna to bring down their tempers to better rationally handle things when something was too stressful. Luykas always drank a lot of it. Growing up in the Empire, his mother had made him drink it every night, just to make sure he never lost his temper and hurt someone. When he'd left, he had a hard time dealing with his Andinna side and continued to drink it, but not nearly every day. He'd weaned himself down to the occasional cup every so often, like most other Andinna. Now he wanted to put it into a waterskin and take it with him everywhere. It helped deaden the bond, or maybe just his need to respond to it.

He sighed happily, downing the glass and having another before deciding he had to get back to work.

He found Leshaun in the healer's home, resting quietly. The healer left quickly at his appearance, knowing he would want a private moment with the old male. Leshaun opened one eye and groaned. "What do you need?" the old male asked.

"I just wanted to catch you up on what was happening. We're leaving tomorrow for the mission."

"I won't be up in time for that. I thought we were taking a few weeks off and I could heal-" The old male looked pretty pissed off now.

"They came after Mave. There's a massive bounty on her head. We need to strike back now. But that's not the important part. Leshaun, we need to talk." Luykas hated being the one with this particular duty, but it was finally time. With Rain recently joining them and now Mave, it was time. "No more missions for you." He laid it out there quickly. "It's time you take a more comfortable position. I want you to manage our resources here at home while we're gone. Everything from our personal supplies, backup sets of armor, weapons, to our homes, so we can come home any day and they're ready for us."

Lehsaun's anger faded quickly and a tired sigh escaped the weak chest of the male. "I know. It's not just this injury. I'm old and tired. Matesh is still in his prime, but he's always helping me when he could be doing more."

"Exactly." And it was truthful of Leshaun to admit. Luykas didn't wound his pride by saying it should have happened a century earlier. Leshaun was an old, grizzled soldier and very few could understand all the things the old male knew. "Rain will be staying back this mission as well, just as we had planned. We don't need the wyvern for this and he needs the time."

"Boy's not been right since we rescued them, that's for sure. I'll keep him close. I'll be up and moving in the next day. That's what the healer thinks, anyway."

"You'll still receive a cut from us. You're still one of us." Luykas hated this. Leshaun wasn't the first they had to permanently leave behind. He hated it, but it was better than the alternative. The Company had lost over a dozen men in the last thousand years. Leshaun didn't need to be another body when they could use him elsewhere. "We just want you in a different role."

"I get it." Leshaun pushed himself to sit up. "You do me a great honor with this, Luykas. It wounds my pride to admit it's time, but I would rather live to see my nephew try for babies than die next to him, or get him killed trying to save me."

"I'm sorry, old friend." Luykas extended a hand and Leshaun took it firmly, proving he still had strength in his old body. He and Alchan had spoken a lot the night before about it. His brother had wanted to deliver the news himself, but Luykas decided he would. He and Leshaun had their disagreements, often. It felt right to him that he needed to deliver this new to the old male, even when it was hard new to deliver. A sign that he did still respect, no matter what. "Now, I need to go speak to Rain."

"Go. Thank you for coming to see me before moving out." Leshaun waved him away.

Luykas retreated, noticing the old male was back in a healing sleep before he made it out of the room. He must have been trying to doze back off when he'd walked in.

He jumped into the air once he was outside and went towards Rain's home with his father. He didn't bother knocking, something he'd never done with the family. He found Zayden in the main room, cleaning his home, not preparing for an important mission.

"Where's Rain?" he asked, eyeing the upset-looking father. He had two hundred years on Zayden, but they never acted like it. Sometimes, he wondered if Zayden was an old man in a young body and sometimes he wondered when the cranky father would grow up. Sometimes Luykas felt too old for his skin. Needless to say, they were never very close. The only thing that brought Luykas close with Zayden was helping raise Rain. Luykas knew what it meant to be a mutt and had grown attached to the little blue bundle when he'd been born. Zayden had to tolerate it.

"Down with the males who keep the patrol. He's getting to work to avoid me." Zayden sighed. "I'm trying, Luykas. I'm not bothering him, letting him deal with whatever is wrong in his own time."

"I know it's hard, but it's good you're letting him." He couldn't say much else. The secret of what had happened to Rain in the pits was one he would keep until the day he died. Rain would decide who could know and who couldn't. His heart broke for the young male, like it had when they had met Bryn and learned what happened to him through the centuries of slavery. Like it broke knowing how Mave was treated. "Well, if he's already getting to work, then I don't need him. You should go down and help Mave and Bryn with the horses. I bet Matesh will be down there soon. Don't stay locked away just because Rain is going through some things on his own."

"I'm his father-"

"But you aren't just his father. You're also an important friend to many others. Maybe getting closer with Mave will help you reconnect with Rain, or sticking close to Matesh. He loves her and she loves him in return. Matesh is his uncle in more than just the adoptive way I am. He looks at Mat like family." Luykas threw the suggestion out there, not liking how Zayden was locking himself away because of the situation with Rain. Zayden watched him, narrowing his eyes, so he continued. "I'm just saying. I am your boss and older than you."

"You aren't that much older than me."

"Zayden, with the way you behave, I'm not even sure Leshaun is as old as you." He snorted, shaking his head.

"Take that back! I'm a male in my prime! I could have any female out there if I wanted any of them." Zayden tossed the broom to the side.

Luykas shrugged. "If they could get over that they're with a grouch, maybe. I don't exactly see any females trying to crawl on your lap. They like Rain's more and he's not even interested in them."

"Says the man who has the only female who talks to him running in the other direction." Zayden smirked. "At least I've been married and had a kid."

He growled. That wasn't the retort he was expecting. For that, he made his suggestion an order. "Go help with the damned horses."

"Before I leave, do you know what Alchan's punishment for Rain will be?" Zayden picked his broom back up and put it away in a small closet.

"No. He hasn't shared that with me. Maybe since Rain's staying here, that's punishment enough. Patrols under Senri."

"Senri is too easy on him. Won't be good enough for Alchan. Well, I just have to hope Alchan has a shred of mercy."

Luykas wasn't worried. He knew Zayden would be, and he knew Matesh was as well, but he trusted his brother to have an appropriate punishment for the first-time offender. Rain wasn't a troublemaker, not like Bryn or Mat could be.

"Put it out of your mind. It'll be okay." Luykas waved Zayden to follow him. "I'll help with the horses too." The bond was still scratching him, but the soothing tea had him in a good place to deal with seeing the other males fawn all over Mave. He wasn't sure why that had started bothering him. It was probably because they got all the attention he wanted. He'd never wanted a female to look his way, not like he wanted her. It wasn't sexual. He just wanted her acknowledgement.

"You know, I haven't felt this good about going on a mission in a long time. I'm tired, bruised from the road, and worried about things, but we're about to bring some good shit back to the village and kick some Elvasi ass where it hurts." Zayden walked out onto the front platform.

"You agree with it?" Luykas hadn't known that.

"Who doesn't? We're mercenaries. Stealing, killing, and having professional grudges is what we do." Zayden jumped off without him, just falling off the platform and spreading his wings to catch the air.

35

MAVE

"We're moving out!" Alchan called loudly, sitting on his massive gelding.

Mave swung herself up on her new blue roan mare. It was a big horse, bigger than the ones she had seen in the Empire. She had learned it was a specific type of horse the Company bred just for their use. They looked for size, stamina, and strength. They weren't the fastest horses, but they could run all day and carry a heavy load.

Like the Andinna. Bigger than the other races, with wings included, they needed bigger horses.

"What do you think of her?" Matesh asked her, pulling his bay gelding alongside her mare.

"She's gorgeous," Mave answered softly, reaching to rub the mare's neck. "Let's go." She gently tapped her heels to the side of the mare, who jumped into action. She held on tightly, swallowing her discomfort. She had to ride for the mission. She could ride a stolen cart on the way back, but she had to ride the mare there.

It was scarier than the mission. A few hours a day of training while they were on the road had helped her get all the basics down, but this was just her and the mare now. There was no other option for her if it didn't work.

She followed the Company out, in the middle of the pack. In front of her, Luykas and Alchan were leading with Kian, Nevyn, and Varon right behind them. Bryn and Zayden were behind her. Bryn, who had barely left her side since the stables, was so close behind her that his horse was getting hit by her mare's tail. The gelding nickered, annoyed.

"Good luck!" Rainev called. "Bring glory back to the Company!"

At that, the Company roared, lifting fists. She joined in, feeling the adrenaline of going off on a mission. It was a heady feeling. She felt indestructible as they rode out, the cheers and watchful eyes of the free Andinna on them.

"Does it always feel this way?" she asked Mat, wondering if this was normal. She didn't expect fanfare as they rode out.

"Yeah, they're always like that. It's an honor to be a warrior of the Andinna. We're a mercenary company, sure. We get our paychecks and we cause trouble, but most of what we do is to help them. We bring back money and supplies so no other Andinna need to leave the mountains and risk capture."

"Are all the free Andinna in these mountains?" She looked back to see that many of the young Andinna had followed them as they left, still hooting and cheering them on. It felt like they were riding off to war.

"No. There's a small mountain range in northern Olost where a small portion of our population ended up. They protect those mountains fiercely. We don't have a lot of trouble happen in that area, so they don't need us looking out for them. Not as much, anyway." Matesh chuckled. "You get used to it. You're a mercenary now, and this is just how we treat our warriors."

"But we aren't heroes," she reminded him, smiling.

"No, we're not heroes. We do what we can when we can, but we're not out sowing rebellion or anything." He nodded slowly, agreeing with her.

She could see it and she disagreed. Weren't heroes. They kept telling her that, and sometimes, their actions proved otherwise. They were mercenaries who helped the free Andinna how they could, but they weren't heroes. She was beginning to believe they were wrong. They didn't try to be heroes, but here was the Company, out to get supplies to keep their people fed - and in the process, get revenge on the Elvasi for coming after them. They were going out to hit the Empire in a way that hurt, to show that coming after Mave was coming after all of them.

She didn't say anything more to Mat. She had a feeling they were more heroic than they wanted to admit, but she wasn't going to burst their bubble.

She was so lost in her thoughts that she didn't notice Kian slow and fall in next to her, on the opposite side of Mat. "So, now that I know the whole story, I think we should talk."

She sighed. "How much did Alchan and Luykas tell you?"

"Everything they know. We don't keep secrets in the Ivory Shadows. I was curious, too." Kian watched her with interest as they rode through the thick woods of the mountains.

"Well, if you know everything, I'm not sure what there is to talk about." She wasn't sure how to feel about Kian's curiosity, so she'd been avoiding it since the day before. This wasn't the first time he'd tried to talk to her, and each time, she found something to do. Now they were riding and she had nowhere to run, no excuse to get out of it.

"He's trying to get a feel for you. Stop avoiding him or he'll get continuously worse," Mat said, cutting in before Kian could continue to speak. She wanted to snap at her male for opening his mouth. He'd teased about how she ran from Kian, but not Senri or her other husbands.

"That," the older male said, nodding to her *bodanra*. "Just wanted to get to know the newest Company member. We have to work together, ya know."

"It's hard for me to open up to people," she said, starting it off. "I spent over nine hundred years with males who would rather kill me than talk to me, so it's been an adjustment to work with a group of males. I've never had much time with other females, so I'm at a complete loss there. I can butcher Andena fairly well, but I'm still trying to catch up. I can't fly. I know who I am and what role I played at the end of the War, so I'm not completely ignorant." She rambled it all off, hoping she got most of his questions answered before he could even ask them.

"You don't like me!" he accused, beginning to laugh. Suddenly, she wasn't looking at the older male with a family to protect and fight for. She was looking at a boy, complaining to a friend. "Nevyn, she doesn't like me!"

"She doesn't like anyone except Matesh and Rain," Nevyn called back. She couldn't see his face, but she heard the teasing note in his words. "Get over it."

"I had fun in Namur with you and Varon," she pointed out. She didn't dislike any of them. It wasn't like that. "I'm just not used to people trying to know me. It's been strange to deal with."

"What did you do with them in Namur?" he asked, his eyes lightened with curiosity again. She pulled her mare away from his, riding closer to Mat, who needed to pull away himself so their wings weren't hitting each other.

"We took her to the fighting ring," Nevyn answered before she could. "Did I forget to tell you that?"

"Oh, that's right. That's where you all pissed off some Elvasi and exposed Mave's identity to them." Kian's booming laugh rolled over them again. "Skies, there's always trouble with you all. You know, I worked with Nevyn and Varon with your mother. She used to get into trouble like this too. We would all hear your father complaining about how she went out and got into a fight and brought home trouble."

She considered him. "Tell me more." It wasn't a request. Many Andinna only spoke of her parents with the utmost respect, even though her father had lost them the War. Kian sounded like he saw them differently.

"Well, your mother's warriors…We were very good at what we did. Very good, but we were rowdier than most of the other warriors. When the army fell, and Anden with it, those of us left immediately joined up with Alchan and Luykas because we still needed the action." Kian shook his head. "Not the point. Your mother. Nevyn, what's a good story about her? I have a few ideas."

Now she was engrossed in every word that came out of his mouth. So many of the males in the Company had known her family. At her current count, Luykas, Alchan, Varon, Nevyn, and now Kian had known her parents personally. Matesh, Leshaun, and Zayden had stories of them from afar, how they inspired the Andinna to keep fighting, were great military commanders, but nothing personal. Rainev and Bryn knew nothing about them.

So she had found someone else who could tell her *more*.

"Tell her about the time her mother got everyone drunk and the impromptu mission we went on." Nevyn was chuckling. "That's a good one."

So he did. Kian launched into the story, and she couldn't stop from laughing at the idea of some female leading a band of bumbling, drunk warriors into an Elvasi scouting camp they knew about. How they flipped the Elvasi out of their beds and wrecked the camp. They didn't even kill anyone. They just had a bit of fun and chased the scouts back out of the mountain.

"Why didn't you take them all out?" she asked when he was done.

"Ah, well, your parents were of the mind that we shouldn't slaughter people. We're warriors, aye, but many were just soldiers who wanted to go home. We never were the best of friends with the Elvasi, but the War came out of nowhere. In the beginning, we tried a lot of ways to show we didn't want it. That was one of them. We let a lot of people go home." Kian shrugged. "I didn't initially agree, but I saw the point. Mercy is sometimes harder than anything, and they didn't want us living up to the vicious reputation the Elvasi were trying to spread."

"Oh." She nodded, seeing the point. She was a vicious fighter, and mercy in her world would have gotten her killed. If she had the choice, would she be capable of showing a bit of kindness to a future opponent? Would she be able to do the unexpected and free an enemy soldier to go home? She put the thought aside to ask him for more. "Do you remember anything else?"

"Have I found a way to make the newest member of the Company my friend?" he asked back, grinning. "Senri would kill me if I made the newest female of our band dislike me. She's trained me better than that."

She couldn't resist smiling. Senri must want to kill this male on a regular basis. "I think you might have."

"Good! Maybe I'll tell you about an old mission I went on with this group. It was in-"

"We don't talk about that mission, Kian!" Alchan roared from the front.

Kian went back to laughing hysterically and launched into another fun tale of her mother.

W̲HEN THE C̲OMPANY bedded down for their first night on the road, Mave curled into Matesh, but couldn't sleep. This was her first real mission with them. She was nervous and knew sleep wasn't going to take her any time soon.

With that on her mind, she left her bedroll and walked away from the Company's campsite. She could stretch and exercise her wings. She had stayed in the habit while on the road, but it had been a couple of days. She didn't want to fall out of it. She could be in the air by the end of winter if she continued to work for it.

She stretched them with extensions on her own, then flapped them twice until a hand landed on one.

"Go to sleep," Bryn told her, walking around her. "Ya need to rest while we're on the road."

"I'll be fine," she replied. They had been on the road for what seemed like ages now. "I want to exercise. It might help."

"Mave-"

"Bryn, don't order me around." She raised an eyebrow. "I'm not hurting anyone."

He narrowed his eyes. "Stubborn female."

"Know-it-all male," she retorted. He was turning into Matesh. She could see it. He really wanted her to listen to him. "Why are you awake?"

"I'm first watch, like always." He shrugged, sitting down on a nearby tree stump. "I don't sleep easy. Ya know that by now."

"I do." She watched him, continuing her exercises. She wasn't going to stop because he was acting *male*. "I understand."

"Oh, I know ya do," he muttered, looking away.

She frowned. They had been growing closer, so what was this? She liked her daily time with Bryn when they worked on her wings. She enjoyed talking to him, listening to his stories. She enjoyed just being near the quiet, leaner male. It helped he was easy on the eyes in ways she never expected.

But now he seemed put out by her or something she couldn't see.

"Have you been drowning?" she asked softly. Over two weeks ago, she'd described her memories and the pain they brought in a way only they would know and understand. Drowning.

"A little, aye," he answered. "The more we talk about yer pain, the more they remind me of mine."

"And Rain's," she added, nodding. "Every time I think of what they did to him..." She had never felt so much rage as she had that day. Now, she could remember old pain with it. Old memories, ones she worked very hard to bury. While they were moving around, it was easier. She knew one day they would all come back and attempt to ruin her. She just needed to keep fighting it. "Talk to me?"

"I was raped by my owner. Ya know that," Bryn said suddenly. "I killed him for it, but that didn't mean it all stopped. I was smaller than the other males in the buildin', so I was constantly protectin' myself. I never got a private space. I got used to it. I never slept in a room where I couldn't escape. I would get cornered too often, so I had to change." Bryn shook his head. "Now, I barely sleep."

She wasn't sure what to say except her own story. "I would find places only I could get into, where only one or two Andinna would fit if they found me. I liked the tight spaces more since I had the advantage. I feel more comfortable sleeping in a small room."

"We all find our own ways to survive," he said quietly. His eyes searched her face now, looking for some solidarity.

"We do," she agreed. "It's easier with others, though. I've learned that." *Finally*.

"Isn't it? I learned that too. Varon and Nevyn taught me."

"Rain and Mat, but you know that." She fiddled with her hands now. There in the dark, they were standing so close now.

"And each other, I think?" Bryn's words sounded strangely hopeful. "We're friends. Ya've got me and I've got ya." He emphasized friends.

"Of course." She looked up to him, taking in the details of his face in the red light of the moon. "You haven't gone far in the last couple of days. You've been right beside me, really." It was the truth. He had barely left her side.

Not that it's a problem...I hope he doesn't think it's a problem.

"I don't like how they tried to take ya," he whispered, leaning down, making their eyes level. "As we get closer to this, I find myself worryin' they might actually succeed."

I'll be fine. That's what she wanted to say, but instead she found herself drifting a little closer to him and his full lips. A strong hand took her waist, and she was certain they were going to kiss. Her mind was warring with this idea that she already had Matesh and did she want to handle a second male? Did Bryn want her, or something more?

Then he was gone, his hand off her. "I need to get to work," he said softly. He walked into the dark, out of her line of sight.

She didn't know what else to do except lay back down next to

Matesh in camp. Her mind stayed on Bryn the entire time, even as she laid her head on the big chest of her lover.

I like him.

The thought was quick and fleeting. It took her a moment to realize she had even thought it.

I want him.

That thought was more natural. She wanted Bryn with her. She wanted him with her and Mat. She wanted the long, deep conversations, the knowledge, and yes, the lean form she found attractive on no one else.

She still felt all the normal things for Mat, curled up next to him, engulfed by his spicy scent. She still felt the deep well of emotion when she saw his eyes. The heat between them. It was all there. She couldn't imagine a life without Matesh in it anymore. She needed him to be her rock as she stumbled through her new freedom.

But she wanted Bryn and his summer-sky-blue eyes, too. His touch of darkness, like her own, and how he kept telling her in some fashion that they were both strong for surviving.

She needed more time to figure this out. She knew it was natural. She had seen Senri and her two husbands, obviously friendly with each other. Kian fit in there somehow. She had seen them around the village. She had glimpsed others who wandered by while she worked. This was normal.

I'm just getting used to having one male. How do I even talk to Bryn about it? How do I admit that I'm attracted to him too? That I want him around Mat and I?

Will it hurt Mat?

She didn't have the answers for herself, and on a mission wasn't the time for these sorts of problems. She wasn't going to distract everyone with it. It would have to wait.

36

RAINEV

Rainev watched his family leave, desperately wishing he was with them, long after they disappeared from view. When he'd asked for the time off, he'd been hurting, fresh out of the pits. Now? He wanted to feel strong, and the only way to do that was to fight. He wanted to test the Elvasi with the Company. He wanted to watch them burn.

He didn't want to be alone, either. Leshaun was still in his healing sleep. The old male probably wouldn't wake up for another couple of days, and that was the only person Rain had.

"It's good see you back, Rain," a male said kindly, walking up to him.

Rain hadn't moved from his spot since the Company left. He continued to watch the road, knowing they were long gone now. "Hi, Cartesh," he said softly, not looking at the attractive young male beside him now. "What can I do for you?"

"I was hoping we could hang out and, uh…well, you were gone and we all thought the Company might not get you back. I was worried."

Rain nodded. "Yeah. Thanks." He stepped away and continued walking, hoping Cartesh wouldn't follow him. He didn't want to see

Cartesh or any of his other friends, really. He wanted to be with the Company. He wanted to be out of the village, burning some damned Elvasi in his armor. The lust for vengeance was running in his blood, and he wasn't out there because he was weak enough to say he would take time off.

Too damned weak. That's all I am without my wyvern.

He took off, flying high to the home he shared with his father. He should have moved out a century ago, but then he and his *bodra* would be put in the community building for the Company, which wasn't much better. As long as they wanted to live as a family, they had a private residence. They all called it a community building for singles to live, but really, it was military barracks. Full of males, all hoping any single female gave them a glance. The females always got their own residence, a space to grow. The males, not so much.

"He'll kill me if this place is dirty when he gets back…" Rain looked around at their dust-covered furniture, the kitchen in shambles. He knew his father tried to clean up a little bit, but didn't have a lot of time before leaving again. Rain knew he wasn't the kindest to his *baba* anymore. Maybe this would be a sign to his father it would be okay in the end.

I hope it'll be okay, anyway.

Rain got to work, starting with the dusting. His father always swept the floor first, which was always a bad move. He had a faint memory of his mother telling him to dust first, so the dirt could all be swept up at once, but his father was always stubborn about it. He would clean the way he wanted to clean, if he was being forced to.

The memory made Rain smile just a little. Maybe some time at the village would do some good - away from the pain, so far removed from the danger the Company always put themselves in.

He cleaned for the rest of the evening, but there was a point when he knew he needed to go find something to eat. They had been away from home so long that they had nothing in their own pantry. He had nothing to eat without going to the hall.

He groaned, looking at the progress he made. It would work. He dusted, swept, and cleaned off the furniture. It would be all the work he could get done. Tomorrow he had to start on patrols, which would be his life every other night until the Company returned.

He left his work there and jumped off his platform, landing easily at the hall where others were flooding in for the community dinner. It was mostly used by singles who had no space to keep their own food, but it was also a meeting ground. The males who were in charge of it made sure to have offerings for each meal of the day, except on holidays. Then there was a never-ending amount of food for everyone all day.

He walked in quietly, hoping not to draw attention to himself, but it didn't work. He was blue; it never worked.

"Rainev!" Senri called out in Andena. Now that Mave was gone, no one would be speaking Common. "Come sit with us!" He sighed and saw the female waving him down with her two other husbands. He dutifully went, accepting the plate dropped in front of him immediately.

"I'll get more." Willen patted his shoulder before leaving.

Rain looked over the plate, seeing it was completely untouched. He called a thank you after the youngest of Senri's husbands then dove in, ignoring the stares he was getting from Kian's family. Like many of those attached to the Company, they treated him like family, the only child born to any member yet.

"So, you didn't go on the mission with them. They probably could have used you, but I'm glad to have you with me, no matter." Senri's comment sounded innocent, but from Senri, it was anything but. She was fishing for information.

"I needed some time off." He didn't really know what else to say. He wasn't going to spill his guts to Senri, of all people. She was one of those mother hen types, but with a battle axe. That combination was terrifying.

"Well, it was your first mission and it all went wrong. I'm glad you decided to spend some time at home and not out there with them."

Senri's smile was warm and endearing. "Young males like you shouldn't be off getting hurt. Let the older boys do it."

Rain nodded absentmindedly. It wasn't a secret that she didn't like him joining the Company. She never outright told him his decision was wrong or bad, but she always made comments. Loving, motherly comments about him staying home, helping the village. Being a warrior here where he could be under her watchful eye.

She's not even my mother.

Rain hated how bitter the thought sounded echoing in his head.

"So, how long until the Harvest Day?" he asked, pushing the conversation in a different direction.

"A couple of weeks. Probably before the Company returns," Willen answered as he sat back down. "Harvest Day. By far the worst festival we ever have."

Rain chuckled. It was. Every able body was expected to help pull in crops, help salt meat for stores through the winter. A big community event to prepare for long, cold winters. With how tight their lives were in Olost, the old feasts he heard about on Harvest Day no longer happened. They saved everything for Winter Solstice and the Spring Festival. Harvest Day was a day of work.

"I'll put you on patrol that day," Senri whispered to him with a wink.

"Thank you." He hated being roped into Harvest Day. None of the Company enjoyed it.

He kept eating as they began talking about what had gone on with the village while he was gone. Gossip mostly. Allaina lost a male from her *mayara*, which was somewhat surprising. The split wasn't amicable, which meant the male moved on to a smaller village to get away from the female.

"She offended him and thought it was okay. He didn't, so he left." Senri shrugged.

"Sometimes things don't work out," Willen agreed softly, nodding.

"It was her fault, and she knew better than to try and keep him but never apologize for the offense."

"What was the offense?" Rain frowned, looking between them.

"He was injured back in the War. That one. She teased him harshly one day in front of several other warriors. They had been together since before the War. It was finally the straw that broke the wyvern's back." Senri shook her head, pursing her lips in distaste. "You never tease a warrior, male, female, lover or not. Warriors are respected. You don't laugh at the wounds of battle."

Rain felt the sting of what Allaina could have possibly said and he didn't know what it was. To drive away a lover of over a thousand years with an offhand, rude joke? He couldn't imagine how cruel she must have been.

"What else is going on?"

"Leeli rejected Cartesh only a few weeks ago." Gentrin began to chuckle. "The young male was so put out. They had been doing really well, but Leeli didn't think it was going to grow, or so she told most of us."

Rain tried not to think of that one. Before he left with the Company, he and Cartesh had been casual lovers, something to scratch the itch. When he left, the other male told him that he wanted to pursue a female he had feelings for.

Now I know why Cartesh was so quick to see me once my family was gone. Damn.

Rain wasn't interested. He once hung out with several males, all around his age, but now, the idea of joking and fooling around didn't appeal to him. He felt like he was over that stage of his life, and over Cartesh.

He finished eating as they kept on with the gossip, only jumping in to make sure they knew he was listening. "I'm going to head out. Senri, what time do you need me tomorrow?"

"Dawn, but feel free to be late. There's no reason to rush to get you to work."

Oh yeah there is. The King expects me to be working while he's gone. Rain didn't say that, though, only heading out after handing in his plate and spoon to the male on duty.

He had little to do. He hated it, after months and months of having a strict schedule, even on the ship - always moving, always working.

Now he was by himself. The world seemed too dark, even under the near-constant glow of the red moon. He wanted Mave there with him. Matesh, or even his father. Any of them would work. Shit, even Luykas or Alchan. Just some sort of company.

He headed out towards the spring, grabbing his supplies at home along the way. He could bathe and then get back to work in the house. That was really his only objective, keeping himself busy.

The male spring was crowded, and although Rainev was gay, he couldn't go to the quieter female spring. That had been established when he was entering adulthood. He was male, and if they made an exception for him, they would have males coming over all the time. The line needed to stay defined.

He stripped, ignoring the others, and slid in on a deeper end, sighing as the heat sank to his bones. This was something he'd missed. The hot springs. Mave had the best bathing in the pits, but the spring water in her pool had been cold. The hot springs were life.

"Rain! Good to see you again!" a younger male called out, waving.

He only waved back, unable to find the energy to start yelling over the other conversations going on. Like everything the Andinna did, bathing was a social activity. If anyone wanted privacy, they needed to come when everyone else was probably asleep or working.

"He's an Ivory Shadow now. Too cool for us?" Another friend threw his hands up, looking particularly offended.

"Tired," he called back, not wanting any bad blood. "You try being captured by the Empire and see how much energy you have when you finally get home."

"Oh, the *raki* has a comeback!" An older male began to laugh. "Leave him be. New warriors always need some time to themselves when they get their first time off. You all will see when you get your first taste of blood. You got blood, right, Rain? Is it time to update your *tatua*?"

"It might be. I saw blood. Too much, even by our standards." Rain sighed, leaning his head back on a rock. "Elliar is a nightmare. The Colosseum? It's a nightmare."

"Ah, that's right. You all brought back the so-called Champion too." The older male moved closer. Rain couldn't remember his name. "Is she as good as the rumors we always hear?"

"Better, but there's a lot the rumors got wrong, too." Rain couldn't stop a small smile. "And she's my *illo amyr* now. Adoptive, of course, but who's counting?"

"Ah, that's nice. If you can see her as family, then I see no reason to get up in arms like the females seem to be." The older male chuckled.

Rain didn't respond, letting everyone go back to whatever else they were doing. New *tatua*. It was that time, wasn't it? This last adventure would probably add detail to his back and chest. He wasn't going to try and guess past that. The magic of the *tatua* did whatever it felt it needed to do.

He wondered who to ask. Leshaun had done his coming of age, and everything since. Rain could technically learn to do his own, but he never cared to train past the basics of being a Blackblood. He knew quick healing techniques, the ability to speed the healing of others, but really, he was already a wyvern in Andinna flesh. Blood magic and the centuries of training many put into it wasn't on his list of things to do. As long as he knew how to control it, no one would force him to learn more.

Late in the night, he was practically alone in the hot spring. He was finished bathing and needed to get some rest if he wanted to meet Senri at dawn.

He was nearly back at his home when Cartesh flew up next to him. "Come hang out!" Cartesh called.

"Not in the mood." Rain landed on his front platform, shaking his head as the other male landed next to him.

"Come on, Rain. It's been months since you left with the Company and we should reconnect." The attractive male stepped closer, forcing Rain to open his front door and move inside so he wasn't pushed against the door.

"Cartesh-" He was pushed against a wall and their chests pushed together. The other male's mouth came down on his, and Rain knew he was in the mood.

A year ago, Rain would have given in, enjoying the forceful nature. Once, he liked how he and Cartesh could go at it. How the other male could bend him, make him want to submit a little, even though he could shift into a wyvern. It was natural, not because he was gay, but because young males liked to test their wills against each other, finding out who they were, and where they ranked with each other. It led to explorations in sex that they would need for when they were with females. Not all males were into it, but Rain had yet to meet a male besides Matesh that had never fooled around with another male.

Now, a bolt of fear ran through him. He shoved, growling, sending Cartesh into the other wall.

"Get out," he snarled.

"Don't play games with me, Rain. You said I was always welcome to come back if things with Leeli didn't work out." The male filled his space again. "You've always liked a bit of force. Leeli didn't. She wanted her males a little softer in bed. A little less demanding."

"Get out!" Rain demanded, shoving again. He resisted the urge to grab a blade hanging on the wall in the main room. He resisted collapsing as the smell of the pits filled his nose. His hands began to shake. "Get out! You can't have me!" He shoved again, this time pushing Cartesh closer to the door and out of it. He felt the wyvern trying to take him, to destroy the threat in front of him, partially shifting as his fangs grew longer and he knew scales began to show up on his flesh. "I won't be owned! I'm not weak!"

Cartesh paled and jumped off the platform, leaving when he realized this had nothing to do with him.

Rain was left alone in the front door of his home, the memories slowly leaving. A reality sank in. Cartesh, if he'd been a real friend, would have backed off and tried to find out what was wrong, what had set Rain off. Instead, he didn't get what he wanted, didn't want to deal with Rain, and left.

I want Mave. I need my big sister.

She would have never just left. Or Matesh. Or any of them. They would have stayed. He closed his door and collapsed. He never made it to his bed to sleep, closing his eyes as the silent tears fell and the memories assaulted him all night.

37

BRYNEC

It took just over a week for them to reach their destination. Bryn spent the entire week focused on all the wrong things. He should have been focused on their mission. They were there now, able to eye the estate they were about to raid. They were tucked in the woods off the property under the cloak of a red night. Much of Olost was heavily wooded, which proved useful most of the time. Bryn *needed* to focus on the cleared property he could see now.

But then there was Mave.

She consumed his thoughts. He stuck close and was honest about why. Seeing her get grabbed by those Elvasi had made him fearful. It had made him angry. He wasn't going to let it happen. He wanted to remain close to her, protect her, even as she jumped headlong into battle. Such was the life of a male Andinna. The urge to protect, serve, and follow, no matter what the female did.

He knew it was hopeless for him. That first night on the road, he'd nearly stolen that kiss. Every night after, he was plagued by the sight of her without a top on or in the springs. He'd seen her nude before, glimpses on the ship, but this had been so much more. The water wrapping around her hips, and how close he got when he helped her with the top. How deceptively smooth her skin was, even covered in small scars from battle. He could still feel her when he'd accidentally brushed against her.

What is wrong with me? Any other female. One who wouldn't mind that I'm smaller than the rest of them. One that didn't have the same terrors I did.

No, I had to fall for her. Of course I did.

He groaned as they all started jumping off their horses, Alchan gesturing for them to stay close. They were just out of the range of the patrol for the estate. This was a place they had watched many times before, thinking it was too big to hit. They had gone after smaller places owned by the same Elvasi, always on his tail, but never this place, his home and base of operations. The fact that they had been considering it before they were attacked was risky.

Now, there was no other way. They were going to end this game with this Elvasi once and for all. He couldn't have Mave. His men couldn't have her. Not if Bryn had anything to say about it.

"You okay? Seem distracted." Nevyn slid up beside him.

"I have been." He couldn't stop his gaze from finding her, only a few feet away, tying her horse up next to Matesh's. "Too distracted."

"Oh." Nevyn didn't seem surprised, but he did seem very curious, looking between him and Mave. "Bryn, you want to talk about this?"

He stepped closer to his friend to keep his voice down and spoke in Andena, so she had very little chance to hear him. "What's there to talk about? We're on a mission. I'm not her type. I'll get over it eventually."

"Sure." Nevyn didn't sound too convinced. He kept to Andena as well, knowing Bryn's idea. "How do you know you aren't her type?"

"Look at…" He gestured very slyly at Matesh. "He's massive, and she obviously loves it. He's the biggest male here. I'm the smallest. Plus, I'm another fucking prior gladiator. I'll never keep her happy like he does."

"Uh huh." The asshole began to smile. "We've been friends for a very long time, Bryn. If you hold yourself back, I'll fucking gut you.

Varon won't stop me, either." He nodded to his partner, the smile never leaving. Varon looked up and grinned.

Bryn knew he would get no support from them.

"So what would you have me do? Try and get fucking tossed aside?" Bryn didn't particularly like that idea. He would rather be as close to her as possible without the risk of being hurt. He'd never really gone after a female, never wanted the attachment. Now he did, but he knew it would never work.

"I think you should try, and if she offers, don't say no." Nevyn shrugged. "How do you know she isn't feeling something herself? You two spend a lot of time together, and Matesh seems like he's not bothered by you at all, even after that incident on the ship."

"Matesh talked to me." He hadn't told the couple yet. "About it… back in Namur…"

"And you didn't say anything to us?" Nevyn's jaw dropped. "Really? Matesh is fine, or he wants you to back off? Explain."

"You two are old gossips," he muttered, shaking his head. He should have known they would want in his business like this. He should have brushed Nevyn off from the start. "He said I could try for *mayara*. He wouldn't stop me."

"Then try!" Nevyn smacked his arm hard enough that the smack drew attention.

"You two, get over here and stop whispering. We've got work to do." Alchan waved them closer. Bryn was grateful for it, even if he knew the hit would bruise. Nevyn glared at him as they walked closer and stopped in the ring.

Bryn knew his friend wanted him happy, but with Mave? Was he crazy? And it wasn't that he wasn't trying. He was, but he had no hope of succeeding. It was a fact for him. He would always be a friend she could talk to, no matter what that almost kiss meant.

Now he needed to somehow stop thinking about her. They had to run this mission as smoothly as possible. They needed a strong showing to show that the mess in the Empire was only the beginning. If they were going to be hunted, they could and would fight back.

And he would never let them have Mave back.

"You and Luykas have a plan, I'm guessing." Kian crossed his arms. He was a no-nonsense man when it came to missions, even when Nevyn wanted to keep joking around. The dichotomy of the two was something to witness, as Nevyn went to his side and leaned on him, grinning. Between the two of them, they had hundreds, maybe even thousands of successful missions, supported by Varon from a distance.

"Of course?" Luykas was looking fairly insulted by the comment. "Come on, Kian."

"Bryn, you're going in as scout. Keep your head down, take out a few stragglers and get into position for Mave and Matesh to follow you. You three will be the kill squad. Go after the merchant and put him down. It's time to end it on that front. The Elvasi need a new fucking ringleader." Alchan pointed between the three of them. "Then meet us in the warehouse."

"The good stuff," Nevyn commented lightly.

"Yeah, the supplies. This is the full intent of the mission. On the eastern side of the estate, the man has a warehouse where the hunters gear up, getting food and supplies, then go out to capture our people. We've hit smaller ones. This is easy. The rest of us will go in and steal carts and horses first. We'll load up and defend it. Kill any Elvasi you come across, unless it seems excessive. No servants, women, or children. You know the rules."

"We ride out together or not at all," Luykas continued where Alchan left off. "Dead or alive, every single one of us is going to leave. This place is three times the size of our normal side jobs. We weren't hired to do this. This isn't a bounty like we normally hunt. This is personal. Because of that, I want you all to keep your heads on straight and don't get caught up in trying to die for it."

"Side job?" Mave piped up, looking around, hoping for an explanation.

"We normally squeeze hits on the Elvasi in between other jobs or when work is dried up," Bryn answered, wanting to be the one who gave her what she wanted. "This is our more helpful work for the Andinna as a whole, since we'll give out much of this to the village and other smaller ones down in the mountains."

"Okay." Mave seemed appeased and went back to watching their leaders, content again.

"We'll get back to that, probably in the spring." Alchan dismissed the discussion with that, getting back on the task of their current job. "Bryn, send the signal when you're in position. You know how?"

Bryn pulled the small stick from his pocket. Luykas made it with sorcery, and Bryn wasn't sure how it worked. He stopped questioning the strange things Luykas could do. "Crack it and it glows. Hold it up from the position, Varon will be able to see it."

"Exactly. Once we see that signal, we move. It means Bryn found a clear path to the objective for Mave and Matesh. The warehouse is easier. We're not going to be particularly quiet, which should be plenty of distraction for you three." Alchan waved him off. "Go get to work, Bryn. Stay safe."

Others said the same as he put away the signal stick and adjusted his belt. He pulled his scarf up to cover the lower half of his face. He'd given Mave some partial answers. It covered his white teeth in the dark, obscured him. He knew how to keep his wings in tight enough to slide in places where others couldn't.

He hadn't always intended to be the sneaky one of the Company, but it was a role that suited him. He once lived like this, creeping around to keep himself safe. The darkness of the docks became his safe place when he needed to get out of his captivity and stretch his legs, but he had to avoid everyone when he did that.

It went hand in hand with the job he now had.

He slipped away from the group and towards the sprawling estate. A few fields of crops were around, specialty spices that the owner sent back to the Empire with new slaves and other goods from Olost. The scent was rich in his nose as he ducked down far enough that the crops went over his head. He found the trails workers used, not wanting to brush against the plants and create any rustling that could draw attention to himself.

He couldn't let this get personal. He knew Luykas' words had wisdom, but damned if he didn't feel this was personal. They tried to take the Company down and leave with Mave. They had set up an ambush right outside their home.

Sure, the Company had been planning to raid here beforehand, but the Elvasi hadn't known that. They had thought the Company would be weak from the trouble in the Empire. They had thought it would be easy, probably, going after several Andinna who had been on the road for too long, tired and ready for home.

The Ivory Shadows were always ready for a fight. It was time to show them that again. The Elvasi had obviously forgotten who they were messing with.

Bryn drew closer, passing the warehouse without a concern. He could hear some of the guards talking. "The ambush the guys set up? We still haven't heard back. Figured that would have gone down by now."

"Who knows? The Andinna probably got sidetracked. They'll come back with the bitch and get fucking rich. I'm not testing the fucking Company. Catching a wanderer brings in better money, in my opinion. More of them than one female who has a fucking small army with her."

Bryn snorted. They didn't even know about the state of their ambush yet. It had only been ten, maybe eleven days before. There was a chance any who did succeed in running were taking their sweet time trying to get back. But, it confirmed one suspicion: the Elvasi hunters that had attacked them on the road were funded by this guy.

He continued on to the main building, the mansion where the merchant was always holed up, protected by dozens of Elvasi who were in his employ. He wasn't the only rich shit Elvasi in Olost, but he was the most influential. Centuries of back and forth led to this. They had ignored this one for too long, that was certain. As the Company lost members, they were slowly losing this invisible war against men like him.

Time to change that.

Bryn found one guard in his way that needed to be dealt with. Silently, he made his way behind the guard and came up, slitting his throat before any fight could be made. He pulled the guard deep into the shadow of the mansion, hiding him in some bushes. Next, he waited. There would be another, and he still needed to keep moving.

The next guard was a walking patrol, like Bryn figured. He tried to break Bryn's initial hold, but surprise was on the Andinna's side. He wasn't able to get his blade up fast enough, so opted to jerk the head of the Elvasi. A quick snap and it was over. He dragged the body and dumped it with the other. He had to keep moving now that those two were out of the way.

Finally, he entered the mansion, jumping through an easy window. He marked the wooden frame with a few gashes, knowing Matesh would understand. After that, he threw his knife into the back of the first Elvasi he saw, a hunter wearing leathers, a net rolled at his hip. He grabbed his dagger and wiped it off on his breeches, smiling. Another silent kill.

He left the room, not caring what it was or what he could possibly steal from it. Other nights, he would have grabbed something valuable to sell later, earn some extra income, but tonight, he just wanted this man. Bryn didn't even know the merchant's name. Alchan and Luykas probably did, but it wasn't something he cared about. He just wanted to see the Elvasi bleed.

He snuck into another room just down the hallway, one that had a perfect view of the grove. He could have come into this one originally, but he liked the roundabout way because he could mentally route escape paths. He would meet Matesh and Mave in the hallway.

He broke the stick and put it on the window frame. The glow grew to a brightness he hadn't expected, an eerie green in the red night. He saw one grow in the grove, probably held by Luykas.

The others were now moving. He just needed to wait.

38

MAVE

"Let's move out," Alchan ordered as the green glow sat in the window of the mansion in the distance. "Before any guards get too curious. Luykas, toss that so Bryn knows to hide his."

Luykas did as he was asked without a word. Mave watched their glowing stick disappear into the dark woods, still dying with curiosity as to how it worked.

Beyond that, she had one thing on her mind nearly constantly: why they were doing this.

She watched the larger group fall out first, trotting out of the grove with a few of their horses and the three draft horses they brought as pack animals. She had a feeling they would be seen coming. The only thing that group had in their favor was that the estate was lightly guarded, with very few wandering guards. If they could be killed fast enough, it could be a while before an alarm was given.

She pulled her right-hand blade, looking to Matesh. "Are you ready?" she asked softly.

"Always." He didn't unsheathe his long sword as they started moving. They needed to get to Bryn. As they made their way out of the grove and into the fields, her mind was still puzzling over the 'why' of the mission. Mat didn't notice her distraction, which she was thankful for, but in the end, she decided to voice her concerns.

"Does the Company normally do this sort of mission?"

"Yeah. We've had skirmishes with the Elvasi before, just never like that ambush. This is just a bigger scale." He didn't seem concerned by her obvious worry or at all. "What's on your mind?"

"We're here because of me," she said softly as they moved through the crops.

"We're here because we need the supplies. And yeah, we're here because if we let them continue to get stronger, they'll come after you harder." Mat leaned close to her, stopping her. They now just stood together, hidden as they crouched out of sight. "Mave, if it had been anyone else, we would have done this. We're the Ivory Shadows. We go after bounties, but we also help the free Andinna. If someone from our village was captured, we would try to grab them before they were taken out of Olost. We take supplies back to them, because we find very little trade with anyone, since the mountains are safe for our people." He gave her a smirk, that arrogant one. "Are you worried?"

"No. Not about any of us. I just don't..." She was feeling insecure, but she wasn't sure how to pinpoint the source of the emotion. It felt like the mission was tied up in her, how they came after the Company because she was with them. If any of them got hurt, she knew she would blame herself. *They can't get hurt. I would never be able to look them in the eyes again.*

"Would it help if I reminded you that most of the Company is only doing the raid? They're letting us go after the grudge match and kill this guy. He might not even be the one behind the attack on us, just our best bet." Mat continued to smirk. "It's not all about you, *ilanra*."

"Ilanra?" She used the distraction of a new word to ignore the small slight he just gave her. He was right. It wasn't all about her. That was what she had to remember.

"Beloved." He kissed her cheek. "Let's keep moving."

"I'm not the one who stopped us. You could have answered while we walked." She growled as he straightened up and started walking away from her. She followed after him, still feeling snarly. "I didn't think it was all about me, but the fact that Alchan and Luykas agreed with me..." She wasn't used to it. She wasn't used to this idea of being part of a group where her words had such weight. It was one thing in the pits, when she agreed to ally with Mat and Rain. She knew everything then. They had to rely on her. This was different. She felt like a respected member of the group.

"Luykas was going to have the same idea as you - you know that, right? He probably already did. He let you give it to the group as a sign that he agreed with it and had come to the same conclusion." Matesh raised an eyebrow at her. "I've known him for a thousand years. He does that for all of us, to help build our confidence and make us feel more important than just Alchan's guard or foot soldiers. We're the Company and we do things together."

She wanted to disagree, but gave Mat a snort of agreement. It made sense, remembering how Luykas behaved while they talked and the other males argued. She didn't like it, though. She didn't need to be coddled and treated like that, whether it was something he did for everyone or not. And she knew Matesh tacked that on to make her feel better.

They slid past the warehouse, hearing the other males swiftly take out guards inside. Mat led her to the side of the mansion, cursing as he tripped over something in the bushes along the side.

"Damn, Bryn. Kill enough people?" He was looking down, frowning.

She drew closer, seeing the two dead Elvasi, and grinned. "Not nearly enough. He probably could have killed more."

"Of course you would think that," he said, chuckling softly. He pointed at a nearby window and nudged her to keep following. "He left us a sign." His fingers landed on a couple of gashes in the wood of the window seal.

"This isn't the window he used, though. It can't see the grove, blocked by the warehouse." Why would Bryn enter here?

"Doesn't matter. This is where he entered. Makes sense. The window is just big enough for us to fit. Well, for me to fit. You should be fine." He pushed it up to open it and waved her to go.

She did so without argument, sliding in the tight fit, even for her. She had no idea how Bryn did it, or how Mat would.

As Matesh fought to get in, she found the dead Elvasi in the room.

"He got one in here too," she remarked casually. "Knife to the back."

"He's like that." Mat groaned and finally made it through. He closed the window, sighing. "Let's go find him."

She walked out of the room first, hoping they saw him soon. She didn't like the idea that he was hiding in the mansion by himself with so many Elvasi around. She didn't want to think about the risks he was taking just so that she could get some blood tonight.

He stepped out of a room further down the hall and leaned on the wall, smiling.

She immediately relaxed just a little. "Glad to see you're safe," she said. "Now where do we go?"

"If my old recon on this place is still good, up the main staircase-"

"Andinna in the warehouse! We're being raided!" an Elvasi screamed from another area of the mansion.

"Are they by the main door?" Mat asked softly.

"Yeah. Come in here. We'll hide out for a minute." Bryn opened the door to the real meeting point and they followed him in. "That's good. The Company can handle anything these Elvasi throw at them. Should leave less resistance for us." They could all hear the stomping and shouting of the Elvasi as they rushed out of the building.

"So where's his office? Briefing on the road said up the main staircase, somewhere on the second floor."

"Yeah. Somewhere up there." Bryn shrugged. "That's really all I know. He could be in his bedroom, also on the second floor."

"I was hoping you had a better idea than that, Bryn," Mat grumbled. "A week of planning-"

"I deal with this sort of thing all the time. Ya want to do my job, ya do it my way." Bryn threw his hands up, like he was daring Mat to question him.

"Leave it," she ordered softly. Bryn had a point. She and Mat weren't the types of warriors who normally did this sort of thing. Open battle, swords in hand - that was more their thing. She watched Bryn carefully; he seemed completely in his element. Hiding out where he couldn't be caught anymore, the hidden bodies he'd left behind. It was being a warrior in a different way, and she could see now how he was just as fine a warrior as her, but in a very different way. For an Andinna, what he did was probably harder.

It was finally quiet again and no one had stumbled on them. Mave gestured to the door. "Are we ready to move out?"

"Aye." Bryn moved first and left the room, letting her and Mat keep up. He didn't stop to check corners or anything. It was like he had a sixth sense for it, knowing what would be safe and what wasn't. They went up the main staircase by the massive front door and ran into no Elvasi.

"Did they really all clear out for the rest of the Company?" Keeping her voice low, she stressed her disbelief at their current situation. There must have been some left to defend their funder.

"He might not be here. We'll find out." Bryn kept moving, putting a finger over his lips as they came to a door. He listened at the door then shook his head, moving on, letting them follow.

It took three doors before he nodded, pointing to the door then holding up three fingers. A countdown. He went to two. Mave held her blade tightly, ready for whatever they were about to find.

On one, his hand went to the door knob. He shoved it open, but then barely dodged a fireball flying out. Mave and Mat were separated by it as it flew down the hall.

"You're going to kill our visitors before we even see who they are!" a male voice said with some humor, a cruel humor. "Come inside! I want to see the Andinna that think they'll kill me."

Mave swallowed and followed Bryn in to see an Elvasi sitting behind a desk, smiling arrogantly. Next to him was another Elvasi, much younger, with a fireball above his open hand, floating only inches from his palm.

"So, you know why we're here," she said looking between them. "You have one sorcerer. There's three of us." She used her blade to point between them. Now that they knew who they were fighting, she was certain they could handle this. One sorcerer? She felt like she had faced worse odds than that.

The door swung shut behind them as the sorcerer smiled.

"Just me? You think we didn't have something like this planned for? Everyone needed to get into position."

Mave's eyebrows went up as a bookcase opened behind the desk. Bryn, moving faster than she could see, threw a dagger across the room. Another fireball came their way at the same time as soldiers ran into the room from the back entrance.

The dagger glanced off the merchant's shoulder as she ripped Bryn out of the fireball's way.

"Damn it!" she cursed, seeing their quarry get away down the back passage. Between them and the merchant: nearly a dozen Elvasi who had been lying in wait and the sorcerer, already growing another ball of fire for them. The one that hit the wall was growing, taking down a painting.

"We're now in a death trap," Matesh said, pulling his long sword. "Fantastic."

"Kill the males. I want her." The sorcerer pointed at her. "Foolish of you to come here. You think I don't know who you are? I'll retire when I drop you back at the feet of the Empress."

"That's not going to happen." She pulled her second short sword. "Bryn, Mat, watch the flames."

"Aye." Bryn pulled a longer dagger, and met one of the Elvasi in a clash. Mat roared as one rushed him.

Mave kept her eyes on the sorcerer, even as an Elvasi stepped up to her. She didn't tear them away until the last possible moment. Her blades clashed with the guard's, sending sparks off them. For every strike he tried, she blocked, stepping carefully around each other. For every strike she tried, he blocked, using his shield to his benefit. With her tail, she grabbed the ankle of another, yanking as she continued her duel. The tertiary Elvasi fell to the ground and she took a risk, diverting to shove her sword down in his chest.

It didn't go her way. The one she was dueling swung at the best time for him, and the worst for her, slicing her wing. She snarled, swinging wide, pulling her wings in. She had grown comfortable letting them relax further from her body than normal. Now she would make sure to keep them tucked to her body where they couldn't be aimed at.

Matesh came up beside her, reaching over her shoulder to take her opponent by surprise. His long sword slid into the Elvasi's chest.

"Get down!" Bryn called. She listened, ducking as another fireball flew over them.

"For someone who wants me alive, you seem to be trying to kill me!" she roared over to the sorcerer.

Another fireball flew at her for that and she jumped out of the way, taking Mat down with her, to make sure he wasn't hit either.

She jumped off him fast, blocking a downward swing from one of the Elvasi, kicking him back. Right after she pushed that one back, another joined the fray, coming over the merchant's desk and nearly landing on her. Mat grabbed him and tossed, roaring as the Elvasi hit another of the bookshelves in the large office.

Bryn was suddenly by her side, driving a dagger into the gut of one of the guards closest to her. Then he was gone in a dark blur, engaging a different one. She was astounded by the speed of his actions.

They were halfway through the guards when the sorcerer could be heard barking more orders. The room was burning, the smoke filling up the top half of the room. The entire wall with the door was engulfed in flames now. She was starting to feel it, a burn in her lungs as the room grew warmer, and the smoke made her eyes water. Every so often, she had a small spell of lightheadedness.

Then the sorcerer disappeared, taking two guards with him. She didn't blame him, even though his act was cowardly. They were all going to die in the room if they didn't get out of it.

"They're running!" she called out, pulling her sword out of the gut of her most recent victim. "Follow them!"

"Hold!" one of the guards screamed. They all fell back to the door. "You're staying here with us."

She did a quick head count. Five left. She glanced at Mat and Bryn, both angling to begin attacks of their own.

The guards' objective was to let them suffocate and pass out thanks to the flames. She knew if she went down, they would just take her and leave with her. That wasn't allowed to happen. She was there to kill them and she was going to succeed.

"Push!" she roared, forcing Bryn and Mat into action. Together, they pressed against the five guards blocking their paths. The flames began to eat the beams on the ceiling. Mave coughed as she fought against two of the guards, moving fast to block and dodge their attacks.

She finally got a hit on one, slashing him open from shoulder to waist. At that moment, the other took the opportunity to aim for her thigh, slicing it like butter. It wasn't deep, but it made her snarl in pain and she knew it would give her a limp until it healed.

The guard dropped after that, though, revealing Bryn, his normally light eyes dark with rage and the kill.

"Thanks," she said, reaching to thump his shoulder.

"Always," he replied.

"Let's go, you two, before we're burned alive in here!" Mat was already in the doorway, his hand out. She sheathed a blade and took the hand offered, squeezing it.

They moved down the spiral back staircase quickly.

"Did you know about this one, Bryn?"

"Nope. Had no idea he had hidden passages. Would have used them if I did." He was at the back of the group now, but when they reached bottom, he pointed over her shoulder. "Stables. Go."

She and Mat began to run. She winced on the first step, then quickly shoved the pain down. They were on the hunt and her injuries would come later. She wasn't stopping unless she was crippled or dead, and being crippled would probably only slow her down.

They made it into the stables to catch the sorcerer on his mount, his guards all still grabbing their horses, all of them unruly thanks to the action around them. The fighting in the warehouse was clear, the smell of blood and smoke filling her nose. A familiar smell. One she had encountered on the sands before.

The sorcerer had another one of those balls of flame and began to throw. Bryn threw another of his hidden blades, hitting the sorcerer in the shoulder and sending him off his horse. The fireball exploded on the earth right in the middle of them, making them all jump out of the way. Mave found herself in a stall with a guard, his blade drawn. She was on the ground and he was over her, ready to deliver a final, painful blow. She rolled from her stomach to her back, screaming in pain as the sword went through her wing cleanly and into the dirt. She kicked up, sending him back. She reached for his fallen sword, yanking it back through her wing, blood going everywhere, and had it up in time to drive it into his gut. He dropped dead next to her.

It took her a few moments to stand up, and then she charged back out of the stable. Mat was fighting two guards, looking like he was doing well. Bryn was fighting against one guard, trying to get out of the stall he'd jumped into to dodge the fire.

She went to Mat, pushing off one of his attackers and going after him herself, feeling like a predator out for the kill.

This one met her swing for swing, obviously one of the most skilled Elvasi she had ever fought. It was a deadly dance as the barn continued to go up in flames. She kept her focus on him, fighting to her best ability, using both blades to try and break his guard while he deftly parried and dodged her every attempt. She tried to grab him with her tail and nearly didn't pull it back in time as he tried to take it off her. She ended up with a deep cut on it for the effort.

He slipped beneath her guard as she tried to refocus from the pain. His sword went into her wing, making her howl and pull them back into her again. The damned wings. She wasn't used to having them move freely like they were. She held them tightly, to the point of cramping, as she continued to fight, her back beginning to ache as she dueled the Elvasi.

While she had been fixing one thing, she was beginning to realize she needed to fix others. She was going to have to learn how to fight with her wings unbound and flexible. There was an aggravation to her fighting now. Annoyance and disappointment in herself, certainly.

A slice across the back of her left hand forced her to drop her offhand sword. She hissed and kicked the Elvasi's shield hard enough to crack the wood and send him back into a post. He dropped the damned thing, and now they were both using a single sword. Her gladius versus his simple short sword. He flipped it in his hand, his keen eyes following her every movement.

She wasn't used to finding someone who fought her so well. He was treating her like any other opponent, where most Elvasi were headstrong against her and used numbers to back them up. This one knew exactly what sort of threat she was and treated her with care. Which meant she needed to continue to do the same in return. There was no cutting this one down quickly.

They clashed again, and she knew it had to be the last. To add power to each swing, he held the hilt of his sword with both hands, proving he had more brute strength than her.

She let him push through her block, sliding out of the way of his swing, dropping her blade at the same time. He tried for a high hit on her chest, while she went for his legs.

It was a test of speed, and she knew she wouldn't lose. The idea of losing meant taking a death blow to the chest. She couldn't lose.

She hit before he did, making him stumble and miss. Before he could regain his composure, she twisted and brought her sword down, sending his head rolling.

Take that, you pointed-ear scum.

Feeling victorious, she knew her next target, seeing Matesh fighting another guard. They were even-numbered versus the Elvasi now, or near it. Three Andinna versus five Elvasi. That wasn't including the sorcerer, though, who was being protected by two of the guards, whispering spells. She didn't know what they were or what he intended, but that's what he was doing.

He met her eyes and grinned.

She felt it first. A shackle clamping down on her wrist and yanking her down. When she looked, there was nothing there. Then another on her neck, pulling down harder, forcing her face into the earth.

"Net her, throw her on a damned horse, and let's get out of here!" the sorcerer fired the orders to his two men.

She struggled, snarling and biting as one tried to grab her. Her tail lashed out and her wings flew out, forcing them away.

This time she wasn't scared. She knew Mat and Bryn were going to come for her. She believed it.

"Mat!" she called, happy there was none of the paralyzing fear in her voice this time. Damn. These Elvasi wanted her so bad. For as much money that was on her head, she really couldn't blame them.

"Bryn, break the sorcerer's concentration!" Mat called out.

She didn't see what happened, but the pull left and she was on her feet in seconds, so fast that the two guards coming for her didn't have a chance to react. She killed the first before he could even see she was up.

"DAMN YOU!" the sorcerer screamed.

She faced off with the second, who barely had time to block her first swing. The duel with this one was quick, because she never gave him the chance to recover. She pressed him to the point that he had no options, killing him quickly.

Then her eyes fell on the sorcerer, another fireball growing in his hand. She ran for him, realizing he wasn't looking at her. He was enraged at something, yanking a dagger out of his thigh as the ball grew bigger.

He began to throw the ball, and she knew its trajectory. As she turned to see how it would end, she saw Mat try to run to block it. He didn't have enough time, and the guard he was fighting was still alive, trying to block his progress.

Bryn's back was open.

"Bryn! DOWN!" she screamed, jumping for him. She had enough time. She was certain of it.

The lean rogue turned and his eyes widened, seeing he didn't have enough time to jump. It was nearly on him. She shoved.

The fireball slammed into her side and sent her flying.

"MAVE!" Mat roared as she went into a beam, her back feeling like it broke from the impact. The air was knocked from her, and when she hit the dirt, she didn't feel like she was going to be standing up any time soon. The landing at least put the fire on her chest out.

Too bad everything hurt so much she wanted to drop into the healing sleep right there.

39

LUYKAS

Luykas walked quietly into the warehouse next to his brother. They had killed four guards together on their way through the field and at the door. Now they were going to raise hell, but they needed to be in position first, somewhere defensible.

He took stock of the warehouse, finding it to be very cluttered. Bags and bags of spices and foods, all ready to ship. Rich fabrics and other materials were lying around. In one corner of the room, weapons, armors, and nets, obviously the gear for any hunters wanting to go out and capture any Andinna they could find.

What he really wanted was the half a dozen carts on the far end. They looked ready to leave for port any day. He investigated further, his suspicions proving correct. Even more food, fabrics, and the like. Things his people couldn't trade for anymore, or create, since they didn't have enough resources or manpower.

Everything in the warehouse would be a boon for their people. He knew if they came home with even a fraction, it would be a successful mission.

"Nevyn, Varon, and Zayden, they have carts ready to ship. Bring the horses here." Luykas waved them over.

"We should have brought our own carts," Zayden said, looking over what Luykas had mentioned. "We're going to have too many carts in the village that we don't need. Stablemaster is going to get pissy."

"We can donate them to other villages." Luykas didn't really care. With this, they would have more than enough for the winter. "There's three carts here, fully loaded. Then we can look at what each of us carries on our own. Bryn is going to want to load more up on these, I bet, with things like the armor and weapons." He kept doing the mental inventory. "We could all use new clothing…" He ran his fingers over the expensive silk.

The merchant must have kept his favorite items here for trade, stockpiling until he had plenty to send back to the Empire. They had never found silk before. They had to purchase it, and it was often too expensive for any of them. On top of that, only Kian had someone to give silk to. None of the Company wore it. It was a favorite among the females, though.

"The spices will please a lot of people tired of the same old shit," Zayden pointed out.

"How long do you think we have?" Alchan asked loudly. "Before someone notices their guards are dead and we're in here?"

Luykas sighed. "If you keep being that loud, not very long." He glared over his shoulder at his brother. "Everyone, start grabbing anything you can. Priority is food, then valuables. In the spring, we can go on a merchant visit in Namur and unload anything our people don't need before we get back to work."

"Yes, sir," many of the males answered back, beginning to move. He shoved his hands into his pockets, walking to his brother. "We probably have a short bit of time. It's late, many of them might be asleep. The guards were lighter than they normally are during the day. What do you recommend for when they know we're here?" Luykas was great at logistics. Alchan knew battle. Together, they could handle an army if they needed to.

"There's three entrances." Alchan pointed them out. Two large ones on opposite ends of the warehouse, then a smaller door on the west side. "The big doors must be for carts to come in, load up, then move out. The small entrance is for workers and anyone gearing up to go hunting. The help, really. It's single story. I want Varon on a cart. He can snipe anyone at any entrance. We can block off the small door with stuff we're leaving behind. Knock over boxes and get that handled. Then, two men at the other large doors. We can escape through this closer one with the carts and they'll be screwed."

"We need to get the doors open and that gives us away." He could see his brother's plan, but he didn't like leaving the escape route open where they could be seen before they wanted.

"We're not opening them until we're caught," Alchan replied. "I'll block the smaller door. You stay on them to keep loading up everything they can."

"Can do."

It was fast work, throwing bags of grain and other items onto the already full carts. Generally, carts were never filled to their capacity to keep from straining the horses or pack animals. The Company never had the same problem. They were going to put as much in as they could. Once they were out of here, they could take things slow to help the animals.

Zayden and Nevyn had the three draft horses hitched to three of the carts. Varon put two more of their mounts on another cart. Four carts out of six. They didn't have any more horses. Their best bet would be to steal some from the Elvasi before leaving. Alchan would hate if his horse was needed to pull. It made Luykas smile, considering having someone run for his brother's gelding, forcing his brother to have to direct a cart.

Varon started whistling as he worked. He couldn't resist a chuckle at the sound. This was the Ivory Shadows. Dirty thieves, waiting for the fight to come to them, no worries in the world. It felt good to be back in Olost.

It was even better when he considered what was going to happen on Mave's end. He could feel her moving through the estate towards her destination, the meeting point. No pain, and she wasn't even feeling any physical exertion.

Thinking of her and her goal, it reminded him. "Have we found any evidence of the Mave problem?" he asked, looking around at the males.

"Not yet, but we haven't touched the armory corner yet." Nevyn wiped his hands on his pants. "I'll do it now."

"No, I've got it," he said, walking over to it. Leather and steel armor, even some expensive and well-made chainmail. Weapons of all types, from battle axes to pikes to daggers - even circular throwing blades. He only knew one Andinna who used those, and they took centuries to master because they could easily injure the user or allies. They also required a little magic to direct, making them very rare.

Then he found it. A crate that wasn't open. He pried it open with his sword - not the best idea but he didn't want to waste time grabbing anything else.

Stacks of paper were revealed to him. It didn't take more than a glance for him to know what he was looking at. Mave. They had made hundreds of copies of her bounty, maybe even thousands. If this was what they were keeping in the warehouse, he couldn't imagine how many were now circulating around Olost.

He snapped his fingers, imagining a small flame, then thought better of it. He shouldn't drain himself using magic before any real fighting started.

"I found it," he called out, trying to keep his voice down at the same time. A loud whisper, really. "They have an entire crate of her bounty. They must be pushing it pretty hard."

"Which means the trouble likely won't be over after tonight," Alchan said, walking over, his task to block the door over. "That's not good. I want her in the Company, but there's a chance we'll be harassed everywhere we go, thanks to these."

"Hopefully, tonight will be enough of a warning that no one thinks to try us again. Eventually someone is going to find all those dead Elvasi."

"There were some survivors on their side that night. There's a chance they'll learn about Rain and decide going against a wyvern isn't worth it." Alchan reached down and snatched one of the bounties. "Her having her *tatua* is a good thing. The image is wrong now, and many get too distracted by the *tatua* to really look at our faces."

"The scar. Her tatua made it black. It stands out." Luykas shook his head. "We're in for a rough time."

"We knew that when we found the bounty." Alchan crushed the paper in his hand and dropped it. "Burn these before we leave. And how the hell did they make so many copies? Isn't that a particularly hard type of sorcery?"

"It is, but with the resources of the Empress behind it…" He shrugged. Nothing seemed impossible when she was their ultimate enemy and the root of their problems. "She probably had every sorcerer in her employment working on it."

"Fuck." His brother walked away, growling and mumbling to himself.

Luykas was starting to worry just a little about them not being caught yet. He focused on his bond with Mave, and there was nothing distressing.

They kept working, until someone tried to open the blocked door.

"Damn it. Something must have fallen over. Hey, assholes, open this! It's time for guard shift!" Luykas understood the Elvasi they used, but didn't translate for the few members of the Company that didn't. It didn't matter, because the sign was clear. They had company.

"Fucking idiots probably fell asleep on the job," another guard mumbled. "Let's use the big door."

Luykas gestured wildly, running for the large door they didn't plan on using to escape. He could hear the footsteps of the guards on the other side of the wall, following them as he unsheathed his *morok*. His brother appeared at his side as the door creaked and began to roll to one side.

"Hey, you-" The Elvasi wasn't ready for the strong swing his brother delivered, beheading him.

The other Elvasi screamed. Luykas tried for him, killing him quickly, but the scream had been enough. Footsteps could be heard by the silent Andinna. Shouts from further away.

They were about to have a lot of company.

"Well, we're the diversion we thought we would be." Alchan flicked his wrist, blood flying off his *morok*. "Let's hope those three know we're about to bring a bunch of shit down on our heads and they need to make their move."

"Bryn will know," he replied. "Pull back. We'll choke them in the door and hold them. Nevyn, here. Varon, Kian, Zayden, stay on the carts. We'll hold out then open the doors as the fight starts to slow down. We can get ready to leave and escape once the others are back."

"Are you two sure we can do this?" Zayden asked loudly. "Sounds like there's a lot of them."

It was Nevyn who gave a laughing response. "We knew coming into this there were a lot of them. Don't get worried on us now, you fucking overprotective grouch!"

Luykas and his brother angled towards the door, their backs to each other. In unison, they pulled their swords up, ready for the fight. Running could be heard, the clang of heavy armor. Luykas watched as Elvasi came around the building.

"We got some trying to pry the door open on this side!" Kian called out.

"Keep them closed!" Alchan roared. An arrow went flying over his shoulder and landed into the closest Elvasi coming their way.

With a grin, Luykas let the feeling of the fight take him. He clashed swords with the first who came near him, then kicked the guard back to break the block and deliver a cutting blow to the man's abdomen. Without pause, he and Alchan shifted, switching places to handle new attackers. They had trained together since the day they met. Brothers born in the same year, they were awkward initially thanks to the story of his birth. What kind of man wanted to meet the bastard his father had in a different nation with a different race? He never blamed Alchan for initially not knowing how to handle him.

General Lorren had seen it and knew the way to correct it. He gave them both wooden training swords and told them to get to work. And every day since, they trained. Seventeen hundred years of working together, learning each other's strengths and weaknesses.

The only pair that fought better than them was Nevyn and Varon.

Luykas found himself against three Elvasi, all hoping to get through him and to his men. He met the first with his *morok*, squaring off. He knocked the second away with a slam with his wing while his tail grabbed the third and pulled, yanking the man from his feet. It was a cheap move, to be sure, but it was a smart one, and he never met an Andinna above it. They had the tail and they were going to use it.

"Fuck!" Zayden's expletive could be heard through all the fighting. "Door's coming open!"

"Hold!" Alchan screamed in return.

Arrows flew by them from both sides. Varon's lightning shot speed versus the now several archers trying to pick them off. One went through his wing, leaving a hole. It would heal in a day, and didn't slow Luykas down as he killed one of the three Elvasi still trying to push through him. Nevyn jumped between them, decapitating one of the foes. Together, they sank their swords into the third.

Without missing a beat, Nevyn spun and killed another coming for them to replace their front line. He roared in satisfaction, making Luykas grin as the advanced warrior began to cut through Elvasi like they were children. Nevyn was one of the greatest soldiers to ever come from their people, without a doubt.

"There's someone running to the stables with more soldiers!" Kian called out. "Going to have Varon take a shot!"

"Do it!" he called back, not really caring. If someone was trying to run from them, they weren't going to make it very far. Not with Varon's watchful eye on them, anyway.

He never stopped fighting as Kian called out that it was a hit. Suddenly, another arrow whizzed past his head, too close to his ear. He glanced back to see Varon grinning, even daring to give a small shrug as he nocked another arrow.

The fight was endless, only broken up for him by the bond pushing pain into him in specific areas like his thigh. She was taking hits, but none that really worried him. By the end of this, he was certain everyone would have some cuts and bruises, and the Elvasi would never kill her, not when she was their biggest score.

There was never really a point where Luykas felt desperate. They had the better positioning, able to funnel guards into the warehouse without being completely surrounded. He and Alchan just continued to cut them down as they came, meeting some challenges along the way, dueling and dodging, with some close calls.

But he knew the mission would be successful.

It was finally slowing down as smoke began to touch the air. Somewhere, something was burning.

"Where's the fire?" he asked loudly, hoping anyone would have an answer.

"The mansion!" Zayden screamed back.

He cursed, knowing they had three people in there. Mave, Matesh, and Bryn, whatever they were doing, were now dealing with a fire.

"Keep an eye out for our people!" He knew someone would, probably Varon. He just hoped they all walked out of the building before any fire got out of control and took the building down.

And so it continued. He kicked back a guard, getting annoyed with just how many there were. How many Elvasi were hiding here? Between the guards, the hunters who weren't going hunting, and the servants they had decided to let live long before the mission start, this felt more like a compound than just a rich man's estate. This was a base of operations, all right, which proved his suspicions correct. If they decimated this place, they wouldn't need to deal with hunters for a long time. It would be a peaceful era for their people and the Company would be riding out with glory.

Everything was going fine, in his mind. They even got eyes on the other Company members.

"I see them running for the stables!" Kian yelled out. "Chasing a few Elvasi down. They're handling runners!"

Luykas was still grinning, until Kian told them the barn was lighting up on fire now as well.

That took his good mood down. He kicked back the hunter he was facing off against, pointing Nevyn to deal with it.

"There's fire in the barn? They just got in there!" Luykas went running towards the other group, who were dealing with their own, smaller group of Elvasi trying to make their way inside. Luykas killed one immediately, then the one Kian was fighting to get the male's attention.

"Look!"

He did, peering out into the red night and seeing the smoke and fire growing at the barn, where there were so many flammable substances, he was sure it was going to be a blazing mess in only moments.

Then a crippling pain slammed into him, just as they all heard Matesh's scream.

He went to his knees. His back exploded into pain. He gasped for breath, dropping his sword. Kian stood over him, protecting him as he tried to push back against the bond.

It's not real. Mave is hurt. I need to get to her and remember this pain is not mine.

He tried so hard. Every second of it was awful. A warmth, burning on the chest just for a moment. He'd nearly missed it. Explosion? No. He would have seen it.

As he pushed the pain down, the fear took hold, along with something else. She was hurt. He was pretty certain that Mat thought she was dead, there was no doubt of that. A scream like that was the scream of a male losing his female.

Luykas stood up slowly, grabbing his *morok*. "Make me a hole!" he demanded.

Zayden and Kian did just that. The moment he could, he went running.

There was a damned sorcerer in that barn. He fucking knew it.

And that damned sorcerer tried to kill his fucking bonded female.

40

MAVE

It hurt. She tried to push up from the ground and it hurt. Mat and Bryn were still trying to fight.

I need to get up.

A hand touched her shoulder. "Don't move yet. Let's make sure nothing is broken. Once I'm sure, I'll let you up."

Luykas' voice was taut with rage, and yet, there was a sympathy and softness to it. He was trying to hold it all back until he knew she was okay.

Then she remembered he could feel everything she did. He had known every injury the moment it had happened. He was probably feeling exactly what she did in that moment.

He's on his feet. I should be too.

She needed to get up.

"Stay down, Mave," he snarled low, leaning over further so she could see his molten gold eyes. Once, she had been told that Luykas was just as dominant as Alchan. She had never really believed it, but in that moment, she knew it. He didn't have the need for the struggles like she and his brother, but he was just as strong, just as forceful as either of them could be.

In the state she was in, she knew better than to fight. For once, she dropped her eyes and did as he asked.

Hands moved over her back. "Keep holding them off, and don't let that fucking sorcerer go anywhere!" he ordered above her. He touched her wings, her back, her tail, every inch of her he could probably see. Finally, his hands left her. "Nothing feels broken, but you're going to be bruised to hell for a week, I bet. We'll talk more about it when this is over."

"Can I get up?" she asked softly, still not sure she could. A hand grabbed her elbow and gave her the support she needed. He helped her balance as she swayed, her back lighting up in pain as if she had been hit by lightning. Fast and immediate, it flared up and receded, then came back.

"We're going to kill that sorcerer, Mave," he whispered harshly in her ear. "Me and you. I need someone acting as my blade while I do magic. Understand?"

"Let's do this," she promised. She just hoped she was a good enough blade. She took a step, limping hard on her right. Growling, she kept walking forward. When the sorcerer threw another fireball, it met an invisible wall, spooking the Elvasi. Luykas was whispering under his breath.

She found a shortsword, not caring if it was hers or not. It was a blade.

"Stay close," her commander ordered. "Hook tails with me."

The moment her tail touched his, her senses were flooded by too much. She gasped and tried to pull away, freaked out by the sensory overload and the emotions that came through as well.

He held her, keeping her tail wrapped by his at their tips. "Get through it. I can stop his attacks, but we need to be on the same page if we want to fight back."

She could feel his stress behind every word. He truly believed they could do this, even with her feeling the pain she was. She could tell he was uninjured from his own fighting. He was proud she was on her feet and slightly hurt that she had tried to pull away. She was confused at how the entire thing was working.

Without a word, she could feel the answer. The bond was doing this, which she figured, but then a completely different image filled her mind. Nevyn and Varon.

This is how. This is what they have from their bond and how they fight.

With that, she realized the bond wasn't terrible for everything. If she and Luykas practiced, they could be like the lovers. Tonight was practice, quite literally by fire.

"Can you fight through the pain?" he asked.

"Yes." She had fought through worse. Now that she was on her feet, she wasn't going to leave them unless she was dead.

Together, they advanced on the lone sorcerer, his last two guards still trying to hold the line of defense against Mat and Bryn.

Each sorcerer was saying something and she wondered what the language was as she pushed forward, going for a swing only to meet an invisible force, rebounding her back. It didn't knock her down, though. She staggered, but somewhere, there was a well of strength waiting for her.

Luykas was calling on water, putting out the fires as she kept the sorcerer's focus on her. The flames were dying now, as the commander wet everything he could, from straw to the wood structure itself. The building would still go down in the end, but now, they had some time.

The entire while, the sorcerer tried to fend her off, not realizing that at any moment, Luykas was going to turn on the man as well.

Now.

She launched into an attack, as Luykas turned. They stayed close together thanks to their tails, moving as a unit. She knew what he was going to do just as he did it and he knew the same from her. They knew how to position their wings, how to step.

She had never in her life been more at one with someone as they fought together. First, she had rarely ever fought with someone.

Second, she had never imagined it would be so fluid. This was like being invincible.

When she was blocked again by that blasted invisible shield, Luykas whispered a fast sequence of words. The next swing she took, power blasted out from the strike, but her sword continued, narrowly missing the sorcerer as he jumped back, creating distance between them with a wall of fire they couldn't cross. A fireball came their way through the flames and Luykas stopped it again with their own wall. She wished she could see the weird invisible things they were throwing up. She didn't know where the line of safety was and that information would have been helpful.

Luykas pointed it out, obviously feeling her frustration. He blew up some dirt with a single word, showing her the wall he'd made this time. Sorcery was beginning to look like a handy skill, in her mind. If she wasn't already being held back by needing to train in her blood magic, she would look at learning it as well.

They advanced again, still silent. Mat kicked down and killed the guard he was fighting. He didn't get into their fight against the sorcerer, though. He helped Bryn with the final guard.

Then they both watched for a moment.

"Go back and help the rest of the Company," Luykas ordered, not bothering to even look at them.

She glanced at them again, seeing the hesitation on their faces. Nodding, she encouraged them to go. She and their leader could manage against this problem. Then it would be over.

Without missing another beat, both of the males ran out, leaving them to the sorcerer and the flames still slowly consuming the barn. Luykas had done what he could to try and save the structure, but in the end, killing the sorcerer was more important than saving a barn they would never use.

The moment they were gone, she and Luykas ran forward.

"We need to get on top of him. Don't stop."

She just listened to the orders, acknowledging with only a nod. The sorcerer was trapped on the other side of the burning barn. They were all becoming trapped in the thick smoke and she coughed, becoming distracted for just a second.

The sorcerer wasn't stupid, throwing a fireball down at her feet through that wall of flame again to stop her advance while Luykas continued to run, nearly breaking the bond. He looked back at her, frowning for a moment, then threw his own fireball at the sorcerer, distracting him just enough that she could jump over the new flame growing on the floor to join the rest of the fire.

"Stay close to me. I won't lead you wrong," Luykas passionately said to her.

She could only nod again. There was a conviction in the words and in his emotions she couldn't deny. He had magic and experience. She was the only one in the barn who didn't.

Looking back at the sorcerer in between licks of red fire, she knew this was going to be one of the toughest fights of her life. She had to completely trust Luykas, or they were probably both going to die.

41

MATESH

Matesh and Brynec ran from the barn. It was falling apart around them. He hated it. He hated how she nodded and agreed with Luykas that they should leave.
She'll be fine.
The hit she took with that post had been bad, very bad. How she was on her feet, he didn't know. It would have put him or Bryn down for the rest of the fight. He was astounded it hadn't broken her back.

Then she told him to go. He turned at the last minute he was out of the barn, looking back to see her and Luykas moving in tandem, like they had been doing it for centuries. A pang of jealousy was there - he wanted that.

Bryn grabbed him. "Don't stop. They need us in the warehouse."

Mat sighed, nodding. With that, he began to haul ass again, running across the property to the warehouse. Varon was standing on a cart, Kian and Zayden defending around him. There were still a dozen Elvasi on their side. He had no idea where Nevyn and Alchan were.

"Shit. Cover with Varon. I'm going to find the others."

"Aye."

They got closer and Bryn didn't pause as he jumped up next to Varon. Mat continued, looking across the warehouse to see Nevyn and Alchan back to back, fighting against even more Elvasi.

He didn't stop running, barreling into two Elvasi at once. He was probably double the weight of one, and the second wasn't very bulky either. They both staggered back, the smaller one unable to stay on his feet. He killed the one who went down first then engaged the second, snarling.

"Well, you're here. I hope that means my brother and Mave are alive," Alchan said calmly, grunting as he took a swing to kill another of the Elvasi.

"They were when I saw them," he answered. "Sorcerer. There's a sorcerer."

"Well, damn. He's going to have fun with that." Alchan snorted. "Idiot brother always has to prove he's better with magic than anyone else."

"Well, Mave's life is in his hands, so he better fucking be." Mat growled in frustration, still upset he'd been sent away.

She'll be fine.

He could only hope Luykas knew what he was doing. He had to trust his commander and his *ilanra*. He never thought to see a day when those two fought together, but he knew they would make it work if they had to. Tonight, they had to.

He kept fighting with his leader at his side. It was something to fight beside the King like this. He'd long gotten over the awe of it and focused on the battle. Tonight, the feeling returned. Something about Alchan was more focused than normal, more regal, more imposing. Which said something, since Matesh was taller, broader, and stronger than him.

Fighting beside him tonight, after his female sent him away, it felt good. Alchan was a silent source of strength for the Company. He was their real leader, with Luykas playing the co-leader and second, depending on the situation. To be in the Ivory Shadows was also to be his.

If I can't fight beside her, my King will have to do.

They continued to push back the Elvasi, and suddenly, the numbers were nearly even.

"We've got runners!" Zayden roared out. "Varon and Bryn are trying to take them out!"

Mat grinned at the Elvasi in front of him, who dropped his sword and turned as well, scrambling off. Mat wasn't having any of that. He delivered a final blow swiftly. He chased after another.

"No survivors!" Alchan called the order.

Mat continued after the Elvasi into the fields, chasing him through rows of spice plants. No survivors. Finally, he jumped and let the wind catch his wings, taking him up with only a few easy powerful strokes. He looked down to see his quarry, who happened to be looking up and over his shoulder in fear as Mat caught up with him.

Mat brought his sword down as he descended, putting the Elvasi down into the dirt, his skull split into two.

With that, he jumped back up and kept an eye out for any more runners, seeing some still trying to break away from Nevyn and Alchan. He dove down swiftly, landing on the back sides of the Elvasi. One turned to defend, blocking him. Mat overpowered him, kicking him onto Nevyn's blade.

It was a slaughter now, as the Elvasi tried to run, dying in the process. He felt good. He felt very good.

This is what they deserve. This is what they needed, after trying to take Mave from him and the Company. If every Elvasi in Olost was dead, the country of city-states would be safe for his female to finally enjoy her freedom without the blood and death.

It was dying down when he walked back into the warehouse. Nevyn was handling the last on their side, while Kian and Zayden had a small group, all trying to leave. He would let them finish it. He looked up to Bryn when he got next to the cart.

"How are you?" he asked, feeling brotherly now with the rogue for some reason. Maybe it was how they spent the night fighting together. He figured it was something more, though.

"Uninjured, for the most part," the rogue answered, looking down for a moment. "You need anything?"

He didn't, not really, but he wanted to say one thing. He'd watched Bryn and Mave dance around each other for too long, and tonight had given him a good insight into how his female felt about the lean male.

"She doesn't save people for just being her friends," he said, reaching up to smack the male's calf. "Just thought you should know that."

He knew from experience. She'd come for him because they had something simmering, because he and Rain were all she had. Desperation, loneliness. She had come. She had saved Rain purely because she loved the young male like family.

Mat, almost a little sadly, knew she cared for the rogue. Knew that he would be *mayara* if they both pulled their heads out of their asses. He was beginning to get annoyed that she hadn't come to him for advice. He would give it. He would give her the world if she asked him for it. If she wanted Bryn, he would grab the rogue and put him on his knees before her.

Maybe his not very subtle hint would give the male the push he needed to act on whatever was going on between them. He had been in the pits, but he also heard their late night whispers, about being survivors. He heard them when they worked on her wings. Bryn gave her something, a companion who understood far beyond what he could. He was a little jealous, and he wouldn't lie about it, but he wanted her to have everything.

Bryn was part of everything in his mind already.

The rogue just watched him in shock before nodding slowly. "Thank ya."

"No problem."

"So if I..."

"You know the answer to that question," Mat said, looking out over the property through the large doors. He watched the burning barn and stables, wondering where his female was. He wanted her back now. Varon lazily shot another arrow, purposefully missing.

Now, the members still fighting were just playing with the Elvasi, tormenting them. Was it a touch cruel? Absolutely. Did Mat care? Not at all.

We're not heroes, that's for sure.

Mat smirked as one jumped back as another arrow hit the ground at his feet. He turned to run, only to get shoved back by Kian, who was having a great time. "Where you going? We have questions."

Mat knew they didn't, but any information was good recon for later. Maybe a little tormenting would get them something they didn't expect.

His chuckles died when the barn collapsed.

"Oh fuck," Bryn mumbled.

Mat didn't realize he was moving towards it until Kian stopped him and shoved, sending him back again. The only male who had more pure brute strength than him stood in his way.

"You run into it now, and you'll be a dead man," Kian said sternly, eyeing him. "If they're dead in there, we're not going to let anyone else commit suicide."

"She's my fucking female," he snarled back, trying again, only to meet strong arms. Another set pulled him behind, then a third pair of hands grabbed his armor.

He was dragged and tossed to the ground several feet from the carts in the middle of the warehouse.

"My brother is in there, but I'm not stupid," Alchan said, growling down in his face. "You'll fucking listen to me, Matesh. You'll wait here. If she's alive, you'll stay here until she's in the damned warehouse. If there's anyone who can deal with the barn, it's my brother, and he's already in there."

Matesh snarled back, but he looked beyond his king to see Nevyn waiting patiently for him to disobey the order. Nevyn, who would have no worries gutting someone for disregarding Alchan's orders in a moment of life and death.

Mat knew he would die if he fought Alchan and tried to go in that fucking barn. He could only wait.

42

MAVE

They ran for the sorcerer again, and this time, when Luykas jumped through the wall of flame, so did she. The sorcerer scrambled back, lobbing another fireball. Instinctively, she ducked but kept running, keeping pace with the mutt beside her.

He blasted the Elvasi with wind, hitting the shield, but distracting the sorcerer for just a moment. She brought her sword down on the shield, roaring as it broke and her swing continued again, feeling power beyond that of her actual arms. It was an unearthly power, one from a deep well inside her and fueled by Luykas. She had no idea where it was coming from, but it was there.

She met another of the walls, bouncing back this time. She hit it again as Luykas pushed the flames away from behind them. The flames that were growing too fast, too wild.

"If I'm going to die, we all are!" the sorcerer screamed. He was fueling the flames now. There was something crazed in his eyes, desperation and power taking control. She had met males like him before. They would go down, but they would try to leave behind as much destruction as possible.

She was one of those types. If she was ever going to die, she was going to take out everyone she could in the process. She wouldn't win, but neither would her enemies.

She continued to bash through the invisible shields, trying to force her way to him. He kept backing away, even though there was no way out. All the while, they could hear the cracking of burning wood. The smoke was beginning to make her lungs burn again, and her eyes watered. Luykas was panting and finally turned away from the flames to help her with the sorcerer again.

"We need to end this before he buries all of us and we burn alive." He was calm, staring her right in the eye. He pushed her back without any sign he was intending to, and a fireball went between their heads.

In unison, they turned on the sorcerer. Luykas snarled. "I hate Elvasi magic users."

"Good to know," she replied, not sure where to go from there. Strength flooded her system again and propelled her with renewed vigor to attack. The sorcerer, his back now to the flames, had nowhere to run.

The sorcerer screamed, jumping back just in time for her to miss the swing, but also into the flames. She didn't let up, following him and slicing across his abdomen as he burned.

With one more overpowered swing, she beheaded him.

It rolled across the barn. The barn, which was cracking and coming down now.

"We need to move!" Luykas yelled, grabbing her arm now. They started running as beams came down around them, slamming into the earth near them on all sides. Luykas pulled her in front of him, shoving as another beam went down, their bonded experience now broken. She then felt the pain, but it wasn't hers. The beam must have landed on Luykas' tail.

"Fuck. Go, Mave!" he roared.

She didn't. She ran back around him and looked at the flaming beam. With a deep breath, she bent down. A hand grabbed her shoulder tightly, bringing the bond back. The strength came back.

She didn't care about the flames. Burns would heal. They would scar, but they would heal.

Yet, when she put her arms under the beam, the flames didn't touch her. She lifted the beam slowly, her muscles and back screaming in pain. She wanted to drop it. When Luykas' white tail was out of the way, she gave up and dropped it, groaning. He grabbed her and yanked, making sure the next beam didn't come down on her head.

They made it out, coughing, the smoke too thick to see anything for a moment. They kept moving and collapsed on the grass. She landed on her knees and rolled onto her back, not worried about anyone coming for her.

"Fuck."

Somehow, their tails were together again, and she could feel his agreement in the bond. Luykas began to chuckle, but she was exhausted and already annoyed with him. What could he have possibly been laughing about?

The power left her, leaving her more confused. What had that been? When her commander looked at her, she saw his eyes were all black, not a drop of gold in them.

"We made it out," he said softly. "Shit. Wasn't expecting that to happen tonight." He rolled his head to the side and looked at her with that annoying Luykas smile. The one that told her he was going to do or say something she didn't like. "We're still connected, so I can feel your curiosity and questions. Blood magic doesn't have too many offensive uses, but you can call it in to give yourself more power. And by the shock, I'm assuming my eyes are black. This is advanced blood magic, not something we teach beginners. Mat doesn't know how to do it either, so before you ask, no, I won't teach you this anytime soon. But, like I said on the ship, when we're connected, the bond lets me tap into both of us. Nevyn and Varon can't even do *this*."

"Why are you laughing?" she asked, narrowing her eyes at him. She wanted to learn. Obviously, this was the best blood magic she had seen yet, the piece she found the most useful. The healing bit Mat had done for her when she was recovering from the collar had been nice, but this was something she could use every fight.

"Because you killed him so easily. Sorcerers are back-line fighters who can't focus on using a sword and using magic. I knew you would handle him easily with some magical backup. How's your back?"

"It aches," she answered. Not nearly as bad as it had, though. "Did...whatever you did help it heal?" She didn't think so, but in that moment, her back was the last pain she was considering. She was alive, and that seemed to make everything feel a little better.

"No, but you're powering through it. You'll be pissed tomorrow, that I can promise. Let's get back to the others."

He stood up first, holding out a hand for her. She grabbed it, groaning in pain as he helped her stand. She stumbled the first steps, but whatever he was doing through the bond was keeping her from slipping into a healing sleep and keeping her on her feet. Now, she was genuinely ready to pass out somewhere. She didn't care where.

But she had to tell him something. One thing was now coming back to her, after all of that.

"The merchant got away," she said finally, looking down as they started moving back to the warehouse. She felt too exhausted to run and he didn't rush her.

"We'll go over everything when we get back." Their tails stayed hooked at the tips, the bond still there. He didn't give her any worry or disappointment. His end was peaceful, accepting, happy even - maybe because they were alive, and hopefully, the rest of the Company would be too.

It felt relaxed between her and Luykas, but it didn't stay that way. As the warehouse came into view, she realized they weren't done with the night yet. The males were still fighting the remnants of the Elvasi. Only half a dozen, most just trying to get away.

She ignored Luykas when he tried to say something, breaking the bond finally and jogging to help. She killed one who didn't realize she was behind him. Now it was clean-up. They didn't want any runners, she was betting, so she took down another, meeting Kian face to face.

"Good to see you alive! You killed my new friend! Why would you do that?" She could tell he was joking by his smile. His smile went from joker to friendly in a second, softening. "We're pretty much done here. Jump on a cart and relax."

"Aren't we going to kill the rest?" she asked, pointing with her sword at two running into the fields now.

"Yeah." He shrugged. An arrow flew over them and hit one in the back, then a second quickly followed it. The second wasn't as on target, but it did the job. She looked up to see Bryn and Varon standing on a cart together now, both with bows in hand.

"Varon's was better," Kian commented lightly. "Still need some practice, Bryn."

"I'm the second best shot in the Company," he retorted, growling.

"Second. You should aim to be the best," Nevyn teased, grinning as he walked around the cart. Alchan and Mat were with him. Mat walked swiftly over to her, checked her body, kissed her passionately, then stomped off. She didn't know what to think of that as he followed Alchan to pick things up. She would need to ask him later.

"No one is ever going to be better than Varon. Stop fuckin' with me." Bryn jumped down in front of her.

She was just enjoying a moment of peace, seeing they had succeeded. She knew orders were about to be dropped on them, and honestly, she was glad they were going to be leaving the same night they arrived. If she never saw another Elvasi, it would be too soon.

"Ya saved my life," he said softly as the other males began to talk and meander, stealing whatever they could get their hands on.

She wasn't sure how to respond except to shrug. "You're…my friend." She wasn't going to let any of them die for her, and she liked Bryn. She liked him a lot.

He shuffled his feet until Nevyn walked over and shoved him. She caught him, hissing as once again her back exploded in pain. Luykas was suddenly behind her, his hand on her lower back.

"Get on with it, ya dumbass," Nevyn said before walking off. Bryn and Mave both cursed at him as he left. Luykas quickly pulled his hand back and walked away, seeming tense.

She was alone with Bryn, whose face was a shade of pink she recognized.

"Thank ya."

"It's not a problem, rea-"

He grabbed her cheeks gently and pulled her face up to his. She didn't stop him. Their lips touched in the softest of kisses, and then he was gone.

She was left shocked, aching in more ways than one, and practically alone near the carts with only Varon, who had watched the entire interaction in an eerie silence. He gestured something, grinning when she flipped him off. He knew she didn't understand yet. She was months away from knowing enough Andinna to start learning the hand signals he used. He patted the cart next to her and offered a hand.

She took it, letting him help her up onto the softer bags of grain. She lay back, groaning.

"I flew into a beam," she explained at his confused expression.

He nodded and spun a finger. She knew from Bryn and Mat, they normally wanted her to roll over when they did that.

If it put her mind off Bryn and that kiss, she would let him look over her back.

As he checked over her back and wings like Luykas did, she found she was watching Mat and Bryn work together to load another cart to the brim. They were working not just in the same group, but as a pair. Bryn smiled sheepishly when he caught her watching. Mat just raised his eyebrows a couple of times, an arrogant smirk on his lips.

Oh yeah, it was definitely time to figure out what was going on with that. On the way back to the village, or when they arrived. She wasn't sure which, but soon, very soon. With this over, she could finally focus on the mundane things again and the nagging feelings she had growing for the rogue to match what she felt for Matesh.

"Everyone finished loading up?" Alchan called out. All of the males yelled back, except Varon, who massaged her wings out. She could already feel the bruises forming, the tight knots of pain she knew would take at least a week to get over. She had never been thrown so damned hard. She didn't answer back either, not wanting to expend the energy on it. No one bothered her to get an answer, especially not with the way Luykas kept hovering close by, almost protectively, and Varon glared at anyone who got around him, his hands leaving to sign for moments to get people to leave. Mat and Bryn never tried, just working and watching her from a distance, both secure and looking good.

After a night of troubles and a successful mission, she knew her new family would keep an eye out for her.

My new family.

She wasn't sure where the thought came from, but it sounded right in her head. She would reevaluate it later.

MAVE REALIZED she had fallen asleep when she woke up. First, she realized the cart was moving. Second, she realized dawn was breaking.

"Shit," she muttered, shaking her head. She sat up, hissing as Luykas was proven right. Her back was on fire. The blow to her back was worse than just a half night of sleeping would fix. She turned slowly to see Mat driving their cart and looked around, seeing how they had six carts, full of supplies. "How long was I out?"

"Only the rest of the night. It's fine," Mat said softly, looking over his shoulder. "You can go back to sleep. We're going to stop at midday, hopefully far enough away that we don't get any trouble. We'll stay the night, everyone will get to heal as much as they can, and we'll go over everything from last night."

"Everything?" she asked softly.

"That depends on you," he responded. "What are you thinking?"

"I don't know how to do this." She moved to sit next to him, trying not to vocalize how badly her back ached. While her comment was vague, he knew exactly what she was saying. It was about another male, but she had no one to talk to about it except Mat. He was the only person she trusted with those types of feelings. He was the person who promised to teach her all about relationships for the Andinna, something she had very little experience with, all of it with him.

"When we get back to the village, there should be a home available for you and me. A family home. Invite him to stay with us." He was whispering, like it was their little secret.

"Okay." She wrapped her arms around her chest, shifting around to get comfortable. "So no one has debriefed from last night?"

"No, we got out of there pretty quickly and everyone's been quiet while we're moving. We'll get back to the village, then do all the celebrating for a successful mission." He smiled and leaned over. She met him halfway, kissing him deeply. "I was so worried last night. We saw the barn go down…"

"Luykas and I helped each other." Something she was going to be thinking about for a long time. She wanted to fight like that again. Her bond was with Luykas, which meant if she wanted to keep trying it, learning to get better with it, she would need to train with him. Then there was the blood magic he did and how it felt for her. She wanted to learn it so badly.

"I know." Mat smirked. "Hate him a little less?"

"A little," she conceded.

They went quiet like the rest of the Company, everyone focused on the road. They saw no other travelers, encountered no other Elvasi.

By midday, she was feeling like she did on hard days in the pits. She was accustomed to being active and injured, but it had been months now since she had to deal with it. She knew she was growing a little softer in some ways, but seeing the Company around her as they all worked together to make camp, she figured the tradeoff was sound.

Luykas gave them all the suggestion that Mave take two weeks off from wing exercises, and they had agreed without complaint. She was perfectly fine not forcing her wings. It would be stiff and difficult to restart, but there was no way she could do anything at that moment without hurting herself further.

Bryn gave her space, something she was a little grateful for. While he gave her space, that didn't stop any of the glances. He'd kissed her, and the next day, it was still on her mind. It was so soft, but she knew there was a strong warrior there. She'd seen it. For his compact size when he was compared to a male like Mat, he was fearsome and fast. He was deadly. He was powerful.

But the soft kiss was exactly right at the same time. Like the coins he gave her, he was very good at small things that had such an impact. Matesh and Rainev were the same, both good at small gifts, ones that shouldn't mean anything but meant so much to her.

Her heart panged at the thought of Rain. They had been away for well over a week now, the longest she'd gone without him around since she met him. They would have a nearly two week trip home thanks to the load they were now delivering. She hoped the time off in the village helped his headspace. She would find out when she got there.

"Let's eat and debrief, everyone!" Alchan called out. "Mave, how are you feeling?"

She narrowed her eyes at the male with the caring words. While he didn't deliver them in a caring way, she knew he meant them in that way. He never asked how someone was. He left that to others and took status reports.

"Fine," she replied.

He narrowed his eyes back and bared his teeth. She returned with a snarl. She didn't need the *King's* care. He could go sit on a fucking stick.

"Sure." He tossed his hands up, rolling his eyes upwards. Again, the not-submissive way. One day, she was positive she would get his eyes to drop. The challenge of it was beginning to get her to keep messing with him. She reveled in the fact that she had free rein to piss off some royal, something denied to her for so long while in slavery.

"Both of you sit down and let's get this done so everyone can relax for a moment." Luykas pointed for them to sit down. She didn't argue with him, remembering that she had decided to put her eyes down just once, for him. Now it stuck and it annoyed her, but she could fix it later. She wasn't in the mood to open that can of worms, but she would, and soon. She hated putting her eyes down. Looking back, she hated the moment of weakness that made her in the heat of battle.

Correctable. I can fix this. He's not above me.

She reminded herself of that as she sat down next to Mat on the dirt like the rest of the Company.

"The raid end went just as planned, so can one of you tell us what the hell happened with your half?" Alchan gave her a pointed look, but she didn't take the bait.

Mat was the one who answered. "The merchant had a hidden staircase and used it to escape, leaving his sorcerer and a ton of Elvasi to deal with us. They had security measures. It was always a risk." Mat shrugged. "He got away. We never saw him again."

She could see Varon's hands moving and tapped Mat, who followed her gaze. He frowned. "Yeah. He was wearing rich shit. Velvet doublet, if I remember right."

Varon's hands continued. Everyone began to laugh, except her.

"What?" she demanded.

"Varon shot him as he was leaving the stables. He's dead."

She couldn't stop from breaking out in a smile. "Thanks."

Varon just shrugged in response.

Bryn picked back up after that diversion. "The sorcerer tried to run when the mansion was burning, thanks to him. We broke through the men he left behind and chased him into the stables. Everything was a shit-show. Mave got hurt…" He coughed a little. She wondered if it was the smoke from the night before. Had he slept and healed yet? "Well, Luykas showed up. We know how it ended."

"And we ran away with everything. So, mission went just as

planned, with some sideways shit. Like always." Nevyn chuckled, elbowing Kian. "Good first mission back with us?"

"Yeah." Kian elbowed him back. "We'll have to celebrate hard when we get back. We've never run a score like this home."

"You sure you want to celebrate with us? From what I remember, Senri-"

Kian whacked his friend in the chest, making Nevyn double over a little and rub his pec. "You don't talk about Senri, plus three weeks away won't be long enough for her to miss me enough, especially if we're wintering in the village." Kian grinned. "I love it when she misses me."

"I bet you do," Nevyn said, laughing, the hit forgotten.

The entire group devolved into talk once they realized there was no getting Nevyn and Kian back on track. She grabbed some jerky and chewed on it. The night before had been fire and fighting. Now, it just felt like friends and family having a good time in the woods.

The only person who was consistently quiet was Zayden. She watched him carefully, seeing he was carving a piece of wood down with a small knife. She wasn't sure what he was doing really with it. Finally, curiosity and the good afternoon got the better of her. She left Mat, who watched her in confusion, and sat next to Zayden.

"May I ask what you're doing?" She nodded to what he was doing, but he never looked up to her.

"I like to carve little things," he said in reply. "When I need time to think." He glanced at her. "Alone."

"Still upset over Rain, I'm guessing." She sighed. "Mat is still your friend. Why don't you come hang out with us?"

"I've been told that more than once, but you and he are keeping secrets about my son. Makes it a little hard just to have a good time like everyone else." He sighed. "And last night. Well, at least I didn't have to worry about *him* dying."

"Excuse me?" She didn't like the accusing note to how he said that.

"I fished you out of an ocean to stick around for Rain and you nearly got killed on your first job with us. Good job."

She growled. "Fuck you, asshole. Fine, play with your wood *alone*." She got back up, deciding she didn't have the patience for this. She found herself sitting next to Mat again, glaring at Zayden with a heat she hadn't had since the pits, like she glared at some of the other gladiators when she was in a bad mood.

"I would have warned you if I had time, but you were off in a flash. The rest of us know better than to mess with Zayden when he's carving. He normally only does it when he's unable to find other outlets for his temper." Mat wrapped an arm around her waist. "Been a long time since I've seen him do it."

"It's Rain. He's fucking cranky."

"He'll be that way until he knows Rain is okay, that he's still the son he was, and that he still loves his father. We just need to give them both time now." Mat kissed her shoulder, trying to distract her. She knew it. He always did things like this, it seemed. "Let it go. He'll be different by the end of winter, promise."

"Okay. I just was trying to keep him company, like we're all hanging out." She felt stupid.

"Don't let it bother you."

"Why not?" she demanded.

"I don't want to kill my best friend, even if he's being a bit of a shitty one right now." He gave her a sheepish smile. "Let's just leave everything until we get back to the village. How does that sound?"

"Perfect." She was ready to get off the road and find this elusive new home they kept telling her was waiting in the village. Over two months free, and she hadn't yet been able to enjoy being able to decide what to do with her own day.

43

MAVE

The road home was slow, but in a way, it flew by. On their fourteenth day, near the village, Mave found herself listening to Kian and Alchan.

"I don't need to send you back early. What are we supposed to do with your horse? We'll be there by the evening meal."

"Fine, Alchan." Kian sighed.

For the first week of the trip, Kian hadn't been missing his female too much. The second week, he was dying for her. She enjoyed the sight of it as much as she enjoyed the male in general. His exuberance to talk and make friends always made her shy, but she knew there was nothing foul in it. He had an open face, an inability to lie, and loved telling stories. Plus his friendship with Nevyn was always funny to watch. They were a better version of Mat and Zayden, since neither of them were cranky assholes. Just two middle-aged males who stopped taking half the world seriously. Varon was always watching them with fondness.

"It'll be okay, Kian," she called out. "Senri will probably be there when we get back."

"Not *probably*. She will. Kian just wants to get home to enjoy her for a moment." Nevyn was laughing. "Sorry, but none of us want to deal with your horse. You are keeping your ass on it, my friend."

"You are a terrible friend," Kian fired back at the warrior. "Mat, surely you would understand. You would pull my horse so I can get home a little before all of you to enjoy my female."

"No, not really." Mat grinned, riding next to her. "Mine is part of the Company and we don't get to fly home early to enjoy some time. We have to ride, too."

"Mave can't fly, therefore that makes sense. I can fly and Senri is right there." He pointed off into the distance.

She sighed, her eyes rolling upward.

For the rest of the day, there was joking and laughing about what they would all do on their return. She gave Mat a look. They had plans, but not ones they vocalized for the group. Some of it was out in the open, but it was the Bryn situation they hadn't let anyone know about.

"We're going to see our new place and sleep in real beds tonight," Mat answered when Kian pulled closer to them. Kian, who spent the entire trip teasing about wanting to have sex but not being able to, didn't this time.

"Ah, yeah. A new home for a family. A good thing to see." He had a soft smile on his face. "I'm really happy for you, Matesh." Before Mat could pull away, the older male reached out and grabbed the back of his head. They headbutted just hard enough that she wondered if one of them was dizzy. They were both fine, though, smiling at each other. The older male turned on her in his saddle. "And you. I'm glad to have you with us, Mave. I hope you and I get to know each other better over the winter. Senri's not here, but she would want me to tell you both that if you need anything to help set up your household, you are more than welcome to ask us. We will do everything we can to make sure you're in a nice place with all the little things handled."

"Well, Leshaun has probably been working on it while we've been gone." Mat rubbed the back of his neck. "Mave, is there anything you want? We can make a list, and if it's not handled, we can do it in the next few days."

"No, I think I'll be fine." Really, she didn't believe yet that she had this new home. She had a room in the pits with a bathing pool in what amounted to a closet. It didn't have a fireplace, and she was never truly dry due to the dampness of her old hell.

Dry, warm, comfortable. Those were the only things she could possibly want and she was certain that her expectations for those were lower than others.

"Are you sure?" he pressed, leaning. He took on that caring tone she knew well, making sure this wasn't a problem.

"I've never had a real home," she reminded him, reaching out to pat his thigh. "How do I know what I want?"

He looked taken aback, then sadly nodded without saying anything. There wasn't much of a response he could have given her, really.

Kian watched her oddly. "I hope your new home is everything you never dreamed of," he said, pulling his horse beside hers instead of Mat's.

"There's no need for all of that," she replied with a huff. "Just don't know what to expect. I've only even seen the inside of Alchan's and I have a feeling he does nothing normally."

"He keeps his a little barren, that's certain." Kian tapped his chin. "Rugs are important. Cold stone floors in the winter aren't pleasant. The main bedroom should be mostly covered, but that's not up to you; it's the responsibility of Mat and whoever else you want in your family."

She knew the importance of the bed thing, so kept her comments to herself.

He continued without missing a beat. "We use a lot of low sitting furniture, things that won't get in the way with our wings and tails. That will all be there for you. Since you can't fly yet, they probably put you in a ground-level house, something like Alchan's, with a staircase. It's not going to be on the ground, but close to it. Actually, it would be a good bit of training as you start learning to get in the air. A short hop, really."

"I have to wait a few weeks, but I'll keep that in mind."

"Don't let Kian go into dad-mode. If you think Zayden is bad... Well, Zayden is bad, but Kian is over-caring to younger Andinna. It's because his family doesn't have children," Mat whispered loudly on her other side. Kian tried to reach over her and whack him. She grabbed the hand before it messed her up on her horse. "I'm just messing with you!" Mat laughed, pulling away and out of reach.

"How are they made?" she asked, turning the conversation away from that. "How does someone dig out and carve the stone?"

"Well, in Anden, we didn't have to make nearly as many. We often expanded and refurbished the older ones with every passing generation. Here in Olost? We traded for digging tools. We had some dwarves help us. The homes were all very small at the time, but there are some dwarf communities in the mountains and we still work with them, bartering to expand."

"Yeah, but how do we make them on our own? We didn't always have dwarves, right?"

Kian frowned, thoughtful. "Anyone want to help me with this? I've never really…"

It was Alchan who spoke up. "Some Andinna become miners and builders, which means about the same thing in our society. To do one is to do the other. It's a well-paying job as well. Many find themselves needed members of their communities. A builder will begin digging out the door size, once a front platform is made. Once they made enough of a dent, they normally hire strong, single, and unemployed males to help with the grunt work. It can take three months to get into a mountain deep enough to have the first main room, the community room in our homes. Humans and Elvasi call them sitting rooms or parlors. After that, they make sure they aren't going to run into other homes and begin building out the bedrooms and storage rooms or whatever else the family needs. There's a lot of numbers and math involved in that. It's slow, back-breaking work, but there aren't enough caves to live in, and none of us like the idea of living on the dirt like the other races. Fireplaces are especially tricky, but the builders came up with some special tools for those to make sure smoke left the home out the side of the mountain. You can look for the smokestacks in the winter, coming out." He never looked at them as he spoke, just rattling it off like it was a lesson from his childhood.

"Remember the summer we spent working on our own place?" Luykas asked, chuckling.

"Yes...General Lorren and our grandmother said we could have one if we were the grunt work. It would teach us to respect the physical laborers, like we didn't already." Their king snorted, shaking his head. "I miss that home, though. We were the only members of the royal family allowed to live outside the palace."

"We were." Luykas sighed wistfully.

"Your grandmother?" She didn't like prying about their family, but she remembered hearing something, and she couldn't quite put her finger on what. Something about their grandmother.

"The queen at the time." Mat was the one who answered.

"Oh." That had been it. They had a general and a queen telling them what to do with their summer, to make their own home. "How old were you both?"

"Three hundred?" Luykas sounded like he didn't really remember.

"Two hundred. We were starting to get into trouble with the rest of the family. We'd both been cooped up for a century. We left the capital completely by four hundred." Alchan sounded like he was reliving it, a strange smile on his face. "Better times."

"Much better times," Luykas agreed.

The conversation dropped as nostalgia took over the older members of the Company. She was silent as the males all began laughing and telling stories about their first places, how it felt good to get away from family for the first time and all the things they did. Many stayed in large ground-level buildings for young males unless they were going home with a female for a night or joined a *mayara*. Alchan and Luykas having their own home was actually a privilege many of them never had. They both knew it too, quick to remind everyone that it was only because they had gotten in just a little too much trouble with the family and were too dominant for the other males.

She could see that, honestly. She couldn't see them living comfortably around other males too long, having to share space like that. She knew in the village, they both kept private homes.

It was reaching late afternoon when they finally saw a familiar face. There was a patrol on the road in the distance, standing between them and the village. Andinna were talking, some sitting on logs and laughing.

But one stood out to her.

"RAIN!" she cried out, pushing her mare forward. She was happy not to be on the cart that day.

The deep blue of those wings was unmistakable. He turned and grinned as she raced towards him, others calling for her to slow down.

She yanked the reins, pulling her mare to a hard stop right before she made it to the patrol. She jumped off, and by the time her feet were on the ground, he was right beside her.

They met in a hug fiercer than any she could remember. She held him tight.

"It's good to see you, *illo amyr*."

"And you, *illi bodyr*," she replied, holding him still, refusing to let go. "I've been missing you."

"And I you," he said, pulling back to see her better. "Is everyone okay?"

"Better than okay," she promised, looking back down the road to the Company. "We're bringing home a lot."

"And the other part of the mission?"

"The hit is dead. Along with a sorcerer he had in his employment."

"Shit." Rain huffed. He turned back to the others, waving them on. "One of you go home and tell the village the Company is back. Tell Senri I'll be with them as an escort."

"Sure." One of the Andinna jumped up and flew fast. Another glared at Rain.

"Oh, the Company is back so the *raki* is too good for us."

Mave snarled. "He's mine and you'll watch your tongue."

Rain grabbed her, shaking his head. "Leave it, *amyr*. There's been no trouble. Senri put me in charge of this unit, over their ranking male. They have some right to be annoyed. As of this moment, you have control of your males again, Lenyc. My apologies for Senri's decision."

"Sure," the acidic male growled. The rest of the patrol just watched the interaction.

"I've missed a lot," she mumbled, grabbing her horse to move to the side of the road. "We'll wait here. Your father is driving one of the carts. I was the only one seriously injured, but I'm feeling fine now. Ready to put my feet up, though."

"I bet. The Company has been moving a lot recently." Rain chuckled. "Yeah, let's wait here for them."

She threw an arm over his shoulder, happy to have him next to her again.

They waited together as she caught him up on the entire mission. It didn't take very long. She didn't tell him about Bryn yet. She didn't want to hope for anything, not yet. He'd kissed her; she'd liked it. She wanted another.

He wasn't easy like Mat was, though. She and Mat just fell into it all together. Bryn was something new. She had to ask him, where she never had to ask Mat. She was pretty sure Matesh was in her *mayara* long before she even knew it.

When the Company got to them, she jumped on her horse while he greeted everyone else.

"Father," he said softly, hugging his *bodra* tightly. Zayden visibly relaxed, holding his son to him like it was the first and last time he would ever be able to.

"I missed you, boy," Zayden mumbled, running his hand through Rain's black hair, ruffling it at the end.

"I missed you too," Rain said. "I'll sit with you."

"Thank you."

Together, those two rode into the village. Mave took in the sight of the homes of the cliff again, smiling. This time, she didn't feel nervous about coming to the village. She knew that if she needed anyone or anything, she could ask the Company. She didn't need to make friends with the free Andinna. She had her community, and they had her.

There were already tons of villagers waiting on their arrival, cheering as the Company rode in. This time, she felt like she earned the fanfare. Jesvena spoke with Alchan first as Luykas told the Company to fall out. Free Andinna took their horses and the carts. Luykas had to repeat to the Company to fall out.

It was time for them to hand it all off. They were done.

"Don't worry. It's all going to be put away into community storage, and we get first choice for any of the fine stuff," Mat told her as they started walking away from the crowd. He looked up and away from her, his face lighting up. "Uncle!"

"Come here, my boy," Leshaun called back. The old male was using his cane, but looking much healthier since the last time she had seen him, which felt like ages ago. "And you, my girl." He added the next words kindly, waving her to join as well as his nephew hugged him. She was slower, but also wrapped her arms around him when Mat was out of the way. She hadn't realized how grateful she was to see him until they hugged. "I'm glad to see my family back. I finished furnishing your home just a few days ago. Here's the key." He held it out to her. "We don't normally lock our homes, but I figured you would want the privacy and contacted a dwarf to come over and set it up."

"Thank you." She took the key slowly, hugging the old male again, this time meaning it. He was treating her like family now because she was with Matesh, but even with that reason, she still appreciated it as if it came from the old male's heart. They were family now.

"Thank you, uncle." Mat dipped his head respectfully.

"It was an honor to do it for you both and whoever comes next."

Leshaun said, smiling. "You're on the end, a bit away from the main bustle of the village. They gave me three choices and I thought that one would suit you most, Maevana."

"Thank you for being so thoughtful." She didn't know what else to say. She didn't want to give him a hard time over her full name now. In that moment, it sounded like he meant it respectfully, as a sign of change. Mave the gladiator had no homes, but Maevana, the free Andinna, did.

"I'll leave you both to it. Mat, you should know the place. On the east end, bottom home with nothing above it." With that, Leshaun patted their shoulders and went to greet the others.

Mave was nervous now and what Mat said next didn't help.

"If you want to do this, inviting him now would be best. You could put it off, but it might make him feel like his attentions didn't pay off." Mat ran a hand over her lower back. "I'll wait here. No worries."

"Are you sure?" she asked, looking up into those emerald eyes. "I've never...had people, not one like you, much less two. Are you okay with this, though?"

"I'm sure. Mave, I promised you...everything an Andinna gets from freedom, and this is part of it. This is our world. Go. If you want him, go and get him. I'll be right here. Tell me what he answers with. He says no and you still want him, I'll go get him for you. Promise." He pushed her away gently now. "I love you, Maevana Lorren, and this is the best way I'll ever have to prove it, by accepting who you want in our family and making it their family too."

She caught her breath. Those were words she had never thought to hear in her long life. She wasn't sure how to respond and something must have given her away. He leaned down to kiss her slowly.

"Mat-" She was so lost for a second. He *loved* her. And she knew she felt the same, but the words didn't come. Never had she wanted to say them, and now they seemed lost to her.

"You don't need to say anything. I know I'm in this for the long haul. Go talk to your rogue."

She went, looking back at him one more time. As she left, other Andinna crowded him, talking about things.

Finally, she looked for her target.

Bryn was sitting on the front of a cart still, laughing with Nevyn and Leshaun. Oh, she had to do this in front of her other lover's uncle, who just gave her a home. Who had put his time and care into it.

And she was going to invite another male into it without ever enjoying it with just Matesh.

Bryn caught her walking up, ignoring the conversation as she grew closer. She knew she was nervous by the way her palms were sweating. She would rather face legions of Elvasi. She would rather be back in the pits with her steel as her only companion. She would rather be anywhere else. This felt vulnerable.

"What do you need?" Bryn asked when she stopped in front of him.

"I was hoping..." She took a deep breath. Why couldn't she find any of her normal courage? If he said no, he said no. She was used to rejection. She had been rejected for a thousand years.

She didn't want to be rejected anymore.

"Mave?" Nevyn turned on her now and Leshaun raised an eyebrow. Varon slid closer to the group.

"Brynec, Mat and I were hoping you would come over tonight and uh...stay with us?" The words flew out of her mouth. She realized she didn't even know his last name, but she could learn. She just knew she was praying he would say yes. She also realized the invitation wasn't to her home. That was the polite public thing to say. No, everyone around her knew it was an invite to her bed.

Oh shit. What have I done?

"And where is your home?" he asked, smiling as his face turned pink. She quickly answered, with Leshaun stepping in to help her explain since she had never seen it. She just kept talking. She was about to head there with Mat, and he didn't need to rush or anything. He was free to say no. He reached out and touched her hand, stopping it from shaking. "I'll bring something for dinner."

"Thank you." She hadn't even considered food.

"We'll talk when I get there?" He seemed so hopeful and nervous now as well.

"We will." She smiled now, her fears fading. He was coming to her. Everyone else was silent, letting the exchange happen.

She felt like running away. Instead, she turned slowly, keeping her composure and walked away like a normal individual would. When she had enough distance, she heard Nevyn scream out in excitement for Bryn, ribbing him, saying he knew it was bound to happen. Other voices joined the mix, congratulating him. She had a feeling that it wasn't settled yet, though. She still needed to have that talk with him. This was just step one of the evening.

She met with Mat again, updating him on what just happened.

"Oh, I could see," her lover said, laughing as they began to walk to their new home. "He'll come and it'll work out. If we need to take things slow, we will. This is however you want this to happen, Mave. This could be temporary - you two might decide it won't work. This isn't signing up for forever, just a commitment to try to be together in a family, together as lovers."

"I'm…not worried," she said finally. "About it not working - that's not what I worried about. I was worried he would say no."

He didn't say anything in return, just taking her hand. When they reached the front of her home, they climbed the thirty feet of stairs to the door and she unlocked it.

Together, they walked in. She kicked off her boots, realizing she could do that since it was hers. This was the place where she could be whatever she wanted, do whatever she wanted.

Home.

And she had the immense treasure of being able to share with others. Not just Mat and Bryn, but all of the Company. She could have friends over. She could have them all in her living room like she had seen them at Alchan's. Relaxed, talking about things.

She took off her armor and went into the bedroom, dropping it carelessly on the floor. The bedroom was huge, the same size as the 'main' room. On the floor was a pile of things, much like she'd seen on the ship in her cabin with Mat. Their bed. Furs mostly, with pillows and quilts added.

"Senri must have added some things for us. The furs are all mine, everything I've used over the years. They're yours now, forever, since you're never getting rid of me." Mat came up behind her, his arms wrapping around her waist. "We can enjoy it before Bryn gets here. He'll probably have stuff to add as well, but that should wait until tomorrow."

Her stomach growled. "No, I think I'll wait for food," she decided, chuckling. "Why does his stuff wait until tomorrow?"

"Because I bet he doesn't want to haul it around tonight along with getting dinner here." Mat chuckled, kissing her neck.

44

ZAYDEN

Zayden sat slowly down at the long table, holding his mead close to him.

"I hurt. Everything hurts. I'm so done with traveling around." He was bitching, but there was no heat to it. He was tired and glad to be home. He was glad that the one person sitting next to him was his son, who seemed lighter than he had in the time before they left. There were still shadows in his boy's eyes, which worried him, but his son was beside him again. That meant the world to him.

"I wanted to be back out there the moment you all left," Rain said, chuckling. "Seriously, patrolling was awful. And everyone kept wanting to ask me about Mave and Elliar, which I really didn't want to talk about. Nothing was normal like it used to be. I like being with the Company."

He listened patiently, understanding his son's point. "Next time, you'll come back out with us. And we're back now. Hang out with the family. Forget the kids." Zayden said kids, meaning the young males his son normally spent time with before he joined the Ivory Shadows. He hoped his words were heard. He meant them. He had hated when Rain joined, going to Luykas to make it happen instead of talking to him. He'd agreed in the end, knowing he couldn't really say no. He had no power over Rain, not really. His boy was an adult, as much as that sucked.

But being on the mission without his son had been as bad, probably worse, than having Rain with them. He could also see his son was growing up, which was something he was fighting.

"Thanks, *bodra*. I'm glad to hear that." Rain leaned into him, elbowing lightly. The most affection he was going to get now that the hugs were out of the way. He would have to deal.

"What were you doing out on patrol today and how did you end up on our road home?" He was curious. He wanted his son to keep talking to him. He would talk about why the moon was red or the stars were white if he had to. Anything.

"Well, Senri put me in charge of them since they're the biggest slackers of the patrols. She knew I was going to talk to Alchan when you all got back and wanted to show she was willing to let the Company make changes, as long as she agreed with them." Rain gave him a sheepish smile. "So, to get them into shape, we patrolled that road every other day and night."

"Looking out for us?"

"Yeah." Rain looked down, using his spoon to push his food around, a habit Zayden knew he gave his son. Summer had hated when they played around with the food. "Speaking of Alchan…" Rain sighed. "I need to talk to him."

"You do. Go now, then come back to me." Zayden wanted to catch Alchan later as well, to make sure his boy wasn't going to get a punishment too hard. He knew he should trust their leaders, especially their King, but it was his son. He would take the punishment for Rain if he needed to, if he was allowed to.

Rain jumped up and walked across the rowdy building. He watched his son's every move as he went to Luykas and Alchan, sitting with Jesvena. Alchan said something quickly and shook hands with Rain. Luykas hugged him. Zayden smiled a little at how Jesvena looked insulted to suddenly be ignored in favor of his son. Company, no matter who, was more important than the rest.

It looked like it went well, as Rain was casually dismissed and came back.

"I have to see him tomorrow at dawn. For both my report on the patrols and my punishment."

"He didn't seem too mad, but just remember to be respectful of him while in his home. It's the one place he won't tolerate a challenge. He's possessive over his space." He'd only ever seen two people challenge Alchan in his home and not get put into the stone floor for it. Luykas, because he was family, and Mave, who probably didn't know any different. Her getting away with it meant the Company dynamics were going to keep changing more than they already had. It meant he respected her, even while they disliked each other.

It meant Mave was above him or Mat in the eyes of the King. Above Rain. It made sense, considering she was such a dominant female.

"Hey Bryn!" Rain called out suddenly. "Come sit with us!"

Zayden followed his son's gaze and saw the rogue holding a large basket with a piece of fabric over it.

"Ah, I can't." Bryn walked over, turning red and Zayden frowned. "I'm going to have dinner with Mave and Matesh."

"Oohhh." Zayden waved him on. "Good luck with that."

"Wait. Are you..." Rain's jaw dropped. "Good for you! And her. Be nice to my sister, Bryn."

"Ah, we haven't talked yet, but um..." Bryn put the basket down and held out a hand to his son. "If all goes well, I'll be honored to join the *mayara*."

"I'm not official, and you know it," Rain replied, chuckling. "I am her brother. I'm honored to have you. Be happy and be blessed by the Skies."

Zayden felt a wave of pride. Brothers weren't official, but they were treated like they were. If a female had no one, she probably had a father and brothers. Mave didn't even have those, really. But she had

Rain, and he quickly realized just how big of a male his son had to be to offer that familial relationship to a female who had no one and nothing when they met.

His son truly was growing up before his eyes, even keeping dark secrets. Ones he knew would come back up. He had no hope that the ease of tonight would last. Rain was probably just too happy to see the Company home.

When Bryn walked off, to cheers from Nevyn and Kian across the building, Rain sat back down.

"That was good of you." Zayden wanted to make sure his son knew how proud he was. "She's blessed to have you, Rain."

"I just wish you and her would start getting along," Rain admitted softly, a smile still on his face. "How's that going?"

He winced. "I was an ass to her on the road and ignored everyone. I was carving."

"*Bodra...*" Rain groaned. "Please. I'm sure you two can find common ground. Try for me. I know you'll never see her as a daughter, but...like just family would work? Just a friend, even?"

"I'll try for friends. I've been a bad one recently to Mat, actually. I'm going to spend the winter trying to fix things." He knew he needed to. He should have seen Mat before this, talked about his new coming life as a taken man. That was something he was supposed to share with his best friend, something they could relate about now. He once had Summer, and his friend now had Mave.

And yet, he'd blown his friend off again, even when he promised he would try to fix himself back in Namur.

"It's okay, *bodra*. We all know you have issues. Mat will welcome you back with open arms." Rain began to laugh as Zayden tried to smack him for that.

They laughed and talked for most of the evening, until his son was barely on his feet.

"Go. You have to be up early."

"It's good to have you home," his son said one more time, a little drunk and leaning on him. Most of the Company was drunk at this point. Nevyn and Kian were singing at the top of their lungs down the table, Varon clapping politely whenever they finished a bawdy song. Alchan and Luykas were even laughing.

"Go, Rain." Zayden pushed him. His son was a lightweight, and nothing would ever change that.

Rain stumbled out, but he had faith his kid would get home just fine. They weren't too high up and Rain wasn't drunk enough to be grounded. Nevyn and Kian were getting there, but Senri would walk in at any moment and help Varon bring those two to heel.

Zayden wanted to do one more thing before heading after his son.

He approached Alchan slowly, waiting for permission to interrupt. It wasn't something they did normally, but he wanted his bosses to know it was professional.

Alchan looked up and sighed. "Come here, Zayden. Let's hear it."

"Rain." He didn't need to say much else.

"Don't worry." Alchan gave him a somewhat drunk, lopsided smile. "He's a good young male who got wrapped up in protecting his adopted sister. Since he's a *bedin*, he'll never have another female, unless something extraordinary happens. I know how important that is. He's also a first-time offender. No need to worry. Have a drink with us. You've been a piece of shit recently."

Zayden laughed now, sitting down with them.

"You know, I'm actually glad you came here instead of moping more," Luykas added. "Now let's drink and forget work for the rest of the fucking night."

Zayden lifted his glass to that. Nevyn, Kian, and Varon joined with them after a few moments. Then Leshaun came, had a drink and relaxed, listening to the tale of their mission.

It felt good. It felt like they were going to make it through whatever strange changes their family was going through. Like he was going to survive them and still have a family.

45

MAVE

Time ticked by and her nerves were making her worse. She paced around the main room while Mat set up their dining area for company.

"Please sit down, *ilanra*." He was losing patience with her.

"I've never felt this." She didn't know how to sit still. It was reminiscent of the first time she took Rain and Mat to her private room in the pits but worse.

"You hate dealing with others, and it's your biggest weakness. I know it. You know it. Bryn knows it, and I promise, he's nervous too. There's nothing you can do to stop what's about to happen. Just accept it's going to. We'll have dinner. We'll talk. We need to set some family rules, small things like chores. Easy stuff will help tackle the bigger things."

"Does this ever get easier?"

"No idea. It was never a problem for me. You should ask Zayden or Alchan, maybe even Luykas. They all need to work a bit harder than most to fit in and handle other Andinna." Mat put the last spoon down and walked over to her. He wrapped his arms around her and held her for a moment. "You and he have feelings for each other. It's probably not love, but something is there. You're attracted to each other. There's no reason for this not to work, not to try. There's no reason to be nervous. If he was going to say no, he would have. He would have never kissed you. This is all set. *You* have no reason to be nervous."

"Why does he need to be nervous?" The intent of Mat's words was clear.

"He might have things he needs in a relationship you don't agree to. You can always turn him away."

"He can always turn me down too, though."

"That's not how this works. If he turns back now, he'll never get another chance."

"Why not?" She had a feeling she would give him a hundred chances to come back. It would hurt if Bryn turned away now, but she wasn't sure she could reject him in the future if he did.

"Because I would never let him," he whispered in her ear. "See, there's things we males do. We protect our female behind her back. If he turns you away now, I have no reason to ever trust him with you. While you aren't watching, I would make his life hell if he came sniffing around again. I would be well within my rights to, because he hurt you. I don't need to let him try again. It's Bryn, though. I don't think we need to worry about any of that."

They stood there for a moment and she let that sink in. There was protective and there was overprotective. She wasn't used to being protected at all.

"We might need to talk about toning that down," she said, realizing he was dead serious. "I mean, something could be my fault-"

"We'll deal with things like that as they come." He pulled away, smirking as if he knew in the long run, he would be right. She narrowed her eyes at his back as he walked back into the dining area.

"Fine." She wasn't going to get into it tonight, not after that.

There was a knock on the door and her mouth went dry.

"Go," he urged softly, nodding towards the door.

She took a deep breath and went, opening the door before she could chicken out. Bryn stood there in the dark holding a large basket, the food covered with a small blanket.

"Hey," she said, leaning on the wall.

"Hey. May I come in?"

She pulled the door open further and held it for him. She felt awkward, but the moment she had the door closed, Bryn turned on her, holding the basket out of the way.

Her back hit the wall as he pushed into her, their mouths clashing together. She ran her hands over his chest, up to his shoulders, and around his neck. His free hand grabbed her hip and she moaned as he broke away, kissing her jawline and leaning to kiss down her neck.

"Let me have that," Mat's voice cut in softly. Her head was turned the wrong way to see him. Suddenly, she had both of Bryn's hands on her.

"Bryn…" She hadn't realized this was how it was going to go.

"I gave ya the coin and I was wrong," he murmured, peppering kisses back up to her neck between the words until he was back at her lips. "Not one. Worth more. So much more."

She melted, her nerves gone.

"Let's have dinner," she said against his lips. He gave her that roguish smile and pulled away, grabbing her hand.

She led him to their dining area. Mat was already putting food on plates, that fucking arrogant smile on his lips.

"Welcome, Brynec." He reached out after putting a bowl down. He and Bryn clasped each other's arms by the elbow. Then they pulled into each other, their free arms allowing them to hug. "Welcome."

"Ya could have turned me away," Bryn whispered. She could only hear because of how close she was. Could Mat have sent him back? Told him no behind her back? She really needed to catch up on what was and what wasn't acceptable for all of them, all of this. She didn't think Mat was lying to her, but maybe stretching the truth.

"I can't do that to you." Mat pulled away. "Thanks for bringing home dinner. Now, let's eat and get some damned sleep."

Mave smiled as the two males finished setting out the food. She just watched them, as they worked around each other like they had in the warehouse. Had they been talking behind her back? The thought crossed her mind.

It was Bryn who grabbed her and forced her to sit down at the head of the table. They each took a side. She felt Bryn kick off his boots under the table.

"Tell me those will go by the door later," Mat said casually, grinning. He put a bowl of soup in front of her.

"Aye. Just got distracted coming in." Bryn added a small plate with a sandwich to what Mat had given her. "Is that her rule or yours?"

She was quickly realizing they didn't find anything weird about this.

"Mine. Leshaun and my parents were sticklers about it."

"Aye. Male rule. Okay. I'm guessing none of the rules are really set though, right?"

"Since we just got here, you're right. I figured we could do it together."

She was never going to get a word in if this kept up. Leaning back in her seat, she began to eat, knowing she didn't really care to. Male rules. So there would be things just between her *mayara*, private rules they kept.

"How about we put it off for the night?" she finally said as they went off about chores, who would do what and when. "Tomorrow, we can worry about it."

Bryn smiled. "I was wondering when ya would get tired of it."

She chuckled, but didn't voice her mind. *I'm not tired of it. I just want to have a quiet night. They've made it so easy for this to be normal.*

In mostly silence, they ate together. She remembered something from earlier and decided to ask.

"What's your last name, Bryn?"

"Lorren."

She nearly dropped her spoon and looked up. "What?"

"I'm in yer *mayara*, right? My last name is Lorren. I'll take yers. Mat, you hadn't…"

"I hadn't yet told her that," Mat said, sighing. He looked at her, guilty. "So much to tell you…Sorry, *ilanra*. We males tend to take your last name while we're with you. It's a not-so-subtle claim. If this ever ends, we just go back to using our birth names."

"Ah. But Bryn…what was your last name then?" Of course she wanted him in her *mayara*. She wanted to see where it went, to try this new thing. To have this family. That wasn't even a question.

"Doesn't matter," he countered, grinning. "Right now, it's Lorren."

She smiled. That was a gesture she hadn't realized would touch her.

They went late into the evening, sharing small moments of conversation, but mostly beautiful, comfortable silence.

When she yawned, Bryn stood up and held a hand out. She glanced at Mat, who started cleaning up the table. He didn't seem tense or worried. When she took Bryn's hand, he reached out and stopped them from leaving.

"Enjoy it," he crooned, kissing her. "I'll be there soon for bed." Once he released her, she was pulled from the room. Exhaustion was riding her, calling her to bed, but it wasn't the only thing. Next to her was a lean rogue who blushed when he saw her topless. Who gave her a soft kiss.

Who obviously wanted to do this right, who had spoken to her male without her knowing to make sure their family would work, she was guessing.

She ended up opening the door to their bedroom and the moment it closed behind them, those nerves came back.

He reached behind her and began to remove her undershirt. "We don't need to do anything," he explained. "But I have no other bed now. If ya need some space, though, I can sleep by the fireplace in the main room. Looks like Leshaun gave ya a lot of nice, comfortable furniture."

"Stay. I'm just…It was easy with Matesh. We just…did."

"And we're different. All of your males will be different." He finished and she let the shirt fall. Again that sweet blush heated his cheeks.

"I hope you never stop blushing," she whispered, reaching out to touch his cheeks.

"It's not because I'm innocent, Mave. It's because I'm imagining all the things I want to do to those." His blush was still there as he gained a devious smile. "And I'm worried you'll be able to read my mind."

That made her throb. "Show me."

He growled. They were doing this tonight. She wanted this now. She wanted to explore his body and see what things could possibly make him blush.

He began to kiss her collarbone as his fingers worked quickly to undo her breeches. He shoved them down and dropped to his knees. She gasped as hot breath passed over her and his tongue swiped between her legs.

She was very thankful she found a stream on the trip back and bathed before they made it back to the village.

He purred between her legs as his tongue pushed into her, exploring. She moaned, running her hands through his hair. He was skilled. One of his fingers ran over her bud and had her seeing sparks. His second hand rubbed her ass, massaging deep. She didn't know she had been sore from riding until he helped her relax.

It continued until her knees felt weak and her legs began to shake. She didn't finish before he pulled away and kissed back up her body.

"We're young. I have plenty of time to show you everything I want to do with you," he murmured, pulling her against his chest. He still had too much clothing on. She fumbled and began to untie everything, stepping away from her own discarded clothing as he moved closer to their bed. "Tonight, I just want us to get to know each other."

"That sounds nice." Really, anything in that moment probably would have pushed her over the edge from being nice to being great.

He stripped now, helping her as she fumbled with his buckle and ties. The moment he was nude, she pulled him to her, claiming another kiss. Now she was growling, possessive. Bryn was hers now, just like Mat was. Her male, her family, her friend. She ran her fingers up the underside of his shaft, making his cock jump. She felt the drop of pre-cum already dripping from it. She touched and licked his scars, memorizing his body.

Hers. Her other gladiator. Her rogue. Her lean lover. All hers.

He was the one who had to pull her down into the bed. Before she had a say, he pushed her onto her back. She growled. She had been enjoying him and he put a stop to it.

"Pick a word, Mave," he hotly whispered in her ear, holding her down. "Pick a word, because now it's my turn."

"Elliar." It was the first thing she could think of. She knew what he was doing. She knew what this was. He was going to take charge, and if she wanted to fight with him about it, that was the word that stopped everything. That was the word that meant it stopped being a game.

He bit down on her breast, making her yelp while her back arched. His fingers explored her, sliding between her legs and sinking deep into her. He explored every inch of her with his mouth. His tail roamed, grazing over her flesh, another limb just helping him make her skin feel like it was on fire. Nothing was nearly aggressive enough to make her worried. Instead, she slipped into a haze of pleasure, her mind only focused on where his mouth would go next.

He moved around her breasts, kissing her stomach, licking her collarbone. She watched with anticipation as he drew closer and closer to her rosy nipple. The room was warm now, but her arousal had her nipples hard anyway.

He hovered over it for a moment, gazing up at her. She tried to lift up, to force him to take it. He just compensated and lifted a little higher, keeping the distance.

"Bryn..." She made his name sound like a warning, not a plea.

He chuckled in response. "Willing to fight me for it?"

She took a sharp breath. He was serious. He had a taunting smile, wanting to see if she pushed.

"No." Not tonight, anyway.

"Good, because tonight, I just want to make ya feel wonderful." At that, he took her nipple into his mouth and nipped it with his teeth, sucking hard.

Her head rolled back and right on cue, she orgasmed, taken by the sensory overload. She couldn't stop his name from escaping her lips, this time a prayer and praise. He sent her over the edge and they were only getting started.

He gave a satisfied growl, and in the span of a heartbeat, his fingers left her and he pushed in.

With a scream, her back arched further as he sank his entire cock deep inside her. She held on to him as he began to rock with a fast, steady pace. Their mouths met as she gasped and moaned, making sounds she had thought only Mat could pull from her. He bit her bottom lip, still giving that low, satisfied growl.

"I never thought ya would want me," he said, shoving her to that peak again, not even out of breath the way she was. "Too small for ya. Too dark for ya. Now ya have me and I'm never letting you forget me."

She nodded desperately. She wasn't going to forget him. Not tonight. Not tomorrow. Not in the years to come. He would have to leave her, because she was never giving him away.

"Mine," she finally said. "All mine."

"All yers," he agreed.

Together, they rocked. She felt every movement of his cock, her world focused on it. Which is how she missed Matesh walking in, stripping down, and joining them in bed.

She tensed for a moment and Bryn slowed.

"Say the word if ya need to, Mave. This is his bed too." Bryn stared down into her eyes. She shook her head, then angled to look at her other lover, lying back near them, his cock standing tall. He watched, smirking with a hooded gaze. Then he wrapped his fingers around that thick thing and began to stroke.

Moaning, she had to turn away, her face hot.

"I know I intend to watch ya and him and do the same. Don't think

I haven't fantasized about it. Remember all those awful things I want to do to those tits."

Bryn's words made her hotter. She felt like any moment she was going to burst into flames.

"Yer safe here, we promise. Ya say the word and it all stops," he promised softly, finally beginning to pant with her. "Ya just let us know when this has to stop."

"Don't stop," she begged. Stopping wasn't an option. A groan echoed over her sounds, and she knew it. Matesh. Matesh was there with them, gaining some pleasure himself from seeing her with another male. This was their bedroom. This was the place where things were private, just for them, her and her males.

Once, she would have been disgusted by the idea of getting watched, but it was *Mat*. There was nothing dangerous about Mat.

Everything about it felt so different from what she had known. Looking into summer-sky eyes, she realized he intended it that way. Bryn and Mat had wanted her to know what being an Andinna was, how the *mayara* really worked, and make her feel safe at the same time.

That broke her.

The climax crashed over her. Quietly, Bryn groaned as she went into that weightless place, her body exploding in pleasure. She clung to him, feeling his cock twitch, and then he spilled as well, coming deep in her.

It was quiet for a moment, as they both rode it out. They held onto each other, and he leaned her back down to the bed. She hadn't even realized she had practically sat up in the process.

When he pulled out, he fell next to her. She was still panting as he kissed her neck more, his hands and tail lazily petting her still.

"Mat," she whispered. "Come closer."

Without a word, he did. She rolled onto her side. Somehow, with all their wings, hers didn't end up on the bottom. She grabbed his still-hard cock and stroked him, wanting the last finish of the night. If this was *mayara*, she could show them she accepted it. She would feel safe in their hands.

"Mave," he groaned out. "*Ilanra*."

He finished in only a few moments, his cum covering their stomachs, kissing her as Bryn rubbed her back and ribs from behind.

"Who gets to clean all of this tomorrow?" she asked, her eyelids suddenly heavy.

"He does," they both answered, referencing each other.

She smiled as sleep claimed her.

46

LUYKAS

Luykas woke up the next morning in a bedroom that wasn't his with something kicking him softly in the foot. He knew it before he opened his eyes. He wasn't sure he wanted to confront it or the body near his. Whoever was kicking him.

What the fuck did I do last night?

He cracked his eyes open, hoping it wasn't too bad. Hopefully, it was somewhere safe. A black wolf pelt greeted him, lush and soft, the warmest thing he knew. It also told him where he was. He tensed.

Shit.

"Good morning, brother mine," Alchan said casually. "Have a nice night? I didn't. I got kicked in the thigh one too many times. If I remember right, you have your own home. Also, you took my favorite fur. You're welcome."

"Sorry," he mumbled, pushing up. He was nude, but that wasn't the problem. If he was in his brother's home, he knew he didn't do anything stupid. Well, too stupid, like fucking a female that wasn't his to bury his cock in anything but his hand. It was still somewhat stupid to come into his brother's space.

"Stop. I'm messing with you." Alchan began to chuckle. "You had too much to drink last night and I wasn't going to let you fly, so I dragged you out here, away from the unfortunate public who had to witness you last night."

"Fuck me," he groaned. "She was with them last night. It…"

"She's not yours. Now, I'm really understanding about how you physically feel whatever she's going through, but drowning in alcohol because it's not you doing it…Next time, I'm just going to put your ass in the dirt outside."

He sighed. Yeah, his brother was being nice to him about this entire thing. While they were on the road, it wasn't a problem. But whatever Mat, and now Bryn, did to her made him go crazy. Even the memory of how she felt was beginning to turn his morning wood into a raging hard-on he was going to need to deal with.

"Do you even like her?" Alchan snorted. "Probably not. The bond is probably just riding you too hard."

Luykas didn't answer that one. He did, actually. He hated her at the same time, though. She was frustrating and glorious. She was a fierce warrior that could meet armies on the battlefield without a drop of fear. She was a Skies-damned frigid bitch who didn't know how to talk to people and disliked him to the point where she was constantly annoyed with sharing air with him.

He wasn't telling his brother any of that. How he wanted to be the male between her legs, who earned her praise and kind words and fought beside her. And damn, they could fight together. The mission had proven it. They could be great together.

There was one more problem, though. He'd promised General Lorren to protect and help his daughter, not fuck her. They were in a good age range of each other. She was an adult. He hadn't helped raise her in any way. His attraction wasn't unsightly in the eyes of their people.

But she was General Lorren's daughter and he knew the general had never intended Luykas to *want* his daughter.

Damn the Skies, I do though.

"It's nothing. I'll get used to this like the rest. No more drinking, promise." He didn't shy away from his brother seeing him or seeing his brother, who was sprawled out nude on the middle of his bed like he ruled the world. He did, in a sense. The Andinna one, anyway.

"Good. Go use my spring to wake up and then get the fuck out of my house." Alchan smiled. "I'm not feeding your ass breakfast, too."

Luykas was laughing as he grabbed his clothing and headed outside. Of course his brother wasn't going to feed him.

It was just before dawn as he stepped into the pool. He bathed quickly, rubbed one out, and got dressed. He didn't want to waste time bothering his brother when he needed to get something to eat and talk to the very female that plagued him about something very different than his problem.

He went back into his brother's home for just a minute to look for something. Alchan was already cooking himself breakfast, but there was more than enough for one person.

"Who's getting breakfast if I'm not?" he demanded, looking over the large pan of eggs his brother was working on.

"Rainev, who will be here any minute." Alchan waved him away. "It's his first punishment. I'm going to feed his stupid ass because it'll make him feel better when I shatter his pride by giving him the first of probably many ass-chewings."

Right on cue, there was a knock on the door.

"Good luck with that," he said to his brother, thumping Alchan's shoulder. He answered the door and let Rainev in, whispering, "Good luck," as he left.

He didn't feel very worried about Rainev, really. His brother knew the line to draw, especially with the young and stupid. Their grandmother had set a good example in the family, and General Lorren only enforced it later on. The real problem was that Alchan always took the punishments on himself and let Luykas fix it later, no matter how soft or harsh they were. It made their king look like the bad guy too much in his mind.

But he took the sign of making Rainev food as well that his brother was going to try and be everything. He would be the judge, jury, and executioner, but also the kind leader who would bandage them up at the end.

Good for you, brother mine.

Luykas was going to find himself out of place if he wasn't careful. It was a good change, but one that would leave him just following Alchan around with nothing to do.

He left quickly, flying to the village and landing at her doorstep. Her first, then food, that way he didn't threaten to lose it later if she punched him or gutted him. He knocked hard, hoping any of them were awake. Any of the three of them would work.

He was a little bitter over Bryn, and he hated that too. He was working so hard to keep her alive, and then to even get her to look at him. Bryn helped with her wings and they talked a lot because he never risked his sanity to help her.

Bitter was a bit of an understatement.

Did Bryn deserve happiness? Yeah. There was no doubt. Luykas knew his own issues weren't Bryn's problem. None of those rational thoughts changed how bitter he was that Bryn was *mayara* now with Matesh and he was there, knocking on her door after an awful night of feeling, too much feeling. It wasn't even about that, either.

It had to be Bryn who answered the door.

"Ya need somethin'?"

"Mave. She and I need to talk about some of her ongoing training."

"Aye. One moment." Bryn left him on the porch, the door open for him to see down the hall. Mat was down there, shirtless, wearing only breeches and looking tired. He cast a curious glance down to Luykas and waved.

With nothing better to do, Luykas waved back. For once, he was at the bottom of the food chain. If he needed Mave, he had to get through her males. They ranked higher in her eyes than he did, no matter if he was her boss or commander, one of the leaders of the Company. In her home, he was the lowest-ranking male.

She was there a few moments later, moving around her massive male to get into the hallway he could see and to the door.

"What do you need?" she asked, stepping out and closing the door behind her.

"You've settled in quickly." *In a single night.*

"We're about to have some important talks about rules. Apparently there are male rules and family rules. I set the family rules and they set rules just for the males, things between them to make life easier." She sighed. "Why does everything have to be so…complicated?"

"Because there's more than two adults in the relationship. It's what we've done for generations." He wasn't there to give her love life advice, but damn, he felt that need to give her the information she wanted. "Look, I'm here to talk to you about your blood magic training."

"Oh, perfect. I was hoping we could talk about that once we were back." She didn't seem annoyed with him. He wasn't sure he particularly enjoyed the excitement she had, either. He should have been glad, but he had a feeling she was going to want something he couldn't give her and that would just put him in a worse spot. "And I want to train with you to fight with the bond. I've never been so in tune with anyone. That could be used on future missions."

He froze, his mind stumbling over what had just come out of her mouth. That was it? She wanted to explore the bond for its combat uses? He should have known. He was the one who introduced her to it while on the mission, and if there was anything that pleased Maevana Lorren, it was being the best fucking warrior she could be.

"We'll start tomorrow," he said, finally finding something to put out there.

"Perfect. That gives me today to work this out. Where do you want to meet?"

"I'll come get you. How's just after breakfast? We'll work until midday. Five times a week."

"Every day works too, but if you need the days off for other things, that's okay."

He didn't like the challenge in her tone, but ignored it. "Five days. You'll want the time off." He didn't ignore it well enough. If she thought he was the one who would need it, he was going to prove her wrong.

They stared each other down. He'd gotten her damned eyes to drop once; he could do it again. Now she faced off with him. He had never wanted to play this damned game more in his life. He normally only had to prove his dominance with Alchan, who needed a reality check every so often. Mave was a different beast entirely.

In the end, the door opened up and they both looked in its direction, the situation unresolved. It would come up every day until they figured it out.

"Yeah, Bryn?" she asked Bryn, who peered out at them.

"Breakfast is ready. There's not enough for more than us, though… Wasn't expecting company."

"I'll be on my way. Tomorrow, Mave, after breakfast."

"See you then," she said, leaving him on the porch to go inside.

"Damn it," he muttered, shaking his head and flying home. What a great way to start their time in the village.

47

TREVAN

It was another day of the same. Another day of waking up in a cramped hole that someone had decided to call a room, without even a cot like the other gladiators had. He had yet to feel brave enough to try and steal one, even just a mattress, for himself.

It felt like he'd been down there for an eternity. He waited a long time after the bell rang for first meal, hoping he wouldn't meet any Andinna on his path there, which he had to change nearly every day. He was thankful that as a guard, he'd been required to learn the paths better than the gladiators that lived in them. It was one of the very, very few things he had to be thankful for.

He made it to the chow hall without incident, glad to see most of the Andinna were relatively subdued. It was a good omen for how his day would go, unless some outside force riled them up. It was always a possibility.

These were things as a guard I had to worry about.

He tried to remind himself that not much had really changed. His life had been chained to these pits the moment he decided he wanted to save the Champion, seeing her fight on the sands. Hearing about her, the way his own people talked about her and the other Andinna. He couldn't comprehend the idea of a woman down here on her own. He'd wanted to be a hero for her.

Fucking idiot, that's what I was.

He partially regretted it, but he kept holding on to the belief he'd succeeded. He'd gotten her out at his own peril. Wasn't that exactly what he wanted? Well, he had wanted to get out too, but he'd decided to stay behind in that blasted alley and give her and those others time.

They better be happy, wherever they are.

He was probably forgotten by them at this point. He tried not to let that thought fester. He was stronger than that.

He grabbed his breakfast and had just enough time to eat before the next bell rang and they had to go up for training.

Another day, same as before. He trained alone, using the wooden sword to beat on the dummy until his arm wanted to fall off. He worked even harder now than he did as a guard. He was putting on muscle mass somehow, even with the basic food they had to eat day in and day out.

The bell rang and he put the sword away, waiting for the Andinna to make it down to the chow hall before him.

"Slave," a lenasti called out. "Stay."

He turned to them, knowing it was him. He was the only one they called 'slave' as a name. The others were addressed by their numbers, but no one wanted to say his. One. He knew the Empress chose it on purpose. It was a reminder of what he did. Helping her property run - her Champion, her whore, her slave. Everything in the Empire was hers and she was a possessive bitch.

"Yes, sir?" He lowered his gaze.

"There's guards here to escort you to the palace." The lenasti shoved him towards the group coming out of the building. He didn't bother fighting. He just let the group surround him and lead him out of the training area and into Elliar proper.

The palace. Why was he being summoned to the palace? Had he done something he shouldn't have?

He didn't get answers from the guards. Men he once worked with. Men who now beat him when they found the chance. Luckily, today they didn't have that chance. He was handed over to the palace guards, who led him deep inside the white marble palace, decorated with rich colors to contrast.

He was led down, down, down. The marble grew darker, until it was an unearthly pitch black and the only light was from the torches.

They were taking him to the palace cells. He'd toured the place once while in training. This was where the greatest of traitors against the Empire were held until their fate.

Was she finally deciding to just kill him and let it be? He had accepted death when he'd let the Andinna run ahead of him. He was hoping for it now. It would end his suffering with his honor mostly intact.

He wasn't locked into a cell. They grabbed him at the last minute and tossed him into a chair with a brutality he couldn't find the source of. He was strapped down, struggling.

They're going to torture me. Why? What did I do now?

One of the guards delivered a slug to his jaw, something cracking in the process.

"Don't. I need him to talk." Cold, feminine. He knew the voice well. The Empress stepped to where he could see her. "Olost. The free Andinna have found a new home there. What do you know about it?"

"Nothing." He knew Olost was their new home, but that was public knowledge. He didn't know anything else.

Someone slugged his gut. He coughed, groaning as a second blow hit him.

"Are you sure?" She didn't seem angry until he looked at her eyes. Her eyes held a fury he didn't want to toy with.

"Yes."

"Make him hurt. Maybe in a few hours, he'll be more forthcoming."

They did. They made him hurt. From blows, to water, to knives. He was man enough to know screaming wasn't a bad thing. They wanted his screams, and no real being would ever be able to survive what they did to him without it.

He was more ashamed of how he begged. He begged them to stop. He didn't know anything, nothing at all. He had no idea where the free Andinna were. He had no idea how they stayed free. He didn't know anything. He had hoped to join them, but he didn't know. They had never told him where they planned on ending up.

"Empress, we know they have most of their population in the southern-"

"I need more!" she screeched. "I need to know exactly where they are! I can flood that damned nation with my men if I knew - I could get into those mountains and find them, but that range is huge! I won't get my men killed for it. You have until the new year, spymaster. Do you understand me? The new year. Come spring, I want to know where they are. I will have her back. I didn't spend a thousand years forging her for them to have her."

"Empress, I don't think she's a threat..."

"Not a threat? Look at what we made her. She's going to be just like her damned father and mother, walking into the Empire, taking what they want like the barbarians they are, and there will be no stopping them. She's dominant enough to get them to kneel to her, and with the Ivory Shadows..." She took a deep breath. "Stop. He's not giving us anything. There's no reason to kill one of our own, no matter what he did."

"Is that why you threw him in the pits? So he would *live?*" The Prince? It was a youthful voice, but Trevan wasn't so sure. He'd never been close to the Prince.

"No, I threw him in the pits to teach him a lesson, which I think he'll learn in time. If he lives through it. And if he dies, it'll be by the very barbarians he cares for so much. It's a win-win to me." She was calm again and walked back into his view. "Actually, that reminds me. I wanted to change your sentence a little. Since you have no information for me, I don't feel like I need to work to keep you alive anymore.

I want to see you on the sands, and I'll make you a little deal in the process." She leaned closer to him. He could barely make out the details of her face. While he knew it was her, his vision was blurry and one of his eyes was swollen shut now. "You'll fight every month. If you survive for one century, I'll change the punishment to banishment and let you leave the Empire. By then, I have a feeling you'll hate the Andinna so much, you'll understand why I keep them down there. If you don't make it a century, well, you aren't really my problem then either." She reached out and gently touched his cheek. "Do you understand what I'm saying?"

He tried to nod. Gods, he understood. He understood so well. A hundred years of the pits and the sands, without a break. He would live her life, always fighting, except he could earn his own freedom, one day.

"I'm only giving this to you because you're an Elvasi. You understand that too, right? You're one of mine, and I should always look to make sure you know who you belong to. Me. You don't belong to them. You don't help them. You belong to me and you help me. I'll let you think on that." Then she walked out of the room, ordering that he be taken back to the pits as she went.

He was yanked from the chair once the straps were undone. He couldn't walk and wouldn't be able to until he found any sort of sleep and healing. It wouldn't be as fast as the Andinna's healing sleep, but he would survive. They had to drag him through the night back to the pits. They dropped him in the training area, where he was told to get moving.

"You can have tomorrow off," one of the lenasti said, his voice laced with the only bit of sympathy he'd heard yet. Then the lenasti cracked his whip and loudly told him to get moving and out of their sight.

He stumbled and tried to find his sleeping hole. He would heal, but he couldn't let the Andinna see him like this. They could easily and accidentally kill him if they decided to jump him now for a bit of fun.

He fell into the first small, dark room he could find and hoped he would be safe for another night. The moment his eyes closed, he was asleep, the Empress' words on his mind. She would free him.

And the hidden message was that she would free him faster if he somehow helped her.

DEAR READER,

Thank you for reading!

You'll notice... No maps this time! I'll bring them back soon, promise. In other news, this was a huge book! When I was writing it, I remember celebrating when I was finally getting the cast off the boat, but it was all just too important! I hope you all enjoyed the ship, the cast, and where their journey may be leading them. I wonder who has changed their guesses for who will and won't be in the harem. And no, I'm not sorry for that ending. Let's all hope together that Trevan doesn't do anything stupid. Until next time, everyone!

Reviews are always welcome, whether you loved or hated the book. Please consider taking a few moments to leave one and know I appreciate every second of your time and I'm thankful.

And if I still have you... Sign up for my newsletter for exclusive content and information on my upcoming works! I send it out monthly. Newsletter Signup!

Or you can come join me in being a little bit crazy in The Banet Pride, my facebook reader's group.

ANDENA GLOSSARY

Feminine- 'am'
　Amin- Female
　Ami- Baby
　Amra- Mother
　Arra- Mommy/Mom (Informal mother)
　Amara- Daughter
　Amir- Sister
　Amrya- Aunt
　Amyra- Neice
　Amran- Grandmother
　Amanra- Lover/Wife

Masculine- 'bod'
　Bodin- Male
　Bodi- Baby
　Bodra- Father
　Baba- Daddy/Dad (Informal father)
　Bodara- Son

Bodyr- Brother
Bodrya- Uncle
Bodyra- Nephew
Bodran- Grandfather
Bodanra- Lover/Husband

Alternative Male and Female
Ahin- A gay female
Ahren- A female that is excessively submissive. Normally isn't strong enough in personality to attract males.
Ahyara- Committed female-only relationship.
Bedin- A gay male.
Bedru- A male that is excessively dominate and possessive. Normally considered unsuitable to females due to dominance issues.
Bedyara- Committed male-only relationship.

General Terms
Ahea- Hello
Ohea- Goodbye
Al- The
Ut- You
Uta- Them
Et- Me/I
Rai- The term for the Andinna temper. No real translation.
Mativa- A 'tradition keeper', or someone, normally female, who passes on important cultural knowledge and leads a community.
Olda- Blood
Oldura- Official Andena word for a 'Blackblood'. No real translation.
Tatua- The Andinna 'ink' normally done by a Blackblood with blood magic.
Mayara- Andinna family unit. The band of males who center on a female to protect serve, and in most cases, love. Generally

husbands/lovers, but can also include brothers, fathers, sons, or just close male friends.

Illo- Big, large (Illon- bigger, larger)
Illi- Little, small (Illin- smaller, littler)
Oto- Old (Oton- older)
Oti- Young (Otin- younger)
Ildan- Friend
Ilanra- Beloved
Ildar- Adopted/Adopt/Adoptive in terms of family.
Raki- Mixed blood/mutt.
Ensam- An Andinna without social place. Forced out by the community or by choice.
Mara- Life
Olmara- Birth
Moro- Death
Somaro- Elite warrior
Morok- Classic Andinna curved blade
Svamor- War group of Andinna.
Semara- Soul
Sema- Skies or just the sky.
Sita- Submit/Submissive
Andin- Dragon
Andinno- Wyvern
Vahne- Strong
Nola- King
Lera- Walk (Lerani- run)
Vorha- Mountain

Curses and Sayings
Kak- Shit
Amov/Bodov- Bitch for female and male respectively
Kuk- Ass
Voek- Damn
Linti- Pigeon

Voek al Sema- Damn the Skies

Na al Sema- By the Skies

Skies/Sema- a way Andinna reference their gods without blaspheming. "Damn the Skies." "By the Skies."

Anvea et- I'm sorry or 'forgive me'

Et anvea ut- Apology accepted or 'I forgive you'

ABOUT THE AUTHOR

KristenBanetAuthor.com

Kristen Banet has a Diet Coke problem, smokes too much, and cusses like a sailor. She loves to read, and before finally sitting to try her hand at writing, she had your normal kind of work history. From tattoo parlors, to the U.S. Navy, and freelance illustration, she's stumbled through her adult years and somehow, is still kicking. She loves to read books that make people cry and tries to write them. She's a firm believer that nothing and no one in this world is perfect, and she enjoys exploring those imperfections—trying to make the characters seem real on the page and not just in her head.

facebook.com/kristenbanetauthor

twitter.com/KristenBanet

instagram.com/Kbanetauthor

bookbub.com/profile/kristen-banet

amazon.com/author/kristenbanet

ALSO BY KRISTEN BANET

Witch of the Wild West

Bounty Hunters and Black Magic

Werewolves and Wranglers

Age of the Andinna

The Gladiator's Downfall

The Mercenary's Bounty

Complete Series

The Redemption Saga

A Life of Shadows

A Heart of Shame

A Nature of Conflict

An Echo of Darkness

A Night of Redemption

Wild Junction

The Kingson Pride Series

Wild Pride

Wild Fire

Wild Souls

Wild Love

The Wolves of Wild Junction Duet

Prey to the Heart

Heart of the Pack

Printed in Great Britain
by Amazon